The War on Silverblood

By C.G. Pennycoff

The War on Silverblood

Content warning: graphic or explicit violence/death, fantasy-based racism, hate speech, suicidal thoughts, violence towards animals and minors, graphic medical descriptions of bodily fluids, implied miscarriage, religious themes, and alcohol abuse.

ISBN 979-8-9920049-0-8 (PB)

For all of my nerdy friends,
this adventure is for you.

Table of Contents

Prologue

THE BATTLEGROUNDS WERE HIS BIRTHPLACE. Just outside of the sanctity of a cave embedded in the snowy mountains' peaks were hundreds of bodies jumbled together in violence and chaos. Dozens of ashen, grey-skinned half-giants broke through steel and snow, separating themselves from their combat-enveloped brethren to push on ahead. As a unit, the moderately sized cluster - consisting mostly of women, children, and injured warriors - clambered up a steep, winding path as battering steel rang out behind them. They were being attacked by a unique subspecies of bearfolk referred to (by mostly everyone) as scarlet-furs.

Long ago, these scarlet-furs were once negotiable and peaceful people. They were bear-like humanoids that loved food and good craftsmanship the same as the half-giants, but over the course of several years, their rage and thirst for vengeance against the half-giants - who supposedly struck them first with an indirect declaration of war - forced them to tear away from their passive lifestyle and take up arms. Their fur took on a reddish tint as war and bloodshed became a part of who they were. The half-giants were no better, assuming the same about the bearfolk. Somehow, this blind squabble turned into an eternity of needless revenge and unyielding hatred over the mundane and the petty that went on for several years.

Shrouded by the leading group of several robust half-giants existed one particular woman deep in labor. Her name was Vergaia, a woman built like a soldier, with brown hair cut short (shaved along one side), battle scars covering her figure, and yet she dressed like an urchin with ebony cloth and wolf hide barely covering her skin. With each sharp inhale of the unrelenting chill that laced the air, Vergaia pressed forward alongside the others, each step heavier than the last. If not for the wind

I

pushing at her back and carrying her forward, she probably would've stumbled into oblivion. The climb neared its agonizing end, and Hope sat at its peak.

An unorganized cluster of pale faces barreled into the cave, a few looking back over their shoulders desperately to evaluate their safety while Vergaia, who persevered thus far, collapsed against the cave wall and let out a heavy sigh of relief. With the weight off of her swollen legs, and enough remaining energy to focus on her own breathing, she could finally finish what she started mid-way through the march up the mountain.

Despite being a woman in labor, few paid her any mind. Her growls and screams of agony sounded hardly any different to those of the brave souls fending off the scarlet-furs that were swiftly approaching.

Eventually, the pillars of stone encapsulated in ice and frost found themselves embracing a young half-giant and her newborn. Vergaia clutched at the weeping babe, looking over his messy, trembling body. With a delicate hand, she wiped away the fluid that coated his skin and wrapped him in the wool blanket she brought with her for comfort. Gazing upon her most beautiful creation, she allowed herself a minute to weep.

Hours passed, and conditions outside worsened as a storm rolling in from the southern coast forced the opposing scarlet-furs to retreat back to their camps in the west. At long last, the fight had been laid to rest. For some time, there was silence. People held onto bated breath waiting for a sign.

Suddenly, from the entrance of the cave, a child chirped, "I can see them! They're back!"

Cheering erupted. Celebration. Applause. Hooting and hollering. A half-giant's definition of "peace". There were no new bodies and no new blood being spilt. After hiking, climbing, running, and fighting, there existed a time to rest one's muscles, wrap up any gaping wounds, and stop any unwanted oozing. To some, that's not "peace", but in the face of unending discourse, that was "peace" enough for them.

To Vergaia, as a new mother, peace was being able to safely look upon her pale, wet, wrinkly son without the fear of a stray arrow piercing either her or the wad of sentient flesh swaddled in wool that she held gently in her arms. Peace was being able to admire her hard work without the screams of agony or the clanging of blades interrupting her every thought. Peace was right then and there, and would only last for that one, irreplaceable moment. Peace was so blatantly interrupted when a big, hulking behemoth strode into the rocky clearing with the tribe's remaining numbers at his side and pride worn on his blood-stained chest. It was the half-giant's glorious chieftain, Mortium.

Mortium stood well over seven feet tall, with massive muscles bulging beneath his tattered furs. His face was scarred and weathered, and his eyes burned with a savage intensity. In his hand, he carried a massive greataxe nearly as tall as him. Runes were etched into the hilt, battle scars enveloped the edges of his blade, and across the shimmering metal, crimson stains. His presence alone was enough to strike fear into the hearts of strangers and enemies alike.

The tribe's remaining warriors followed Mortium into the cave's icy clearing with heavy breaths and a mix of familiar yet unfamiliar blood staining their clothes. Their faces were a mix of battle-worn discomfort and immediate relief.

"Great news," Mortium huffed, voice echoing throughout the cave. "We've sent them into a retreat going down the mountains past the border. It should be safe to return to our homeland by sunrise tomorrow."

"I'll do you one better, Brother," the new half-giant mother interrupted, voice cracking and straining from discomfort. "A little one just joined our clan today. Oomphga, my son."

Mortium strode over to the swaddled baby to perceive its features in finer detail and fell to his knees before it. When Vergaia passed over her son to Mortium, he clung to him, body still quaking. Little baby Oomphga fit snugly into Mortium's stiffened forearm and his calloused palm but sunk uncomfortably deep in the thick wool wrap that enveloped him. Atop of Oomphga's head rested wavy brown hair that hardly covered Oomphga's crusty scalp, two fuzzy lumps along his crown, and a strange dark brown patch consumed the skin around his right eye. Despite these medical abnormalities, the infant received nothing but words of admiration from the battle-worn chieftain.

"I see you gave him a name similar to that of our ancestor. You wish for him to grow up to be as great of a warrior?" Mortium inquired, his softened gaze never breaking from the child.

"I wish for him to grow up to be whatever he wishes to be. Let's not forget how many skills our grandfather had. I'm sure he'll pick up one of them," Vergaia jeered in response.

"You wish for him to be a guildsman then?"

"I wish for him to be as good of a man on the battlefield as he was off of it. I have no doubt he'll do great things for his family, for his tribe, and for his people."

"I...suppose that's a fair enough request. Very well, Oomphgor..."

"Oomphga."

"...Oomphga," Mortium restated to himself aloud as he picked up the newborn into his burly arms. "*Ahem.* May Obak, Creator of the Giants and Eternal Chieftain of the High Peak Mountain Clan, oversee you and your future role in the tribe. May Laniara, Mother of Nature and Creator of the Land protect you as you grow to withstand the snow, sleet, and hail of frigid mountains. And may Neodashkus, General of War and Champion of Combat guide your blade from your fifth year of life and beyond."

He paused for a moment longer to look back again on the nephew he held so close to his chest. For someone so strong to hold something so soft and yet so fragile in comparison - it felt incomprehensible. One could only imagine the pain and adrenaline Mortium still clung to in that moment. His heart thrummed, and though his arms ached from combat, he held his nephew firm. His safety was guaranteed. He laid his hand on the baby's chest and uttered a continuation of the giants' sacred prayer before he lowered himself to pass the child back to Vergaia. Before the baby parted from his arms, he gazed upon his beloved sister, his eyes - once full of excitement - now reflected something far more grim. Then, within a single breath, he uttered to her:

"Take good care of this one."

She knew what he was implying. Everyone knew. Vergaia created a notorious reputation for herself amongst the half-giants as being the only unmarried woman, now mother, in the clan. She had several miscarriages, the father's name unknown throughout each and every one of them. Most people probably assumed the worst about her and her partner, but worried for her all the same. She was family, after-all, and a hard-working woman: strong but stubborn. Little did they know, she traveled many miles to see her husband and faced many perils equal to that of the High Peak Mountain tribe's strongest, most capable warriors. If anything, this child was a miracle, one that should've perished along with all the others during one of his mother's hikes.

What purpose or motivation she clung to, however, no one could even begin to understand. After all, why would a woman, so bold and capable of doing wonderful things at home, travel so far and risk the lives of so many of her unborn children for a mere man? This only Vergaia knew.

"Now, come. Let's get you and the others home. This is the cave where grandfather died, after all. We wouldn't want to stay long enough to bear witness to whatever beast dwells here," Mortium muttered.

Twenty-one dawns passed, and Vergaia began her trek down High Peak Mountain with little Oomphga firmly strapped to her back. She passed through a few villages in the mountains, stopping only for meat and drink. The company served little interest to her. After ten more dawns, Vergaia, now at the base of the mountain, continued the journey through the Bristlethorn Forest.

To most, Bristlethorn stood as a sad reminder of the first battle that started the conflict that would bring about ruin for decades between the half-giants and the scarlet-furs. The trees - though burnt and charred - still stood tall covered in battle scars and charcoal-stained bark. The rivers - though frozen around this time of year - hoarded arrows, teeth, and shards of weaponry beneath its icy shell. The remains of the poor bodies lost from one of the countless battles still littered the open fields. Most were buried by time. The vultures gathered had dined more richly than kings with bodies to consume unending for years. Whatever remained, the maggots came along to clean off of the bones. Whatever bones remained became a treat for the wolves or coyotes. If anything remained after all this time, the earth had swallowed it up, allowing the vicious cycle to continue.

Despite the horrors of Bristlethorn, there existed one place full of joy and hope, a shining beacon in the darkness that consumed the land, and that place was Sergei's humble cottage. In comparison to the shadow-covered landscape that stretched for miles of forest past the front porch, Sergei's house brought to light the beauty and life that existed within the nightmare. The amber glow seeping through his windows illuminated a garden rich with healthy vegetables, vibrant wildflowers, and dozens of burrows and nests set up along the border between Heaven and Hell. Even Vergaia seemed far more at ease the closer she got to her partner's cozy residence. After a total of thirty-one days, she finally arrived. Hand firm and heart heavy, she knocked on the door.

For a moment, she waited patiently with her heart caught in her throat, glancing at the name etched into the door frame and then back over her shoulder at little Oomphga who squeaked happily at the sight of his mama. Then, with a click and a turn, the love of her life swung open the door.

A tall, well-rounded bearfolk man standing at six and a half feet tall greeted them at the door. He was not like the other scarlet-furs. He was a foreigner, one from distant, southern lands, which is why his fur still bore its rich, chocolate brown color. His broad shoulders and muscular build gave him the appearance of a well-fed grizzly which was only accentuated by his thick brown fur fluffed to perfection around his neck and his plump belly. The only physical abnormality he had belonged to his right arm, missing from one of his adventures overseas and replaced by an old, rusted, steel prosthetic. A sailor no more, he dressed in simple clothing, favoring loose-fitting tan linens that allowed him to move freely. He also fashioned two red scarves, one around his head and one around his torso, adding a touch of color and naval flare to his otherwise drab attire. With the scent of blueberries hanging from his lips and his heart worn on his sleeve, he stood there by the door with the giddiest and toothiest smile plastered across his face.

"My dear wife, Vergaia! Oh, how good it is to see you!"

"Great to see you too, Sergei."

"It has been quite some time! I see you are keeping your hair short, and...you are thinner!" He happily hollered, ignorant to the denseness of this comment as well as the still sensitive youngling curled up in the hood of his spouse's fur mantle. It was only until he heard the whimpers and whines that realization struck. "You come to bring our little one! Come inside! Let me see them! Let me see them!"

Without saying a word or cracking the faintest smirk, Vergaia stepped inside the warm and beautifully lit cottage, and she wandered over to the fireplace ignoring the rest of the heartfelt decor. Taking great caution, she sat down in front of one of the cushioned seats, untied her mantle, laid her son down on the couch, stood up, and stepped away so Sergei could get closer. Eagerly, he leaned in, his round, bear-eyes fixated on Oomphga, his round ears perked up in excitement, and his fuzzy muzzle nearly pressed up against his exposed belly the closer he got.

"Aww! Look at you! Are those bear ears I see? And your eye! Looks like mine with all the fur! And you got my papa bear tummy!"

Sergei pressed the edge of his lips against Oomphga's stomach and playfully blew into it. Baby Oomphga wriggled his arms and body, eyes wide open. His small, thick, grey hands batted at Sergei's nose, but Sergei hardly felt a thing.

"Three days," Vergaia interrupted.

"Eh?" Sergei paused to look over his shoulder.

"You get three days with him, and then I have to return to my tribe. I told them I would be showing Oomphga the mountains and collecting supplies. That's. It. I've already been away for almost two weeks. Any longer…and they'll get suspicious."

Sergei scooped Oomphga up into his arms and embraced him gently, his brow furrowing. He looked upon his wife and son, gaze shifting skeptically. Every word brought a sad mix of confusion and agony, and every glance at his ignorant, baby boy - void of thought and blissfully unaware of the war that tore his family in two - made his wife's demand all the more unbearable to hear.

The couple had many discussions before about running away together and forging a new future in a world where only the two of them existed. Sergei would offer his house and home to Vergaia, but she refused.

Vergaia always stood firm in her beliefs, and she believed that her place among half-giants held more importance than any other place she had in the world. Call it traditionalist nonsense, but it was her culture and her creed. Her ties to her giant ancestors, her half-giant kin, and her tribe in the mountains were unbreakable by spirit and by law with roots that stretched to her core. As if the consequences for betraying the tribe weren't enough; if anyone knew she traded her role and her people for Sergei, she would be slaughtered like the boars she cooked and served to feed her people. She knew this better than anyone else. Sergei did not, and for years, he wouldn't understand.

Sergei Silverblood grew up with his bearfolk kin in a place he always called "Old Country". Their morals and traditions were usually rooted more in blind love and the celebration of life. Much like the local scarlet-furs (before the war), they would gorge on the forests' natural offerings; rivers filled with fresh water and even fresher fish, berry bushes as far as the eye could see, and the freedom to roam between the untamed wilderness and the civilization that stretched far into the western territories. What wasn't there to love? Who wasn't there to love? And Sergei, for his entire life, believed the same thing all bearfolk believed in: tales of the truest kind of love.

One fateful day, Sergei met Vergaia during one of her hunts in the Bristlethorn Forest. When the two first laid eyes upon each other, Vergaia saw a threat while Sergei saw the love of his life. Luckily, fate worked in Sergei's favor. Some heartfelt rambling later and Vergaia laid aside her axe in favor of living a happy life with this truly innocent bear. At first, it worked out alright with the two of them marrying in secret, seeing each other whenever Vergaia went out for a bountiful hunt on behalf of her people, and now…

The edges of Sergei's lips hung low as he stared upon his dear wife with glistening eyes. Vergaia, stone-cold in expression, cracked under the weight as the creases alongside her lips and brows gradually softened. She couldn't deny a deeper sorrow of her own - let alone hide it - but she thought about it for months after they eloped. It was the only way given the circumstances.

"We can...visit every so often. Maybe every other month?" Vergaia suggested.

"Every other month?! But I'd miss most of our little boy's life. His childhood. It'd vanish in the blink of an eye. Surely, we can do-"

Vergaia's statuesque stance reminded Sergei once again of their predicament.

"Every other month will do, but I expect to keep my boy for half a month, at least! He deserves plenty of time with Papa Sergei! Wouldn't want him to become a barbarian...N-NOT THAT ALL HALF-GIANTS ARE BARBARIANS, o-of course! I just think our little baby-"

"Oomphga."

"-Oomphga deserves time to live and enjoy life! Emphasis on the 'live' and 'enjoy' part! He deserves to be happy and do whatever normal kids do like...fishing! He could go on adventures and catch fish! Maybe he'll do both at the same time! Who knows~?"

Slowly, Vergaia started coming around to Sergei's ideals. Fishing sounded practical, and adventuring would provide Oomphga with plenty of life skills. He could learn how to survive in the wilderness, foraging plants and hunting animals. He could learn how to set up traps, cook food over the open flame, and slay monsters the same way her grandfather, Oomphgor, did long ago. After a moment of thought, Vergaia nodded in approval and pulled Oomphga up and out of Sergei's arms to look upon him.

"Adventuring. That's what I'll tell the tribe. Oomphga will grow into a warrior the same way his great grandfather did. He will adventure outside of the mountains and learn how to survive independently. He will grow up bigger and stronger the more experience he has fending for himself. Just think of all he'll learn. All he'll see. All he'll do."

Oomphga chirped happily, flailing his arms and legs with excitement. There was something magical about this boy. The sparkle in his chestnut eyes, the equally cheeky smile he wore looking upon his mama and papa, the way his bear ears flickered up and down every so often, and the squeaks hidden in his laughter. Vergaia convinced herself that no matter what Oomphga became, she'd always love every part of him all the same.

"So…is that a 'yes' on me keeping him for three weeks rather than three days at a time?"

"Of course you can. Make it a whole month, minus ten dawns between the both of us to account for travel. Just promise me you'll teach our boy something of value while he's here."

"Yes, ma'am!" Sergei cheered, looking over his wife's boulder shoulders. "Don't worry, my little Oomphga, you're in safe bear paws and half-giant hands! We're going to take good care of you, together (but not really) forever and ever! Papa Sergei promises!"

Chapter 1:
Through the Mountains

WHEN OOMPHGA'S FIFTH YEAR ARRIVED as anticipated by his mother and uncle, he was far from prepared. Around this stage of life, he could do a lot of things half-giants expected of kids at his age. He could carry a handaxe, craft arrows, sharpen sticks, and start a campfire. All pretty standard expectations in the eyes of the tribe. However, there were a lot of things that he couldn't do; the biggest being that he couldn't let anyone know about his "scarlet-fur heritage".

To mend this issue, Vergaia drilled into Oomphga's memory that he had to tuck back his bear ears at all times and cover up the fuzz around his bear eye with wool bandage wraps. Time and time again, she reminded him and pulled back the leash whenever he had forgotten. There were times when going outside became forbidden because of how forbidden the family secret was, but this made Oomphga long for freedom even more.

He craved the fresh air running through his nostrils, the wind blowing through his matted hair, and the warm embrace of the sun's light on his skin. If not for this longing, Oomphga probably wouldn't have learned how to hide his differences - at least, most of them - but there was one difference that there was no hiding: his speech.

While Oomphga's mother taught him how to survive and how to fit in with the half-giants, his father was left teaching him about the more basic things like colors, shapes, how to speak, how to read, manners, what was right and wrong, etc. Unfortunately, Oomphga never had the time to properly learn and absorb even the most basic things which led to quite the interesting combination between what he learned from "Papa Sergei" and "Mama Vergaia".

"Mama. Mama. Mama Vergaia, Oomphga does not want food right now. Oomphga would like to go outside. Can Oomphga go outside, please and thank you?" Oomphga chimed, clinging onto the fur wrap Vergaia wore draped across her waist. He jumped up and down, his eyes fixated on his mother rather than the meal she swiftly began preparing.

"Oomphga can go outside if he can stomach boar for lunch. You've skimped on eating meat for the past couple of years and your uncle wants you to grow up as a big and strong young man." She gestured to Oomphga's small and stout frame. The sting in her voice reflected a cruel sarcasm. "And big, strong, young men eat their boar."

"Uuugh! But Oomphga will throw up and end up outside anyway! So, can Oomphga go outside now, please and thank you? ...Also, what's the celebration for?"

"The celebration in question is part of half-giant tradition. By partying in their names, we show our gratitude towards the three most powerful gods of the giant pantheon, Obak, Laniara, and Neodashkus, who came together to create the eight half-giant tribes of the world. Each tribe was created based on one of Laniara's eight elements and our people were blessed with Neodashkus' eternal strength. Every year, a celebration is held by all of the tribes of the world on the same day to reinvigorate the power of the gods through feasting, hunting, song, and cries of prayer that last through the night. This is our honor and our tribute to them."

Oomphga stared up at his mother blankly. Words overlapped in his mind, jumbling and mashing themselves together in ways that Oomphga couldn't understand. His question was probably answered somewhere in his mother's response but got lost in the jumble of words morphed into one long sound. Vergaia noticed this and reworded her explanation plainly.

"We give thanks to the gods by throwing a party."

"Oooh." Oomphga's interest dwindled. He didn't care much about parties. Most of it was drinking and eating anyways, two things that Oomphga had no interest in unless pear juice and berries were involved, so after a few thoughtless blinks, his attention switched back to his earlier request:

"Can Oomphga...celebrate outside for a bit? Please...and thank you?" he asked hesitantly, his eyes alight, hoping to hear those three magical words.

Vergaia sighed in defeat. "Yes. You may."

"YAY!!!"

Leaping to action, Oomphga threw himself across the small, wooden hut they lived in to grab all of the traveling tools he had to his name: a knife, a rope, a bag of herbs, and a small roll of bandages. Then, he gave his mother's leg a big bear hug
and rushed to the front door.

"Oomphga! Aren't you forgetting something?"

"Mmm...no?"

Vergaia gestured to her right eye, immediately prompting Oomphga to conceal his eye with the wool bandages he packed away. Unable to take care of this duty himself, he waddled over to Vergaia and held them out for her to wrap around his head for him. Not only did she cover up his eye, but she also fluffed up his hair so his bear ears didn't show. The moment the wraps were secure and Vergaia drew her hands away from his long locks, Oomphga bolted through the front door and bounded up the snow-covered path of their little tribe like there was no tomorrow and no time to waste. He ran past the houses, his vision of them blurred while his focus on the road ahead remained clear. The speed at which he ran kept his ears back and his eyes sharp as he headed up into the heart of the mountains.

Oomphga barreled through the thick snow and hurdled these rocks dozens of times before, his steps getting lighter and his muscles reacting faster than the last time he scaled this part of the mountain. With rhythmic breaths, he clambered up cliff-edges and made bold leaps over pits in the stone. From this height, one could imagine how painful the drop below would be if one's body remained intact after such a fall, but Oomphga never calculated that possibility. He was confident in his youthful vigor. The wind, growing in intensity - the steeper he climbed - barreled past him and stung his face. He could feel the cold seeping into his bones, but Oomphga pushed on, driven by a determination to reach the top. By this point, he forged a clear path of his own to the one place he loved exploring more than anything in the world: the ruins of an old church.

What remained of the church was scarce. Pieces of white and gold tapestry hung from the broken upper windows, cobblestone still littered the old, worn road leading up to the church's doorstep, and crimson quartz littered the fields outside. The first time Oomphga arrived at these desolate ruins was to look deeper into this "creepy old human church" that he heard in passing conversation between the adults, but when he came to investigate for himself, he saw something he never expected to behold: a raven massive in scale.

It towered over him and stood to be about nearly the size of the church itself from the foundation to the peak of whatever religious symbol was stationed on top of the roof. The bird's feathers glistened like fresh ebony, and its eyes shimmered like polished gold. It had a beak longer than a greatsword and thicker than a greataxe's blade. It was probably just as sharp too, but these ominous and dangerous features didn't discourage Oomphga from the bird at all. No. He was infatuated with it. Practically, obsessed. Oomphga wanted to see this majestic creature again more than anything in the world. To call it special was an understatement. This raven felt like a creation hand-made by the divine, and Oomphga longed to admire whenever it reared it's feathery head.

Before he could make it to the familiar staircase, the repetitive thoughts running through his imagination were abruptly silenced by the deafening cry of an anonymous wolf. With how close it sounded, Oomphga could've sworn that he was right on top of it. He looked around and waited until he heard the sound once more. The sound pierced his right ear and when Oomphga looked to his side, sure enough, there sat a steep dip in the path. He inched closer to the edge and looked down. Below him, covered in snow and patches stained red, was a grey dire wolf pup huffing and whimpering. Though Oomphga recognized this as a wild and dangerous animal, his heart ached for the poor creature.

Without hesitation, he slid down into the small ditch alongside the wolf and cautiously approached it, his palms inching outwards towards the canine's injury. Thick crimson flooded from a deep incision stretching from his neck down to his chest, drowning him in his own blood. His gaze, fixed on oblivion, appeared empty and sunken, but still sparkling with life. In all of Oomphga's days of watching wolves, deer, mountain goats, and even bears from afar, he's never seen a creature act so submissively in the presence of man. If it were starving, desperate for a taste of survival, it'd bite; if it sensed a man or fellow beast's intentions and felt threatened by them, it would growl, but this poor creature…

This creature - if anything - looked ready to accept whatever fate befell upon it.

As slow as he could, Oomphga lowered himself down onto the dire wolf's level. He could see color slowly dissipating from its eyes as all hope began to die with it, but Oomphga wasn't going to let that happen. He brushed back the wolf's mucky fur to examine its wounds. Before him appeared a deep gash leading from the chest to the neck. The scar was about as deep and as thick as the edge of an axe. From this point, it was easy to draw to the conclusion that this lone wolf found himself at the end of a half-giant's blade, and - judging by the color of the blood - the hunt was recent.

Deep as the wound itself was, it was mendable. With the right herbs and medicine at Oomphga's disposal, he could bring the wolf back to health. With this in mind, Oomphga reached into his tiny herb pouch hanging from his waist side, and without a second thought, he offered up a handful of corydalises, praying the creature would eat it.

"Eat this herb, please and thank you. Oomphga promises it will help you feel better."

Upon Oomphga's command, the wolf lapped the herb up off of his hand. Oomphga's eyes widened in surprise at the wolf's obedience, but he quickly regained his composure and began to work on the wolf's injuries. His hands were shaking, but he knew that he had to be careful not to make the wolf's injuries worse. He dabbed at the wounds with a cloth, applying a healing salve that he had found in his pack. He then began to bandage the wolf's wounds, taking care to make sure that they were secure.

The wolf watched Oomphga intently as he worked, its amber eyes filled with gratitude. It had never felt such kindness from another creature before. It had always been hunted by humanoids and half-giants; it had never known what it was like to be cared for, but Oomphga was different. He was a kind and gentle soul, and the wolf knew that he had found a friend in him.

Oomphga continued patching up the wolf. Its breathing steadied and its eyes cleared. The healing salve was working its magic, and based on how active the pup was trying to be, it probably felt somewhat better. Oomphga beamed, realizing that the wolf's condition was improving.

"There we go. You probably won't feel better for a while, but Oomphga will make sure you heal! In fact, Mama is making boar meat! Maybe she can give you whatever is left over! With food in your tummy, surely-"

Examining the exhausted creature once more, Oomphga felt a strange connection with the wolf pup, and not a necessarily pleasant one. Perhaps it was a feeling of empathy or - maybe even - some kind of mystical bond, but he could sense its discomfort and yet its eagerness to go with Oomphga wherever he wished.

Of course, Oomphga wasn't going to leave the pup all by itself when it still was in a semi-stable condition at best. So, wanting to make the wolf pup feel the most comfortable it could during its recovery, he inched closer, allowing it to use the heat lingering on his skin for whatever warmth and company it desired. Willingly and without any sign of hesitation, it buried itself deep into Oomphga's small frame, adjusting its head so it rested on his lap.

"Mama will be worried if I don't make it back in time for the celebration. But…Oomphga will stay with you. When you feel better enough to walk, we'll head back to Oomphga's village together! alright?"

The wolf let out a tired hum in agreement. So, for what felt like hours, there Oomphga sat with a dire wolf curled up in his loving arms. He let his mind wander as a means to pass the time, his attention fixated solely on the creature lying close by his side. Now that he had a dire wolf friend to protect, surely, he should have a name, right? Like Graffnor or Dargus. No…this was a curious and adventurous little pup. Not some blood-thirsty monster. Oomphga began sounding out different letters and vowels, hoping something would stick.

"Barn-…Burnu-…Bup-…Buppy. Buppy! Oomphga's gonna call you Buppy, lil' guy! You are now Buppy!" he repeated aloud, giggling every so often. "Buppy. Buppybuppybuppy-"

There he sat petting Buppy on the head all the while. A little bit more time passed. Patiently he waited, letting the creature have a moment's rest. Then, when he finally began to stir, Oomphga piped up.

"You ready?"

The pup let out a long yawn, its tail wagging eagerly. And that - if anything - was a good enough response for Oomphga. So, he scooped the dire wolf up into his arms and carried it all the way back down the mountain with a giddy smile on his face.

He marched with eagerness, energy revitalized. The thick snow that clung to his baggy, forest green pants stood no chance against him and his quest home. The closer he got to his house, the livelier Buppy appeared. His tongue hung from his mouth, his tail patting Oomphga on the chest with each flick. When he arrived back at the tribe, everything was transformed. The once barren and dull village of half-giants was now filled with laughter, music, chanting, and the strong scent of fresh meat of all types roasting over a spit.

Oh, the meat. Just the mere mention of such a thing made Oomphga queasy. His stomach knotted and his throat clenched as the gunk locked in his gut demanded release. He frantically denied his body's request and desperately picked up the pace. As much as Oomphga sensed Buppy's pain, Buppy took notice of Oomphga's nausea. Trying to help his newfound friend, Buppy licked Oomphga's face. This distracted Oomphga but did little aid. When he finally made it home, he raced inside, laid Buppy down onto his bed cot, and made a mad dash to the back of the house.

"Welcome home, Oomphga. You made it back just in time. Your uncle will be arriving any minute." Vergaia noted aloud, hardly taking her eyes off of the boar she prepared. "How was your time celebrating outside?"

There was a long silence.

"It was great..! Oomphga made a new friend!"

He stumbled back into the house, wiping away any residue that lingered upon his lips. He picked up Buppy off of his bed and walked up to Vergaia. Patiently, he stood there waiting for Vergaia to look at him while he held Buppy close.

Eager to see this new friend, Vergaia finally pulled her gaze away from the meal to look at Oomphga. Her eyes widened and her brow furrowed.

"Please, tell me this isn't your friend."

"His name is Buppy!"

Buppy let out a few short woops and howls.

Vergaia stared at Oomphga blankly, her scowl reflecting her unspeakable shame. Oomphga could read his mother's disappointed expression perfectly fine, however, he was determined to keep the pup whether she agreed to letting Buppy stay or not. Taking a second to collect her thoughts, she set aside the boar she was cooking, and she knelt down.

"Oomphga, you know I love you, right?" Vergaia uttered, her voice only a little louder than a whisper.

"Mhm."

"You also understand that this…this is a dire wolf. This is not a dog or a puppy. This is a wild animal. A dangerous, wild animal."

"But he's not dangerous to Oomphga! Buppy likes Oomphga! He was in the mountains injured and all alone and…" Oomphga trailed off.

A wave of emotions mixed with an indefinite number of continuations to that sentence hit him all at once. To pick one reason of many to excuse his display of compassion wouldn't even begin to justify his intentions. He shifted his sights onto Buppy who still hung from his arms contently. He and Buppy, though they knew each other for an hour or two, felt like friends. Best friends. Friends for life.

"Oomphga didn't want to leave him there to die," he stated, his voice soft and solemn. Not forceful, not demanding. "He needs Oomphga, and Oomphga is going to do whatever it takes to take care of him whether you like it or not. Please…and thank you."

Before Vergaia could refute his objection, Oomphga carried Buppy outside. As he wandered off to a quiet place, he hoped that something stuck with her. He wanted her - more than anything - to open up her heart and reconsider the audacity of her own request. Even if she didn't agree, he wished that she would reflect the same way he did in that instance.

Taking a deep breath, Oomphga sat down in the snow just outside of their front door, setting Buppy on the ground next to him. He sat there, passing the time by staring at the other half-giants enjoying the festivities. Buppy curled up and whimpered, calling Oomphga's attention to him.

"Oomphga is sorry," he murmured. "Oomphga didn't think that Mama Vergaia would say 'no'. Mama Vergaia always wants Oomphga to make friends with other half-giants, but they're too…different?"

Looking over at Buppy, he realized just how different Buppy was in comparison to him, and he let out a little chuckle.

"Guess Buppy is different too. In a good way!"

Oomphga pulled Buppy in close and rubbed his head playfully. Buppy accepted this kind gesture and let out a long howl.

Suddenly, casting over Buppy, Oomphga noticed a growing silhouette that seemed to sway to and fro. He recognized the frame and build that silhouette belonged to before he looked up to see who it was.

"Oh! Hi, Uncle Mortium!"

Uncle Mortium looked down upon little Oomphga with a crooked grin. He clung to the door frame as if that was the only thing keeping him on his feet. The burning scent of mead poured off of his personage from the ram horn that hung from his belt to his teeth. Judging by how much of his drink coated the fur draped around his shoulders, saying he had too much was an understatement. To Oomphga's surprise, another figure stood alongside him - someone he didn't recognize.

The old man's face was a roadmap of his long life, with wrinkles etched into every corner. His pale, green eyes were sharp, intelligent, and they twinkled with clear foresight. He held a long, birch wood staff wrapped in lavender cloth and herbs in one hand, and in the other, he held a rolled-up piece of parchment.

"Oomphga, my boy! Good to see you again!" Mortium slurred, his head hovering inches from the wall as he shifted and squirmed uncomfortably. "I…umm…I have a special, family friend I'd like for you to meet! This…is Seirah." Oomphga watched with amusement as sweat dripped down Mortium's brow. He almost looked just as sick as Oomphga an hour or so ago.

Was he alright? Should Oomphga ask?

"He's our tribe's shaman, in case you were not informed. He was hoping to meet with you! Somethin' about annn…apprenticeship or other-"

Apprenticeship? His mother told him about apprenticeships once or twice. Oomphga tilted his head, his curiosity peaked. Buppy, equally as curious, inched closer to Seirah with his nose pointed up towards him. The towering sage gripped onto his glorified walking stick tightly and lowered himself in front of Buppy and Oomphga, a glint of mirth in his hazy pupils.

"Is this wolf pup yours?"

Oomphga scooped Buppy into his cushioned arms and held him close against his chest for a moment. Then, with a cheery smile, he held him out to focus his heartfelt gaze on his blissful expression.

"He's…Oomphga's friend! His name is Buppy. Oomphga found him in the mountains today."

"I'm guessing you were the one that patched him up as well?"

"Mhm."

"Where did you learn medicine from?"

Oomphga shrugged. "Life."

Life, a timeless teacher. You eat enough random plants and you learn what they do. Of course, being gifted with a sixth sense for danger and a seventh for magic helped as well. That Oomphga couldn't deny.

"I see. Well, I'm impressed. You're very young, and to have such a vast understanding of the natural world," Seirah hummed. "I can also sense an impressive amount of magic growing within you. You should consider tapping into that one day."

Oomphga blushed and looked down at his feet momentarily. "Thank you, Mr. Sea-rah, sir!" He chirped.

"No need to thank me. I'm just stating the obvious. Now, about that apprenticeship…" Seirah leaned back in his walking stick and looked at Oomphga thoughtfully. "I've been watching you for some time now, Oomphga. I've seen the potential in you. You have a gift, a rare gift. I believe that you could be a great shaman one day. That's why I'm offering you an apprenticeship with me."

Oomphga's eyes widened in surprise. "Oomphga? An apprentice?"

"Yes, you. I think you would be a great fit for the position. You have the skills and the aptitude. All you need is guidance and training. I can provide that for you. One day, when you have all the knowledge and resources required, I believe you will become a shaman worthy of replacing *me* one day."

Oomphga was silent for a moment, considering Seirah's offer. He had never thought about becoming a shaman before, but the idea was starting to appeal to him. He loved learning about the natural world - plants and animals alike - and he was always fascinated by magic. He could see himself being a great shaman one day. He turned his attention to Buppy.

"What do you think, Buppy? Do you think Oomphga would be a good shaman?"

Buppy let out a short, happy howl just as Uncle Mortium slipped. His back hit the ground with a crunchy *thump*.

"I'll do it!" Oomphga replied proudly.

Seirah chuckled and extended a hand to the drunken chieftain, swiftly pulling him to his feet.

"Excellent. I'm glad to hear that. We'll start your training next week on the same day, bright and early in the morning. I will meet you here at your home. From there, we will walk together back to your future place of work. Here." He extended the piece of parchment towards Oomphga only for Buppy to snatch it up into his slobbery maw. "It's an outline of what you'll be learning. I want you to go over that with your mother. I'm sure she can help you read it."

"Thank you, Sir!"

Seirah nodded and slipped his quarterstaff into Uncle Mortium's hand, letting him use it as a crutch to help him walk back up the hill and into the bustling village.

Oomphga smiled upon the two, letting out a short giggle with each stumble and slip Uncle Mortium made as he pathetically trudged through the ice and snow. Excitement consumed him. He was ready to begin this new journey of his. He was determined to become a great shaman and to use his gift to help others. Eager to tell his mother the good news, he rushed back into the house, still holding onto Buppy all the while. He told her all about the apprenticeship, his eagerness rising even more as hundreds of fantasies ran through his mind.

A shaman! How exciting! Oomphga's gonna be a shaman!

Chapter 2:

A Little Boy's Plea

OMPHGA COULD BARELY CONTAIN HIS BLISS. The idea of an apprenticeship to the shaman, the tribe's healer, had consumed his mind and he could think of nothing else. Mama Vergaia, likewise, agreed. She had never felt that her child would be picked for an apprenticeship under the shaman, all things considered, and she was excited. So excited, as a matter of fact, that she allowed Oomphga to keep Buppy. Her stern, cold heart had thawed in that moment of elation as she came to understand truly just how much Oomphga loved the little wolf pup. So, just this once, she willingly broke from her orderly and unchanging ways to make room for her son's happiness.

"Thanks Mama. Oomphga won't let you down!" Oomphga vowed, pelting his hand against his chest.

"Now, shall we join the other half-giants in celebration?" his mother asked, extending her hand out to her son.

"Yeah!"

So, as the sun stepped down from its peak, Vergaia along with Oomphga and Buppy, joined the other half-giants in their rambunctious revelry. Most of the older half-giants already had their fill of grog and ale. They sang and danced, laughed and shouted their praises to the heavens amidst their drunken stupor all while the bonfire roared at the village's heart. The younger half-giants, however, played ramball; a pretty dangerous game of "who can pelt each other with the ball the hardest" where everyone kicks a ball - made of ram and mountain goat pelts tightly stuffed and coiled up in rope - at each other. The goal was to dodge the oncoming projectile, but some kids got a weird sense of amusement getting hit as hard as possible that Oomphga never understood. After all, who would deliberately **want** to get pommeled with something that usually left rope burns and bruises on their skin that wouldn't go away for days? Not Oomphga.

"I'm going to go get us drinks. Why don't you play with the other kids in the meantime?" Mama Vergaia encouraged.

Before Oomphga had a chance to state his rebuttal, his mother was gone, wandering off towards the bar where a bunch of warriors all sat around drenched in their own drinks.

THUMP.

With a thwack, the ramball hit Oomphga in the side of the head, knocking him off of his feet and onto his back. A choir of high-pitched cackling erupted from the group of kids as they all pointed at Oomphga. Oomphga rubbed the side of his head where the ramball left its agonizing mark. Buppy approached to lick his face until, out of the corner of their vision, a lone figure approached them: Tuthjorn Thundrak, son of Mortium, and Oomphga's cousin.

Oomphga hardly knew his own cousin. They only met each other once or twice whenever Mortium would come over to check in on Oomphga and Vergaia, but he was a good kid at heart. Oomphga's best - if not only – friend among the half-giants. A little rambunctious and a bit bratty, but he had noble dreams just like his cousin and just like his own father.

"One day, I wanna be a warrior just like my dad! A good one! One that will kick butt and keep you and…and EVERYONE safe! Those scarlet-furs won't know what hit them!"

That's what he always used to declare with the confidence of a warrior. Now, in this moment of humiliation, Tuthjorn stood over his dear cousin with a warm smile and an outstretched hand.

"You alright, 'cos?"

Oomphga returned the same expression and grabbed onto Tuthjorn's arm so he could pull himself onto his feet.

"Oomphga's…been better," he chirped in reply.

Tuthjorn scooped up the ramball and tucked it under his arm while he used the other to ruffle Oomphga's hair. Without even realizing it, he brushed his hand over Oomphga's bear ears, but with all the mats and knots in Oomphga's hair, it was impossible to tell the difference between the two.

"Hey, we had a kid get absolutely walloped earlier and he's out of the game. Didn't know if you would be interested in filling in for him!" Tuthjorn chortled.

"Ah! Um…er…well, Oomphga-"

"Come on, Tuthjorn!" One of the other, tougher-looking kids whined. "How long does it take to fetch a ball?!"

"Yeah, yeah! I'm coming!" Tuthjorn sassily hollered over his shoulder before fixing his attention back onto Oomphga. "So?"

"Oomphga would, but he's not very good at ramball. He'd just get in the way…"

Tuthjorn shrugged and passed the ramball to one of his teammates.

"Suit yourself."

Without fuss or retort, he returned to the group, and as he sauntered off towards the other half-giants, his eyes flickered with hostility towards the kid that tried to rush him moments prior. With Tuthjorn's short temper, Oomphga worried shoving and yelling would ensue, but instead, his lips curled upwards, and he playfully batted his buddy's shoulder.

Oomphga looked over at Buppy with confused and disheartened eyes. Something about the festivities made Oomphga feel like some sort of outcast: a reject that didn't belong. Maybe it was the realization that his mother left him alone to go spend the rest of the night with her friends and Oomphga's other relatives (of which he knew very few aside from his uncle, Mortium, and now his great, great uncle and future mentor, Seirah), or maybe it was the lack of things suitable for Oomphga and his personal interests. Either way, at the very least, he had Buppy, and hearing his pants while watching him bounce up and down on his paws, made him happier than anything else at the celebration.

He grinned and wandered over to a nearby bench. Though it was covered in mead stains, it served as a perfect resting place for Oomphga and Buppy. Not even a second after he plopped down, Buppy hopped up and sat on his lap. The curious wolf pup looked around at everything, his tail wagging eagerly.

"You know what Oomphga just realized?" Oomphga asked as he began rubbing and patting Buppy's head and back playfully. "We're like…we half-giants are like one big pack of dire wolves. Yeah, we look big and scary, but we're family, and we stick together. And now, you're a part of the pack too! …How do you feel about that, Buppy?"

Buppy didn't respond. He just looked up at Oomphga with his big, yellow eyes.

"Yeah. Oomphga's pretty happy too~"

As the festivities continued, Oomphga's mind drifted to the future. He imagined himself as the tribe's shaman, creating potions and curing the sick and injured. He imagined the joy that his work would bring to others as loved ones rejoined and connected with one another after recovery. He imagined his mother, his uncle, Seirah, and Buppy all by his side to support him and praise him for his generosity. Gradually, the daydreaming drifted into an ignorant slumber.

Profoundly entwined in cherishing embraces and lively faces, Oomphga envisioned himself wandering down the straight and narrow path of success and compassion. The skies were bright, never dreary, and everyone around him was healthy and happy. Any scrape Oomphga saw was immediately mended by his magic-marked hands and any symptom of illness he spotted was cured with the right combination of ground herbs and elixirs. Peace and prosperity were easy management. However, without warning came an eerie silence in Oomphga's dream interrupted by a deafening screech. Oomphga looked around at his fantasy world, unsure of where the cry came from and from whom. The longer he paced, desperately looking for the creature or person in need, a burning sensation overwhelmed him until he found himself paralyzed from head to toe.

With a jolt, he woke up, sweat pouring from his skin and heart pounding fiercely. Buppy was growling and howling loudly, his snout pointed towards a thick silhouette standing at the top of the hill. It was humanoid in shape - no doubt about it - but it had a thick frame that was covered in...fur? It was a scarlet-fur. One with a flaming spear in one hand and something round hanging from their outstretched palm.

Is...is that a-!?!

A head. The head of another scarlet-fur. The detailed features on the bear's mangled face were impossible to perceive when the firelight behind the figure only illuminated its shape. Judging by the shape of the head alone, this scarlet-fur had its head hacked off. It was no clean cut. The bits and pieces of bone - the muscle jutting out of the bottom - was evidence of that. They also appeared to be young. Very young. Much more so than the individual holding the head itself.

"WHERE IS YOUR CHIEFTAIN!?!" The silhouette cried out.

Her voice was deep and mellow. It echoed through the bustling village and received only silence in response. That was until Mortium, still drunk with a tankard in one hand and his iconic greataxe in the other, lumbered forward.

"THAT...would be me," he grumbled. "What is your business here, Scarlet-fur?!"

"I demand retribution for my son, Grey-skin! Your blade took his life, and now, you will pay the price dearly with a son of your own-"

She pointed her spear toward Tuthjorn standing not too far away from the bench Oomphga sat on. Mortium stumbled in front of

Tuthjorn, shielding his son from the burning steel pointed in his direction.

"Over my dead body."

"That's what I was hoping to hear."

Beyond the rooftops were a small band of more visible scarlet-furs, all carrying varying weapons, each marked with dents, chips, and faded ruby stains. The malicious glint in their eyes spoke volume. They wished to take as many lives as they could for their leader. With so many half-giants drunk and vulnerable, they knew this was going to be an easy slaughterfest in the name of their fallen brethren.

Before the first step, Seirah thrust his quarterstaff out towards Mortium. A blinding emerald beam struck him, and a much softer band of visible magic enveloped him. Oomphga could feel some of the energy emanating from the mesmerizing glow. When the light dissipated, Mortium was in perfect condition with a sound mind and bulging muscles. Not a second after the spell was cast, the scarlet-furs advanced.

Vergaia swiftly raced to Oomphga's side to drag him away from the fray. Her grip on Oomphga's hand was tight and her yank dangerously strong. Buppy fell off of Oomphga's lap, letting out a yelp, but he swiftly brushed off the snow that cushioned his fall and he hopped back up onto his feet to follow after Oomphga and his mother.

"WHERE ARE WE GOING!?!" Oomphga cried out in confusion, his voice cracking and breaking on each syllable.

"Don't ask questions, Oomphga! Just stay by my side!" Vergaia demanded.

Forced into a state of silence, Oomphga had no choice but to helplessly observe the chaos. Twisted visions surrounded him of mothers dragging their children to safety while the fathers either aided them in their escape or raced to their chieftain's side in defense. Screams of terror and despair echoed from all directions and infected Oomphga's mind. Children were decapitated, their mother's forced to watch in horror before they were run through themselves. Bearing witness to such gory atrocities, Oomphga couldn't think, could hardly feel his hand the tighter Vergaia held onto it, and couldn't utter a word. Before he knew it, they were crossing the border of their small village and making their escape, but something out of the corner of his wide eyes gave him the impression that their exit wouldn't be easy. Buppy noticed it too. He stopped to bark at the scarlet-fur standing with a longbow and an arrow coiled around his round, fuzzy fingers. He was gonna shoot - not Oomphga - but another kid that was by herself making a mad dash towards safety. That was until he caught a glimpse...of Buppy.

His howls and barks would blow the cover of this assassin eventually. He knew it. So, he swiftly refocused his aim, pausing for a moment - most likely to see if the wolf would be smart enough to move or if he would stay a still enough target. Oomphga noticed and tried to break free of Vergaia to scoop Buppy up into his arms so he could - at the very least - shield him with his thicker and tougher skin, but Vergaia's grip was too strong, and she barreled through the snow too quickly for Oomphga to catch his footing.

"BUPPY!!! COME ON!!! PLEASE!!!" Oomphga hollered, his voice cracking and aching from the strain. The second time he called out to Buppy, there was hardly a sound.

The arrow sprung to life, piercing the sky, and with deadly precision struck Buppy between the ribs. Oomphga let out a silent cry, his body aching and straining to use every ounce of strength to tear from his mother's hold. With his other hand, he dug his nails into Vergaia's fingers and ripped them open just enough so he could bolt to Buppy's side. As the scarlet-fur prepared his second arrow, Oomphga ran after his mother, holding onto Buppy firmly.

His throat clenched and his heart dropped a thousand feet as he slowly came to realize how soft Buppy felt in his embrace. Blinded by tears and fueled by sorrow, Oomphga raced alongside Vergaia, weeping and sobbing.

"Oomphga is sorry..!" Oomphga repeated to himself, knowing full well that Buppy couldn't hear him anymore. "He's sorry. He's sorry! HE'S SORRY!!!"

The bearfolk assassin fumbled with his arrows. His bow put up a fight. While he struggled to get an easy shot of the mother and son, Oomphga and Vergaia made their escape.

By now, the village was out of sight as were the threats that invaded it. Finally free from the battlefield, Oomphga threw himself down into the snow with Buppy so he could finally look over the damage. His hands twitched; his vision was hazy. All he could see were whites, greys, and reds. He wiped away the tears that clouded his sight. Once his eyes focused, all he could do was look on in horror and disbelief at the innocent pup that lied before him. Buppy's eyes were still open but lacked all heartwarming glow.

"Oomphga can save you," he lied through gritted teeth. "He can fix this!"

He scrambled for the bag of herbs that still hung from his side and he grabbed a tear-soaked handful of corydalis.

"Eat this, please and thank you..! …Come on..! PLEASE..!"

But there was no reaction. Not a sign of movement. The glaring truth stared Oomphga dead in the face and spoke with a subtle cruelty: "abandon all hope." Huffing and whimpering, Oomphga's hand reeled back towards his pouch. He had no choice but to accept his defeat and the anguish that followed. He pulled free the arrow lodged into Buppy's chest and buried his face against his side. Every inch of his body aching with grief, and he hated it.

Vergaia looked on at the village they left behind. The bonfire grew in size, rising up towards the moon high up in the sky. She glanced over at her son - damaged beyond all recognition - and with a fraction of the sadness he felt reflected in her expression, she approached him to lay a loving hand on his shoulder and squeezed gently. Oomphga looked up at her, his eyes red and swollen.

"Oomphga is so sorry," he uttered as loudly as he could.

Vergaia shook her head. "It's not your fault," she said warmly. "You did everything you could."

Oomphga sniffled and wiped his eyes with the back of his hand. "He knows, but it wasn't enough. Oomphga could've done more and-"

"No. No, you couldn't have. You did your best, and that's all that matters." Vergaia wrapped her arm around her trembling son and pulled him into a gentle hug. "We'll get through this together."

Oomphga nodded against her shoulder. He knew that his mother was right. They would get through this together, even without Buppy. For a long time, the two sat just holding each other and grieving over their loss. Finally, Vergaia released Oomphga and brushed her scarred fingers through Oomphga's long, brown hair.

"Come on," she said. "Let's take you to your father's."

Oomphga clung to Vergaia, using her as a support to pull himself onto his feet. Without complaint or rebuttal, he followed his mother towards the trail leading down the mountain. As they walked, he glanced back over his shoulder at Buppy to see the cold, lifeless corpse of his friend one last time. An eerie silence lingered in the air as his lifeless eyes stared back at Oomphga. An unforgiving wave of sadness washed over him as he reflected on the short time he shared with the young pup that he held in his arms so dearly mere moments ago, but he buried those memories deep. He knew that Buppy would want him to be strong, and if he could speak from beyond his snowy grave, he'd tell him to grow even stronger in the years ahead.

And so, that's what Oomphga vowed to do.

He would never forget his best friend, but he would also never let his death drive a stake through his compassion the same way the death of the scarlet-fur's son transformed her and her allies into entities that reaped nothing but heartache onto the innocent lives of their enemies. He would live a kinder life for both of them. He would protect and preserve those alive the same way Buppy did no matter the sacrifice or the risk.

Oomphga will make you proud, Buppy. He promises.
...Thank you.

Chapter 3:
Mother Nature Beckons

AFTER THE PASSING OF BUPPY, time felt hazy. The color that used to enthrall Oomphga felt so void and lifeless now. The sunshine-y faces of passerby in the other mountain villages mocked him, and the animals that sang far off beyond Bristlethorn forest cut his memories deeply. Never has the youngling held such a long expression of mourning throughout several dusks and dawns.

Oomphga would often find himself staring off into the distance, observing the vastness of the universe - of the many creatures of all shapes and sizes, predator and prey, living in their ignorant freedoms while he moped around "thinking" his youth away. His time with Buppy was so short, so why?

Why did he feel such a gaping hole in his core? Why did he feel so different now? What could Oomphga have possibly gained in those few minutes with a lone wolf pup that no other experience in his five years of living could compare? The memories he made with Buppy hardly covered the span of a day, but it felt like a lifetime passed.

Perhaps, it was the volume of the events that stuck with him the most. From making his first ever friend to the moment he lost him, he asked himself: why? And Tuthjorn, Mortium, and Seirah! What happened to them? They were thrown smack dab in the middle of the fray. Maybe Seirah used his magic to escape and maybe Mortium survived his battle with the scarlet-fur leader, but Tuthjorn…he was just a kid about as old as Oomphga.

More thoughts wriggled and squirmed inside the depths of Oomphga's mind, burrowing deeper and deeper.

"Talk to me, Oomphga. You've been quiet for days now," Vergaia said.

Realization finally struck him. Was he really zoning out for that long? Ten whole days. Where did the time go?

"So...so have you," Oomphga stammered.

"Yes, I have. I've been worried about you."

Oomphga looked down at his feet. They were wet, cold, and sore. Leaves, mud, sticks, and rocks clung to them, digging into the skin on his heels.

"Oomphga's sorry. He's been thinking."

Vergaia brushed her fingertips against one of the small, round ears that protruded from Oomphga's matted hair. The other flinched every so often. This feeling always soothed Oomphga and yet, something about it now caused every muscle in his body to grow tense. He let out a long, shaky sigh and fixed his gaze onto his mother.

"He doesn't understand," Oomphga admitted. "Why do the bearfolk and the half-giants hate each other so much?"

Vergaia sighed. "More often than not, we find that we each suffer our own losses, yet instead of moving on, some of us try to mend what's broken by breaking the hearts of other people in return."

"But it's not fair!" Oomphga whined. "Why do people that didn't do anything wrong have to get hurt?! It makes no sense! It isn't-" Oomphga let out a quiet huff, his voice growing quiet, less arguable. "It isn't fair, Mama..."

"War isn't fair, and yet we must fight battles that aren't our own and grow strong to protect those we love. That is what we must do. That's what you will have to do when you're older, my little Oomphga." Vergaia extended a hand to Oomphga, but he pushed it away.

"But Oomphga doesn't want to fight! He just wants to help people! He wants people to STOP fighting!"

"You'll understand when you're older."

Oomphga broke into tears, sniffling and panting through gritted teeth. *Why does Mama have to be so pessimistic?! Doesn't she see?! Can't she hear herself?!*

A silent resentment started to fester in Oomphga's mind that day. He would show his mama that life didn't have to be this way. It could be so much different if people just accepted things for the way they were and moved on.

Moving on. Why did it have to be so hard? And yet, even for a kid like Oomphga, he felt a part of him forcibly trying to push through the grief and aggravation, to suppress the darkness he perceived and seek out the innocence of his childhood that his father promised him. One day, if Papa Sergei was right, he'd feel all better.

Vergaia reached for something along her waist. It was her handaxe. She pulled it out of the leather loop that held it in place, and she held the handle out towards Oomphga. He looked down upon the dark wooden handle blankly.

"Take it," Vergai uttered.

"No."

"Take it!"

Oomphga, unwilling to argue with his mother, did as ordered. He could feel the pressure building up tears as the handaxe entered his possession. Out of confusion and stubbornness, his ember eyes traced along the hefty weapon in his grasp. From base to hilt were beautiful streaks of wood, smoother than paint brush strokes, and along the chipped blade were old runic carvings. He had no idea what they meant, but he gazed upon them with sincerity as if they were the most interesting thing in the world.

"I know you don't want to fight, Oomphga, but one day, you will. Whether it's in self-defense or to protect another person or to stand up for what you believe in, you will have to fight. Do you understand me?" Vergaia asked.

Oomphga nodded, suddenly understanding all too well.

"Oomphga understands…"

"Good. Now, come along, we're almost at your father's."

Vergaia took Oomphga's free hand into her own and walked with him through the woods.

"Chin up. We wouldn't want your father to worry."

When Mother and Son finally arrived at the warm, inviting home of Papa Sergei, Oomphga paused to look at the vaguely familiar garden and front porch with a weather-worn rocking chair swaying back and forth. He glanced up at his mama, waiting for her to take the first step. She approached the door, energy draining from her face each and every second she had to wait. Eventually, Sergei opened the door with the same cheery smile, old linen clothes, and the faded, red scarf he always wore whenever he greeted Vergaia and Oomphga.

"My beautiful wife! My wonderful son! Look at you, you've…" It's clear, he wanted to state the obvious: he grew. But something held him back. Something drove a stake through his chest. Solemnly, he got down on one knee to see his son eye to eye. "You've changed. What's wrong, my boy?"

Oomphga hardly uttered a word. He was tired and emotional. Plus, he didn't want to lie to his papa or shrug off his feelings, but he was so close to his face, his expression practically begging Oomphga for an honest answer.

"Oomphga…um…" he mumbled, shrinking into his own anxiety. "Things happened at home - a lot of things - and Oomphga doesn't feel very good about them."

"What happened?" Sergei's face softened, his paw reaching out towards Oomphga's cheek. He accepted his father's gentle touch; would've been rude to refuse.

"War happened," Vergaia interrupted, her voice flat and monotonous. "Oomphga bore witness to a battle for the first time. At least...one that he can remember."

"Oh...that's-"

"Can Oomphga go to bed? He's tired. Please and thank you."

"I...suppose you could-"

Without giving Sergei a chance to further elaborate on what Oomphga could do, Oomphga squirmed and shimmied past his father, pushing past the fluff and fur to make a swift dash to the small upstairs bedroom in the attic he called his own. The presence of moss and flowers scattered about his room usually comforted Oomphga, giving him a breath of fresh air even when he was cooped up inside, but he pushed past the plants he cared so deeply for day in and day out. His aching feet brushed against his bright purple butterfly rug as the weight of his body got heavier and heavier.

Everything felt so draining. So soulless. He tossed his mother's handaxe aside, plopped down face first onto his bed with a thud, and clung to his bright olive bedsheets. The familiar scent of his papa's cottage - his sanctuary - brought the faintest sense of relief. He was safe here. Hardly anyone visited him or Papa Sergei. No one would ever hurt them here. *Why couldn't his parents just stay here together away from it all?* It was all so...unfair.

"But he's just a kid, sweetie. I understand, for you, the whole...half-giant-tradition-is-important-and-all thing, but he's five and the mountains aren't really a safe place for a kid like him. I think, maybe, he should stay with his Papa Sergei until things settle down! Surely, things will get better soon. After all, it's been - what - 50-ish years since this whole bearfolk half-giant war started? And my cottage is a pretty safe place for him to be."

Oomphga lifted his head, entranced by the faintest traces of his father's voice. After he stated aloud Oomphga's similar idea, there was a long pause in the conversation. He wondered if maybe his mother gave a hushed response since he couldn't hear her through the floorboards. More than eager to eavesdrop a little more, Oomphga shambled out of bed and sprawled himself across the ground, bear ear pressed tightly up against the wooden panels below.

"I bet someone will come around eventually to straighten things out! A politician. A foreign diplomat. A representative between our people. The druid. A wandering adventurer eager to dig deeper into the conflict. Someone. Anyone! And sometime soon-"

"Stop." Vergaia interrupted. Her voice cut through Sergei's light-hearted ramble with relentless precision. "Do you realize just how dense and insulting you sounded, just now?"

"W-well, I-"

"Not only are you brushing aside our half-giant heritage, but you're underestimating your son's capabilities, putting faith in non-existent aid that has yet to resolve anything between our people, and you're expecting me to - what - abandon our son, who's just as much mine as he is yours, here with you for an indefinite amount of time because you think he isn't safe with me?"

"You don't have to abandon our son. You could move in with me, and we'll raise him here together away from-"

"My people? My tribe? My friends? My family?"

Sergei replied, his words strained: "Are we not your family too?"

"Sergei, I don't think you understand my predicament. If I were to leave and move in with you, my brother would worry. He would send his best hunters and trackers out to find me and they would find me. They would find you. They would kill you, maybe even me, and Oomphga...his life would be left in the hands of fate, and that is not a risk I am willing to take."

Oomphga reeled back, shaking his head to and fro. He didn't want to hear anything anymore. He couldn't bear to listen to his mother's pessimistic perspective for another second. He scrambled to his feet and frantically glanced around at his bedroom. His wooden animal figures stared back at him from the floor, their painted eyes staring spearheads into his soul. The padded mattress that sprawled across his bed frame yearned to support him, but he could see through its facade. The springs creaked and groaned whenever they accepted his weight. The lantern sat on his bedside table without its flame patiently waiting for that spark it remembered so fondly, but the glass casing that enveloped its wax and its wick was empty aside from those, and the dozens upon dozens of plants Oomphga hoarded - they reminded him too much of the forest.

Ah, yes, the forest - the long-running expanse of woodlands that resided just outside crying out to Oomphga. He pulled open the window next to his bed, eager for some sense of relief, and suddenly, he was absorbed in the scent of fresh air and pine trees. In the sky beyond, the sun laid itself to rest. Its warm glow broke forth through the fog that covered the landscape and cast about a soft blanket of orange woven together with marigold. The brooks peacefully babbled amongst themselves, and Primavera's breeze whispered tales of magic and wonder into Oomphga's ears.

Oomphga longed to be out there, in the forest, away from the confines of his small, cramped room. He wanted to run and play with the wildlife, climb over rolling hills, discover new flowers, and swim in the river. He wanted to be safe, and yet he longed so deeply for freedom.

Without further contemplation or delay, he fetched the rope out from under his bed, tied one end around his bedpost, filled his backpack with his bear plushie and a few essential supplies, and then he whisked himself out the window and down the siding of the house. His toes were inches away from the grass below when, suddenly, he paused to listen in one last time.

How could he not?

"I still don't understand why we couldn't just run away together! I can get us a ship! We can sail to a far-off island where no one would be able to hurt us!"

"My people need me, Sergei! We lost several of our chefs last year, and I'm the only one left! Without me, the half-giants could starve! And besides, let's not forget what happened the last time you went out sailing..!"

What...did happen?

Oomphga peered in through the window, catching a glimpse of his mother gesturing to his father's missing arm. Sergei clutched it tightly, head hanging low, and ears pressed back against his head. Then, he turned to look up at Vergaia, eyes narrow and teeth warped to create a forced smile.

"You can be...quite cruel sometimes, luv."

"And you as well...in your ignorance."

As much as Oomphga wanted to run into the room and calm them both down, he didn't have the strength nor the energy to force a smile that he refused to wear.

Just a few minutes to relax, and then Oomphga will be back to fix everything!

He plopped down onto the grass and adjusted the pack slung over his shoulder. Beyond the bright, well-defined clearing around his father's house was a path riddled with uncertainty. There was no definitive road or trail for Oomphga to walk on, but nevertheless, he trudged forward into the mist. He shuffled past the bushes, weaved through the weeds, and kept a sharp eye out for jagged rocks and thorns along the trail. Taking great caution with him, he delved deeper and deeper into the dreaded Bristlethorn forest, and yet - even as the light faded from the horizon - he felt less and less dread the deeper he wandered. The trees of the Bristlethorn forest loomed over him, their branches reaching out like arms to grab him, but the way the branches weaved and twisted overhead intrigued little Oomphga. He loved how alive Bristlethorn forest felt, even when not a single spec of life stirred.

With no direction, he continued his walk, his feet guiding him wherever they could safely go. Of course, as darkness consumed the woodlands, following any sign or sense of familiarity became near-impossible as the milky-white fog grew thicker. Now, Oomphga couldn't even see the way forward, let alone find his way back.

Before Oomphga could begin to realize the potential dangers of this situation, he spotted - there - inches away from his face flickered a spark of light that danced through the silver clouds. It was unnatural in its appearance like the teal core of a piping hot flame, or the heart of an aquamarine illuminated by stars. It danced before Oomphga, swirling and swaying across the sky an arm's length away. His jaw hung in astonishment, his eyes locked onto the teal wisp gliding around in the air with such majesty, such grace.

"What in the world...?" Oomphga muttered to himself, his voice barely a whisper. He had never seen anything like it before. The light danced with such energy, such mirth. It was almost as if it were alive.

Teehee...

Oomphga's eyes widened as he heard the sound. It was so soft, so delicate, yet it was unmistakably a giggle. He glanced around, trying to find the source of the sound, but he could see nothing but the light, now closer than it was a second before.

"What's so funny?" Oomphga asked the light.

Teeheehee!

The teal ball of radiance inched closer to Oomphga, its playful energy almost palpable. It swirled and twirled, the faintest twinkle echoing amidst the silence.

"You are a cute little...uh...floating light, aren't ya?" Oomphga said, his voice still a whisper. He held out his finger towards the light, imagining it somehow perching itself onto his nail, but instead, it suddenly drew back and flew off into the depths of the woods, letting out a slight *whirr* as it cut through the mist.

"Wait!" Oomphga called out, but the glow was already gone.

Oomphga stood there for a moment, staring at the spot where the gleam had disappeared. He couldn't believe what he had just seen.

A talking light? It was impossible. Nevertheless, there it was before his very eyes.

"What was that?" Oomphga asked himself.

He shook his head, trying to clear his thoughts, but his imagination took hold of any sense of reason he had. It must've been some kind of magic. Maybe it was a spell or a mythical creature. No matter what it was, it made Oomphga feel something unexplainable. It soothed his soul and waned his worries. He trudged forward, taking care with each step. Gradually, the familiar glow returned, stronger than ever.

It was almost as if…there were more of them!

Oomphga stopped in his tracks and looked around. The teal lights were everywhere, dancing and swirling through the air like a thousand fireflies. They were so beautiful, Oomphga couldn't help but stare.

"Woah…what are you? *Who*…are you?" Oomphga asked, his eyes alight with wonder.

The light seemed to pause for a moment, as if they were listening to him. Then, they began to move again, this time in a more organized fashion. They formed a half-circle around Oomphga's back and ushered him forward, a few trailing ahead. Once they had him where they wanted, they rushed over a slender, endlessly deep moat filled, and swarmed the tall, winding willow tree before them. Their glow illuminated the peace lilies around its roots and the teardrops of greenery hanging from its winding branches. The rustling of its leaves whispered a welcome to the boy, beckoning him to sit under its shade. So, Oomphga found a place by the crystal-clear waters to sit and stare upon his reflection.

It was strange. This was the first time he's ever truly seen himself. He hesitantly brought his palm to his rosy cheeks. Were they always this soft? And the small, white crescent moon under his left eye. Did he always have that? He brushed his fingers through his hair. Sure, it was a little matted, but it was so long and fluffy. It was like a pillow that supported his head. Oomphga's fingers traced over one of the two brown lumps that stuck out from his scalp. So those were his ears. They really did look like his papa's. All these features felt so unique. All these features belonged to Oomphga, and Oomphga alone, but there was still one feature that Oomphga had yet to perceive: his right eye.

Ah, yes. The eye he was always told to hide as if it was some atrocity that no one could bear to see. It certainly felt like an atrocity with all the fuss his mother made over it whenever he stayed with her in the mountains, and with all the itching and discomfort it caused. The white cloth he wore over it didn't help a bit. Thank goodness he wasn't in the mountains anymore. He was by himself in the forest...all alone.

Oomphga reached behind his head and, after a moment of fidgeting with the knot holding the cloth to his face, he unraveled it. And...

...there it was. His eye, the one his Papa Sergei always spoke fondly of. The whites of this right eye were black, but his russet iris matched the other perfectly. The one thing that caught Oomphga's attention the most, however, was the fuzz. There was so much brown fuzz around his eye from cheek to his brow. It nearly consumed half of his face. No wonder why his mother wanted him to cover it. No wonder why he felt so special whenever his father complimented it.

Mama Vergaia...Papa Sergei...he missed them.

"You're quite a long way from home, kid," echoed a voice from behind. It was deep and mellow, booming with a hint of authority.

Oomphga swiftly turned around and there stood a tall, dark-complexioned gentleman. His eyes shimmered in contrast with the lights that illuminated his subtle presence. Shadows dripped down from his beady eyes onto the long, feathery cloak draped over his shoulders and down his back. Upon his chest rested an insignia resembling that of a raven that loomed over a rose-covered moon.

"Hello, Sir," Oomphga uttered as he gazed upon the stranger, enthralled by his appearance. "My name is Oomphga. And you are..?"

"Omen, a messenger."

"A good messenger?"

"I would like to consider myself as such. I come on behalf of a friend of yours."

"Oh…" Oomphga dipped his head and brushed his palm up and down his arm. "Mr. Omen must have the wrong person. Oomphga doesn't have any friends."

"Buppy, I believe his name was."

Oomphga suddenly shot up from the grass. "You know Buppy?!"

"Of course. We spoke together in the mountains the day before and after his departure." Omen paused dramatically. "He wanted to let you know that he believes you'll make quite the great druid."

"Druid? But…Oomphga's supposed to be a shaman when he grows up. That's what Mister Sea-rah said. Also! Also…what's a druid? Whatever it is, it's not a shaman."

"You're going to be apprenticing under a shaman, yes, but the Mother of Nature and the Mistress of Misfortune want you to be the new druid, the soul protector of the land and the animals.

The Mother of Nature? THE goddess, Lanniara, herself?! And this Mistress of Misfortune…who was that? Was she important? Was she a friend or ally of Lanniara?

Disregarding this Mistress of Misfortune lady, the messenger spoke supposedly in Lanniara's name so maybe - just maybe - Oomphga was going to be a druid after all. And this "druid" job didn't sound half bad! In fact, the idea of being the "protector of the land and the animals" sounded more appealing than being a shaman. It certainly aligned itself well with the oath Oomphga took to defend those in need, and if the plants and animals needed Oomphga, then who was he to deny the call for action?

"Oomphga…will do it! Oomphga will make sure nothing bad happens to the innocent creatures!" Oomphga cheered triumphantly, putting his hands on his hips and raising his head up towards the moon. Noticing a stick lying nearby, he picked it up and pointed it at the edge of the clearing, eyes sharpened and arm crossed in front of himself defensively.

"Danger better watch out, because Oomphga got some mixed blood! He got giant strength and bear senses! Grr! Raaawrg!!!"

Oomphga barreled forward towards the center of the clearing, but Omen deftly caught him by the shoulder to pull him back. His grip was firm, his palm radiated a cold chill up Oomphga's neck and spine.

"Woah, easy there, tiger. I have one last thing I need to give to you before I go: a blessing from the goddesses."

Before Oomphga could react or respond to the messenger, a wave of dizziness and nausea hit him with full force. The world felt like it was caught up in a tornado, spinning so fast one could hardly make out the difference between the ground and the sky. When Oomphga was finally able to readjust his vision, he took in the new sights. Everything had changed. The trees, once tall and lanky walls of ebony bark, were now rose-tinted towers of peach petals. The bushes and grass, a plethora of weeds and thorns stretching as far as the eye could see were now filled with peonies and irises.

Where Omen once stood was now a peachy-skinned giant with flowing pink hair that danced in the breeze. Sitting atop of her shoulder was an albino squirrel that leapt from her side and clung to Oomphga's arm.

"Mr. Omen,…sir?"

This - whoever it was - was not Omen. She gave Oomphga a different feeling. One of reassurance and compassion. The way she smelled of cherry, the way her rosebud lips curled softly across her face.

"Please, call me Lani," she giggled. "I come to present my gift, my blessing."

"A blessing?"

With a knowing smile, the tall woman gestured to the squirrel that clambered up onto Oomphga's shoulder.

"The squirrel?"

The squirrel's lips moved in the shape of syllables. "The name is Dexterous," it chittered.

"You can talk!" Oomphga declared, eyes widening.

"You can understand," the squirrel corrected.

Lani nodded with a satisfied grin lingering in her expression. "If you wish to be a druid, you must be able to talk with the animals. They will provide you with some of the wisdom you'll need to become more attuned to the world around you. As you grow, you will learn more of your capabilities. Your magic."

"Magic? But Oomphga doesn't know magic."

"Oh, but you do."

With a flick of her palm, a flower stem sprung forth from the ground until it stood almost as tall as Oomphga. At its end lay a faded yellow flower bud sealed shut.

"With the will you pull from your heart, you can make this flower bloom. All that's left is a wave of a hand."

There was no way it could've been THAT easy. Brushing aside his doubt and uncertainty, Oomphga did exactly as instructed, waving his hand over the flower bud. A green aura fluttered from his palm onto the flower, and, within a few seconds, it blossomed into a healthy daffodil. Oomphga stared at his hands. He hardly felt anything aside from a cloud of warmth.

"Keep practicing and experimenting, and you'll find that you can do many wonderful things."

"Wow! Thank you, Miss-...oh! Lani," Oomphga corrected himself shyly. "Thank you, Lani!"

Without any sign or warning, Oomphga felt the nausea and dizziness hit him once again. This time, it was stronger than the last. The ground beneath him swayed and swirled, causing Oomphga to stumble back into the moat around the tree. The squirrel on his shoulder vanished into thin air, leaving Oomphga to fall.

With a crash, he plunged into a seemingly endless pit of water. Oomphga clenched his nose and clamped his mouth shut. His body, knowing full well that it was without air, flailed and ached in yearning for it when none was to be had.

"My turn..." a disembodied voice echoed from the deeper depths below.

Like a whisper among the ripples in the water, this speaker cut through the water into Oomphga's ears. Though this individual sounded authoritative and yet "familiar" in some bizarre sense of the word, the way they spoke felt like needles digging into Oomphga's neck and spine. Whoever they were made it unclear whether they were friend or foe.

Overhead, Oomphga caught a glimpse of light. The color of the once soothing teal wisps transformed into an abrupt blast of scarlet and orange. Fire. No glorious bonfire either. A wildfire that roared so loud, Oomphga could hear it from a few feet below the surface. His heart pounded. His hands trembled. He reeled back, trying to cover his ears as haunting silhouettes wormed their way into his memories. Sparks of red splattered across the vivid theater of his mind. Why? Why did it have to be red?

Then, there were streaks of grey and brown coming down from the sky. Falling rocks? Meteors? Whatever it was sounded heavy, like marching soldiers making their way into battle, and it shook the lake to its very core. Bits of broken stone crashed down into the water, nearly hitting Oomphga in the process. As a boy that was never taught how to swim, he responded by frantically flailing around his arms and legs. One rock, the shape of a spear, grazed his shoulder.

His chest was getting tighter, his heart and lungs felt like they were going to collapse at any second if he didn't breathe soon. The depths reflected his restlessness and tossed him around. The waves knocked any sense of direction out of him. Now he could hardly tell the surface from the bottom of this seemingly endless lake. Then, when all hope of recovery seemed lost, an underwater current swept him up and brought him up towards the land, filled with colors and light that completely blinded him.

After that…

…there was nothing.

○ ══════ ○ ○ ✸ ○ ○ ══════ ○

"Aymus!" The voice of Omen echoed through the darkness. "Aymus, wake up!"

Who's Aymus? Is Oomphga…Aymus?

Choirs of cataclysm, screams of sorrow. The taste of blood danced across his taste buds, its warmth embracing his skin in more than one place.

Is this how he dies?

"Look at what you've done!" Omen snapped; every inch of his features twisted to conceal something deeper than rage.

"Look at what I've done?! Look at what HE'S done!"

Who is Omen arguing with? Is that…a devil?! Why are the devil's fingers bleeding like that?!

"He didn't bring about the Calamity, Martin!" *Martin…why does that name sound so familiar? Why do I remember it so fondly and yet…my neck throbs just thinking about him?* "You've doomed us…you've doomed us all! Laniarra…the Mistress of Misfortune…they will remember. They will remember what you've done, and you will pay for a thousand eternities if I have anything to say about it..!"

No…not yet. Whatever I was sent here to do. Whatever it is that needs to be done, I'll do it even if my body fails me! It can't end like this. Not yet…

For the longest time, Oomphga couldn't see, hear, or feel anything aside from the cold water that covered him from head to toe. After a while, he could faintly make out the sounds of someone speaking to him, but the words sounded muffled. He couldn't make out anything that he could understand aside from his own name, but then again, he didn't have the energy to make much of an effort understanding what was being said even if he could hear the words.

"Oomphga! Oomphga!!!"

Five more minutes…Oomphga is tired…

"Oomphga, my son. Come on. Wake up, please! We don't want your mother to-"

"What did you do? WHAT DID YOU DO!?!"

Oomphga tucked back his ears. The fighting. He couldn't bear to listen to it anymore. He tuned out the voices and denied all familiarity by letting out a raspy groan in rebuttal. He flailed his hands around until his palm met with warm linen and furry fingers that curled around his and forced his hand against his chest. It felt like he was being swaddled in a big heavy blanket of some kind. It was so comfy, and it smelled like Papa Sergei's house.

An indefinite amount of time passed. Oomphga eventually pulled himself from his deep sleep, letting out a long groan. His eyes fluttered open. There was the fireplace, and there was Papa Sergei sleeping on the floor. He could hear footsteps coming from behind the couch. Was that-?

"Ack-!!!" Oomphga clung to his bear ear as something - or rather someone - pulled on it.

"What were you thinking!?!"

"Oomphga is sorry, Mama! Whatever he did, he's so sorry!"

"You don't know!?! You ran off last night, almost drowned, and nearly gave your father and me a heart attack thinking you were dead!!! What were you doing outside playing in the dark, giving us a scare like that!?!"

"Oomphga was taking a walk! Honest! *Ow ow ow...*"

"In the middle of the night when it's foggy out!?! Oomphga!"

"Darling! Sweetie Pie!" Papa Sergei startled himself awake and placed a gentle paw onto Vergaia's hand and Oomphga's ear. "Why not - instead of yelling at the poor boy - we be happy that he's alive, da?"

Mama Vergaia snapped her hand back, letting go of Oomphga's throbbing ear. With the pounding headache, it was hard to remember what exactly happened. Was everything just an elaborate dream? Was it real? That's when he spotted him past his huddling parents: Omen. No longer was he the dapper, dark-skinned man that he met in the woods. No. He was Omen, the towering raven with beady eyes - eyes of cold recognition - feathers brushed back, and wings hanging low. He peeked in through the window, staring back at Oomphga intently.

"Oomphga. Oomphga look at me," Vergaia commanded. Swiftly, Oomphga re-focused his attention on his scowling mother. "Don't you EVER run off like that again. Do you understand me?"

"Yes, Mama. Never again," Oomphga swiftly responded, not fully realizing in the moment what he was agreeing to.

With a loud whoosh, Omen was gone, leaving Oomphga distraction-less.

"...I trusted you to be better." Vergaia straightened herself and let out a quiet huff. "Sergei, keep an eye on our boy. We can't let him out of our sight. It seems you were right to be worried...for his sake."

"Y-yes, my love! Anything for you, my dearest~!" Sergei chirped, voice trembling.

Sergei flashed Oomphga a grizzly stare. Until it was time for Oomphga to return home to his Mama Vergaia, he could say "good-bye" to the forest and re-acquaint himself with the four interior walls of his cramped bedroom for the next two weeks.

But one night, after Papa Sergei finished reading a chapter of his personal memoirs, Oomphga spoke up.

"Papa?"

"Yes, my son?"

"...What's a druid?"

"It's...well...it's someone that does really good things. Many many good things...Why?"

"Oomphga's gonna be a druid when he grows up, Papa."

Chapter 4:
Sticks, Stones, and Half-Giant Bones

EIGHT YEARS HAVE PASSED. Other than his parents, who would've imagined eight years of Oomphga's youth would've been spent going back and forth, from mountain tribe to forest cottage, between Mama and Papa? By now, Oomphga had grown into independence as a traveler and wandering outcast much like his great grandfather at the age of thirteen.

From handholding and the excessive use of manners to adventuring alone and exploring the mountains on behalf of the duties he had to his tribe. Though he still lacked the same tough-guy energy all the other half-giants' kids had, his mother spoke nothing of it since she and his mentor, Seirah, understood better than anyone else that if Oomphga was to become the tribe's shaman, he would need gentler hands in contrast to the others. While all the others fought tooth and nail, Oomphga's place was alongside Seirah, revitalizing magic at the ready, to mend their brethren's wounds.

However, after the first scarlet-fur attack that Oomphga could remember (and each attack following), he took the time to form a stronger bond with his rambunctious cousin and loyal protector Tuthjorn. Tuthjorn didn't change much from his usual ways. He still boasted and bragged plenty, but he always had a special spot for Oomphga in his life. Since not many other half-giants liked his abrasiveness and arrogance (despite most of them being abrasive and arrogant themselves), no one seemed to spend as much time with Tuthjorn as Oomphga. Of course, this meant whenever Oomphga was enjoying himself somewhere in the mountains or off running errands for Seirah as part of his apprenticeship, Tuthjorn would find him to scream about some big find of his.

This was another one of those days.

Oomphga sat by a patch of toadflax, drawing it and marking it down in a worn, leather book he had since he first started his apprenticeship when, from off in the distance, a familiar yet melodic cry rang out.

"Oooh, Oooomphgaaa~!"

Oomphga let out a cheerful huff, sitting aside his quill. "Whaaa~aaat?" he echoed back.

Tuthjorn bolted across the patchy snow, heavy duty boots crunching with each step. When he finally reached his cousin, he looked him over, glancing back and forth between the herbs, the messy scrawls in Oomphga's journal, and the goofy yet restful expression plastered on the giddy half-giant's face.

"What are you doing, 'cos? Looking at flowers again?"

"Oomphga's doing work for Seirah as per usual. *They're herbs, by the way.* What's Tuthjorn doing?"

"I'M GLAD YOU ASKED!!!" He plopped down onto the ground next to Oomphga, eyes alight and lips curled. "I was getting the usual earful from my father - you know the spiel - about what it means to be a good chieftain, making tough decisions, making sacrifices, that kind of thing - yada yada yada…whatever - BUT, at some point, he mentioned this girl coming to visit the tribe from overseas, and…" Tuthjorn took a moment to hype up the big reveal. "…she's our age. You know what that means?"

"Uh…that Oomphga and Tuthjorn should be the ones to tell her about the tribe and the fights that have been going on for…*57, 58, 59, 60 years?*"

"No, you bone-head, it means that you gotta stop smelling the roses and get yourself some muscle, so you don't completely embarrass yourself when she arrives! We gotta show her exactly how powerful the High Peak Mountain tribe really is!"

Oomphga forced an affirmative smile.

"Alright, alright. Will do. Say, when will she be arriving, anyway?"

"A month or two from now."

Oomphga blinked a few times letting out a strained chuckle. "…Oh! And you were going to tell Oomphga…when?"

Tuthjorn snickered, his lips crinkling. "Eventually! *Ahem.* REGARDLESS, no slacking on that training! After you're done with your studies *or…whatever*, I wanna meet up with you sometime to help you brush up on combat stuff. By the end of the day, I want you breaking boulders with your fists, ya hear?!"

"Oomphga doesn't think that's-"

"No, ifs, ands, or buts about it, Cousin! We'll get you whipped into shape! You'll be the biggest, strongest shaman there ever was. Well, stronger than Seirah, at least."

That's not saying much considering how ancient Seirah was.

"So…was that the only reason you came to visit Oomphga? He's…um…" Oomphga paused to look over his journal. Though the current entry still remained incomplete, he made some progress on other things; hopefully enough to make his mentor happy. "…he's done with his nature studies, so you could escort him back to Seirah. After that trip, Oomphga and Tuthjorn could - he supposes - do some training. All depends on what Tuthjorn wants to do, really!"

"I…guess I could tag along with you, then," Tuthjorn groaned. "As long as it doesn't take too long! I got important things of my own I need to do."

"Important?"

"Chieftain things. Important."

Tuthjorn threw his arms behind his head and began wandering off towards Seirah's cabin, leaving Oomphga scrambling to collect his belongings. Once Oomphga had his bags, books, quills, and colored ink, he trailed after Tuthjorn, following close behind in his footsteps.

Tempted as he was, he hardly averted his gaze from his cousin. Every confident step he took, every thrust of his body up the steeper hills and cliffsides, and every part of who he was screamed, "warrior". Going by the standards of half-giants, he was a living and breathing idol - golden paint streaks poured down from his pale blue eyes and his muscles...*gods his muscles*. With grace and ease, he navigated over the rocky terrain, looking back every so often to see Oomphga lagging behind (of course). Whenever he had to drag Oomphga along, he would always grumble and groan about it, but Oomphga could tell he wasn't really annoyed or upset. He tried as hard as he could to hide it, but deep down, he imagined in the confines of his mind that Tuthjorn appreciated the travel company. Who else would he ramble on to?

"Oh! Oomphga, I finally remembered another thing I wanted to tell you!"

"Go on..."

"I keep hearing rumors going around, you know," Tuthjorn grunted, hoisting himself up onto a ledge. He held out a hand towards Oomphga.

"Rumors? About..?" Oomphga jumped up and grabbed Tuthjorn's arm, nearly dragging him down with him, but Tuthjorn endured the weight bearing down on his arm.

"Rrrrgh...You!"

"Oomphga?"

"Yes!" Tuthjorn let out a tense sigh, pulling Oomphga up to his level. "Apparently, Seirah's been talking about you behind your back."

"Good things or bad things?"

"Eh...both? It depends on what you consider to be a good thing being said about you. He talked about how good you are with plants and animals, how well you've been doing with your apprenticeship stuff - great job, by the way - but…"

"But?"

"I don't know. 'Said your goals were too…ambitious. Unrealistic. Whatever that means."

Unrealistic?

"Is…wanting peace between the bearfolk and half-giants too much to ask? Is the mere concept of peace really…unrealistic?"

"…You know, I think I can see why Seirah said such things about your goals."

"But…is it?!" Oomphga whined. "Look at it this way, the half-giants and bearfolk have no reason to fight anymore aside from the occasional family feud, so why bother making it anyone else's business?"

Tuthjorn scoffed. "I don't know. They just do. Even still, what can we - correction: *you* - do about it?"

"Something. Anything." Oomphga huffed, his lungs working harder as Tuthjorn swiftly trudged onward. By this point, Oomphga could hardly keep up. "It's better than doing nothing."

As they crested over mountain ledges side by side, Oomphga longingly took in the view of the rocky crests and the trees meeting together in harmony on the horizon: mountain and forest together as one.

"Look, Oomphga," Tuthjorn uttered, "if you want my honest advice - my honest opinion - I suggest you don't even bother with *those* beasts. They're not like the run-of-the-mill wolf or polar bear you seem to care so much about. They're vicious and vile…"

Those. Oomphga didn't like that word very much. *Those.*

That word - that sickeningly repulsive five letter word - struck Oomphga in the chest with a dagger that burned the skin off of his bones. In this context, Oomphga couldn't have hated hearing that word any more than he did. Every muscle in his body stiffened, every hair and every follicle of fur stood on ends, and yet his expression remained soft. As soft as the tuft of hair hanging down his back from his makeshift ponytail.

"...And Tuthjorn would've been dead because of them if not for his papa. Oomphga knows."

Patting Oomphga on the shoulder, Tuthjorn stood close to his cousin's side, a small grin inching its way across his cheek.

"That-a boy. Look at you, coming around to despising those scarlet-furs! I think there may just be some hope for you yet!"

Before the two knew it, they were cresting over a hill that led them straight to the clearing where a cozy shack covered in fauna and dusty, white snow sat. Oomphga eagerly rushed to lead, running with journal in hand up to Seirah's door. He knocked a chipper beat - as per his usual - and stood by. When Seirah finally opened up, he looked down upon his apprentice, his face alight with a natural glow at the sight of an equally excited Oomphga.

"Good afternoon, Oomphga, and good afternoon to you as well, Jarl Tuthjorn. Come in, come in."

Seirah stepped aside and beckoned the two younglings into the warm embrace of his home. Oomphga graciously entered, arms coiled around his leather-bound collection; Tuthjorn politely shoved him aside as he walked past. With a gentle click, Seirah closed the door behind him and sat down in the rickety, handcrafted chair that sat within an arm's reach of a shelf packed with potion ingredients and medicine. Realizing that Seirah was finally comfortable, Oomphga handed his journal to Seirah and patiently stood by, watching him skim through his most recent pages.

"Only two today?"

"U-uh, yes..! It's getting a lot more difficult to find new plants in the mountains, see, and today, Oomphga has some very important duties he needs to take care of with Tuthjorn."

"Duties that are more important than the assignments I give you?" Seirah raised a suspicious brow.

Tuthjorn coughed loudly next to Oomphga.

"Well, training. Strength training," Oomphga uttered. "It's Oomphga's duty to the tribe to be strong and fit for battle, isn't it?"

"A shaman? Fit for battle?"

Suddenly, he could sense an eerie, judgmental aura enveloping the room as all eyes were on him and all ears tuned in to his next words. The power - the authority - these two individuals had over Oomphga nearly overwhelmed him, but something changed. Something unnatural. Oomphga peered over to the window and heard, off in the distance, the coos of a very large yet very familiar raven: Omen. Despite being a soft purring, Omen's voice boomed and echoed across earth and sky. Oomphga understood this voice.

"You are the druid," he solemnly chirped. *"It's all about balance. Tell them. Tell them it's all about balance."*

Oomphga returned his attention to Seirah and Tuthjorn. They were waiting ever so patiently for him to elaborate.

"Well, yes. Oomphga…thinks it's pretty important to balance strength of the mind with strength of the body. Being big-brained means nothing without being big-muscled, and…vice versa?"

Almost simultaneously, they cocked their brows in intrigue and looked over at one another. As slowly as Seirah sat down, he stood up and approached Oomphga, his towering figure obscuring the light seeping in from the windows.

"And your magic..?" he whispered.

"What about it?"

"Do you wish to train that as well?"

It had been quite some time since Oomphga did *anything* with his magic. Despite getting his powers a few years ago, it still felt new. Fresh, even. He learned something new about it whenever he experimented with tapping into it.

"Yes, sir..!"

Seirah extended Oomphga's leather journal to him, letting him look through all the pages worth of progress he's made. Every page had colorful illustrations, handwritten text, and remnants of nature stuck between the bindings. It was all lovingly procured in this one book: Oomphga's pride and joy.

"There are a lot of things Oomphga would like to learn about and improve upon. His studies, his strength, his magic-"

"Then I think you've nearly reached the full extent of your nature studies in the mountains. As Shaman of the High Peak Mountain tribe, I grant you a warrior's freedom to explore the vastness of the forest. Perhaps, there you will find more wisdom to learn and more space to grow."

While Oomphga's expression remained unchanged, (if anything, he was more relieved to be granted the luxury of freedom), Tuthjorn laughed. He laughed and laughed until he was practically wheezing.

"Sorry! Sorry, but it sounds to me like you're telling Oomphga to waltz into scarlet-fur territory!"

Seirah reiterated his statement with his stern, serious gaze. "He is allowed freedom to resume his studies in the forest. Yes."

"Wait - *by Obak* - you really do mean-! You want to send my cousin into the dragon's lair?!"

"Oomphga's never seen a dragon. Think they're friendly?" Oomphga asked.

"Yes, but...you forget, Oomphga," Tuthjorn began, "scarlet-furs are not friendly. They're not like a wild animal that you can look at from afar and admire. If you look at one of them, they'll bury arrows into you and then roast you over a spit for supper, so if Seirah's going to send you on trips into the forest, I'm coming too! I'll protect you! I'm the chieftain's son, after all! It's my duty as a warrior and a leader to be! Besides, I'm good with a blade! I'm-"

"Too cocky." Seirah growled, forcefully slamming the base of his quarterstaff against the partially degraded floorboards. "Hasn't your father taught you about the importance of humility? Besides, this is Oomphga's field of study as a *shaman* to be. Not a chieftain's and certainly not yours."

Tuthjorn reeled back, fangs bared. He hated a lot of things, but one thing he hated more than anything was belittlement. Backlash. If he were in front of the other half-giant teens or his father's friends, he'd hate it even more, but seeing Oomphga in just as uncomfortable of a state, wriggling and squirming with anxiety, washed away his distaste. He never admitted it out loud, but seeing Oomphga make a bigger fool out of himself ALWAYS made him feel better.

Magic. There was something about having magic that made Oomphga uncomfortable. Yes, he wanted to improve upon his abilities using it for the sake of helping others, but there was something that irked him about possessing magical abilities. Maybe it was the sense that he, the freak of nature, was undeserving or that the idea of potentially powerful magic - capable of creating irredeemable damage - was at his fingertips. Or maybe - just maybe - it was an ill-omen in disguise; a sign that something terrible was weaving itself into the line of fate and Oomphga would end up being the only person capable and responsible enough to prevent it. For this reason, he had no choice.

"So, what do you say, Oomphga? Think you'd be ready for such a jump in your studies?"

"Y-yes, Seirah, sir."

One by one, Tuthjorn and Oomphga filed out of Seirah's hut, and they both, simultaneously, let out a much-needed sigh of relief.

Tuthjorn glanced over at his cousin and friend, his gaze the softest it's been in a long time.

"Are you alright there, 'cos?" Tuthjorn asked, gently patting the back of his hand against Oomphga's shoulder.

"Yeah. He's fine." Oomphga clawed at the curly mats in his hair. "He's fine. He's ready to do strength training with Tuthjorn now."

"No, no, no. You focus on your magic and apprenticeship stuff for the rest of the day. We'll just focus on strength stuff another day."

"But what about-?"

"Oomphga, look at yourself."

Oomphga looked himself over. His appearance looked fine aside from the obvious deformities of the face that he knew he had. It's not like Tuthjorn could see it though so maybe it was…

"No, not physically. Just-…it's all about-…" Tuthjorn huffed. "You don't have that…FIRE right now that you kinda need to do strength training. You don't have the-the hype, the adrenaline, the burst of energy you get whenever you do something you're REALLY passionate about! And I get it. Fighting isn't your passion, and it sucks that Seirah demolished whatever amount of ambition you had with his huff and puff about the work you have to do for your apprenticeship, but you can't work on your strength when you're this upset about it. Not like this…unless~"

There was a pause. Oomphga recognized that devious spark in Tuthjorn's eyes, and he didn't like it one bit. Tuthjorn bounded off to the middle of the clearing in front of Seirah's house where he stood with a cocky grin on his face. From a pocket embedded in the blue cloak around his shoulders, he pulled out a slingshot (along with its respective pebbles) and stepped back, broadening the gap between himself and his cousin.

"If you wanna stand there and sulk all day, go ahead, but I'm gonna go pop a couple of birds out of the sky," Tuthjorn bragged.

"Tuthjorn wouldn't-!"

"Oh, he will, unless Oomphga does something about it~"

With a snarky smirk, he turned tail, running off down the path as he readied his slingshot. Frantically, Oomphga threw himself off the steps of Seirah's home and made a mad dash after Tuthjorn. His legs buckled under the weight placed in each step down the slope, but Oomphga kept running. He wouldn't stop until Tuthjorn's slingshot was out of his hand.

Tuthjorn led the way back towards the tribe, his attention on the skies and the treetops above. He knew he'd come across a bird to shoot at eventually. He already spotted a few as the two made their way into the thick, rolling grove of pine trees. As they ran, sliding down the hills and leaping over rocks, Tuthjorn laughed with glee while Oomphga lost his footing from behind.

He stumbled, the gap between him and Tuthjorn getting larger and larger. Every muscle in Oomphga's body cried out. The sting of the chilled winter air dug its fangs into his flesh, and yet there was Tuthjorn, paces ahead. He sprung down the trail, flying through the air and landing without skidding or sliding an inch.

"Come on, Oomphga! Wouldn't want an innocent bird to get hurt, now, would we?!"

Almost as if on cue, a bird caught Tuthjorn's eye. A mourning dove. It was a tufted titmouse. If a pebble the size of a thumb hit it, Oomphga couldn't even begin to calculate the possibility of a creature that small surviving Tuthjorn's deathly aim. He readied his slingshot as he got closer and swiftly came to a stop. The bird was ignorant, nestled in the branch's creases. It was now or never. Oomphga burst through the physical anguish and threw himself forward with all of his might. Swift steps: quick breaths getting quicker the longer he endured. Without warning, and through no control of his own, his body suddenly felt lighter. His skin was enveloped in a blanket of fur. His hands and feet -

calloused, trembling, and tense - were smaller and buried themselves into the inches of snow rising from base to joints. A wave of energy rushed through his veins and, without hesitation, Oomphga threw himself at Tuthjorn.

His body cut through the air and slammed into Tuthjorn's side. He burrowed his claws into Tuthjorn's shoulders and reached his neck around to sink his fangs into Tuthjorn's wrist. The slingshot slipped out from his cousin's fingers and dropped to the ground. He reeled his head around and stared deep into the amber eyes of a dire wolf. This was not Tuthjorn's friend anymore. This was a monster with only the faintest shred of Oomphga left in it.

"Alright, Oomphga! I give up! I give up! You can let go now!" Tuthjorn pleaded through tears.

Oomphga's toothy grip loosened, but he still held onto his back with his claws. He let out a long, guttural growl in response as his eyes, sharp as daggers, imbedded themselves into Tuthjorn's gaze.

"I promise! I won't shoot any of the birds. You have my word. As the son of Chieftain Mortium, you have my word!"

After careful consideration, Oomphga dropped down from Tuthjorn's back and stared up at him. At his arm. What a nasty bite Oomphga left. Blood oozed out of the dozens of tooth marks embedded in his flesh. He could taste it now. The sickening substance that coated his teeth. Oomphga slowly lifted his head up towards his cousin until his muzzle pressed up against his skin. He parted his lips and let his tongue run across the wound, whimpering as he cleaned it the best he could.

"Ah, don't worry about it. I'm sorry I riled you up like that, buuut it *did* work, didn't it?"

Oomphga let out a whimper.

"Gah...looks like you do have some bite to your bark after all," Tuthjorn hissed as he squeezed at the area around his wound to bleed it even after Oomphga finished cleaning it. "I know I technically started it and all - and I technically deserve this - but we gotta take care of my arm before I go home to dad. Otherwise, he's gonna yell at us for playing around with dire wolves, and neither of us want to get in trouble, now do we?"

Shaking his head, Oomphga stepped back a bit. Wisps of golden light danced around him, allowing him to turn back into his half-giant self - clothes, equipment, and all. Before Tuthjorn noticed, he tucked back his bear ears.

"Right. Tuthjorn is right," Oomphga stated, bringing his palms to Tuthjorn's arm. The same soft light enveloped Oomphga's hands and seeped into Tuthjorn's arms, restoring the skin he had lost leaving only the faintest sign of bruising where the scars were.

"There. Like nothing ever happened. And nothing did happen today, right Oomphga?"

". . ."

"Don't look so glum! You did great today! You might not have muscles like mine, but you sure showed me that you're strong! Maybe not as fast, but pretty darn strong. Would give our great grandpa a run for his greataxe, that's for sure!" Tuthjorn cheered.

But Oomphga did not feel the same pride Tuthjorn expressed. Despite the appraisal, nothing about what Oomphga did sat well with him. If anything, the thought of injuring his cousin in such a way only for him to shrug it off ate him up inside. As he stared at the bruise that lingered across his arm, he could only feel a crippling sense of dread and sorrow. Along with the taste of blood still lingering on his teeth and tongue, it all made him sick to his stomach.

"Oomphga is sorry," he uttered briefly before burying his head against Tuthjorn's chest. "He's...so sorry."

"Hey. Hey, it's alright, 'cos. It's all water under the bridge, and with your healing magic, it really is! Hardly felt a thing!"

Tuthjorn let out a soft chuckle and coiled his arms around Oomphga, holding him in a brief yet gentle embrace. When he drew back, he ruffled Oomphga's hair and ignored the feeling of his bear ears - the same way he always did.

If only he knew. If only Oomphga didn't keep it a secret, then maybe...

"Come on," Tuthjorn began. "Let's head back to the tribe, yeah? We'll go back to your place, have some food, and grab a pint of pear juice. You're favorite!"

Oomphga nodded. With one arm around his back and a hand on his shoulder, Oomphga trudged back home nestled close into Tuthjorn's side. There was a long silence from Oomphga that hung in the air, but Tuthjorn - being the bold, talkative sort that he was - didn't let that linger. He found a way to stir up a conversation about that girl again and rambled on about her without end, throwing around speculation after speculation about what she was like, swooning over the made-up illustrations of the imaginary, pretty girl that he painted in his mind. It was amusing. It definitely took Oomphga's mind off of earlier events of the day.

"Oomphga, if you end up catching her fancy more than me, would you be willing to put in a good word for me?"

"Catch...her...fancy?"

"Yeah. If she likes you more than me!"

"Oh! Uh...well...Oomphga doesn't think he'll be 'catching anyone's fancy', but sure. If she likes Oomphga more than Tuthjorn, Oomphga would be willing to brag about Tuthjorn if he cares that much about impressing this girl. Although...how does Tuthjorn know that he'll like her?"

"Huh?"

"Sorry! What if...*you* don't like her? What if she's bossy or mean? 'Cause if she's anything like the girls around here then you have nothing to worry about! She definitely won't like Oomphga!"

"Haha! She's not gonna be bossy. She's from the Violet Sun tribe, and Dad says their customs are different from ours, so I don't think she'll be ANYTHING like the girls around here!"

"Well, Oomphga and Tuthjorn won't know anything about her until she gets here, now, will they? Until then, have patience."

Patience was never a strong trait of Tuthjorn's, but the two had no choice. They had to wait, even if their imaginations and uncertainties were restless.

By the time they were done conversing, Oomphga and Tuthjorn stood by the front door of Oomphga's small hut of a home. As suggested, they had food and juice, laughing and carrying on about other things, until the sun set and the moon rose.

"Oh! It's almost curfew. I gotta get home. Thanks for hanging out with me today, Oomphga. I hope you get better with your magic stuff, and if you're gonna take Seirah up on his offer, be safe! I don't know what I'd do if I lost my favorite cousin!"

"Oomphga will be fine. He'll just be looking at plants in the woods anyways. Nothing too crazy~"

Before Tuthjorn could step out the door, Oomphga coiled his arms around Tuthjorn and pulled him in for a tight hug.

"Oomphga will see Tuthjorn again in a few weeks."

With a pat and a salute, Tuthjorn bounded off towards his family's longhouse at the top of the hill overlooking the tribe.

As Oomphga lay awake that night, staring up at the arched ceiling of the hut he and his mother called home, he let his mind weave colorful tapestries of this new girl coming to the mountains. Unlike the men and women of the High Peak Mountain tribe, he envisioned this girl being slimmer, maybe more dexterous in her build with flowers lacing her hair and a waterfall of feathers draped over her shoulders and hanging down her back. Slung around her waist was a bag filled with herbs, and peeking out over her shoulder was a bow that she used to keep herself safe. As well as a physical appearance, he contemplated her voice, deep yet gentle on the ears, her mannerisms, cool and collected, and her interests, maybe hunting (as it was with all half-giants) and - *what's another random yet incredibly reasonable interest - stargazing?*

Regardless, with a clear and concise image in his mind, he could begin planning out the potential conversations they'd have about the different types of flowers and the many animals they've seen. Oh, how wonderful that would've been: to finally be in the company of someone that shared the same interests as him.

His colorful imagination came to an abrupt halt when his mother stepped close to his bed, her eyes sunken.

"Sleep. Now. You have a long day of traveling tomorrow."

"Aww…alright, Mama…"

"And don't forget to tell your papa how much I love him."

"I won't forget, Mama. Don't worry~"

Mama Vergaia cracked a small smile and trudged over to her cot. With a loud *thump*, she collapsed onto it, falling asleep instantly the moment her head hit the pillow. Meanwhile, Oomphga burrowed himself into his bed, letting the feeling of his warm, fur blankets envelope him as he slowly drifted off into dancing dreams about girls, flowers, and magic.

Chapter 5:
A Quicker Way Down

*A*QUICKER WAY DOWN...
Oomphga thought about this everyday throughout those ten painful days alone on the long, familiar road to Papa Sergei's passing between the mountains and the forest. At first, the trips he made across the glacial passes and through the villages weren't so bad, but now they were getting to be the most boring part of Oomphga's life. If his mother were here with him, things would be different, but now, he was all on his own.

There must be a quicker way down!

With heavy breaths and tensed arms, Oomphga decided that - today - he wanted to try scaling down the mountain's more natural paths. He didn't expect it to get him there much quicker, but he didn't think there would be any harm in trying. So, with courage across his chest, he climbed down several large rocks and wandered through fields of heavy snow, taking in the beautiful sight of the clear blue skies above and the sun-kissed treetops beyond. A warm radiance embraced his snow-buried legs and brought about a soothing bliss with each step he took through the heavy powder around him. If he didn't have a father that worried so deeply for him, Oomphga would stop and drown himself in sunlight and snowdust. Alas, he had to firmly remind himself: he was looking for a way home that would cut the time he spent on the trail.

So, he continued his trek down the mountains until he eventually spotted - concealed by piles of winter fluff a few paces away - a large, gaping hole that appeared to lead down deeper and deeper into a craggy abyss. To most people that lived in the mountains, this would be considered hazardous and deadly if treated with ignorance, but to

Oomphga this looked like an opportunity for efficiency - a quicker way down!

The only question was: what was at the bottom? Oomphga peered over the edge only to be met with a long tunnel with no answers. Plopping down his backpack full of things into a mound of snow beside him, he dug through a pouch containing his essential traveling gear, wriggling and squirming his hand around in one of the bigger pockets until his hand brushed over a large spool of hempen rope. He pulled it out of his backpack with ease and then looked it over. It was definitely sturdy enough to hold the young half-giant - this he knew - but how far would it get him down this seemingly endless chasm? Without a way to see or gauge the depth of the gaping hole, Oomphga put his trust in his instincts and tossed down the length of rope he had, securing the other end to a "pretty sturdy" rock he found close by.

Then, taking a deep breath, Oomphga swung his backpack back over his shoulders and he began his descent down into the deep, dark unknown. The sun he once basked in seconds prior was now barely in view, and the only thing that embraced him now was a frigid breeze that occasionally swept down his bare spine. The rocks his bare feet pressed up against for support were sharp and unforgiving, cutting his toes and heels. The further down Oomphga climbed, the more he felt his arms tremble. Maybe climbing down this mysterious hole was a worse idea than he had originally thought.

Down . . .

Down . . .

Down he went . . .

Deeper and deeper into the depths below. The lower he hung, the more the rope seemed to swing. There was a faint purring coming from above. When Oomphga looked up towards the light, he could see the rope begin to strain. He had to be close to the bottom now, right? He clambered down a little quicker, his upper body clinging to the rope while he outstretched his leg beneath him until… there it was. Solid ground. With relative grace, Oomphga let himself drop two or three feet down, the fall reminding him that his knees needed as much time to recuperate as the rest of his body, but first, he had to establish where exactly he was. Oomphga fumbled around in the darkness, trying to collect a torch or something from his bag. That's when he heard a gruff snort echoing from deep within the bowels of this foreign cave.

Oomphga paused. He wasn't sure what kind of creature made a noise like that. Whatever it was sounded massive in scale. Oomphga intensely peered into the dark, hardly able to see a thing until he spotted a faint silhouette shambling towards him. A raspy growl echoed out in tandem with a deep yet feminine voice.

"Stay where you are, intruder. Let Mama see you."

A twinge shot through Oomphga's body, spreading through his spine to his hands. His search became all the more frantic now as he wriggled his hand around in his bag trying to find something that he couldn't even see. Metal bits and bobbles clinged and twanged as his knuckles brushed up against everything within his satchel.

Come on..! Come on! Come on!!!

There! He grabbed hold of his torch and yanked it out of his bag.

"Yes..!" He exclaimed softly.

Now, a light. With a whisper and a snap, there was a spark and soon a flame hanging from his fingertips. He held it up to the pale cloth coiled around the head of his torch and, within a minute, the flame grew in size. The ground, his bag of traveling trinkets, a couple of sparkly rocks on the ground, and a long, brown snout were all illuminated by the torchlight.

He could see clearly now; this was no beast before him. It was a bear - a mama bear - and it had its sights set on Oomphga. Its mouth hung agape, teeth sparkling like citrines against the warm light of the fire.

"H-hello," Oomphga uttered, reaching for his chest. "M-my name is Oomphga. Are you…a mama bear?"

"…You have ears like mine," she huffed.

"Yeah. Oomphga got these ears from his Papa Sergei. He's a bearfolk guy."

The bear reared her head back and stood up, eyes alight and ears upright. She turned her head from side to side to look around before pointing to herself.

"You can understand me?"

"Oomphga can understand all animals. He's a druid…he thinks."

"I've heard of those." The bear plopped down onto her paws again and leaned in close once more, the edge of her snout brushing against Oomphga's neck and cheek. "If you're a druid, then why were you afraid of me?"

"Oomphga has had…back luck with animals in the past-" Oomphga whispered, his voice trailing off. The warmth of the grizzly bear's fur enveloped him, and her moistened snout tickled his skin. Oomphga remembered this feeling all too well. His throat clenched and he grit his teeth as his gaze followed a small, furry figure scurrying off in the distance.

"Oomphga had best get going. He needs to get home." Oomphga uttered, his gaze realigning with the bear's. "Where does this cave lead?"

"Here, hop on my back. I'll get you out of here."

Oomphga snatched up his bag, briefly extinguished his torch, and carefully climbed onto the bear's back only to reignite the flame. After taking a few deep breaths, Oomphga readjusted his focus onto the female grizzly. In everything she did, she was so gentle. He could hardly imagine what would've happened if she somehow misinterpreted Oomphga as some kind of threat. He couldn't even hurt a fly let alone her, but with half-giants and their history with wildlife, there was no telling what went through her mind.

"So…does Mama Bear have a name?"

"Goodness, no! We bears don't have distinguished names or titles like the hairless ones or the animalfolk do."

"Then…if Mama Bear had a name, what would she call herself?"

"You call me whatever you see me as."

"Hm…Bear Friend."

"Bear Friend?"

"You're a bear and you're friendly. Bear Friend. Do you not like it?"

"No, no! I am actually relieved that you see me as a friend," she chortled, glancing back over her shoulder at a much happier Oomphga. "I suppose I expected a more…hairless name."

"Oh, Oomphga doesn't like giving animals people names. In fact, he doesn't like 'naming' animals at all anymore since it's…bad luck!"

"Is it?"

Oomphga let out an affirmative hum as he refocused his attention on the surrounding cave. Torch held high, he stared intently at the shadows that danced across the wall.

"Does Bear Friend have cubs?"

"One. Would you like to meet him?"

"Yes! Please."

She shifted her neck and turned around to hobble down a branching pathway. The clearing she took Oomphga to was huge in scale. Patches of glistening stalactites hung over an open pool of water, and every so often, a soft *plink* or *plop* would echo over the torch-light's crackling. Oomphga looked around, his eyes following the natural pillars of stone and the winding path that lingered above them against the wall off to their right only to see the road trail down at the end into a rolling pile of rocks. Past this pile of rocks was a thin gap that led to a much smaller, more snug clearing where there a small bear cub wandered around until it spotted Oomphga.

"Hairless! Hairless!" The bear cub cried, belting out his voice in both confusion and warning to his mother.

Oomphga carefully hopped off of Bear Friend's back and knelt down before the bear cub. He extended his hand towards the cub and it cautiously began its approach. Nose outstretched it took tiny steps closer and closer until it was close enough to lift its front paw to bat at Oomphga's hand.

"Your paw smells like fish," the bear cub mumbled. "But I don't see any fish."

"Probably just Oomphga sweat. He does that a lot," Oomphga confessed.

"What's an Oomphga?"

"Oomphga is me. It's his name."

"But what's a name?"

Bear Friend sat down and let out a grizzly chuckle. Her cub responded with furrowed brows and a scrunched-up nose.

"Mama, what's a name?" The bear cub repeated, this time addressing his mother. He bounded over to his mother's side in a huff, climbing into her warm, fuzzy lap.

"It's what he's called. Like you calling me Mama or me calling you Baby or Sweetie, he goes by Oomphga."

"Oomphga…what a weird name. He's Hairless. That's what I'd name him," the bear cub sassed, raising his head proudly.

"And how would you separate him from all the others?" Ears perked at the question; the bear cub paused. Confidence drained from his expression, and he bowed his head.

"Well…I…"

Seeing that her son wasn't going to respond, she looked over to Oomphga to see his reaction.

"He could…call Oomphgaaa…Fuzzy!"

"Fuzzy?"

"Since Oomphga's not really hairless yet he isn't covered in hair, you can call him Fuzzy! A good in-between, if he does say so himself~"

"Alright…so…Fuzzy," the bear cub began, eyes squinted. "What are you doing in OUR cave, anyway?"

"Oomphga - or rather, Fuzzy - was looking for a quicker way down the mountains. He saw a big hole that led straight down, and since it was so close to the edge of the cliff overlooking Bristlethorn Forest, he was hoping it would take him home. If it did, Fuzzy would be saving days of travel time so he could spend more time with his papa!"

"You WANT to find your papa?"

"Well, yeah. Fuzzy likes spending time with his papa. They pick berries together, go on hikes through the forest - Papa Sergei always lets Fuzzy talk about the plants he found. He has a whole book of them that he keeps on hand in case he finds something new," Oomphga rambled happily.

With his free hand, he pulled out the small journal he had tucked away in the deep pockets of his baggy green pants and opened it up to a random page of his entries where a small, pink flower was drawn next to words that read:

Herb Robert (Stinky Bob)

Known for being one of the stinkiest weeds, herb robert is an invasive species that can be identified by its small pink flower petals, its fuzzy, red-ish stem, and the odd number of rounded points on its leaves. DO NOT CRUSH THE FLOWER. It triggers the stinky.

Reading it in his mind, Oomphga giggled before showing the page to the bears.

The bear cub stuck his tiny nose deep within the book binding, sniffing the ink and the flattened flowers. "What's all this?"

"This is Fuzzy's notebook. He has to do this mainly for his studies, but...kind of like how your Mama taught you how to do things, Fuzzy's papa taught him how to make it look pretty with these things called illustrations. That's why..." Oomphga paused, lost in a sea of memories.

Over the years, there were so many fun things he used to do with his Papa Sergei. Whenever he wasn't there, sitting beside his papa, he was terribly and utterly alone with only the things his father taught him to keep him company. This journal - this compilation of all the things Oomphga loved - served as the unbreakable bond between his colorful, fun-loving papa and his wise, down-to-earth mama, and he couldn't even begin to imagine a place in time without either of them or the leatherbound book he held in his grasp.

"...that's why Fuzzy would like to find his papa. He wants to spend more time with him painting and writing and playing! That's why he wanted to find a quicker way to his house. That's why he risked climbing down the spooky hole that brought him into your home."

Bear Friend carefully picked up her cub by the scruff of his neck and moved him aside so she could stand up and allow Oomphga to climb back up onto her backside.

"Well, then, let's get you to your papa."

"I wanna come too! I want to play and spend more time with you after Fuzzy leaves, Mama!" The bear cub whined, jumping up and down next to his mother's front paws. He occasionally stumbled in front of her, but his gaze never diverted from her face even as she began walking towards the cave entrance.

"Alright, alright. You can come along, Sweetie. Just stay close to Mama," she warned.

And there we were, traveling back through the deep, dark cave until we inevitably reached the great outdoors. Oomphga extinguished his torch and took in the sights. The warm glow of the sun was all he needed now to illuminate the path home.

"So, where to next?"

Chapter 6:
Like Father, Like Son

PAPA SERGEI'S HOUSE sat a few paces ahead. Oomphga could recognize the healthier, home-grown trees, the brighter patches of grass, and the diverse collection of natural wildflowers that littered the fields. As they reached the edge of the meticulously well-kept yard, Oomphga paused to take in the view. His eyes scanned the house, watching for any signs of life beyond the windows.

"Thank you," Oomphga uttered as he dismounted from Bear Friend's back and rearranged his satchel over his shoulder. "You and Small Bear were both a huge help to Oomphga! He…hopes it wouldn't be too much trouble to pass through your cave more often to reach Papa Sergei's."

"We'd be delighted to see you again!" Bear Friend cheered.

Her bear cub, on the other hand, looked significantly less enthused about the idea, rolling his eyes and letting out a faint huff.

"Mamaaa…" he whined. "Can we go catch fish now? I'm hungry…"

"Yes, yes. We can. It was nice meeting you, Oomphga!"

With a smile, salute, and a spring in his step, Oomphga bounded up the hill past the vegetable garden and the stone well; up the oak steps and onto the weathered porch. He didn't even get a chance to knock on the front door before Sergei opened it to greet him, eyes bright, ears perked, and happy as a lark to see his son again after so long.

"Oomphga! You are early! Come in! Come in! Can I make you anything, my beloved son?" he asked, clasping his hands together celebratorily.

After entering Sergei's house, Oomphga paused next to his papa, looking up at him with a cheeky grin.

"Oomphga would like…bear-berry pancakes, please!"

"Pancakes? At 6:00 in the afternoon?"

Oomphga shrugged. "Why not?"

Sergei sighed, but cracked a one-sided smile, brown eyes softening. "Alright. Bear-berry pancakes it is then!"

"YES!!!"

Together, the two rushed to the kitchen to get out all of the ingredients and soon began their pancake-making dance. Father and son worked in tandem, the two gracefully sliding across the stone tile back and forth between counters and cabinets to fetch whatever was needed for their recipe. Every so often, they would cry out a chipper reminder to the other to turn down the heat at just the right moment and voila! Perfect bear-berry pancakes.

Every. Single. Time.

With one last flip and a tap of wooden plates, the fruits of their labor were laid before, them just out of arm's reach, perfectly stacked with butter and maple glaze oozing down the edges.

The two sat across from each other, prepping their plates until their hard-earned feast rested between their hands and their respective wooden utensils. The moment the sunset's orange beams of light accentuated their gluttonous desires, their animalistic instincts yanked back the veil and revealed its toothy maw. They ripped and tore into their pancakes with their forks and knives desperate for a mouthful of that sweet blueberry and golden fluff. Once they both sank their teeth into their first bear-sized bite, they let out complimentary hums, signifying that room for conversation just opened.

"Sooo? Has anything new or exciting happened in the lives of Oomphga and his Mama Vergaia?" Sergei belted cheerfully from the other end of the table.

"Not too much." Oomphga replied, mouth still half full of half-chewed bites. "Let's see…Oomphga found a shortcut down the mountain, met a bear and her cub (they were really nice), discovered twelve new types of plants up around the old church ruins, picked up totem crafting a while back, but...he's not too sure he's gonna do anything with that-"

"That's nice! How is Mama Vergaia doing?" Papa Sergei asked, eagerness in his tone.

"She's doing alright. She's the only chef in the tribe, so she's doing all she can to feed everyone at the moment," Oomphga giggled and smiled across the table at his anxious father. "She says she loves you!"

Papa Sergei let out a big sigh of relief. "And Papa Sergei loves her too, very, very much! He also loves his little Oomphga!"

"He's not so little anymore now, Papa!" Oomphga laughed back.

"I know! He's such a big boy, he might even be old enough to try and go fishing again with his old man," Papa Sergei replied, poking a big forkful of pancake fluff that he shoved into his toothy gob. "Maybe this year, he'll be able to catch and release something without getting too squeamish."

Oomphga recalled back to his fifth year when he tried to go fishing with Papa Sergei. He gagged every time Papa Sergei put a worm on the hook and cried whenever a fish bit the line, got reeled into the rowboat, and started flailing around as if its life depended on it. His father saw it as harmless fishing, and Oomphga saw it as aquatic torture.

"If he's old enough to go fishing again, is Oomphga also old enough to go into the market again with Papa Sergei? He needs to pick up another journal for his nature studies. The one he has right now is getting kind of full-"

Papa Sergei paused, eyes darting across Oomphga's ashen skin. He harshly swallowed and let out a raspy cough.

"Oomphga, it's...not about your age. It's about-"

"Oomphga has a sweater and long hair. He can keep his half-giant features hidden." Blissfully unaware of his father's concerns, he resumed eating his breakfast, one hungering bite after another. "Come on, Papa! Oomphga hides his bear features all the time at home with Mama. He's used to it. Why is it any different with you?"

"Because unlike your mama, I don't think you should have to hide any part of yourself..!" Papa retorted; his voice slightly raised. "It's not...normal for kids like you to grow up hiding who they really are all the time. It cuts me deep, little Oomphga, watching my boy, who's already self-conscious as it is, hiding himself in plain sight all for – what? To fit in? To be like everyone else? Is that what you want? If so,...I worry for you, my little Oomphga. Please, don't be mad."

"So, what would Papa prefer? Oomphga plays with grass in the backyard and never steps foot in the city ever again?"

Oomphga let out a long sigh, pulled out his journal from the small, leather pouch by his waist, and he sat it aside before he slowly resumed eating his brunch. He dragged his fork through the pancake, tearing it apart in small flakes that drowned in thick syrup on his plate. Sergei stared at his son from across the table, scratching the fur across his jaw as an awkward silence filled the kitchen.

Hesitantly, Sergei reached across the small, round table to pat Oomphga's hand.

"I love you, son. I love you so much that I'll...I'll think about it. If going to the market is something you REALLY want to do while you're here with Papa Sergei, then...I *might* let you go with him."

Oomphga's face lit up, his ears springing to life atop his head.
"Yeah?"

"Yes. So, how about it? Will you let your papa think about it for a night?"

Oomphga finally cracked, a smile inching across his face. "Of course. Anything for you, Papa Sergei."

With little daylight left, Oomphga finished his pancakes, put on his baggy pajamas, and checked in on each and every one of his plants before he clambered into his bed. The sheets were recently washed. He could feel it. The warmth embraced him, practically begging him to doze off into a heavy slumber, but there was still so much on Oomphga's mind.

Firstly, Oomphga reflected on the long road ahead. He had so much to do for Seirah and his apprenticeship, he nearly forgot about all the things he wanted to do for himself - no - his people. His homeland. His community. Tuthjorn, although bold and brash, had noble goals and he wasn't wrong when he implied they were more "realistic" than Oomphga's. Being able to punch boulders and defend people in a fight seemed far more doable than ending a war, bringing about world peace, or protecting every living creature under the sun, but it's what Oomphga wanted, as unrealistic as it all sounded.

If documenting plants would somehow make him a wiser shaman for his tribe and druid for - well - everyone and everything else, Oomphga wanted to do it. Plants, animals, magic, learning the history of where it all comes from and how the world worked - it all sounded like an adventure fit for a keeper of balance and representative of nature.

In all of his vivid imagination, Oomphga couldn't even begin to paint a picture of everything he's seen already and all he'd witness in the years ahead.

Silhouettes of nondescript creatures, big and small, humanoid and bestial, approached Oomphga with curious, hungering eyes. They weaved and danced across the darkness, and yet Oomphga hardly worried about their intentions. They were just his imagination, after all, and his imagination couldn't hurt him even if it wanted to. So, for what felt like hours, Oomphga stared vacantly back at them, admiring them and their life-like vigor until his attention snapped onto the ladder leading up to his room. There was a gentle pat followed by a creak.

Then it happened again.

Pat. Creak. Pat. Creak.

Peering over the floorboards, Oomphga spotted two bear ears and big, brown eyes that glistened in the void. Oomphga could recognize that lamblike gaze from anywhere: Papa Sergei.

"Oomphgaaa~! Are you still awake~?" Sergei sang quietly.

"Yeah," Oomphga whispered in response. He wasn't afraid of his father knowing that he couldn't sleep, nor did he feel a compulsion to fake sleep like he did for his mama.

"Is Oomphga...still hungry?" Sergei asked.

Oomphga shook his head.

"Is Oomphga...not sleepy?"

Once again, Oomphga shook his head.

"So, you *are* sleepy. Is Oomphga...thinking about stuff? Is that why he can't sleep even though he's tired?"

"Yeah..."

Sergei clambered up the last remaining steps on the ladder and walked over to Oomphga's bed, plopping down onto the mattress and blankets by his feet.

"Papa? Were you ever expected to be anything special when you grew up?"

"Well, I was expected to be a merchant by my mom and dad! Of course, I made a couple of...questionable decisions growing up, and I ended up being a pirate, but...I was a good pirate! Literally! Everyone on board the F.F.S. Whiplash called me the bestest boy!" Sergei let out a heartfelt laugh, but Oomphga didn't reciprocate.

"Do you think...Oomphga will make a good druid one day?" Oomphga asked, his mind and body already entering a daze.

"I think..." Sergei plotted his next words carefully. "I think you'll grow up to be a good *person* one day. Whether you grow up to be a druid, or a shaman, or a warrior, or a painter, or whatever! As long as you do your best and you keep being as kind and compassionate as you are now in the years ahead, I think you'll end up being the person that you're the most proud of. No matter what happens, just know that I'll always love you and be proud of you because you are my son! And nothing is ever going to change that."

"Thanks, Papa."

"Now, you better get some sleep, little one."

"Papa?"

"Yes, Oomphga?"

"Could you...read 'The Animalfolk of Eustella' again?"

"Again? Starting from the beginning or-?"

"Yeah. Starting from the beginning~"

Papa Sergei let out a heartfelt sigh, stood up, and lumbered over to one of the tables in Oomphga's room where a few books sat alongside his collection of mossariums. "The Animalfolk of Eustella" was the thickest book of the bunch, but it was always Oomphga's favorite. From beginning to end, it was 328 pages of intricate storytelling and educational bliss. As interesting as it was to analyze, Oomphga always preferred listening to his papa softly speaking every line as he regaled his son with the true tale of how the animalfolk came to be.

Line after line, Oomphga's body melted further and further into his mattress. His eyes got heavier; his brain became emptier until a peaceful slumber finally overcame him.

The next morning, Oomphga awoke to the sound of Papa Sergei's voice.

"Oomphga, I came to a verdict last night."

"Mhm?" Oomphga tiredly hummed.

"Grab your sweater. We're going into town together!"

Oomphga's eyes shot open, energy overtook him. The second his father left Oomphga to his own devices, Oomphga clambered out of bed, wandered over to his dresser, and dug through piles of heavy clothes until he picked out a baggy blue sweater he wanted to wear along with his baggy tan pants. He threw them on and fluffed up his hair, making sure it was nice and poofy so he could use it to cover his facial features. Then, he collected a bag of gold pieces his father gave him, his bag of herbs, and his plant journal. Feeling lighter than air, he scurried down the ladder, rushed to the kitchen for a swift breakfast, and after he was done, he cleaned his dishes and stood by the front door, waiting for Sergei to meet him there.

"Got everything?" Sergei asked.

"Yep!"

"Alright, then let's go!"

Father and son traveled together, hand-in-hand. Along winding paths and babbling brooks, they took a scenic trip through Bristlethorn forest, talking and laughing along the way. While Oomphga rambled on about all the plants he's discovered and the fun facts about them he mysteriously knew, Sergei would ramble on about fish and the stories he had tied to each and every one of them. Just like his father, he never actually paid too careful attention to what he said, but he kept his ears pointed towards him even if his eyes wandered to other things that caught his interest.

"And that's how I knew your mother loved-!"

"Papa! Papa! Look at this stick!" Oomphga picked up a long branch off of the ground. It was the perfect size for a quarterstaff and the branch at the end spiraled in the most perfect way where the end came to a nice circle.

"Oh, Oomphga, what am I going to do with you?" Sergei chortled, a fuzzy, bear paw on his hip.

"Love and take good care of Oomphga forever and ever?"

Sergei patted Oomphga's shoulder as Oomphga walked with the quarterstaff still in hand. With each step, he awkwardly dug it into the ground, occasionally dragging it along whenever his arm grew too tired to lift it. Eyes now on the path ahead, Oomphga could hear chattering and saw - at the base of the rolling hills - tall buildings and sparkling lights: the city of Endinerose.

It was the beating heart of the Nature Faction, one of the largest, most bustling cities on the West side of High Peak Mountains, and one of the only places in the area where they (both bearfolk and half-giants) existed in the same space (under very strict regulation, of course).

Treading down the streets, his hand burrowed into Sergei's paw, Oomphga looked around aimlessly all while taking in as many sights and sounds as he could as he skipped down the sidewalk. As majestic as Endinerose was, it still had all the same aspects - both good and bad - as a big city. In other words, it was filled with as much bliss as there was chaos. With each note from a minstrel's melody came an infant's cry; for each child babbling to their friends was a whiney drunkard complaining to theirs; for every ounce of laughter was an ounce of distasteful bickering, and so on and so forth.

For some, these sounds of the city alone would drive someone mad - all the hustle and bustle, several conversations ringing in your ears at once, people hollering just to be heard over the more natural noises of the city - but to Oomphga, he didn't mind it. (He preferred it much more than war drums and chanting, anyway). And if there were any sounds of the city that brought Oomphga the most joy, it was the soft pitter patter of the fountain in the heart of the market district.

They were so close to it now. Just had to pass the Eat and Sleep Inn and they'd be there!

Of course, as Oomphga and Sergei made their way down the street parallel to the inn, Oomphga's eyes fell on a half-giant standing

idly between a door and the - unfortunately - oh, so familiar sign that
stated in bold, red letters:

Bearfolks allowed to drink: 5 a.m. - noon.

Half-giants allowed to drink: 1 p.m. - 6 p.m.

And if I catch any of ya fightin' within 30 feet of my property,

I'm reportin' all of yous to the NFC.

The NFC (Nature Faction Counsel), a huge organization with
multiple representatives chosen to stand in for each of the different races
that coexisted East of all the other elemental factions and West of No
Man's Land. Most of the council agreed to keep out of war unless it
interfered with the well-being of commonfolk or nobles that didn't
deliberately involve themselves, which is why businesses were forced to
post rules like this.

With every passing of this sign, Oomphga could sense trouble,
and this time, trouble came in the form of two female bearfolks that
stood still as stones on the opposite side of the street:

The taller of the two looked on at the inn, emerald eyes piercing
through the curly, crimson bangs that covered half of her head. Her
thick, furry fingers were coiled around a decorative gold and green spear.
Etched into the metal beneath the socket that held the silver, leaf-shaped
blade firmly in place were the words, "Love and Loyalty Eternal". Across
her chest was a blinding, heavy, metal plate with a prominent amethyst
embedded near the collar and hanging between her legs was a thin piece
of green cloth that stretched down to her ankles.

The bearfolk beside her was black-furred with a cane and pearly-
white pupils vacantly fixated on the same inn. Unlike most of the
bearfolk in the area, she was a descendant of black bears, ones that have

not yet been altered or tainted by the bloodbaths of war. In contrast to her companion's cold, metallic, battle-fit attire, she fashioned mostly long, flowing, rags that draped down her shoulders. Clinging to her waist was a long skirt that hung down to the sandals on her padded, fur-covered feet. The faded blues, purples, and golds of these robes brought more life and mystery to this woman than anyone else in the entirety of Endinerose.

The former of the two bearfolks glanced over at Oomphga. Her gaze reflected a shared sense of friendly familiarity.

Chapter 7:
Fear Fighting

ELADDA SWIFTCLAW; FAITH TRUEZ. Those were their names and Oomphga knew them well - which is the exact reason why he got so concerned seeing them both standing across the street from a menacing-looking half-giant meandering about outside of the Eat and Sleep Inn.

"Papa Sergei, can Oomphga go talk to his friends for a bit?" Oomphga asked.

"I suppose you can. Hey, try not to get yourself into any kind of trouble! Play safe!"

Without giving an affirmative response, Oomphga bounded over to Eladda and Faith, skidding to a halt close by with the help of his new stick to stop him in his tracks.

"Hey, guys! Whatcha…um…" Oomphga swiftly glanced back and forth between his friends and the half-giant idling along the side of the road. "Whatcha doin'?"

"Waiting for my dad to come crawling out of the inn," Eladda grumbled. "He was gone ALL night with a couple pals of his. I suspect they partied hard and waited until the inn's bar opened up at five just so they could grab a drink."

"Jeez. And that's why you're-"

"Standing here patiently waiting? Yeah-" Eladda let out an irritable sigh and leaned against her spear.

"Why haven't you gone to do something else in the meantime?"

"And miss catching him?"

"You're making him sound more like a mouse than a man, Eladda."

"Hmph. I wonder sometimes…"

Oomphga brushed his sleeves together a bit nervously as he joined his friends staring at the door to the inn. He hoped he wouldn't be here for too long.

"We expect he'll be out any minute now, right?" Faith asked.

"Yes. And if he doesn't come out at noon on the dot, we go in."

"Go in..?! Are we...even allowed to do that? Oomphga doesn't think we're of age and the sign says-"

"Don't know. Don't care. Gonna find out," Eladda interrupted.

"I think it'll be fine, Oomphga. It's not like we have any intention of drinking anything," Faith said.

"True. True." The longer Oomphga stared at the door, the more he felt the urge to hype himself up before going inside as if entering an inn at the age of thirteen would end up being some kind of "big deal". He waved his sleeves, hopped on his feet, took deep breaths, and spun his quarterstaff around in circles until...

BONK!

"Ow..!" Oomphga yelped as the heavier end of the staff landed between his ears on top of his head.

"It's noon. He's not out. We're going in."

Eladda led the charge towards the door with Faith and Oomphga trailing behind her left and right side. Swiftly passing by the half-giants standing outside, Oomphga could feel their unrelenting stares burrowing into the three of them, stalking their movements even as they scurried into the Eat and Sleep Inn.

Once inside, Oomphga and the others paused to take in the new perspective. There were so many different types of people occupying the tables scattered across the room: humans, elves, dwarves, orcs, angels, demons, and animalfolk dispersed across seats, chatting, conversing, and intermingling with one another. The inn was packed with so many people that looked different from one another talking and having fun together as if they were one in the same.

However, within this jovial scene of merriment, one expectation - one assumption was met: bearfolks (specifically "scarlet-furs" as the half-giants would call them) sat *almost* exclusively amongst their own kind. There they sat clustered in the corner of the inn, most of them in a droll, exhausted state with empty, wooden mugs inches away from their paws. At one table was a particularly interesting bunch of bearfolk that consisted mostly of men. Some dressed in formal attire while the others wore clothes that reflected a bizarre set of professions. One was a mage, another was an archeologist, and the third was, well, definitely a foreigner of some sort considering black robes and bits of silver armor that masked most of his appearance.

Amongst this crimson-furred crew, one sat with his cup in one hand and his head in the other. Dark circles clung to the bottom of his eyes and his fingers dug into the skin of his temples like earthworms trying to burrow into cracks in the road. He appeared distraught, almost mad, his attention intently fixated on the trails of dark wooden lines between the oak boards that made up the table.

"Father!" Eladda's voice cut through the room, instilling a brief moment of silence.

In a huff, she recklessly stomped over to the familiar drunkard and slammed her fist down on the table. Slowly, the man turned his head to Eladda and, somehow, every vaguely visible feature on his fluff-covered face dropped.

"Oh, it's only you, Eladda..."

Oomphga took Faith's hand and rushed over to Eladda's side, apologizing on her behalf to the guests and drinkers trying to enjoy their time at the inn. The moment he arrived, the foreign bearfolk dressed in black flashed Oomphga a crooked stare. He could see his glowing, ruby eyes behind the mask he wore.

Unappreciative of the attention, Oomphga shyly cowered behind Eladda's bulkier frame. She'd keep him safe from the mysterious man.

"I can't believe you left me alone last night and you didn't even tell me where you were! You could've been eaten by some kind of monster or had a stroke while you were out or..." Eladda paused, sporadically looking out the window at the half-giant peering in. "...or SOMETHING!!! If you wanted to go out and drink? Fine! That's fine, but leaving me, your daughter, home alone worried sick about you?! That's irresponsible at best and- ARE YOU EVEN LISTENING TO ME!?!"

Eladda crossed her arms and stood tall, gazing down upon her father with iron-clad disappointment beyond measure.

"You sound just like your mother." Mr. Swiftclaw slurred. "Always on my rump about this or that..."

"Well, someone's gotta look out for you, you old mule," Eladda hissed. "Now, let's go. You're cutting it a little too close to half-giant drinking hour..."

"Oooh. Is it?"

Mr. Swiftclaw buried his scratched-up paw into the faded orange cloth around his waist and dug out a silver pocket-watch. Oomphga inched closer to his shoulder and peered over it to read the funny little numbers around the inner rim of the metal circle. There was still roughly about an hour left.

"Oomphga, help me get my dad home, please-"

Oomphga's ears perked up at the sound of his name and he snatched a glance at Eladda. "Hm? Oh! Yes! Of course!"

Without warning, Mr. Swiftclaw stood up, his chair sliding back into Oomphga's abdomen. Oomphga let out an audible grunt and stumbled back, but quickly recovered his composure and rushed to Mr. Swiftclaw's front, dragging his left arm to his shoulder while Eladda grabbed the right. Together the two hauled him towards the door, occasionally calling back to Faith as a means to guide her towards the entrance. Despite exiting the tavern, Oomphga could still feel the cloaked bearfolk's eyes piercing through his psyche, but more eager to aid his friends, he suppressed it with every ounce of strength he had to his name.

"Oomphga's not gonna lie-"

"Do you ever lie?" Faith asked.

"Oomphga feels bad that Eladda has to babysit her own dad. If Oomphga had to babysit his dad, then who would keep Oomphga out of trouble?" Oomphga asked as he pushed open the door for the four of them.

"We would," Eladda replied. "Happily. For me doing this with my dad? It's not ideal given the circumstances. He's the general, after all. He's supposed to be responsible, but you. You're my best friend, Oomphga. I'd kill an army of half-giants for you if it meant keeping YOU out of trouble~!"

Oomphga nearly choked on his own spit. Not just out of fear for himself, but out of fear for the half-giant they were standing right next to. Oomphga flashed a crooked smile to the tall, burly man in a desperate attempt to keep the peace.

"She doesn't mean that!" he laughed. Immediately turning to Eladda, he belted a whisper. *Tell him you don't mean that!*

Instead of getting offended, the half-giant let out a barely audible chuckle, his gravelly vocals ringing in Oomphga's ears. He stared daggers at him, his twisted grin inching across his face the deeper he tried to gaze past the long, wavy locks of hair that shrouded Oomphga's humanoid facial features, leaving Oomphga no choice but to observe the strange burn mark that coiled around his neck beneath his scruffy beard in return.

The two of them could sense Eladda's bitterness increasing by the second the closer he got to her quivering companion. She turned away, her attention fixated on Faith and her father. Left alone at the mercy of the rugged stranger, Oomphga shrunk down and slowly tried to back away, but without warning, the half-giant grabbed him by the neckline of his sweater and held him firm - his grip on the fabric tight and unrelenting.

"Looks like you bearfolk are all alike after all," he hissed. "Pathetic."

"Pathetic..?!" Eladda snapped.

"Eladda, don't-!"

Suddenly, Eladda's clenched fist flew past Oomphga's cheek and into the man's yellow teeth with a loud *CRACK*! The sound rang out so close to Oomphga's ears, he couldn't tell if it came from the half-giant's jaw or Eladda's knuckles. The half-giant threw Oomphga back towards his friends and dropped to his knees. Blood trickled down his lip and marked the stone beneath him. Meanwhile, Eladda shook off the pain running through her hand and readjusted her stance. Fearlessly, she stood by Oomphga with one paw on his shoulder and another across the spear on her back. Faith hovered behind them both, paw resting on the rapier she had tucked away in her guide cane.

"Stay down, sir. Please," Oomphga begged politely, taking a few skittish steps back towards Faith and Eladda's drunken father.

But Oomphga knew, no matter how much he pleaded or tried to reason with the half-giant, his stubbornness would get the better him and thus, get the better of Eladda as well. Gradually, the grey-skinned man rolled back his shoulders and stood tall until he was - once again - towering above them only, instead of chuckling and brushing off the outburst, he growled and pulled a greataxe from his back. The blade dropped onto the cobblestone with a loud *clang* followed by a gentle, metallic *hiss* as he approached Eladda one step at a time.

"Stay where you are!" Eladda threatened, her spear tip pointed towards the half-giant's gut.

A crimson flame ignited in her jaded eyes. Her bloodlust beckoned her, and since the half-giant didn't fall back upon her demand, she prepared herself for a potentially lethal strike. Her feet dug into the ground; her hands gripped tight around her polearm.

Just as the half-giant raised his greataxe, Oomphga lashed his quarterstaff outward towards the ground at his feet. The heavy fabric that consumed his hands up to the rugged branch were illuminated with a faint, green light and, without further warning, the cobblestone plates on the streets shifted making way for weeds that sprung up from the earth and snapped around the half-giant's wrists from behind.

He barely twisted the staff, fighting against forces beyond his control, and watched as the plants curled tighter. With a sudden jolt of his hands back towards his chest, the vines suddenly sunk back into the ground, pulling the half-giant along with them. He hit the stone beneath him with a loud thud, his greataxe clattering out of his grasp. He furiously wrestled and squirmed with the foliage that had him pinned.

"Oomphga said 'please'!" Oomphga shrieked, voice cracking at the last possible second.

"Oomphga? Did you do something?" Faith asked.

"He did! What the heck is that?!"

"A good opportunity to leave! Let's go!"

"No!" Eladda interjected. Her attention immediately turned to her father, slumped over on the ground next to the Eat and Sleep Inn. "My father! What about him?!"

"What about him?!"

"We can't just leave him here like-...like THIS!"

Mr. Swiftclaw drunkenly mumbled to himself, fidgeting with his pockets as he hazily looked around. The man's senses were null and void to danger. He clearly had no sense of it.

"Fine, fine, fine! Eladda and Faith can carry Mr. Swiftclaw to safety aaaaand Oomphga will stay here and make sure that Mr...half-giant man stays down, alright~?" Oomphga smiled anxiously.

"You think you can handle him? By yourself?"

Oomphga looked back towards the half-giant. He seemed to be momentarily stunned, squinting in suspicion at him.

He recognized the name, didn't he? He's finally catching on, putting pieces together.

Oomphga turned to his friends and forced as confident of a smile as he could muster.

"YEP!!!"

He needed them to believe in him. He *needed* them to *go*, because he assumed - if they heard any kind of accusation this half-giant made – his friends would probably get the wrong impression of him.

"...Thanks, Oomphga."

Eladda patted Oomphga on the shoulder and rushed over to her father with Faith, guiding her hands and arms so she could hold up Mr. Swiftclaw's one side while Eladda supported the other. Once Mr. Swiftclaw got on his feet and began hobbling away, Oomphga refocused his attention back onto the half-giant as he remembered his current predicament.

"Vergaia's boy-" he let out a guttural growl, tearing away weed by weed, stem by stem. "I had my suspicions, but this...Mortium's gonna have a field day when he hears about this..!"

Oomphga froze up. His heart lodged in his throat. The fear of the unknown consumed him.

*No...Oomphga doesn't want Mama to be in any trouble with Uncle Mortium. **Oomphga** doesn't want to be in any trouble with Uncle Mortium!*

Cautiously, he took a few steps back, legs and arms tense. He readied his body for whatever was to befall upon him next.

Oomphga had to act fast, but what was he to do?

...Turn tail and run in the opposite direction towards the marketplace. That's what.

Kicking up stone and dust, he made a mad dash towards the bustling city streets just as the axe-wielding menace broke free of the last vine. He could hear the blade skidding across the ground and the thundering of heavy footsteps trailing close behind him.

Oomphga huffed and puffed, dodging and weaving between passerby as gracefully as he could with quarterstaff still in hand. His attacker barreled through them without a second thought. Even though he had his youthful vigor on his side, Oomphga knew he stood little chance against this rage-fueled warrior. Then, spotting an alley, Oomphga swiftly diverted off of the road, completely changing his course. He lunged down the narrow path, hoping for freedom at the end, but there was nothing. Nothing more than a brick wall several feet high. Oomphga's eyes darted across the long stretch of stone surrounding him, hoping to find an answer in the cracks.

Then, from behind, sonorous steps echoed. Metal clattered against the gravel. Displayed on the brick and mortar in front of him, a silhouette grew in shape and size. Oomphga turned to face the half-giant. The man raised his blade high and, in a flash, Oomphga threw himself to the earth beneath him just as his opponent's shimmering blade met the wall where Oomphga's head was a second ago.

"You little snake!"

A snake! That's what Oomphga needed to be!

His body shifted and morphed into that of a grass snake, and he slithered down deeper into the alley, but by the time that the half-giant realized, he grabbed Oomphga by the neck and squeezed tight. Oomphga flailed helplessly in his grasp, hissing and jolting around vigorously until the edges of the stranger's greataxe rested across his scaly neck.

"So…the rumors were true. Vergaia really did sleep with a scarlet-fur after all. You know, you might as well surrender now, kid, or else things could get ugly, and I doubt your mommy would want me to bring home her freak of nature *dead-*"

Oomphga lost his animal shape. He gasped and wheezed, clinging to the half-giant's hands as his quarterstaff clattered across the cobblestone, far out of reach. The sadistic look in his icy gaze gave him the impression that he WANTED things to get ugly.

Windpipes clasped shut, Oomphga held his breath and reached towards his waist.

"You lied to us, Aymus! You two-faced snake! You get Camellia killed, you challenge my judgment - the gods' judgment, you transform me into THIS, and to top it all off, you LIED to us ever since the beginning! You traitor!"

"Put him down, Martin!" Omen hollered. His voice barely broke through the howling winds and roaring thunder.

Aymus wheezed and kicked at Martin's kneecaps, desperate to close the gap between his feet and the ground hundreds of feet below. Even if Martin were to let go, falling freely into the hellscape beneath them seemed preferable to suffocating at the hands of his misguided companion.

"I never lied to you and I never- ack! I never betrayed you, Martin!" Aymus huffed. "Never!"

"I can't trust you anymore, Aymus! If I were any wiser, I'd say you're in cahoots with those infernal monsters! You and your goddess were working together to bring about the destruction of mankind, weren't you!?!"

"The only one bringing about ANY destruction will be you if you don't put Aymus down!" Omen physically interjected, pulling the angel back towards the wide expanse of rocky mountain behind them, but Martin rejected Omen. He pressed his palm against Omen's chest and tried to force distance between himself and everyone else.

"I'm sorry, Martin, but you leave me no choice!"

A burst of flames engulfed Aymus' calloused hand and - within his palm - appeared a sword forged out of a fiery essence. He pressed the scorching blade against Martin's knuckles and sliced through his fingers. If the sword were any hotter or sharper - or if any amount of extra strength were put into the cut - Aymus would've slit his own throat. However, in the heat of the moment - in the face of the Calamity - Aymus took his chances to seize the sweet release of freedom.

"AYMUS!!!"

With the last of his remaining strength, Oomphga drew forth his mother's handaxe, brought it up to the fingers around his neck, and burrowed his blade into the half-giant's knuckles. The scream he heard in his bear ears made them ring, but he had no time to dwell on the agony. The second Oomphga's feet met the floor, he scurried away.

Along the way, he eagerly picked up his quarterstaff off of the ground and bolted towards the crowd gathered around the center of the market district. Wind pelting him in the face as he ran at full speed, he finally had a second to collect his thoughts. Granted, he had several, but he had to figure out his next course of action wisely if no one in the monstrously large crowd of people were going to intervene. He looked up towards the clear, blue skies, praying for some kind of sign of what to do even as his world came crashing down. He asked for a blessing. A message? A hint? A fragment of hope. A next course of action. A plan to escape the horrors of the tangled web that was unweaving itself under his skinny little legs. Anything.

Gazing upwards and not forwards, Oomphga hit the edge of the fountain in the middle of the market. He nearly fell in, but in the water, he caught a brief glimpse of an idea. Extending his hand once more, he accumulated a decent-sized orb of fountain water packed like a snowball, but this wouldn't do. Not at all. He needed more, so he wiggled his hand to and fro until he had amassed a hefty wave - roughly about a gallon of water - that he hurled back into the crowd towards the half-giant chasing him at full force. Oomphga's pursuer stumbled back and wiped his face dry with his arm, but when his vision was finally cleared, he couldn't find anything. It was almost as if, by *magic*, Oomphga had disappeared.

Oh, if only you could see the stumped look on his face, soaking wet and red with envy. The longer he stood gawking in the town square, eyes bulging, head thrashing back and forth like a fish out of water, the more time the soldiers of Endinerose had to apprehend him. They rushed him from behind. Some kept the pointed tips of their halberds at the half-giant's back while others forcibly restrained him. He hollered and wailed in rebuttal, but once the soldiers slapped on a pair of specialty handcuffs, it was all over for him. They dragged him away, the owner of the Eat and Sleep Inn trailing behind. He was a goblin. Short, stout, and sucking on a lollipop stick. He stood idly by with his hands tucked in his rugged jacket's pockets and a crooked grin plastered across his face.

"EXACTLY 30 feet, and ya know what that means, pal-" the goblin cooed.

A trip to the N.F.C.

"You traitor! I'll kill you for this! I'll kill you! You and your mother both will pay with your lives! Just you wait!" the half-giant barked and wailed, sparing no ounce of dignity to continue spouting incriminating threats. As the soldiers hauled the stranger away, the goblin paused to look back towards the fountain. Maybe he expected to find Oomphga, but all he found, sitting up on the ledge of that fountain, was a tiny house mouse.

Oomphga laid across the stone bricks that surrounded the water fountain. He huffed, gazing up at the bright, blue sky. He couldn't tell if he was relieved or mortified knowing that, now, someone was out there that knew his name and his face. Someone knew the truth of the matter and brought to light the consequences the Silverblood family hoped would never come to pass.

Mama was right all those years ago…they're gonna kill us. They're gonna kill us all.

Brushing back his fur with his tiny fingers, he breathed in deep, trying to reassure himself that the one person that would pose any threat to him and his parents would be put behind bars. Theoretically, he and his family were safe…for now.

Chapter 8:
No One Listens to Oomphga

OMPHGA KEPT HIS EYES open wide, his attention fixated on the people in the streets. He knew his own luck (or lack thereof) better than anyone else. It was only a matter of time before something came up. After finding Papa Sergei in the marketplace, he clung to his prosthetic arm and stuck close by him as they went to fetch his journal.

"Are you okay, little Oomphga? You look nervous. Did something happen with your friends?"

Oomphga's ear twitched, his anxiousness held his attention captive. He peered through his locks and kept a sharp eye out for any more half-giants roaming about in the streets.

"Oomphga is…alright. He just…missed Papa Sergei is all~" he breathily chuckled.

Papa Sergei smiled at this response and kindly guided Oomphga through the current of people to the leatherworker's shop where he let Oomphga pick out his journal of choice. The one he picked was fairly plain in appearance: a brown, leather book with an ornamental design on the cover, but what made this journal special was a little pouch on the inside for Oomphga to put his writing or painting instrument of choice into. With his new journal safely in his grasp, Oomphga was content and had nearly forgotten all about the scuffle moments prior.

"Is my little Oomphga ready to head home?" Papa Sergei asked.

"Oomphga is ready," he chirped. *He's ready to curl up in bed and scribble away in his new journal. Hopefully, he'll be able to forget today ever happened and, with any luck, he can go back to having fun with Papa Sergei tomorrow!*

Hand-in-hand, the two walked out of the city and back down the familiar path back home. However, shortly after their departure,

Oomphga caught a glimpse of something along the side of the road, down a branching path.

It was Eladda and Faith. They were trudging along and hauling a stumbling Mr. Swiftclaw towards Whistling Woods, a humble village outside of the hustle and bustle of the big city. It was where the animalfolk lived and thrived.

"Hey, Oomphga, aren't those your friends?"

"They are."

"What are they doing with Artyom?"

"Probably taking him home," Oomphga replied. "We found him in the bar."

Father and son stood side-by-side, watching the semi-awkward display of two girls carrying a poor, ignorant drunkard on their shoulders. His furry feet dragged through the mud behind them and caught on every stick and rock laid out before them on the road leading back to Eladda's house.

"…Do you want to help them?" Papa Sergei asked.

Oomphga stared at Eladda and Faith as they struggled to walk with Mr. Swiftclaw. They were doing the best they could, but at this rate, it would take them hours to carry him home on their own. Looking at the situation from an outsider's perspective, Oomphga concocted the perfect idea to help his friends out.

"Yeah. Can Papa Sergei take these home for Oomphga? He's gonna help his friends." Oomphga asked as he handed his new journal over to his beloved papa.

"Of course, Son. You go be a good friend!"

The two smiled at each other briefly before Oomphga bounded over (once again) to Eladda and Faith. Faith was the first to acknowledge his approach.

"Oomphga! We were starting to get worried about you," Faith said with a smile.

"Huh? How did you know it was Oomphga and not someone else chasing after you?" Oomphga asked.

"You have a certain cadence in your huff when you run."

"Oh."

"You keep forgetting that don't you?"

"Yeah…" Oomphga fixed his attention onto Eladda. Her eyes batted in the opposite direction, and she didn't even look at him. Not once.

"Hey, Eladda," Faith began, catching Eladda's attention. "I believe you had something you wanted to say to Oomphga."

"Um…I'm sorry," Eladda uttered.

"Hm?"

"I said, 'I'm sorry'."

"Oomphga heard Eladda the first time, but what is she sorry for? She didn't do anything wrong~!" Ooomphga let out an audible giggle before thousands of devious deeds popped into his mind. Things he could easily see Eladda doing. "…right?"

"I guess I just…feel a little bad about leaving you back there. Alone." Eladda let out a defeated chuckle. "I said I'd fight an army of half-giants for you and then - the moment things started getting dicey - I got caught up with helping my dad over you. I was trying to look out for him, but if something happened to you back there-"

"It's alright, Eladda," Oomphga interrupted. He stepped up to Eladda's side and gave her a big, bear hug. "Oomphga forgives you. Eladda was very smart, putting her dad first! Honestly, despite everything being really scary, Oomphga did alright too, and, hopefully, Eladda won't have to worry about the half-giant man anymore! The man running the Eat and Sleep Inn caught him for Oomphga! He won't be bullying or threatening people like us any time soon!"

"It's always a relief when the bad guys get their just rewards, huh?" Eladda snickered.

Oomphga snapped out of his trance of positivity. "Huh?"

"Ah, nevermind."

"Oh, would you two like a break from carrying Eladda's dad? Oomphga can carry him."

"Could you, now~?" Faith playfully interjected.

Nodding cheerfully, Oomphga backed away from his friends briefly before shapeshifting into a stocky draft horse with a long, wavy brown mane and a spotted grey coat. With all the grace of a toddler, Oomphga plopped down, rump first on the grass, his horse-y legs outstretched in front of him. Eladda pulled her father over and pressed him against Oomphga's back so, when he stood up, Mr. Swiftclaw was slouched across his spine. The grizzly, old man hardly stirred aside from letting out the occasional uncomfortable groan whenever Oomphga moved.

"We're heading to my place. You remember the way, right Oomphga?"

Oomphga nodded inelegantly, unable to speak. It was one of the many downsides to taking on an animal form, but he didn't mind the sacrifice (as impractical as it may be sometimes). Cautious of a clueless and unconscious Mr. Swiftclaw sprawled out on his back, Oomphga walked slowly and steadily. Step by step, he made an effort not to sway until he knew for sure that his rider wasn't going to slide off of him.

As the three friends treaded down the road, Eladda and Faith engaged in friendly banter amongst each other while Oomphga listened intently.

"You know, Faith, the Endinerose Autumn Festival is coming up soon," Eladda said. "Didn't know if you wanted to tag along with me and Oomphga again this year."

Faith let out a faint hum in response.

"Is that a…yes or-?"

"Maybe. Probably not."

"If you don't like the sound, I'm sure we could get you some earmuffs or we could celebrate in a quieter part of town - just the three of us."

Oomphga couldn't help but let out a soft yet excited whinny at the idea.

"I guess that would be alright, but if it's still too loud, I'm probably going to-" Faith ended mid-thought and stopped dead in her tracks. Eladda and Oomphga both did the same, their attention on Faith, watching her silently as she stared blankly at the trees off to her right, but her round, black-furred ears twitched and turned so they were pointed behind them.

By the time Oomphga noticed what she might've heard, it scurried away, giving him the briefest glimpse of what appeared to be a person's cloaked backside. The half-giant's threats in the city came to mind. Oomphga's heart pounded, his breathing got heavy. If someone truly was following them, who were they and what did they want? He kept a close eye on the bushes and the branches.

There they – no – *she* was. Shrouded by the leaves she must've rushed behind for cover sat a young, grey-skinned girl with a golden glint in her eyes.

"It's probably just an animal you heard," Eladda uttered, shrugging at the prospect of danger.

Oomphga snorted in an attempt to subtly deny Eladda's assumption.

No, it was definitely a person Faith heard. Oomphga can see them..!

"Maybe."

Oomphga neighed in rebuttal, determined to support Faith. She heard them, he saw them, but with no way to translate his animalistic noises…

"You're probably right. It's nothing of concern, and if Oomphga's agreeing-"

What?! No! Oomphga is not agreeing!

He neighed once again, his horse voice cracking from the strain. He stomped and thrashed his head towards the trees, practically begging for Faith to reconsider. Eladda rushed to his side and pressed her paws against her father's back and Oomphga's side to keep Mr. Swiftclaw from falling off.

"Easy there, Oomphga. Faith has great hearing. I trust her judgment."

When Oomphga looked back towards the girl's hiding spot, he lost sight of her. This must've been what the half-giant from before felt like when he lost sight of Oomphga. Oh, what a horrible feeling it was. Thinking back, Oomphga could feel his throat clenching, red consumed his vision. He panicked. The fear of getting caught overwhelmed every organ, every nerve, tied to his senses. He huffed, body trembling and heart racing faster than his thoughts - a roaring plethora of words and noise. No one could hear his pleads, and no one believed him. Nausea. Dizziness. If he could reach into his bag of herbs to grab his lavender, he would, but he couldn't. Not in this state. No one could hear his screams. *Not in this state…*

"Oomphga, look at me," Faith uttered, but Oomphga didn't want to listen. He had to know where that girl went. He had to find her before she snitched on him to his uncle in the mountains!

"Look at me!" Faith repeated, forcing Oomphga's head in her direction. Her pale eyes - Oomphga lost himself in them. Even after raising her voice at him, her gaze softened in an instant. Her touch - gentle. Her voice - almost a whisper. "Breathe. Deep breaths. Listen. Don't just listen to me. Listen."

Oomphga did as told. He continued to stare at the only thing he could - Faith's uncomfortably close face - as he listened to the forest. He could hear the sweet, melodic chirps of birds as they sang songs of love and happiness amongst each other. He could hear the humming of the wind as it passed, announcing the arrival of spring's beautiful weather.

"Jeez, Oomphga, I've never seen you get this-"

"Shh…" Faith politely shushed Eladda, never breaking her blind stare.

As Oomphga slowly backed away, his ears caught the faint sound of Mr. Swiftpaws' belongings jingling in the pouch tied to the cloth wrap around his waist. The clinking of coins rang out, but the sound of something else revealed itself to be hidden in the mix. Usually, Oomphga wouldn't dare to think so deeply about another person's belongings, but this "something" sounded like stones tapping together.

The thought of rocks made him happy. The sounds they made, the different colors, shapes, and sizes he found them in, each one gorgeous and unique to the others. His thoughts drifted off to a land filled with these special rocks.

"Feeling better, Oomphga?" Eladda asked. Impatience made its way into her tone.

He hummed in response.

"Alright, well, we still have a ways to go until we get to my place. Maybe, once we're there, I can pour you a cup of pear juice. How does that sound?"

Oomphga's body stiffened. His long ears sprang up and his long, rugged tail swung loosely to and fro.

Oh, yes, please!

Who would've thought that a nice, cool cup of pear juice would be all Oomphga needed to take the edge off? The playful fizz danced across his taste buds, and the accentuated taste of pure pear juice refreshed and rejuvenated his energy. He sat in a cushioned chair by the window, gazing at the bustling animalfolk village beyond the clear pane of glass all while comfortably drinking his beverage inside. Faith and

Eladda sat not too far away on the floor next to the couch where Mr. Swiftclaw laid still as stone.

"And you're sure you saw someone?" Faith asked.

"Oomphga's sure that he's sure. He saw a girl. She had black hair, wore a black cloak, had dandelion eyes, and grey skin."

"You sure did get a pretty good look at them-" Eladda muttered, glancing over her shoulder every so often to check on her father.

"Yeah! And after everything that happened in town with the half-giant guy..." Oomphga nervously took another sip of his juice.

"Judging by how scared you got during the trip home, I'm assuming things got pretty hectic, right?" Faith asked.

"Far from pretty. It was *very* hectic. The guy almost choked Oomphga out. If it weren't for the goblin running the Eat and Sleep Inn, that half-giant probably would've found Oomphga and executed him in front of everyone in the market, he and his father both if he knew where he went, and because it was in the market, Oomphga suspects-"

"-that someone saw what happened, knew the guy that attacked you, and is now following you to get revenge?"

"Exactly! Either that, or someone is after Mr. Swiftclaw considering his state. Oomphga doesn't know what kind of enemies he might have, but still! It's all too coincidental for Oomphga's liking!"

"Father does have a lot of enemies. It's to be expected given his position-" Eladda noted aloud, her padded fingers brushing away the specks of dirt in Mr. Swiftclaw's fur.

"I wonder..." Faith began. "I wonder what he was talking about with his friends before we showed up. Being someone with authority, it could've been important."

"Over a drink? I doubt Father said anything 'important'."

"You would think it might be if he left Eladda alone so early in the morning..."

"Even so, important or not, I'm sure he's forgotten about it by now."

A torch went off in Oomphga's mind. He lunged to the edge of his seat, eyes alight with inextinguishable excitement.

"Unless he had something to remember the conversation! While Oomphga was doing the thing that Faith asked him to do - listening - he heard rocks in his coin pouch! Smooth rocks, not the rough kind! Oomphga could recognize the higher pitched tippy-taps from anywhere, and they didn't make the quiet squeaking or scratching sound - you know - that coarser rocks do!"

Slowly, Eladda turned to look at Oomphga. Her expression couldn't have represented the festering pit of her disappointment-mixed confusion more. "...rocks?"

"Hold on, Eladda. Maybe he's onto something."

"No, but...rocks?"

"Yeah!"

"I'm sorry, but what do rocks have to do with remembering things?!"

"Could be a rock. Could be a polished gemstone. Either way, if someone gave it to him, when he goes to reach into his pouch, he could be like, 'Oh, wow! Mr. Swiftclaw remembers! So and so gave him this rock and when we were talking about that one thing!' It's hard to explain, but Oomphga knows the feeling."

"No, no, Oomphga. When someone gets blackout drunk, they don't remember *anything*. He could be missing coins in his pouch and not remember what he spent it on! What makes you think that he'll remember anything because of a rock?"

"Just humor Oomphga. He knows rocks. He knows what he's talking about. In fact, Oomphga bets Eladda a gold piece that he could probably figure out what the conversation was about based on what kind of rock Mr. Swiftclaw has in that pouch."

"You-!" Eladda briefly covered her face with her paws and let out an annoyed sigh. When she pulled her hands away, she blinked a few times and then, suddenly, she cracked a wide grin. "Oomphga, you are my friend. You know you are my friend, and I care about you a lot, right?"

Oomphga happily nodded.

"We've been friends for - what? - eight years now? In those eight years - I'm gonna be frank - I don't think I've ever heard you say anything more idiotic in my entire life, and if this is yet another excuse to go on an hour long tangent and flex how much you know about a vague thing in nature, then - respectfully - I'm going to punch you."

"Alright, alright…" Oomphga uttered, slinking back into the chair. "But if Oomphga left out all of the details, kept that stuff in his brain, and just said the important parts, would that be better?"

Eladda responded with a loud groan.

"I think it would be fine," Faith said.

Oomphga carefully pulled himself out of the chair, sat his cup of juice aside, and approached the couch where Eladda and Faith sat.

"Permission to look through your father's things?"

"Permission granted," Eladda growled.

"Yes..!"

Extending his sleeves, he worked out the knot holding Mr. Swiftclaw's pouch to his waist. Once he unraveled the string, he drew the bag back towards his chest, cradling it like a newborn pup. Oomphga, now free to explore the contents within, smiled and sat in front of Eladda and Faith. With a dainty touch, he pushed open the edges of the cloth and reached inside. After making contact with the stone, Oomphga knew this was no ordinary rock. Resting across his sweater-covered palms lay a partially red, partially transparent gemstone.

"A crimson quartz," Oomphga whispered, bringing it close to his face. Past locks of hair, Oomphga could see swirls of blood encased within, he could feel the gem's warmth spreading through the seams of his baggy clothing, and he could sense the life forces that went into its natural formation.

"So, Oomphga, the all-knowing rock expert, what does this rock tell you about the conversation my father had at the inn?"

Oomphga didn't respond, captivated by the sensations and information flowing from his hands to his hippocampus. The pressure to find accurate answers and the sudden rush of knowledge overwhelming all sense of thought made deducing the subject near impossible in the short amount of time Eladda gave him to come up with an answer.

Time after time, Eladda tried to force an answer out of Oomphga, calling his name and asking again for a response, but he couldn't verbally reply. He was too busy listening, his divine allies and druidic senses speaking to him, filling his memories with all the information he could've ever needed and more. It was during this process that Oomphga uncovered the gemstone's origin and painted a mental image of a journal filled with every ounce of wisdom he obtained in that brief moment of staring.

Hemogem (Crimson Quartz)

Commonly found in Bristlethorn Forest, Hemogems are quartz crystals that form when combined with silica and the oxygen in blood during a magic transfer between a creature and nature. Most hemogems have been excavated and repurposed as a concentrated arcane source for spellcasters but can also be used as external energy for magic-centered machinery.

This particular hemogem, being about 4.5 inches in length, grew in (roughly) about 5 years. The cold temperature and strong, irregular energy pulses emanating from it suggests that its host possessed a strong mix of wild and dark magic. Chances of its source being a necromancer, monster, or infernal creature are high.

"Hellooo, earth to Oomphga," Eladda waved her hand between Oomphga's face and the crimson quartz.

Putting his thoughts on hold, Oomphga put the crystal back in the pouch and sealed it up. "Yeah...Oomphga got nothin'."

"Nothing? You don't know ANYTHING about this thing?! All that time staring at it, and you don't know a thing about it?!"

"He does. Nothing that would help him figure out why Mr. Swiftclaw has it though. It's a hemogem from Bristlethorn Forest. It has magic properties, so Oomphga speculates - whoever gave it to Mr. Swiftclaw - either wants him to remember something about Bristlethorn Forest or is giving him this arcane source to do something with. Didn't think Mr. Swiftclaw was the magic type though. Unless...this is all part of some kind of political hoo-haa."

"That's a little more than nothing. It's nothing precise, but even still...that's pretty impressive. If you're correct, that is." Eladda brushed her paw up against the back of her neck. "And you got all of that from a gemstone?"

"I'm assuming it's just a hunch considering we won't know anything unless we ask him about it," Faith politely interjected.

"And in this state…" Eladda turned once again to look upon her father, sprawled out across the couch cushions. "I'll ask him later whenever he wakes up. As for you two, you should probably be getting home. It's getting late. Oomphga, I know Sergei is going to be worried about you if you're away for too long."

"Yeah. He's getting better though at letting Oomphga do things on his own! Granted, he's still skeptical about Oomphga whenever he's alone, but given the sporadic war stuff still going on, Oomphga doesn't blame him."

"Well, maybe if he sees you walking home by yourself, he'll be more trusting," Faith suggested. She clambered up onto her feet and made her way towards the door. Somehow, she always found a way - whenever we visited Eladda's house - to avoid all of the furniture in the house.

"You really think so? You don't need anyone to walk you home, Faith?"

"I'll be fine. I know the way back to my house from here. I've taken the path hundreds of times before."

Oomphga rushed over to the table beside the chair where he sat prior, swiftly finished his pear juice, and collected his things before rushing up to Faith from behind. "But-"

"I know you're worried about me, but I insist. I'll be alright. Just because I'm blind, that doesn't mean I don't know how to find my way around. Thank you for being considerate and wanting to help, but I got this. See ya tomorrow, Eladda!"

"See ya!" Eladda called back.

As Eladda and Faith gave a playful salute good-bye, Oomphga fidgeted and stumbled out the door behind Faith without saying a word.

"Oomphga's not worried about Faith getting lost or hurt or anything. Oomphga's worried about Oomphga getting - you know - attacked or something. Being the most perceptive, Oomphga was hoping that Faith could - uh - keep an ear out for trouble like how she did before."

"You want to be independent, don't you?"

"Yes."

"You want your dad to see that you're capable of being in the woods at night alone, right?"

"Well, yeah, and Oomphga has literally traveled by himself before. It's not anything new, but given the circumstances of what just happened, Oomphga would like-"

"It's not that dark. You know the road home from Eladda's. I think you'll be alright~" Giving Oomphga a pat on the head, Faith made her way down the street back towards Endinerose. "Bye, Oomphga!"

By himself, Oomphga adjusted his bag of things over his shoulder, patted himself down, realized he left his nature journal with Sergei, and - letting out a shaky breath - he began his journey home all by himself.

Chapter 9:
The Dreadwalker

BLANKETS OF SHADOW covered every inch of the road back to Papa Sergei's leaving only the faintest streaks of sunlight to illuminate each step. Despite being cloaked by the darkness, Oomphga had the nagging feeling drilled into his mind that something kept its eyes on him. With no nature journal to keep his head in and no one to remind him that things will be alright, Oomphga had nothing but the throbbing in his chest to focus his attention on. Every jump in his pulse incited another deep breathing exercise and every quiet snap immediately caught his attention. At this point, assuming that someone or something was stalking him, Oomphga tried to accumulate a plan in the midst of his silent and painful panicking.

Why don't you just say "hi"? Show that you're friendly and mean no harm. Acknowledge the person or creature may or may not be following you, and if there is, surely, they'll be intrigued enough by your demeanor that they'll just let you off the hook and go away, right?

Or you could turn into an animal and just blend in with the other forest critters, no problem! That is…if this someone or something doesn't see you turn into an animal and know that you're pretending.

Or - you know what? - how about they just show themselves already?! Good or bad, it's clearly worse off not knowing, so, push comes to shove, we draw our handaxe and defend ourselves! Spit some magic fire at them! Turn into a wolf and show our teeth!

Several voices spoke amongst each other in Oomphga's head in tandem with the erratic pounding in the center of his tightened chest. The harder Oomphga thought, the worse off his body felt. Suppressing his imagination and painfully swallowing back the uncertainty, Oomphga called out to the trees.

"Hello!" Oomphga paused to briefly mutter a few words of reassurance to himself. "Hi, forest creature, cloaked girl, or anonymous monstrosity! Oomphga just wants to say that he is friendly and totally not defenseless, so if you attack first, Oomphga is…probably going to run away because he doesn't like physical violence but will definitely resort to it if he has to, and that is NOT a bluff!"

…Nailed it!

Then, there was a snap, a loud crunch, a sudden scream, and aviary cries as a nearby flock of birds rushed to the heavens.

Was that Oomphga? Did he step on something? Did he scream and not notice or feel a thing? He probably did. His voice felt a little hoarser than it did a second ago, so maybe. Hastening his step, he continued his hike down the path leading into Bristlethorn Forest. The weathered, oak trees, still more dead than alive, towered over Oomphga. Their branches faintly swung to and fro from the breeze, creaking and popping like old joints.

It's alright. Oomphga must be pretty close to home now. He can recognize these trees from anywhere, so as long as Oomphga continues down this path, he'll make it back onto more familiar soil and everything from there will be fine…most likely…Oomphga hopes.

A sudden, thunderous boom rang out. It shook the ground Oomphga stood on and stopped him dead in his tracks. The rumble continued for about a minute, and an unnerving silence followed. There were no howls and no rustles in the bushes - only the deafening thump spreading from Oomphga's heart into his ears. With a loud gulp, Oomphga took a few steps back and silently whispered through a half-giant's prayer:

"May Obak, Creator of the Giants and Eternal Chieftain of the High Peak Mountain Clan, oversee Oomphga and his future role in the tribe and forest as shaman and druid."

Multiple thuds followed, gradually increasing in volume, but

Oomphga continued, his voice trembling as he quickened his speech and held on tight to his quarterstaff.

"May Laniara, Mother of Nature and Creator of the Land, protect Oomphga as he confronts whatever made that horrendous noise..!"

The rumbling would not stop. Oomphga huffed through his words, sweat pouring down his brow, drenching the hair that masked his face. His grip grew tighter.

"And may Neodashkus, General of War and Champion of Combat, guide Oomphga's blade if he finds himself in need of self-defense..!"

Caged by trees, Oomphga waited impatiently to gaze upon the dreaded behemoth stomping about, but his worries passed when he finally saw...*it*.

Pushing past charcoal trunks and teal leaves stood a tall, lanky, humanoid creature made of inky flesh and dancing shadows, baring the faintest hints of deer and wolf with its claws - scythe-shaped blades longer than swords, its teeth - scattered rapiers covered in saliva and mucus, and its face... - its wolverine skull-shaped face with antlers that protruded from its skull just above empty sockets in the side of its head. Deep, blue eyes fixed onto Oomphga, it lumbered forward, each step shaking the earth under his feet.

Oomphga could hardly grasp the horror approaching him. It moved like an animal stumbling around on its hind legs, but its body and fingers looked like that of a person Oomphga somehow knew in another life. The closer it got, the more suffocating the scent of death emanating from it became, but Oomphga couldn't move. His feet wouldn't let him, his hands refused to reach for the handaxe nestled against his waist.

The monster hissed and lowered its head towards Oomphga, black smoke flowing down between its jaws. The stench made Oomphga gag and wheeze. He half-expected it - whatever *it* was - to lunge forward to take a bite out of him the second it was close enough to do so, but it didn't. Instead, it held its head close by, and the look in its innocent eyes - its beautiful facade - begged Oomphga to reach his hand out to try and pet it. To pet Death.

With a face like this, how could Oomphga refuse? His heart, captured and bound by the submission of the poor creature before him, demanded connection and encouraged Oomphga to show kindness to this lonely, wandering monstrosity. A wave of calmness washed over him as he reached out to touch the creature. Fingers inches away from its glistening, inky skin, Oomphga found himself whisked away into time immemorial.

Aymus sat by Omen, hands clasped and heart heavy. His gaze pierced through the flames that danced across the logs of wood at their feet, sparks and ashes making their way towards the blood red sky. The blackened clouds cast a heavy shadow over the forest, but the warm glow of the campfire remained a beacon of their survival against the cataclysm that reigned, but not for everyone. There was one soul lost, their corpse mutilated and lying just beyond the campfire by the line of trees that surrounded the two, and beyond the trees lingered Martin howling to the heavens. Thank goodness the other soul in need of protection was close at hand, arms coiled around Aymus' as they slept against his shoulder.

Aymus blinked away the horror he still faced and shifted his attention to the little demon girl sitting next to him. She clung to Aymus' silky robes very gently and rested her head against his bicep. While Omen poked and prodded at the fire's only fuel, Aymus turned his head left and right to shift his attention to the forest only to find nothing but gnarled branches swaying in the breeze.

"He's been trying to talk with them for hours now," Aymus said. "Do you think he's actually gotten anywhere? Received any new instructions?"

"I doubt it'll be anything we haven't already heard. You and I both know how the gods are. Martin, clearly, does not. They have their secrets, and they have their truths, and they told us all they can given the circumstances." Omen turned to Aymus, gaze solemn.

"I don't know what he's expecting at this point. Laniarra sent her druids, the Maiden of Misfortune sent her spies-"

"And Neodashkus sent us Martin~" Omen cracked a hint of a smile. "The most arrogant, irritable, and whiny angel I've ever seen. If he cries any louder, the Maiden of Misfortune might turn his windpipes into a ribbon and tie them into a nice little bow for us."

Aymus covered the little girl's pointed ears amidst Omen's ramble, and let out a heavy sigh, growing sick from his friend's cruel attempt at humor.

"Omen, not in front of the child, please. Spare her innocence," Aymus politely requested.

"Aymus," Omen hummed, "it's going to be alright. In the eyes of the gods, we're giving it all we got and we're doing a good job."

"Really? I got Camellia killed by a dreadwalker, and you call that a good job..?"

"She's...in a better place. Surely. Who knows? Maybe she'll be one of the lucky souls brought back after the Calamity to-"

"That doesn't change the fact that someone is DEAD all because of *me* and *my* negligence..!"

Man or monster, it didn't matter. Anything that touched that sad creature was doomed to die. Lucky for Aymus, he wasn't the one that learned the hard way. He looked to Omen, his expression one of grief and genuine sorrow, one that Aymus had not seen Omen reflect in a long time.

"I'm sorry," Aymus uttered under his breath. "I'm sorry, that-"

"Was a small mishap. We've all had our own, but you've learned. We all learned. Not all creatures in these forests can be saved or tamed.

Not now. Not yet. You did your best, Aymus. We all did our best, and that's all we can do."

The little demon girl beside him fidgeted and squirmed, shifting her body on the log so she could lay her head on Aymus' lap. As she moved, she didn't speak a word; only let out a yawn to show her tiredness. Aymus grinned and softly brushed his fingertips through the girl's hair, watching her doze off on her makeshift bed. So, too, did exhaustion eventually take its toll on the young druid. Beautiful groves and smiling faces - a distant prospect in the face of such a bleak reality. Trying so hard to restore what was lost drained Aymus of life more than fighting and more than the monsters, and yet he smiled along all the while.

"I miss the peace," Aymus hummed.

"All the more reason for the three of us to stay alive so we can keep fighting for it," replied Omen.

Oomphga swiftly drew his sweaty palm away.

A dreadwalker.

The grim creature snarled. He could sense Oomphga's faltering desire to make contact.

"No. Oomphga is sorry, but…he can't pet you. Oomphga knows what will happen if he does and he doesn't like the idea of dying. He has a lot to live for, after all, so…"

Without warning, an arrow split through the air overhead and embedded itself into the dreadwalker's back. The dreadwalker, now enraged, lunged forward. Oomphga leapt back, summoning a thick wall of stone to rise up out of the ground between him and the creature's toothy maw. The rocks crumbled at the dreadwalker's might, but it reeled back right after the impact and before the tip of its nose made contact with Oomphga's chest. In the brief window of time Oomphga had, he retreated back down the winding trail, panting and stumbling in the dark.

His feet turned to hooves. His form and weight shifted as he took on the figure of a white-tailed deer. With grace, he jumped over any roadblocks in his way and weaved through clusters of dense foliage leaving the dreadwalker in clouds of dirt and dust.

Rumbling. Rustling.

The dreadwalker hastily pursued, but he hardly stood a chance. The monster could hardly keep its balance running on nothing but hind-hooves. Sure, it had twice the strength of an ox, capable of destroying anything in its wake, but it couldn't keep up. Its body was designed to be big and deadly, a stalker in the night. Even despite its slower pace, Oomphga had no intention of stopping. He had the energy to spare. He dodged and weaved his way through the forest, trying to get himself back on the path to go home.

The trees! That's where he will go! He'll find a way back through the trees!

With one last powerful stride, he shifted into a flying squirrel and scurried up the nearby tree. He leapt from branch to branch above the dreadwalker, gliding as he extended his furry wings to soar. This was the closest Oomphga had ever gotten to flying since the concept was still far too advanced for him to learn - much less learn under pressure.

The dreadwalker, unlike the half-giant in Endinerose, caught sight of this transformation and followed. Being nearly as tall as the trees himself, he covered their distance at an alarming rate. Having such a small frame and even smaller organs Oomphga stopped at a tree and changed back. Fire consumed his palm, and he threw it at the dreadwalker's head, hitting it with a burst of flame, but its flesh didn't burn, nor did it seem phased by the force of getting pelted in the face with such a strong, concentrated gust of heat. The beast reeled back its twisted claws, giving Oomphga a few seconds to decide what to do next.

He was stuck in a tree, the elements were of no use, he couldn't become a bird and fly away and attacking it with a weapon would require him to get up close and personal. *Unless...*

Oomphga drew his handaxe and, with all of his might, he threw it directly at the dreadwalker's head. The blade lodged itself between its eyes. It stumbled back, possibly stunned by the direct brain damage it received (if it even had a brain).

"Ha-HA!!! So long, stinky!" Oomphga hollered, determined to take his chances and try flying for the first time here and now. He took on the form of a raven, extended his wings, and dropped off of the branch.

For a minute, it felt like he was…actually flying! The wind pelted him in the face, brushed back his feathers, and daintily held him up by his wings. It didn't feel too much different from being a flying squirrel, actually. However, being a bird, flapping your wings is essential, something that Oomphga forgot to do. In other words, instead of flying, he was gliding down to the ground in the middle of a clearing.

Feeling the ground beneath his feet was not something Oomphga wanted, especially when he turned to see that the dreadwalker did not look very happy. With its claw-hands, it ripped Oomphga's handaxe from its own skull and tossed the blade aside.

Why didn't Oomphga just stay a deer?!

The dreadwalker screeched and Oomphga reverted back to his deer form in the hopes of regaining that distance between him and the monster, only this time, it was enraged. Horns forward, it charged after Oomphga. Sensing it so close behind him, Oomphga jumped to the side and allowed the dreadwalker to race past him.

THUMP!!!

Its horns were embedded deep into the charcoal bark of a massive oak tree. Abusing his blunder, Oomphga skid and scurried in the direction of Sergei's house, praying to the gods that the monster would give up the chase.

By this point, every bone in Oomphga's body screamed for relief. He longed for the comfort of home. He wanted to brew himself a soothing cup of chamomile tea, prop his legs up on the couch, and write about this horrendous creature in his journal before burying this memory in a place where he would never have to think or worry about it ever again.

Galloping along, the world around him felt like a black and white blur passing by faster than he could recognize. In a world of varying shades of grey, all of the trees blended together and - all of a sudden - spotting something like a hole was all the more difficult. One wrong step and that's where he ended up: at the bottom of a ditch.

Slipping down the ledge with stones leaving scars on his sides, his body endured the undignified, floppy tumble down the steep wall of dirt and rock as his front right leg (the equivalent of his right arm) twisted and contorted beneath his weight. There was a loud snap. At first, Oomphga thought it was a branch, determined to continue his run, but dizziness, nausea, and shock hit him hard and fast.

Gradually, the world around him became much clearer. Oomphga reverted back to his old self and clutched his arm close to his chest. Hearing the heavy steps in the distance, he knew, somehow, the dreadwalker wrenched itself free already. So, eagerly, Oomphga bolted for cover. It made him sick to his stomach realizing that he had to wait until he regained a solid consciousness again. If he tried to stumble around seconds after injury, he'd be caught for sure, but if the dreadwalker found him, he wouldn't stand a chance.

But he was disoriented, sore, and desperate for safety; desperate for a safe chance to rest and recuperate. In his injured stupor, he reached for his herb pouch and buried his hand inside. It flailed about, fingertips whacking against herbs with no way to tell the difference between them.

The dreadwalker arrived. With quieted steps, it skulked around the ledge where Oomphga tripped. Its head swayed as its foreboding, azure eyes scanned the horizon. Oomphga held his breath, lungs tight and aching the second after he silenced himself. It felt like suffocation.

A long moment of silence. Then, belting a painstakingly loud cry, the dreadwalker lumbered back towards the thick of Bristlethorn Forest. Oomphga let out a loud huff and a whine, squirming and jolting around, desperate for some level of comfort. The faintest touch upon his arm - the slightest movement - hurt worse than anything Oomphga's ever felt before. The sting of scars and the dull aching in his legs after days on them hardly compared to the intense, concentrated agony consuming the entirety of his right arm. He tried to hold it still and tried to support it with his other hand, but nothing would make the pain stop.

Snap.

Oomphga froze. His eyes widened, his body tensed, and his ears peaked atop his head. He could hear a faint shuffling coming from nearby. It wasn't the dreadwalker; Oomphga was certain it left. It couldn't have been Papa Sergei either. There was no way he would find Oomphga in the dark without aggravating the monster that followed him here. Whatever it was, their footsteps were too soft. Too delicate. When Oomphga looked up to the ledge, he saw…her…

"Oomphga Silverblood. There you are."

Chapter 10:
Duties and Destinies Intertwined

IT WAS THE GIRL that followed him earlier. She peered down at Oomphga, dandelion irises glistening in the moonlight. The girl in question resembled Oomphga in age and a raven in aesthetic. She had short black hair brushed back over her pointed ears and a long, ebony, feathered cloak draped down her backside like a pair of wings. Dark brown leather pouches coiled up her left arm and a hunting bow occupied her hand, but she didn't aim it at Oomphga. In fact, she lowered it off to the side.

The girl reached to her side and drew forth Oomphga's handaxe. Her body sunk to the ground, her arms outstretched. She extended the handle towards him.

"I believe this is yours."

An inky red substance covered the blade. It was thinner than paint but still smeared and splattered across the silver. Oomphga gagged and shuddered but smiled anxiously in his best attempt at showing appreciation.

"Uh…thank you."

He feebly reached out and coiled his fingers around the cloth-wrapped base of his mother's handaxe. Oomphga's stomach did cartwheels and somersaults, twisting and turning. He loosened his grip and tossed the weapon aside in the grass before his eyes darted back towards the soft-spoken stranger.

"So…what do you want with Oomphga?"

"You're the druid?" she asked.

"Yes?"

With a smile inching across her face, the young, grey-skinned elf tucked away her bow and hopped down into the ditch. Feet firmly planted in the soil, she turned towards Oomphga and puffed out her chest.

"The name is Marigold. I'm a hunter."

"Oh!" Oomphga's eyes lit up. The name sounded so familiar to him. He brushed his hand across the soil. Flowers of all shapes and sizes blossomed at his fingertips. Even in the darkness, he could see their vibrant yellow and orange colors. He carefully pulled at the root of one of the flowers - a flower of his own creation - and presented it to the girl.

"Marigold~!" Oomphga cheered. "Here."

Marigold paused. Past his thick strands of hair, it was hard to tell if the expression she wore was one of astonishment or a lack of words to follow up the odd gesture.

"Wow. I…can see why Omen spoke so highly of you. Although, he didn't say you'd be this…"

Oomphga inherited her hesitation. He looked himself over, thinking maybe she was caught off guard by his baggy sweater, rugged appearance, or mixed features. She could've been referring to anything. Was it his dumb smile? His clear lack of confidence in everything he did? His scrawny frame? Was he too..-

"Different?" Oomphga uttered.

"I was going to say young," she chuckled as she took into her hands the marigold that Oomphga happily presented her with. "And sweet. I don't know why but…I imagined someone that went by the name of Oomphga and knew someone as old as Omen to be some kind of…equally-as-old man. A big, tall, buff guy with a full beard and massive muscles. Maybe even a little intimidating, but I have to say, I've been colored impressed. You must be a pretty good druid already to have been chosen by Laniarra and the Mistress of Misfortune at such a young age."

He watched in awe as she slipped the stem over her pointed ear. Poor Oomphga felt himself getting swept up in the moment for so long, he could hardly speak.

"Oh! Uh - about that - if you're looking for Oomphga, the capable druid, then - um - you're sort of out of luck 'cause - you see - Oomphga still has a lot to learn. His teacher says he needs to do more exploring and training if he ever wants to be a good shaman or druid…or both. He's hoping he'll be worthy of wearing the druid title with pride one day, but he has a long way to go and…wait, where are you going?"

Marigold stood up and walked over to a cluster of sticks and leaves. She picked up a few and - still wearing a playful grin - she brought them over to Oomphga. She reached into the leather pouch on her arm with her dainty hands and pulled out a roll of cloth bandages.

"I wouldn't say that. You seem pretty capable to me. I mean…you outwitted a dreadwalker."

"Outwitted is a HUGE overstatement~"

"You confronted it, enraged it, and somehow managed to escape it. Still, pretty impressive~"

The two let out quiet laughs that died out into an awkward, lingering silence.

"Oh! Here, let Oomphga heal his scarring before Marigold does anything."

Oomphga held his palm against his arm and let the soothing warmth of golden aura envelope his injuries. The light seeped into the fabric and dispersed across his skin. Taking as much care and caution as he could, he drew back his bright blue sleeves and looked upon his arm. It didn't look broken or out of place, so that was good. It definitely felt…off to some degree.

"You have healing magic."

"It can only do so much. It can't get rid of diseases, relieve joint or muscle pain, reattach anything that's been detached, or reverse full-body damage. It's practically only good for mending and curing broken bones, rashes, burn marks, or scars."

Marigold pointed a twiggy finger at Oomphga's face. His features were obscured by clusters of matted hair, all rugged and filthy, no doubt, filled with twigs and dirt.

"What about that?"

"His hair?"

"No. Your eye."

She parted his long, wavy locks, and blessed him with the ability to see her other facial features with more clarity. Her face, a soft diamond shape, had plenty of tiny chips and scars across it. One hung from her rosebud lips down to her chin. Smeared, ashen paint dripped down the underside of her sharp eyes and yet, despite these dark, gothic qualities, she wore an expression sweeter than that of an angel's.

Her thumb ruffled the short strands of fur emanating from Oomphga's bear eye.

"It's…uh…genetic."

Oomphga could hardly speak. His heart got caught in his own throat. If he said another word, the little froggy might've croaked. The way she poked and prodded at his hair and his cheeks, tickling his skin with her fingertips made him feel at ease.

"…You're a strange guy, Oomphga Silverblood."

"That's probably genetic too~"

She focused her attention on Oomphga's arm and gently cupped it into her hands. It ached, sharp pain rushing through his muscles and joints every time he moved it an inch in any direction. Getting him patched up became a war on tears as Oomphga fought tooth and nail to keep himself from becoming a whimpering mess in front of his company. Sometimes, he couldn't keep quiet and let out a bit of an anxious whine, but Marigold didn't care. If anything, she giggled and made a clear effort to resume her duty without delay up until a certain point. Without warning, her expression darkened and, slowly, she reached for her cloak, pulled it off her boney shoulders. She traced her fingers thoughtfully over every stitch and seam as she made it into a makeshift sling that comfortable cradled Oomphga's arm.

"This is my great grandmother's cloak," she murmured.

"You're trusting Oomphga with it?" Oomphga asked.

"I trust you won't get yourself into any more trouble while you're using it. However,…"

"However?"

Marigold let out a disquieting huff. "What are we going to do when you're done using it?"

"…If you walk Oomphga home, you'll know where he lives. How about, every week, you stop by to check in? When Oompha's arm heals up, he'll be able to give Marigold's cloak back without running all over the Nature Faction looking for her."

She nodded and took Oomphga's hand - luckily, the one not tied up in a sling - and yanked him to his feet. She was even so nice as to pick up Oomphga's handaxe and tuck it into the small wrap around his waist where Oomphga usually kept his handaxe.

And so, the two ventured back onto the path leading to Papa Sergei's house. Marigold kept a watchful eye with her bow at the ready while Oomphga let himself become attuned to his surroundings. His bear ears flickered at every sound and his nostrils flared with each steady breath.

"So, you're…training to be a druid."

"Yep."

"Yet you know that you're the druid already?"

"Yep."

"So, what's the training for?"

"To be better. Oomphga wants to bring about peace between the half-giants and bearfolk one day, so he's trying to get to that point where he's good enough of a druid."

"And what does that look like?"

"He's not sure, but he's hoping people will actually listen to him because right now, he's 'just a kid' and...no one listens to 'kids' unless they're really smart or really strong, so Oomphga's trying his best to be both. If he's smart enough and strong enough, then maybe, just maybe, he'll finally be able to talk out the feud."

"Have you tried to talk things out before?"

Oomphga pulled down the collar to his sweater to show off the black and blue marks that embraced the grey skin around his neck. Marigold breathed in sharply; her dandelion eyes widened.

"He's tried," Oomphga sighed. "Time and time again, Oomphga's tried. He's tried convincing his mom, his dad, his cousins, his friends, and anyone else involved, but...nothing. He's always met with 'it's more complicated than you think' or 'you'll understand when you're older' or 'it's simply too unrealistic'. Oomphga...wishes there was more peace. He's hoping maybe - just maybe - if he does his studies and gets better at his magic stuff...maybe he'll uncover something great! Something that'll give him a boost! Get his name out there! Prove to everyone that Oomphga's a great druid worth listening to!"

"Shh..!"

Oomphga lowered his head, ears flopping to the side.

"Sorry, but...you know what he means, right?"

"I...can't say I do. I can only imagine. To be fair, I guess druids never really have much to go off of since there's usually one druid in a faction at a time..."

Oomphga straightened himself. Marigold walked with such confidence and such grace. Oomphga tried to mimic her motions, but being a bulkier fellow, his steps fell a little short. Too heavy. Too stiff.

"Maybe...Marigold could help Oomphga be a better druid. She's always in nature. She knows a lot about a lot of things. She's also probably really good in a scuffle."

"Now, you're giving ME too much credit~"

Oomphga inched a little closer to Marigold.

"Come ooon~! We can learn a thing or two from one another! Besides, Oomphga could use another friend outside of the bearfolk and half-giants. Could use as many friends as he can get with how much he has to learn!"

The way her cheeks lit up when she finally turned to look up at Oomphga. The edges of her lips curled upwards; a spark of fire ignited in her expression.

"I will consider it...if you return my grandmother's cloak to me."

"Oomphga promises to return her cloak, and Oomphga never breaks a promise~!"

The longer they walked, the smoother the journey became. The trees, the soil beneath Oomphga's feet, and the cozy scent of homemade beetroot soup - home. From here, Oomphga walked Marigold up the winding path and onto the porch. He couldn't shake his own heartfelt smile as he took Marigold's hand into his own and shook it.

"Thank you for getting Oomphga home. Thank you for...practically everything," Oomphga chortled.

"I look forward to getting my cloak back."

"And Oomphga looks forward to fulfilling that promise of his!"

A wink, a wave, and she was gone, but Oomphga knew he'd see her again. There was not a shred of doubt in his mind about it.

Chapter 11:

Her

"**Y**OU BROKE YOUR ARM running from a WHAT!?!"
Sergei wormed his way into the truth eventually
uncovering Oomphga's accidents in the city *and* on the
way home from Eladda's. To think that he could somehow become even
more overbearing. The mere prospect left Oomphga gasping for air and
begging for room to breathe. What wall of defense did Oomphga have
against his father's will?

"It's not broken...anymore! Oomphga will be healed up in no
time!"

"No time!?! I-...You-!"

"Yes! Just give him a few days - maybe a week or two - and he'll
be feeling right as rain! You'll see! And then Oomphga and Papa Sergei
will be able to laugh about this by the riverbank over the cute little fish
swimming up and down the stream, and everything will be o-kay!
AHAhaha!"

Pins held up Oomphga's lips and desperation held up the dead
weight hanging from his shoulder. That stare. That brutal stare Sergei
had. Oomphga knew this meant one thing and one thing only.

"You're not going anywhere in that week or two. You hear me?"

Oomphga sunk down into the couch cushions.

"Yes, Papa..."

"No going outside, no 'adventures', no exploring..." Sergei
grabbed Oomphga's new journal off of the mantle and held it up with
an iron grip, "...and no magic!"

"But-!"

"No complaints about it either! I don't care what Seirah says,
and I don't care what your mother says! You're just a kid and I won't let

you get yourself into any more trouble!" The firelight danced across Sergei's face; the moisture in his eyes glistened. "For as long as you are under my roof, Oomphga Silverblood, you will listen to me and the other bearfolk because you are in too hot of waters with those half-giants!"

Those. Once again, the mere word rang in his head and brought a discomfort similar to that of a silver utensil scraping the bottom of a frying pan. *Those.*

Oomphga helplessly and obediently sat in the stomach of a bronze bull. Even as steam poured from its nostrils, Oomphga remained – externally - calm and well-collected. He silently brushed his hair back - showing off his mostly half-giant facial features - and crossed his arms, unaware that he stoked the fire.

"Don't give me that look!" Sergei huffed. "It's ten o'clock at night. It's bedtime. BUT, if I wake up, and I catch you doing something you shouldn't be doing, I'll-! I'm gonna-! And then you'll-!"

Oomphga raised a curious brow. What punishment would match his crime? What even was Oomphga's crime?

"It's…it's too late at night to think of something, but you'd better not go outside or do anything dangerous!"

"Yes, Papa," Oomphga uttered sharply.

Sergei lumbered into his bedroom and slammed his door shut. All was calm and all was quiet. Slowly, Oomphga took the deepest breath his lungs could handle and belted out the loudest yet most quiet scream he could muster.

"*Grr! Rawr! Raaaawrg!*" He whispered aloud, trying to subtly mimic the deafening cries ringing through his head. Tears welling up in the half-giant bearfolk's eyes, Oompghga plopped down, his body sprawled across the length of the couch.

It's not fair.

But then again…nothing was. Such is life.

Time passed by as slowly as it could in the Silverblood house. The clock - it's *tick tick* ticking - started to tick Oomphga off. With an injured arm and nothing to do, not a sound in the world could compete with the obnoxiousness of that sound in particular.

Tick. Tick. Tick...

The sun rose and set each dusk and each dawn of each day. Sergei would make his passes between his bedroom, the bathroom, the kitchen (to make food for Oomphga and himself), and the front door. Meals were often brought out to Oomphga, served on a stained, wooden cutting board, and tasted of second-hand disappointment.

Late one afternoon, Sergei left with little notice and - not even an hour later...

Knock! Knockity! Knock!

Now, THERE was an exciting sound: the oh, so, familiar knock of a friendly face. Oomphga ruffled his hair so it masked his face, threw himself off of the couch, and raced to the front door as quickly as he could. FINALLY, something to do, someone to see, and Sergei couldn't lift a paw to stop him. Energy. Life found itself in the physical husk of the young druid, at last! Tearing the door open, Oomphga's smile couldn't get any bigger.

"Eladda!" Oomphga cheered, ignoring the very obvious accompaniment of Mr. Swiftclaw behind her.

"Oomphga!!!" Eladda cheered, pulling Oomphga in for a tight hug. "Where have you been!?! You've been gone for - what - two weeks!?! And...BLEUGH! You smell terrible!"

"Has it...has it really been that long?" Oomphga asked, bringing his nose to the pit of his sweater. Sweat and body odor flooded Oomphga's nostrils, yet he hardly noticed a wretched stench. At least...not more than usual. Still, this strong "natural" scent repelled Eladda.

"Yes, it's been that long!" Eladda squeaked through her pinch nostrils. Gazing upon Oomphga, she pointed a short, fuzzy finger at his sling. "What did you do to yourself this time?"

"He tripped and fell into a ditch. He was running…" Oomphga leaned in close and whispered into Eladda's red-furred ear. *"From a dreadwalker…"*

"A dreadwalker?" Mr. Swiftclaw asked.

"Mhm. And now Oomphga is banned from going outside for as long as he wears this sling."

"Banned from going outside, huh?"

"Mhm."

"For as long as you wear that sling?"

"Yep."

"Hold on. Let me fix that for you."

Reaching forward, Eladda undid the knot and pulled back the cloak, setting Oomphga's arm free of the dangling hammock it rested in. He flexed his elbow and rolled his shoulders, wondering if he ever really broke or sprained it in the first place.

"Eladda! You can't just-"

Mr. Swiftclaw tried to firmly interject, but Eladda wore a proud smirk on her sleeve.

"How do you feel?" she asked.

"Better..?" Oomphga hesitantly replied.

"Wow, it's almost as if wearing a sling and resting your arm for a week makes it feel better!" Eladda laughed. "Jokes aside, my father and I came over because we wanted to tell you something."

"Oh?"

"My daughter informed me that you made assumptions regarding a certain object in my possession," Mr. Swiftclaw noted, "and, although I don't very much like the idea of a bearfolk hermit snooping around in my things, as the son of my friend Sergei, I must confess…your assumptions were correct."

"Correct? In…what regard, might Oomphga ask?"

"You were right about the political stuff involving using the gems as a source of magic! Just the other day, my father told me that he and some arcane inventor came up with new weapons to use in the fight against the grey-skins!" Eladda chuckled heartily. "And I suppose you were right about him keeping the gem as a means of remembering, soo…"

She tossed Oomphga a gold piece, and, although holding the chip of rare mineral between his fingers felt nice, his stomach knotted; his face suddenly got hot.

"That's…good?"

"It's great for us! As long as the grey-skins don't come up with something like that, we might just be able to put an end to this war once and for all!"

"What…um…what kind of weapon is this exactly?" Oomphga leaned against the door frame and showed off his teeth in a crooked grin.

"The hemogem will make up a spearhead," Mr. Swiftclaw clarified. "One cut or scar and the magic decays the flesh until it inevitably melts the muscles and tendons down to the bone. For the safety of you and your father, I have sent out orders to this inventor companion of mine to mass produce as many as possible before our next invasion. Speaking of your father, where could I find him? There's a matter of some urgency I would like to discuss with him."

"Market," Oomphga murmured, "he assumes."

The taste of vomit climbed up Oomphga's esophagus and clung to the back of his throat. He could hear the screams and feel the agony crawling through every inch of skin on his grey arms. The heat flashes alone simulated the feeling of melting all too closely.

"Father! Did you have to get so graphic?"

"I…forgot graphic violence greatly upsets you."

"Um…on a different note, the half-giant that attacked you in Endinerose! Remember him?"

"Mhm…" Oomphga hummed silently, vigorously holding back the urge to dry-heave where he stood.

"Well, he got executed, so you were right about us not having to worry about him ever again too!"

Vision blurry. Palms sweaty. Knees shaky. Body…going numb. Shadows crept up on his vision and seized control of his perception. Before Oomphga could sit himself down or catch his breath…

Thud!

"Aymus, are you alright?" Martin sat beside his friend Aymus, his hands cupped around a steaming, metal tankard.

"I…I think so. How do I look?"

"You *looked* hideous," Martin sassed, "but you seem fine now after healing you up a bit. Those hags are no joke." Martin happily extended the cup towards Aymus.

"What's that?"

"Just…chamomile tea. I made it the way you like it."

"Not scorching hot?"Aymus let out a faint hum and delicately scooped up the warm mug.

"Not scorching hot."

"With honey?"

"Yes. Granted, it was honey from your bag, but you're the only one that has any. It's not like we're gonna go back to the forests and milk make-believe beehives just so you can have a cup of tea."

"Why are you getting so pressed about how **you** *made* **my** tea?"

"I'm not!"

"Right, right..~"

Aymus pressed the heated metal against his lips and let nature's dew flow across his tongue. *Ah*...the taste of home: where chamomile and honey once existed in abundance. Now, it's all liquid magma and ash as far as the eye can see (especially from up here). The blistering cold felt no different. Snow and ice, the kings and queens of High Peak Mountains, ruthlessly devoured every ounce of life along the east side of the Nature Faction, and with the colder climates came the bitter pain that followed any amount of warm, fleeting embraces. This pain gradually returned to Aymus' body. It attacked every inch of him relentlessly with a frozen knife and an icy stake that the Mistress of Misfortune drove through his brain, blessing and cursing him the lobotomy of a lifetime that he didn't even ask for.

Breaking through the befuddlement that clouded his cognition, Aymus hardened his physical shell and turned to Martin with dry eyes and an arched brow.

"Is *she* still with us?" Aymus asked, bobbing his head towards one of the four currently vacant tents gathered around the roaring campfire.

"Where do you think Omen is?"

"Keeping an eye on *her* hopefully," Aymus muttered, looking off towards the mountain pass.

Martin resituated himself atop his rocky seat and followed Aymus' distant stare. "They went out hunting together, actually."

"And you didn't want to go with them~?"

"It's not that I didn't want to as much as...I couldn't. Someone needed to look after you and wake you up, and I wanted to be the one to do it! We need all eyes open up here," Martin chortled and playfully ruffled Aymus's shoulders. His emerald cloak swayed and shifted, dripping down his arms the more Martin shoved him around. Shrouded in the two's laughter came voices up over the winding road.

Him and *her*.

○ ══════ ○ ○ ✸ ○ ○ ══════ ○

Her. Oomphga could barely make out her figure, but he knew she sat nearby. He could recognize her lilted voice parrying with Eladda's bolder tones halfway across the room. Oomphga kept an ear turned towards them, listening intently even as he slowly regained consciousness.

"You talk about him like he's all that and a plate of prince biscuits. I'm starting to think you love him or something," Eladda jeered sarcastically.

"I'm not here out of love," Marigold refuted. "I'm here to collect what is due to me and to request his aid in return for my own yesternight."

"Aaah…I think I understand. So, you're just here to extort him for favors. Unless he knows about this? What do you even want from a guy like Oomphga anyway? Flowers? Herbs? Rock facts~?"

Oomphga smiled at the thought. If Marigold wanted to know anything about any of those things, Oomphga would've been more than happy to fill her in on the details. A giddy energy rushed through his body and into the stubby, bear tail attached to his rump.

"You're not too far off. I need him to fetch a flower for me in the High Peak Mountains."

"What?! The mountains?! But that's where-!"

"If what my feathery friend says is true, then he's the only one with the knowledge and the skills necessary to even find this particular species of magic flora. I need *him*."

Oomphga pulled himself upright and rubbed his tired eyes weighted sleeves as unquantifiable amounts of bliss bolted out of his chest and into every crook and crevice of his face. His ears perked up, his eyes flashing with a glint of gold, and his crooked smile stretched beneath his nose from ear to ear masked only by bulks of his long, bronze hair as he sat erect on the couch where he once lay.

"Did someone say *magic* flora?" Oomphga asked.

"There ya go. Great. Now you've got him started-"

Marigold nodded. "Ever heard of the crystium catastrophe?"

"Ooh! Yes yes! Oomphga has heard of it many-a-times before! Who hasn't?"

Eladda let out a low growl and covered her ears before she gave Oomphga the go-ahead to continue his ramble.

Crystium Catastrophe

A rare subspecies of camellia with properties so different, it's considered to be the only of its kind. Firstly, its petals are a pinkish-white with glowing specs (visible only at night) and a pearlescent, crystium (or "crystal" in Fae) coating (visible only during the day). It grows solely in harsher climates, but it thrives off of magic and direct sunlight in the center of a ruined old church near the peak of the High Point Mountains.

Rumor has it that the crystium catastrophe was planted by Aymus, the first druid, after reaching the eye of the Calamity. He planted it there to be a beacon of hope, a sign of better things to come, evidence of survival amidst something as bleak and deadly as the Calamity itself. Some say that, because it was blessed by Aymus, omen, and the paladin, Martin, the flower has the capabilities to protect those near it from misery, misfortune, and even death itself, but nothing has been proven...yet.

"So, you do know about it. As I expected," Marigold replied smugly.

Oomphga nodded. "Okay. Eladda can uncover her ears now!"

Eladda carefully pulled her stubby fingers out of her ears, glancing back and forth between Oomphga and Marigold with shifty eyes. She seemed to squint between the two, her nose wrinkled as if their chemistry gave off a filthy stink that flooded her senses.

"What do you even want this flower for anyway?" Eladda asked, tucking her paws in between the metal plates covering her burly arms.

"I cannot say. It'd be too hard to explain…"

Considering its powers - its supposed magical capabilities - Oomphga could only assume one reason and one reason alone: she needed hope. She needed reassurance even if it was in the form of a flower, she craved an artifact - an idol - that promised her happiness. Oomphga could see it in her eyes and hear it in her solemn vocals. He knew the feeling all too well, but he never imagined the desperation needed to turn to anything tangible for the will and the courage to be a better druid. Even if he did believe in the rumors and superstitions, worshiping them as though they were fact, he convinced himself that things weren't that bad and that he didn't need it.

Now, he pondered the idea. If he had this flower for himself, he'd thrive as the druid. The number of people he could help without fear or worry would be astounding. He could gather together a crowd of people and call off the war without the need to run any more errands or listen to anyone. He could probably end the age-old feud just like that.

But no...

Whatever Marigold needed it for probably impacted her more than the violence of war impacted Oomphga (or anyone between the bearfolk and half-giants, really). Death was nothing new. Not anymore. Not to Oomphga.

"In a few days, Oomphga will make the trip."

Eladda snapped, eyes bulging as she turned towards Oomphga. "You won't be going into the High Peak Mountains ALONE, will you?!"

"Yes. Yes, he will," Oomphga blinked. "Eladda doesn't have a problem with that...does she?"

"Yes, I have a problem! You recently broke your arm, from what I've heard, and now you want to risk your neck in grey-skin territory for a FLOWER of all things?!"

"Well, Marigold is counting on Oomphga to fetch it for her, and Oomphga is the one that owes her for letting him borrow her cloak as a sling. Which - that reminds him..." Oomphga patted himself, being careful with the use of his arm, trying not to move it too erratically so soon. Realizing that it wasn't on his person, he checked the couch cushions.

"*Ahem.*" Marigold gestured to herself where the feathery cape resided, draped around the base of her neck and hanging from her back.

Oomphga hummed. "Oomphga owes Marigold more than her cape back. Oomphga owes Marigold his life. She saved him from the dreadwalker whether she realized it or not. Besides, maybe Oomphga will get a chance to talk things over with the half-giants while he's there!"

"Diplomacy? With those barbarians!?! Have you already forgotten what happened a few days ago?!" Eladda stormed over to Oomphga, her face inches from his. Though hair clouded her vision of him, he sat and stared upon her stern glaring with all the clarity in the world. "You've been lucky - escaping the grey-skin, escaping an apparent dreadwalker (whatever that is) - but you'll be walking straight into the hornets' nest with this one, and I believe, if I remember right, they're not very friendly to outsiders, now, are they?"

"Yooouuu never know until you try," Oomphga let out a breathy chuckle and shrugged.

"And you'll know for sure I'm right when you end up dead," Eladda replied coldly. "Listen, you know I'd go with you if I could, but my father needs me with his drunken political escapades. Faith needs me. You need me. This war is no joke. You won't be treading through fields of sunshine and roses. You'll be walking through frost, hiking up a mountain, and onto a literal battlefield where you will be slaughtered heartlessly like cattle where you stand!"

"You worry even more so than Papa Sergei," Oomphga interjected, "and Oomphga doesn't think-"

"Well, Sergei is right! So just-!" Eladda took a deep breath and clasped her hands in front of her muzzle. "Oomphga...you are my best friend. Last week, I did you a disservice as such. I left you to your own devices right after a grey-skin threatened you, and I left you on your own to head home when it got dark! I care about you. I worry for you. You got hurt because of me. That's one too many mistakes that I am willing to accept, so spare me another and do NOT go up to High Peak Mountains!"

Oomphga looked over to Marigold. Her golden eyes whispered the meaning of hope across the hollow gap between them. Even despite his cowardice in the face of danger, she openly trusted him - Oomphga, the druid with all his imperfections - to do something.

Swallowing the knot in his throat Oomphga stood up from the couch. Light broke through his hair and fell upon his beastial eye and a new, clearer voice fell upon a warm breath of air.

"Oomphga can do this."

Tomorrow...

Chapter 12:

Fuzzy's Mate

A BRIGHT NEW DAWN. A day of destiny. Oomphga brushed his fingers through his long hair as he sat gazing out at the early morning sunshine and the horizon painted in red and gold. Pulling strands of his hair tight, he tied it up in a red ponytail and let it flop down his backside with a sigh.

Pat. Creak. Pat. Creak.

"Oomphga?" Sergei peered at Oomphga beyond the floorboards, his expression lacking any sign of its usual morning glory. "You've been very…quiet."

"Don't forget what you have to do. Remember: after you say your 'hellos' to Tuthjorn and the new girl, make your way straight up to the abandoned church, get the flower, put it in a pot at home, and keep it safe until you have to bring it back here."

"Oomphga?"

"He's been thinking," Oomphga mumbled in reply.

"You've been doing that a lot lately, I'm sure. Thinking of…good things, I hope."

"Just…things Oomphga has to do. What he can and can't do. Stuff like that."

Sergei clambered up into Oomphga's attic space and crouch-walked over to the side of his bed mattress. Oomphga could sense how close he was. His presence dominated the bedroom.

"I'm…sorry if I hurt your feelings, my son. It's just that-"

Oomphga braced his ears for the impact of slander.

"I'm worried about you and your safety. I don't mean to ruin your fun or discourage you from going outside and doing your nature studies, but the world is very dangerous right now. Your mother and her people don't understand that you're young and fragile, but I do. I guess I'm just trying to protect you while giving you a chance to be a kid and it ain't easy. So, please promise me that you'll try to stay out of trouble while you're in the mountains. Because if something happened to you-"

"Oomphga will be safe. It's okay. Oomphga will probably just keep to himself anyways-"

Sergei pulled Oomphga into a bear hug from behind. His warm fur and heavy arms enveloped Oomphga, dragging him into that same safe and comforted feeling he remembered from way back when.

"I love you, son. You be careful now, ya hear?"

"He'll be as careful as the world lets him be," Oomphga whispered through the cracks in his voice.

After an awkward pat and a smile, Sergei straightened himself only to bump his head on the ceiling.

"Now, I'm gonna make you some bear-berry pancakes while you get ready with your things!"

His things. Crawling off of his mattress, Oomphga grabbed his traveler's pack and opened it up to put in a few extra things. He strategically stuffed a blanket into his backpack followed by the special set of gardener supplies his papa got for his tenth birthday and his beloved bear plushie. With little room left, he closed the main part of the backpack and carefully slid his two journals into one of the smaller pockets before closing it up. He grabbed a hair tie, tied back his long brown hair, wrapped a bandage around his bear eye, and tucked back his two, fuzzy bear ears. A confident nod later and Oomphga playfully scooped - *no* - eagerly lifted - *no, that's not right either* - painfully lugged the backpack up onto his back, hauling the full weight of his baggage down the ladder and down the stairs to drop his things with a loud *thud* by the door.

He let his body fall against the wall, giving his muscles a brief second to rest and who did he see out the window? Marigold. She sat along the hillside, watching the clouds roll by. Her raven hair fluttered against her back; the sunlight illuminated her face. Oomphga caught himself staring. Why did he do that? He gazed upon her, excited by the mere thought of spending a minute - a moment - outside basking in the autumn air with her.

"Oomphgaaa!" Sergei called out. "Your pancakes are ready!"

Oomphga rushed to the kitchen and finished his breakfast as quickly as he could, shoving spoonfuls of fluff, butter, berries, and syrup into his mouth with little time to taste or properly digest the food. The second his plate was empty, he ran to the door to grab his things and felt a paw pulling him back.

"Woah! Slow down! What's the rush all of a sudden? This is your last day with your Papa Sergei."

"No, it's not."

"Well, not technically, I guess, but still! You won't be seeing him for another month, and I've never seen you in a bigger hurry to leave. Is it about your injury? Was I too harsh in scolding you? Did I hurt your feelings?"

"What? No! No, Oomphga just...he's a busy boy, and has a lot to do! Long LONG ways to travel!"

"You're only thirteen. How do you have a lot to do?"

"He just does!" Oomphga squeaked.

As he turned to put on his backpack, Sergei's eyes lit up. His eyes evaluated Oomphga's stance, his physique. He stepped off to the side to look out the window. He even flared his nostrils to take in his natural odors.

"Wait a minute...I think I know what's going on here..."

"Nothing is-" Oomphga's voice cracked again, and he let out a quiet cough. "Nothing is going on here. Nothing unusual."

Sergei knelt down and looked upon Oomphga with a smile.

"You're going through some changes, aren't you~?"

Oomphga blinked. "Eh?"

"Puberty! My little Oomphga is going through puberty!"

Oomphga looked around. He had no idea what that even meant. "Uhh…sure?"

"Don't think I haven't noticed! The itty bit of peach fuzz on your chin, the shifts and squeaks in your voice, the rebellious attitude, the nasty stink of cut grass and smoke coming from your pits!"

Oomphga brought his nose to the underside of his arm again. He couldn't smell anything. No matter who said what about his stench, he couldn't smell it. Not even a whiff.

"Ah, you don't understand because you are little and a lot is going on in your life to keep you busy, but Papa Sergei gets it! Oh! While Oomphga is gone, Papa Sergei should probably think about how to talk about the birds and the bees with little Oomphga-"

"But Oomphga already knows about birds and bees! He practically studies them for a living!"

"No no no! Not THOSE kinds of birds and bees!"

Oomphga squinted. "Not those kinds of-? …Oookay, well Oomphga's gonna get going now-" Picking up his things, Oomphga pushed himself out of the door, Sergei trailing behind him.

"Good-bye, Oomphga! Don't forget to take frequent breaks! Maybe stop by the lake to take a-"

Sergei's voice faded into nothingness, but it caught *her* attention. The second she glanced over her shoulder at Oomphga, he froze up. He didn't understand why, but the outdoors felt a billion times hotter.

"Marigold!" Oomphga squeaked. He fidgeted and twitched, patting down his sides hoping to find something to hold for comfort. "What are-uh-what are you doing here? Oomphga returned Marigold's cloak and-and he hasn't gotten the flower yet! So…"

"I just…figured I'd tag along!" Marigold replied. "I want to see the druid in action out and about in the wild!"

"In the wild~" Oomphga chuckled aloud to himself.

"Also - um - pardon my asking, but are you okay? Your voice is a little-"

"That! Oh! That~" Oomphga coughed, trying to clear whatever was causing that annoying cracking in-between his words. "It's...been like that all day. Probably a sore throat from sleeping with his mouth open. Not that he does that often, but...maybe he did and didn't notice? There was no drool on his pillow so, probably not-"

Marigold laughed at him.

Why was she laughing? Did he say something funny? Was it his-? Oh, yes. Definitely his voice.

Instead of taking offense, Oomphga laughed along and readjusted his backpack strap over his shoulder. As Oomphga wandered off in the direction of Bear Friend's cave, his gaze bounced between the trees, the dirt road, and the birds that occasionally flew overhead.

"Sorry if I'm quiet. I've never traveled with anyone before," Marigold said.

"It's fine. Oomphga kinda knows the feeling. Whenever he travels up the mountains to his mama's-" Oomphga paused. *Could he really tell her? Yeah. She isn't a half-giant nor a bearfolk, so what does it REALLY matter to her?* "-to his mama's...house, he travels alone. Well, mostly alone. Sometimes the animals join him, but..."

"Animals...join you on your travels?"

"Ah! Marigold will see soon enough~" With confident strides, Oomphga made his way into Bear Friend's cave with a chipper grin plastered across his face. The darkness wasn't all that inviting, but the spaciousness and the bit of plant-life along the entrance did. "How do you feel about bears, by the way?"

"Bears as in bearfolk? The people? They're alright. They have their faults, but they're a friendly bunch to outsiders like myself. Bears as in the animals? I've thought about hunting one or two in the past, but...I couldn't do it. They're too big and their hides are too thick. Plus, the way they move. The way they act. They feel all too close to people. Innocent people. Why...do you ask?"

One by one, step by step, Oomphga could hear them approaching. Marigold heard it too. Almost instinctively, she reached for the bow on her back, her eyes sharpening, her sights focused solely on the large figures moving in the darkness. Suddenly and without warning, Small Bear ran forward before slowing down and stopping.

"Mama! I told you! I told you it'd be Fuzzy! And he brought company this time!" He peered around at Marigold and belted as loud of a warning cry as he could. "BAD COMPANY!!!"

"No no no! Fuzzy didn't bring bad company! This is Fuzzy's friend! She's not gonna hurt you!" Oomphga pleaded.

"You can...understand them?" Marigold inquired, turning to Oomphga with an inquisitive expression.

"More or less."

"Oomphga, deary!" Bear Friend waddled forward; her lips curled into somewhat of a smile. "You're back! And - how cute - you've brought a friend! A...female friend! Is this your mate?"

"What?!" Oomphga reeled back. "NO!!! No no no! She's not-! No. Cute, but no."

"I'm not what?"

"What's a mate, Mama?" Small Bear asked.

"Nothing! Nothing at all! Regardless-" Oomphga coughed, still trying to clear away the squeaking in his voice. "We're just looking for safe and swift passage through. We got things of great importance to get done, mountains to climb, things to find, and...and...why is Bear Friend looking at Oomphga like that?"

Her stare. Her doubtful stare. She padded over to Oomphga, nose flaring and steps heavy. Even Small Bear mimicked his mother's motions, sniffing and circling Oomphga.

"What is even happening right now?" Marigold whispered.

"Oomphga has no idea-"

Bear Friend wandered over to Marigold and did the same thing. After doing her little "sniff test", she began trailing deeper into the cave with her head held high. "Deny it all you want, deary, but you two are gonna be mates! I can smell it!"

"So...what did the bear say?"

"She wants us to follow her. That's...that's what she said."

Oomphga let out a breathy sigh and trailed after Bear Friend, Marigold and Small Bear following close behind. Gazing down at him, Oomphga could see, fading into the darkness the deeper they traveled into the cave, a cheeky little grin smoothly spreading across his face like butter on toast.

"Fuzzy's gotta ma~ate! Fuzzy's gotta ma~ate! Haha! I don't even know what that means, but the look on your face is too funny!"

Oomphga could feel the warmth cooking the underside of his cheeks and his half-giant eye twitching before he summoned a bright, burning flame in his hands for torchlight. Gracefully, Marigold spared Oomphga some of the mocking and stepped between him and Small Bear.

"You're Fuzzy's mate. Ya know that?"

Oomphga cracked a faint chuckle. "She can't understand you, you know."

"I could if you translated them for me," Marigold said in a soft, cheery tone.

"Yeah! Tell her! Tell her what Mama said! Tell her!"

"He-! Well-!"

Oomphga's eyes lit up and his ears fell flat. Now, he was *really* caught between a rock and a hard place. As much as he wanted to be honest, he didn't want to make her writhe in mutual discomfort, but at the same time, she was probably the only defense he had against the allegations. If they truly weren't true, she would say the same thing he said, but if they *were* true then…

No. She had to know. Oomphga couldn't keep a secret or tell a lie to save his life.

"They…think we're mates."

Marigold paused as if she wanted to calculate her next words carefully. "I suppose it makes sense for them to make that assumption. After all, it's not too often that male bears are seen with female bears without there being some kind of relationship between them."

"That's-…that's true. Unless they're family, of course, but chances are, if they're not directly related in a biological sense, they're-"

"Right."

"And then…yeah! Because we're not directly related, and they could smell that, they think we're-"

"Yeah!"

"Yeah!" Oomphga nodded and brushed back his hair. "Yeah."

He couldn't get over it now. The idea, that is. As much as he tried to deny it, if there were ever someone Oomphga wanted to be with for the rest of his life, gosh, how nice would it have been if it was *her*? The way she caught on - the way she seemingly knew as much as he did about the natural world - it left Oomphga feeling seen, heard, and understood. Of course, part of that knowledge probably came from all of her experience in hunting these animals in the past, but even still, Oomphga rode on the tidal wave of excitement for as long as it lasted. It's been years since he felt so in-tune with someone. The last time he felt this kind of connection was several years ago with…Buppy.

But here stood a person, one with wisdom and a cheery aura around her, and as cold and dark as her raven-like appearance made her seem, the amber glow in her eyes reflected a life that Oomphga missed and a hope that - in that moment - he would be willing to fight and die for.

"It's kind of cute that they think that," Marigold hums.

"It is, isn't it?"

Trying to avert his attention to other things, Oomphga looked around at the faint, bluish glow coming from gemstones protruding from the walls and floors of the cave and the mushrooms sprouting around them. Beautiful things, all of it, however, nothing in that cold, rocky tunnel could compare to the innocence and beauty of Marigold's expressions as she oohed and aahed at the spectacle surrounding them.

"Hey, Oomphga," Marigold whispered, leaning in close. "Maybe you can answer this question for me, but…why are some of the gems in here red?" She gestured over to a patch of hemogems that were growing through the skeletal remains of a humanoid being: a human, elf, or something in between. By now, it was impossible to tell.

"They're…hemogems," Oomphga explained. "It's crystalized blood. Like all of the other gemstones in here, its glow is a reflection of the magic within it."

"So, these are all arcane crystals!"

"It would appear so."

"Does that also mean that the blood belonged to someone that could use magic?"

"Well, yes and no. Everyone has magic in them. Whether they know how to use it or not is a different story. Like, Marigold! Marigold COULD use magic if she-"

"Could you teach me?"

Oomphga paused. Was the druid-in-training really being asked to suddenly become the druid-in-teaching? Surely-

Her eyes shimmered as she stared longingly at the flame enveloping Oomphga's hand. That's when Oomphga realized: he didn't earn his powers or the skill to use them - it was given to him. For him to teach Marigold anything wouldn't be possible, but he could feel her longing to try. She clung to Oomphga's every word, and Oomphga didn't second-guess himself on this "all creatures have magic" theory either. He knew it was true, but to actually use a part of yourself that you never knew you had - he couldn't formulate the level of difficulty.

"Well, could you?" she asked once more.

"Maybe. One day."

Still following close behind Bear Friend, the four of them made it to the small clearing where sunlight beamed down into the cave and Oomphga's rope still hung down.

"How good is Marigold at climbing?" Oomphga asked.

"I'm an archer. I climb up a lot of trees to get the best shot."

"Good news, then. That's how we get up into the mountains. Oomphga will let Marigold go first since she's-"

"A lady?"

"Oomphga was gonna say lighter, but...sure?"

Approaching the rope, Marigold gave it a cautious look over. She gave it a bit of a tug, watching the stones and the steep cliff edges above. Aside from the few small rocks that dropped down, not much else happened. Without further delay, she hopped up, grabbed on tight, and began clambering up the hundreds of feet of rope Oomphga left behind.

"So?" Bear Friend asked.

Oomphga looked over at Bear Friend. "So...what?"

"Did my senses deceive me? Are you two not truly mates after all?" She purred.

"We're-" Oomphga scrunched up a little, his hands digging into his green pants' pockets. "It's complicated, but whatever it is, Oomphga's gonna be by her side for as long as she lets him. Even though he's known her for such a short amount of time, he's gonna look out for her the same way he'd look after you two."

Bear Friend let out a warm purr and nestled her head into Oomphga's side. Instinctively, he wrapped his arms around her to pull her in for a warm embrace. Then, slowly, by his feet, Small Bear slipped between the two of them and looked up with his big, beady brown eyes.

"Hey, I'm…sorry for making fun of you. Could you - maybe - forgive me?"

Brushing aside his rascality, Oomphga scooped up Small Bear into his arms to hold him near. The furs atop his head brushed against the underside of Oomphga's chin and he burrowed all of his weight into his chest.

"Of course!"

A few minutes of sitting with the bears later, Oomphga stretched his arms and legs, hopped up onto the rope, and began his climb. His muscles ached and his hands tensed as he slowly began clambering up towards the light.

"Bye, Fuzzy!" Small Bear cried out.

"We look forward to seeing you again!" Bear Friend added sweetly. "Be safe!"

Don't worry. Oomphga thought. *He will.*

Chapter 13:
The Frigid Night Out

OOMPHGA PLOPPED DOWN face first into the snow, the weight of his backpack nearly crushing his spine. He loved the cold and missed it dearly, but this hefty luggage - this agonizing baggage - had to go. After a moment of letting the chill soak into his skin, he squirmed out of his backpack straps, rolled off to the side onto his back, and glanced around at the rigid mountainside. The rustling of the pines, the light of the stars, the growing chill as the moon pursued the sun's place in the sky, and from this view - from this high up - one could make out all the wonders of the world.

"So, you travel this road often?" Marigold asked, sitting down beside Oomphga.

"Every few weeks," Oomphga hummed, "and the sights never get old."

"Never?"

"Never. Not once."

"You never get tired seeing the same trees or the long expanse of snow or-?"

"Nope!"

Marigold sat for a moment, twiddling her fingers and patting her legs. Looking over at Oomphga, she playfully cocked her head to one side, her lips taking a crooked, upward stance between her ruby cheeks.

"If we're going to camp here, we should probably make a campfire to keep us warm throughout the night, should we not?"

"Oh! Right, right!" Oomphga rolled onto his feet, stood up, and brushed the snow off of his pants. "Oomphga forgot! You're an elf, and elves don't do very well in the cold, do they?"

"We do not." Marigold began her walk towards a cluster of pine trees over yonder. Her leather boots paved a trail and Oomphga followed in her smaller footsteps. As she walked, she looked down at her rosy-red hands, hardly taking her attention from them.

"My hands," she uttered with a heated breath, "they're freezing."

On cue, she extended her hands out towards Oomphga, letting him take them into his own. They were small, soft, frigid with most of the cold lingering in her fingers, and they fit perfectly in Oomphga's much larger and more calloused palms.

"How do you keep your hands so warm when the mountains are so cold?"

"It might be because Oomphga was born and grew up in the cold, so his body is used to it. Or it could be because he can summon fire at will." He let out a faint chuckle that trailed off into silence. "Why are…Marigold's hands so soft if she's a hunter? Shouldn't they be rougher from climbing trees and stuff?"

Marigold chuckled a bit louder than Oomphga.

"I guess…it might be because I take really good care of them whenever I get the chance."

Oomphga gently rubbed her fingers between his palms. Once they felt as warm as his hands were, he drew them away with a smile (and an awkward pat as a treat).

"There! Good and ready for tinder and wood collecting, yeah?"

"I think so," she brushed her now warm hands against her arms and rubbed them against her face.

Humming a jovial tune, Oomphga approached the closest pine tree he could and began scraping off some of the flakes of bark into his hands. He also snapped off a couple of low hanging twigs and tucked them away into his arms. Marigold did much of the same thing, only she climbed up into one of the other pine trees close by and began snapping off twigs from higher up.

Once a reasonable sum of tinder was acquired, Oomphga returned to the patch of snow where his backpack lay and brushed it aside to reveal the dark green grass beneath. Then, with a snap, sparks flew from his fingertips, creating a shower of sparks. The sparks danced through the air, gracefully landing on the tinder.

Within a matter of seconds, it ignited and grew into a small flame. Oomphga watched as the fire grew in size, spreading to the surrounding tinder. Soon, the small mound was engulfed in a humble blaze, casting a warm glow across the snow-covered ground. Oomphga nodded and began to unpack a few of his things just as Marigold knelt down beside him. She deftly drew forth a dagger from a holster at her side and began scraping off the moist, wooden exterior of some of the larger sticks she acquired, tossing the remainder into the flames. Piece by piece fluttered down into the campfire before them.

"Well," Marigold mused, her voice soft and contemplative, "this might last us for - what - three hours?"

"Probably," Oomphga replied. "If Oomphga notices it dying, he'll fetch more tinder to keep the fire alive."

Reaching into the largest pocket, Oomphga pulled out a rolled-up woven blanket, handful of hardtack, and a jar of chestnuts. He cracked open the lid and extended the jar towards Marigold. Happily, she took the jar into her hands, her fingertips brushing against Oomphga's.

"Thank you," she purred, "for offering up your food, I mean..! I would've gone hunting a bit earlier, but it slipped my mind, and I must've forgotten. Would be harder to do it now when the sun isn't out."

"Oomphga has food for days. No worries. It won't be meat (like what Marigold is probably used to), but it'll be enough for the both of us."

"Does your food consist solely of biscuits and nuts?"

Before Oomphga could even answer, Marigold flashed him a knowing smile, sending Oomphga into a frantic defense.

"What? Pfft! No..! He has other things! Like dried berries and…and…pear juice."

"Pear juice? And…no dried meat?"

"Oh," Oomphga brushed the back of his neck and curled up under the blankets. If he weren't so big, he'd hide himself in them. "Meat…makes Oomphga unwell, but for a ranger like Marigold, it's practically her breakfast, lunch, and dinner, huh?"

"I like berries for breakfast."

Oomphga's bear ears sprung up one by one as his expression softened. "Oomphga does too!"

Her eyes, sparkling like the stars, bound Oomphga's mind in a trance. Seeing her look upon him so sweetly and so compassionately, there was no better feeling in the world. His body, cold from an icy embrace a moment ago, all of a sudden felt all warm and fuzzy like the cozy embrace of his bed at Papa Sergei's. Oomphga let out a yawn and flopped down onto his bedroll.

"Do you…not need your blanket?"

"Marigold can keep it if she'd like. Oomphga's used to the cold."

"If you'd like, we could maybe…share it. That is, if you want to, because I think I'd be alright-"

And just like that, Oomphga was fast asleep, snoring loudly with his body draped across his bedroll.

What a wonderful home his mind concocted: a cabin on top of a hill overlooking the sea that Sergei spoke so fondly of. The waves danced and leaped, crashing against the rocks peering out of the blue below.

"Oomphga!" a familiar voice called. Looking towards the hill's crested peak, Marigold stood by dressed in a beautiful floral gown holding a medium sized box tucked in her delicate arms. Oomphga wandered up the trail leading to this house, heart humming a peaceful tune.

Oomphga wonders what the special occasion is...

"Happy birthday, Oomphga, and welcome home!"

Oomphga blinked. Was this HIS house? Did he really forget his own birthday? Wait a minute...*isn't that still a few weeks away?*

But her gestures, her smile, the decorations lining the front edges of the porch. Perhaps he truly did forget. As he sauntered up to Marigold, she extended the box in his direction.

"Marigold, what is this?"

"Your gift. Come inside and open it."

Oomphga stepped into the cabin and took in the sights. It felt so spacious and yet the perfect size for the two of them. Almost as if he knew where he was treading, he walked into the living room and sat down on the couch, the firm yet soft cushions brushing up against his back as he let the seat hold his weight. Carefully, he placed the box onto the ground, an audible yip sounding when it met the floor.

"What-?"

He turned to Marigold, hoping for an explanation, but she didn't say a word. Instead, she gleefully gestured towards the box over and over again.

"Open it. Open it."

Parting the lid of the box, there sat the, oh, so familiar pup.

"Buppy..?"

He scooped up Buppy into his arms. He was just as small and happy as he remembered, still smelling the same healing salve he covered his injuries with many many years ago. He yipped and yapped, tail wagging, eyes wide, face still reflecting innocence at its heart. Oomphga couldn't believe that the one thing he loved more than anything in the world rested in his embrace once again. Tears burning the edges of his eyes, Oomphga curled his body around Buppy defensively. His fingers ran through his fur and his cheek pressed back his best friend's pointed, grey ears.

"Well, what do you think?" Marigold asked.

"Oomphga thinks that being with you and being reunited with Buppy…it's a dream come true." He turned his attention to Buppy's wagging tail and goofy grin. "It's good to have you back…"

"Baaa!"

"…What?" Oomphga paused and held Buppy out. "Did…you just…?"

"Baaaaa!!!"

Oomphga's slumber was abruptly interrupted by the same piercing wail he heard from Buppy in his dream. Opening one eye, he found himself face-to-face with the short-furred face of a baby mountain goat standing on top of his chest. Its cloven hooves left imprints and markings all over his skin.

"WAAAAA!" It screamed.

Before the young druid could fully register the surreal encounter, the startled creature bolted back to the safety of the rest of its herd perched along the nearby mountainside.

Taking a deep breath, Oomphga laid back down onto his back and stared up at the morning sky, admiring the colorful arrangement of pinks and oranges intertwined behind the streaks of white, puffy clouds. The fresh scent of natural pine and stone washed through his lungs, the wind brushed against his bare chest, and the orchestra of animal sounds filled him with a rush of eagerness to continue his travels.

Rolling his arms forward, Oomphga made an effort to pull himself up off of his bedroll, still a little groggy and definitely a little sore, but suddenly, he noticed a curious sensation holding him back. Glancing over his shoulder, he spotted Marigold curled up underneath his blanket. The fabric kept the two wrapped up and tangled together in a warm embrace - warmth that savagely spread through Oomphga's cheeks. Whether this feeling came from admiration or nervousness, Oomphga had no idea. All he knew was that he had to find a way to politely wake up Marigold from her peaceful slumber somehow.

With a gentle hand, he patted Marigold's shoulder.

"Marigold. M-Miss Marigold. It's morning time."

Almost immediately, she woke up and - without saying a word - she collected her belongings. Judging by the sluggish way she unraveled the blankets and stood up, Oomphga sensed that she, too, was still half-awake.

"Did Marigold sleep well?" Oomphga asked.

"I did," Marigold droned.

"She wasn't cold?"

"I wasn't."

"Did Oomphga keep her warm all night?"

"You-" She froze up and cocked her head to the side. "You...um...you did. Th-thank you."

"Don't mention it!"

Marigold, teeth chattering, sat motionless by Oomphga's side, coiling Oomphga's fuzzy blanket around her body for warmth while she woke up. Seeing her so desperate for comfort, Oomphga pulled out a small bag of dried berries, a metal flask filled with pear juice, and two small wooden mugs from his backpack, handing one to Marigold. Happily, she accepted, and held out her cup while Oomphga poured the juice. She brought the cup to her lips and let out another shaky sigh.

"Cold?"

"A little."

Oomphga crawled over to the remnants of their campfire and extended a hand towards the sticks and twigs, alighting them with his magic fire. Much like last night, it sparked to life, the small spark now a roaring, crackling flame. Marigold inched herself to be by the warmth, her side pressed fiercely against Oomphga's. For what felt like an eternity, the two sat close to one another, Oomphga's skin a fiery blaze while Marigold inherited his heat.

"So, Oomphga was-" he squeaked and coughed, "Oomphga was thinking…how would Marigold feel about scaling the mountain on Oomphga's back?"

"I appreciate the offer, but I'm fine. My legs are a little sore, but-"

"Well, Oomphga actually had this idea - and this might sound a little crazy - but Oomphga turns himself into a mountain goat and Marigold rides on his back? It would probably be a lot quicker, Oomphga's assuming. And he wouldn't want Marigold to be cold, so she could just hold onto Oomphga's blanket until we make it to the top!"

Marigold looked at Oomphga, her brows furrowed. Then, she looked past him. That's when she noticed the mountain goats behind him scaling the mountain as a group in the distance.

"You want…to climb all the way up the mountain…like that?"

"…Yes."

Chapter 14:
Part of the Herd

ONE HAND ON HIS BLANKET, the other pressed gently against Oomphga's neck, Marigold held on tight. Her small, delicate fingers dug into Oomphga's wooly curls as they navigated the treacherous mountain path. Oomphga, a sturdy and surefooted mountain goat, carefully followed the other goats ahead, his hooves gripping the narrow ridges with precision. His attention was fixated on the rest of the herd, his keen eyes observing their every move.

How do they make it look so easy?

"Come on! That's it," a powerful, raspy voice bellowed out. "No one will get left behind, now! My fellow bucks, keep an eye on the nannies and the kids!"

The voice belonged to the herd's leader, an old goat with a long, flowing silver beard and impressive horns that, although damaged, surpassed those of all the others. Despite his age, he exuded an air of flamboyance and vitality that set him apart from the rest of the herd.

"How much longer until we get to the green fields, Mama?" a smaller and younger goat bleated.

"You see that ridge at the top where there isn't any more cliff to climb on? That is where we are going," their mother replied.

Oomphga glanced in the direction of the kid, squinting his eyes as he looked along the cliff edge almost directly into the sun that loomed above them. *That high, huh? That's not too bad.*

"There has to be some kind of magic that would get us up quicker than this," Marigold grumbled directly into Oomphga's ear.

But Oomphga couldn't reply. Not with the common tongue, anyway. So, silently, he persisted in his climb, his eyes on the rest of the mountain goats ahead.

The journey seemed endless, each step a testament to the grueling nature of their ascent. Suddenly, without much warning, one of the kids slipped on a rock. The nanny close by extended her neck, trying to grab onto her little one, but her movements were too slow. Then, as if fueled by instinct, Oomphga leapt across a ledge, letting the kid fall onto his neck and into Marigold's lap. Chunks of rock and stone broke off beneath Oomphga's weight as his hooves struggled to grasp onto the rocky face of the mountain. Marigold deftly drew forth her dagger and lodged it between two stones, her grip on Oomphga tightening.

"She's-she's alright! Oomphga got her!" Oomphga called out to the herd above after finally regaining his balance.

The mountain goats paused, staring blankly at Oomphga and the elven woman seated across his back. She coiled her arms around the mountain goat. It screamed and flailed about. Poor thing probably didn't recognize either of Oomphga or Marigold's scents, but with a careful and gentle hand, Marigold brushed the kid's coat, easing it into a more soothing embrace.

"Shhh…it's okay. You're going to be okay."

"Who are you?!" The elder finally snapped. "And why do you carry a predator atop your back?!"

"The name is Oomphga!" Oomphga admitted. "His - uh - his herd is further up this mountain near the top. And this is Marigold! She's a friend! She's here to help Oomphga during his travels!"

A choir of gossiping ensued, each of the nannies and bucks turning to one another to discuss the strange new addition to their traveling party.

"Hmm…how good are you and your companion in the face of wolves?"

"Wolves?" Oomphga repeated solemnly. "Oomphga has handled wolves before…"

The wind howled, sweeping across Oomphga's coat. A chill

seeped into his skin and sucked the formation of teardrops straight out of his eyes. If he could, he'd brush his face against his arm to wipe away the pit of grief accumulating in his head, but there he stood on thin slabs of stone. Hiding his emotions wasn't worth the risk of plummeting thousands of feet down to his death.

"Whatever your situation is with the wolves, Oomphga and Marigold would be able to help, surely."

"Very well. You may stay with us for now."

As they neared the summit, the air grew thinner, and the wind whipped around them with increasing ferocity. The goats pressed on, their determination unwavering. Finally, after what felt like an eternity, they reached the top of the ridge. Before them, a vast expanse of lush green fields stretched as far as the eye could see. A collective sigh of relief swept through the herd as they gazed upon the verdant paradise that awaited them. As they entered the green fields, they were greeted by a symphony of sounds and smells. The gentle rustling of the grass, the sweet fragrance of wildflowers, and the laughter of the children in the herd filled the air. The goats frolicked and grazed, savoring the abundance of food and the newfound freedom.

Oomphga dropped down onto one of the many dense patches of grass and let out a relieved sigh. Eagerly scrambling to her feet, the kid, once slung over his neck, now stood proudly atop it while its mother approached slowly and cautiously alongside the herd's elder. When they were both near enough, the kid leapt off of Oomphga and rushed to more familiar company.

The elder let out an approving hum and smiled upon the two weary travelers resting at his hooves.

"So…a druid and a dark elf traveling among my herd. Never thought I'd see the day."

Oomphga's ears shot up. "How did you-?!"

"Haha! I could tell by the name you went by! We all could! It's-"

The goat paused to catch his breath, and then - to Oomphga's surprise - he bowed his head. "It's an honor to meet you personally, Druid Oomphga."

An honor. Oomphga looked back at Marigold with identical levels of confusion. This feeling - these introductions as of late - Oomphga didn't want to admit it, but it all felt nice. Nicer than the feeling of being battered by his half-giant brethren or babied by his bearfolk kin. However, there was something about it all that the druid-in-training couldn't comprehend. This sudden appraisal from out of the blue - has he been missing something, or has he been missing from a time and place he can't remember? The lack thereof knowledge about what a druid was or why he had considered one added to the inquiries he had accumulated thus far, but still, this "honor" thing left him a barrage of even more questions.

"Thank you," Oomphga finally replied. "The feeling is mutual. You said you had wolves you needed help with?"

The elder nodded. "Yes. It shouldn't be any of my concern, but this quarrel between the half-giants and bearfolk - I think the discourse has been making them far more…aggressive as of late. Far more like…man."

"Far more like man? What does that mean?"

"The wolves, our natural enemies, usually hold some level of respect for us. My biggest fear is their agitation getting the better out of all of us, not just my herd. I've seen them atop the mountain on two legs. From afar, they seem like strategists and tacticians fighting to survive, but now I watch as they gang up and kill creatures with no intent to feast, tearing their bodies apart to devour their insides like starving hunters. They have evolved into monsters. Though…perhaps it is only the season. Some of our own nannies have been far more tense as of late."

Oomphga could hardly envision it. Wolves, loyal and familial creatures at heart, killing so relentlessly and pointlessly, and on two legs?

This all sounded far too unnatural to be common evolution. Wiping the deep reds and sparkling silver from his mind, Oomphga envisioned the crystium catastrophe - the beacon of hope itself. He's never seen it for himself yet knew of its existence. How it worked or what it did, truly, was far beyond his comprehension, but something must've been wrong if the half-giants, the bearfolk, the mountain goats, the wolves, and even Marigold were all in desperate need of peace.

"Oomphga thinks he can help."

"You know what's causing it?"

"Oomphga's on a quest to look for a flower, one created by one of the first druids ever to walk the earth. It was supposed to keep hope alive after a terrible calamity that happened hundreds of years ago. Maybe something is wrong with it and that's why everyone's been acting strange."

The goat's eyes widened. "And…you can fix it?"

"Maybe. Oomphga's certainly going to try if that's the case. The only problem now would be…explaining that to Marigold."

"Your friend?"

Oomphga let out an affirmative hum as the two goats looked upon her. He couldn't get over her silly yet shocked expression; she still had no idea what was happening.

"Why are you both looking at me like that?" Marigold asked skeptically. Oomphga tried to come up with a reply but couldn't.

"I suppose you'll only know for certain when you get to this crystium catastrophe you speak of, won't you?" the elder goat asked.

When? If the world was truly in a growing state of discord, the prospect felt more like an "if" if anything at this point. And if something were to happen - if another battle or fight were to break out the moment Oomphga returned home to the half-giants - what then? What of Marigold? What of Oomphga if something happened to him? If the crystium catastrophe, all along, was the source of the war and all it would take to fix everything would be to nurse it back to health, then he HAD to make it there, for Marigold, for the animals, for the half-giants and bearfolk, for potentially everyone in the world.

The world needed the druid, and it needed him alive.

"It won't be easy. Oomphga might need help," Oomphga uttered, solemnly looking upon the elderly mountain goat beside him. "If Oomphga were to need help during his journey because something bad happens along the way, could Oomphga call for Leader Goat or his herd?"

"Maybe. There was someone a long time ago - a tall half-giant with long hair - he used to have a horn. A special horn. We could hear it across the mountain. Maybe you could ask the half-giants if one of them still has that horn, that is...if they're willing to speak with you."

"Well, Oomphga knows three (maybe four) of them that'd at least be willing to talk with him. Maybe one of them will know!"

The elderly goat cracked a faint smile and turned tail. "Then I wish you luck! I'll be waiting to hear from you, Druid Oomphga!"

With that, he stumbled back over to his herd, already starting up a new conversation with one of the nannies. Happily, Oomphga clambered up onto his hooves and with a shake of his coat and a wave of magic light, Oomphga was back to his usual self. What he didn't realize was that Marigold fell off of him in the process and plopped down into a fluffy pile of snow.

"Oh! Sorry!" Oomphga hollered, reaching a hand out to Marigold to pull her back onto her feet and dust her off.

"A little more warning would've been nice~" Marigold rolled her eyes and let out a quiet chuckle under her breath.

"To be fair, what could've Oomphga done aside from look at you and bleat? Should he have let out a short and sweet baa or a loud, scream-like baa?"

"I don't know. A little wiggle and a baa would've been nice~?"

"Alright. Duly noted~" *A wiggle and a baa. Oomphga will have to remember that.*

By the end of the week, Oomphga and Marigold made it to Oomphga's half-giant village. It was significantly smaller than what it once was many years ago, but it still had shops and hubs for the different craftsmen. Marigold looked around at the quaint little village, watching the half-giants go about their day with a very off-putting expression.

"Is...something wrong?" Oomphga whispered.

"They're...staring at us."

Sure enough, looking around at some of the half-giants, there they stood gawking at the two as they walked down the main road. Oomphga curled his fingers around Marigold's and held her hand firmly in his own.

Off in the distance, Oomphga heard screams. Both him and Marigold turned to look and see what was happening and, sure enough, horrors awaited them. Two half-giants were in the middle of torturing a female bearfolk. She was weeping and sobbing, blood soaking her fur and burn marks across her back. Their yelling was incomprehensible from afar, but knowing the bearfolk's recent discoveries of the hemogem's destructive properties, he wouldn't be surprised if they were trying to extract that from her.

But her resilience was strong. Even though her unconscious or dead husband's corpse laid outside, she refused to say anything. The half-giants, annoyed with her tight-lipped stubbornness, then proceeded to beat her...to death.

"Oomphga Sage Thundrak!" A familiar voice boomed.

Suddenly jolting towards the sound, Oomphga caught sight of Tuthjorn with his arms outstretched. He ran to Oomphga and pulled him in for a tight hug. A young lady, about their age, trailed behind him. Her expression was very stern, almost chilling. She wore metal plates over her chest and waist, both covered by long, flowing purple scarves, and hanging by her waist side: a long slender blade unlike any kind of sword Oomphga had seen before.

What an agile weapon of choice. Oomphga wonders if it's all for show or if she actually uses that.

"Cousin! You made it back from your studies alive!" Tuthjorn cheered, grinding his fist against Oomphga's scalp roughly. "I was so worried a manticore mauled you to death or a scarlet-fur caught you unawares, but…you live!"

"Of course! Oomphga is all-right!" Oomphga laughed anxiously from Tuthjorn's ruffling and nudging. The image of the bearfolk still lingered in his mind. He couldn't shake the thought. The moment he had a second to catch his breath, he cracked a forced smile. "Did Tuthjorn really doubt Oomphga's-?"

"Gah! You've missed out on so much!" he interrupted. "Our special guest arrived just yesterday morning and she's just- …she's so…you have to meet her for herself!"

"The special guest? Oh! The-" Oomphga smacked himself gently upside the head. "The girl from the Violet Sun tribe!"

"YES!!! Yes…" Tuthjorn let out a bawdy chuckle that diminished as his attention focused on Marigold who was still standing stiff and silently next to Oomphga. "And…who might your companion here be, 'cos?"

"Hm?" Oomphga curiously looked over his shoulder at Marigold, his lips naturally curling into a goofy grin. "She's…she's a really good friend Oomphga made. Her name is Marigold. She technically saved Oomphga's life in the woods once~"

"Your…cousin, technically saved himself," Marigold replied.

"Oomphga broke his arm," Oomphga admitted.

"*Oomphga* confronted a dreadwalker," she mocked.

"Oomphga accidentally ran into one in the forest," he added.

"He spit fire at it and buried his blade into its skull."

Oomphga gagged at the thought, and Marigold caught on quickly to the sickening sounds he made.

"What's wrong? Too much?"

Oomphga nodded. "It was…out of self-defense."

"By Obak's might…" Tuthjorn's eyes widened as he grinned mischievously. His eyes shifted back and forth between Oomphga and his elven company. All too quickly, he recognized the look his cousin wore.

Please, not you too..!

"I don't know what I'm more impressed by, 'cos. The fact that you fought a monster or the fact that you were brave enough to waltz into the tribe with your elven love interest. Why if I were any wiser, I'd say you-"

"OOMPHGA!!!" A gruff voice cried out.

Tuthjorn and Oomphga flinched as they both slowly looked in the direction of the bellowing scream. With footsteps that shook the mountains, Mortium approached. His eyes lacked the fun, cheery glow they usually had as he stormed past his fellow half-giants, hardly paying them any mind as they watched the spectacle he put on, and tucked under his arm was a copy of the Endinerose newspaper.

"You…" he growled. "You have some explaining to do, young man." He unfolded the newspaper and there - staring Oomphga in the face on the front cover - was the half-giant man that attacked Oomphga in the city.

Oomphga painfully swallowed back his guilt. He hoped he wouldn't have to see those dark eyes and gnarled teeth ever again, but the Endinerose illustrator did his attacker justice and spared no detail in the portrait he made of him.

"What were you doing in the city, Oomphga Thundrak?!" Mortium belted.

"But that isn't-"

"ANSWER THE QUESTION!!!"

Oomphga felt every inch of his body cave in on itself from the pressure. Tears filled his eyes as the struggle for words - for an excuse - grew harder and harder until it became a painful lump in his throat. Helpless, he stood before his uncle practically suffocating from shock. From over Mortium's shoulder, Oomphga spotted Seirah. His color-faded eyes shot daggers into Oomphga's chest.

"One of my best warriors is dead because of you! I had to sit alongside the NFC, listening to him ramble about how he saw YOU making merry with the scarlet-furs, helping one of their leaders! All the other representatives laughed at him as he hung from the gallows, but I...I believe him, so tell me..."

"Stop it..." Oomphga begged.

"What were you doing in the city with the scarlet-furs!?!"

"STOP IT!!!" Oomphga lashed his hands out as a wave of rocks and snow swept everyone back away from him.

He panted, a surge of desperation filling his mind with words - a lot of them. He could feel a crackling under the skin of his fingertips. Something felt terribly wrong.

Was it hormones? Was it the crystium catastrophe? Was it...Oomphga?

He shook aside the doubts, tossed aside his bag of things, and rushed over to Mortium as he rolled onto his side, his fangs bared and his hands tightly gripping onto his greataxe that he used as a crutch to lift himself onto his knees.

"Oomphga...is so sorry..!" Oomphga squeaked. "He didn't mean to lash out like that. It's just-...he was so overwhelmed by everything. If Mortium was a little gentler with his words - if Mortium didn't yell - Oomphga would've been more than happy to-"

A sharp pain enveloped Oomphga's left side as he watched Mortium swing his greataxe outwards towards him. Several voices rang out, each of them crying out Oomphga's name.

Why are they yelling at Oomphga? What did he do wrong this time?

Feeling the cold steel part from his side left a deep gash where the icy winds let themselves in. Head throbbing, he grasped at his side and stumbled back. His legs buckled under the weight as they tried to keep him steady. Despite holding his hand directly against the wound, he couldn't feel any of his healing magic taking effect. It was almost as if his body was going weak too quickly for him to think or act upon anything.

When his feet finally slipped out from under him, he fell into a pair of big, soft arms, his head resting against someone's soft chest. Looking up, he caught a blurry glimpse of who he tumbled into.

"Mama…" Oomphga huffed through strained breaths. "Tuthjorn…Marigold…"

Mama Vergaia looked at Oomphga, but her expression was far from a happy one, and it only got grimmer and more aggressive as she focused her attention onto her brother Mortium. She started yelling a bunch of things at him, but Oomphga couldn't make out a word of it. He could hardly even hear his own thoughts as they tried to talk him through what to do.

Hold tightly.

Oomphga's hand trembled, his fingers burrowing into the skin around the injury to latch on.

Keep holding. Now, Breathe. Take deep breaths.

Though his throat pulsed, and his nostrils flared at the slightest touch, he tried to keep breathing in and out through the mouth, but his eyes grew heavy. All this thinking made him tired.

No! Whatever you do, Oomphga, DON'T close those eyes!

He couldn't help himself. The idea of taking a nap and waking up to everything being all better seemed so tantalizing - so tempting. His grip faltered and his head sunk deeper into his mother's breasts. They were so soft and warm. He was practically curled up in his bed and on the road to recovery. All he needed was his blanket.

Stay awake! Stay alert! We're so close! You just need to focus! You just need to heal yourself!

Letting out a faint hum, his fingers traced over his injury. Though they were cold a moment ago, they left a warm sensation behind on his skin. Everything felt so comforting - so perfect for a nice...little...nap. If only Marigold was in his lingering sight, it'd be even nicer.

Upon his silent wish, there she appeared. She got down onto her knees and politely offered to take Oomphga from Vergaia's arms - *at least, Oomphga thought that's what she asked* - because not long after, there he was: head resting across her lap and eyes focused on hers. She was crying, and Oomphga didn't like seeing her cry.

With every ounce of strength he had left, he pushed past the shadows overtaking his vision, let out one last breathy chuckle, and mustered the wisest words he could think of:

"Did...did you know that...marigolds are very sensitive to the cold. At least their petals have anti-viral, anti-bacterial, anti-fungal, and..." Oomphga choked back the nausea that coursed through his body "...anti-inflammatory properties. Pretty crazy for a flower to be able to do all that, huh~?"

Oomphga rambled on, eyes glistening with happiness.

"W-...what?!"

And that's all Oomphga could remember succumbing to the hazy darkness that infected his senses.

Chapter 15:
Behind Violent Eyes

W HEN OOMPHGA'S FIFTH YEAR ARRIVED as anticipated by his mother and uncle, Oomphga was far from prepared. How could he have known? How could he have foreseen such a grim, violent future when all he ever knew existed in the present? How could he have readied his defenses for a path of betrayal, blind justice, and silent cries into the void?

Step by step, Oomphga ventured forward through the mist, following close behind the teal wisps that guided him along the way. The fresh scent of chamomile, honey, and pine permeated through the woods, only growing stronger as Oomphga continued down the winding path. Then hints of berry and fermented grapes invaded his senses. Sounds of howling, laughter, and merriment filled the void of silence. It grew louder and louder until, peering over bushes, the young druid caught a glimpse of a festival filled with bearfolk and half-giants. They were all happy, smiling and drunkenly embracing one another. Out of the corner of his eye, a young half-giant girl came into view along with a slightly smaller bearfolk girl. One of the two grabbed Oomphga's hand and began dragging him along with them.

"Woah! Slow down, now~! Where is this place?" Oomphga asked aloud.

Is this…the afterlife? Oh, gods, please, don't let it be so..!

But he received no response, only visions of unfamiliar faces dancing and singing in tandem in front of an old, wooden cottage overlooking a large lake. There were so many colorful conversations taking place in tandem with several different activities to take part in: musical performances, improvisation games, ramball, apple bobbing, and even flower crown making.

The two small children ignored all of these delights and lead Oomphga into the cottage. They weaved through the halls and guided him up the familiar staircase and into the master bedroom, empty of hosts.

"Look! Look there!" The bearfolk girl cheerfully whispered, pointing off towards the other end of the room.

There sat, alone by the window, a woven cradle where a small half-giant bearfolk baby lay wrapped in a fuzzy pink swaddle. Oomphga cautiously reached out and laid his hand across the baby's blanketed stomach. His palm and fingers outstretched were practically almost as big as the newborn herself. His thumb brushed against the soft fabric, grazing over the baby's hand tucked away underneath.

"You act like you've never interacted with a baby before!" The half-giant girl giggled.

"Oomphga hasn't," he whispered and cautiously pulled his hand away. "Who is this baby girl, anyway? Is this Papa Sergei's house and is this-?" Oomphga gasped. "Is THIS gonna be a baby sister Oomphga is gonna have?"

"No, but..." the bearfolk rolled her shoulders with a half-smile, "you are to keep an eye on her for the next couple of minutes while her parents are out. Okay?"

"Hm? Why Oomphga?"

The half-giant and bearfolk girls began moving in unison as the two of them backed up towards the door, both still smiling.

"Because you're good at hearing things..."

"Seeing things..."

"Learning and knowing things..."

"Things that no one else can..."

Oomphga stood stunned by the two's choreography.

"...What?"

They both flailed their hands at the dumbfounded druid and grinned. "Bye-bye!" they cheered in a whisper as they closed the door quietly.

And there, Oomphga stood, jaw hanging, and brows furrowed. After witnessing all of the merriment - all of the fun going on just beyond the cottage walls - he was given the task of...babysitting? He gazed longingly at the window. Happiness and peace existed just outside of his reach, but he denied it. With the edge of his lip curling upwards, Oomphga let out a heavy sigh before turning his full attention onto the sleeping newborn.

Stepping towards her cradle, he paused to look upon her features. Many of them were similar to his own: the bear ears, the fuzz around the eyes, the thicker, grey skin covering most of her body. Carefully, he scooped her up into his arms of medium thickness and cradled her close to his chest.

"Don't worry," he hummed, "Oomphga will take good care of you."

Curling up in a rocking chair by the open window, he basked in the warm glow emanating from the festivities with the child coiled in his cozy embrace. It was so peaceful, Oomphga couldn't help but let his body sink deep into the chair, his muscles resting against the wooden dowels supporting his back,...

...but peace didn't last for very long.

What was once a soothing ambience with dancing lights and singing instruments slowly drifted into a blinding light and screaming that Oomphga couldn't ignore. His brown eyes shot open, and he glanced out the window and down at the roaring blaze consuming the half-giants and bearfolk below. As Oomphga watched on in disbelief, he caught sight of a cluster of devils ripping and slicing their way through the crowd leaving a gory mess of bulging, blood-shot eyes and crippled corpses scattered across the once lush green fields.

Overwhelming his senses was the presence of the newborn as it cried its tiny lungs out and squirmed underneath its swaddle. Hardly able to control the tremors in his chest, Oomphga pulled himself from the rocking chair and held the baby against his shoulder, his mind frantically trying to come up with his next course of action.

Hide, flee, or fight. Those were his choices.

His attention fell on the baby-sized basket in the corner of the room and rushed over to it, laid the child down close, tore off the crimson ribbon holding up his hair, and he weaved it between the straw of the basket. His bear ears twitched at every sound, his hands trembled, and his heart felt like it was going to burst out of his chest.

Creeeaaak…Slam!

Oomphga turned to look towards the door. It was completely unlocked, and the fiery, cloven hooved guests had just entered the cottage.

"The beast is up here. You know what you need to do," a quiet, rusty voice commanded.

"Beast..?!" Oomphga whispered. "What beast? Is Oomphga the beast? Is Baby the beast?"

He looked over the crying infant lying next to him with sharpened eyes and noticed not an innocent detail out of place. Then, quicker than before, he roughly finished his little crafting project. Using his hair ribbon, the basket, and a belt he found in one of the drawers in the bedroom, he made a makeshift saddle that he strapped the baby girl into using the swaddle that she was wrapped in. Once he had it wrapped around his body, he immediately noticed that it didn't feel sturdy on its own, but the tighter Oomphga had it strapped to his chest and above his waist, the more secure it felt. Suddenly, his ear twitched again. He had no more time left to waste. He got down onto all four, his body shifting and reforming into the shape of a young, grey and brown-furred dire wolf.

"It should be in here," the same rusted voice noted. *"Cinth, I need you to promise me that no matter who or what you find in this room, you will show them no mercy."*

Oomphga looked between the back window and the door, his heart beating faster the longer he thought about his next move. There was a long pause in the intruder's conversation.

"Is…that a baby I hear?" another, much softer-toned man inquired.

It is! There is no one else in here, so…so go away, please!

"You hear the future demise of the Fire Faction if left to its own devices," the sterner man hissed.

"How…how do you know?" asked the other.

"Because that is what the soothsayer has prophesied. Now, get in there before any local authorities arrive. We do not want a whole war on our hands, now do we?"

"…Very well."

Oomphga took a step back from the door, his back paw pressed against the dresser. With a faint creek, it gradually opened up before him. He watched intently as the gap between the door and the doorframe slowly got wider and wider. Then, when it was just wide enough to fit through safely with the basket on his back, he bolted and scurried right between the two intruders!

"After them! NOW!!!"

The baby cried louder and louder, a siren on Oomphga's back as the desperate chase between Life and imminent Death ensued. Panting and huffing, Oomphga made his way down the stairs and out one of the windows into the carnage, his claws and soft paw pads scraping against the wooden ledge.

Without hesitation, he charged head-first into the field of gore. The blood curdling screams and ripping of flesh with steel nearly made Oomphga gag. His judgment was clouded. Every color and object in his sights blurred. His desperation to survive assaulted his pulse. His yearning for safety nagged his senses.

But these intruders - these "hunters" - were no fools. They came prepared with wolves of their own. The moment Oomphga heard the same animalistic huffs and pants coming from behind him, fear took over.

He dodged and weaved around the bodies, both living and dead, both half-giant and bearfolk. His feet scratched and scraped against the earth as he turned violently in different directions, trying to make a nimble escape, but the brown wolf at his tail followed his movements more efficiently by barreling through his obstacles.

At the edge of the carnage sat the oversized, looming trees of Bristlethorn Forest. Familiar trails lie in wait for Oomphga to follow them. He burst forward through bushes with the still trailing close behind.

He ran...and ran...

His body cut between the trees and the wind brushed back his fur and cleared his vision and amongst the silence of the forest, it was easier to hear how close the wolf as well as the cavalier that joined the chase on horseback.

The crackling of twigs, the moonlit sky, the soothing presence of the baby strapped in on his back; Oomphga - for a moment - let himself get lost in the feelings. It certainly took the pain away from the aching muscles in his arms and legs as well as the growing side stitch he acquired somewhere along the way.

Where was he even going, anyway..?

"Cinth! He's heading towards Endinerose! We can't let him get onto the main road!"

He is?

He was, and the main road was only a sharp-turn-left away. With a powerful push of his front right paw, he turned to start heading that direction, but then…he heard it.

The tap of an arrow. The faint twang of the bowstring. Then, the lodging of the arrowhead between skin, muscles, and bones.

Oomphga fell to his side, the baby tumbling out of the basket. Its screams of agony were deafening, only adding to Oomphga's anguish the longer he laid across the grass with the arrow buried into his body. With his original form unveiled, he used his half-giant strength to endure the suffocating pain as he turned to face the little girl he swore to protect lying at the feet of the brown wolf that shifted into that of a tall, wolf-eared man with a twisted dagger in hand.

"Wait! Don't hurt her! She's just a baby! A harmless, innocent baby! She's done nothing wrong!" Oomphga squealed, his arm outstretched.

The man looked back at Oomphga, his cruel eyes softening only a fraction of what Oomphga would have hoped. Even as black, inky tentacles enveloped around Oomphga's legs, spine, and wrists, holding him pathetically against the earth, he spared only an ounce of sympathy.

"She doesn't deserve this! It's not-!"

A tentacle stole the voice from Oomphga, gagging him until all that could escape from him were screeches and raspy breaths.

The wolf man shifted his attention to the cloaked figure that stood behind Oomphga, his hand enveloped in malicious, crackling shadows. The chanting. The voice. Oomphga…recognized it.

"…*Martin? Martin, is that you?*" Oomphga could hear himself ask, his words echoing in the confines of his mind. "*Why? Why are you doing this? How could an angel who fought alongside me for the innocent people of this planet do something so vile?*"

"*…I don't want to die, Aymus.*" The cloaked devil replied, yet his mouth hardly moved. It was almost as if they were speaking through telepathy.

"*Neither does she. You must control yourself, Martin. Control your fears. As long as we're together, I promise, you won't die.*"

"*I can't.*"

"*Yes, you can!*"

"*You lie! You're a liar!*"

"*You're uncertain and afraid! Please,…call off this genocide. Spare her…*"

All fell silent, the final judgment falling upon the man concealed in black robes.

"Spare me your sympathies. Kill her. I'll take care of this one."

"*Monster! I thought you were better than the monsters, Martin! I thought you were-*"

As everything began to fade, the wolf-eared man got down on his knees before the weeping child, raised his blade, and…

Chapter 16:
Deep, Familiar Roots

COUGHING AND WHEEZING, Oomphga awoke with a start. Adrenaline coursed through every inch of his body, his nostrils burning from the intense floral scents that enveloped him as - towering above him - stood Seirah holding a handful of dragon lilies.

"Good. You're responsive," he commented aloud. "A good sum of people have been worried about you."

Carefully, Oomphga sat up from the fur-padded cot and wiped his face with his dirty hands still covered in his own dry blood.

"Seirah. Seirah, Oomphga had an awful dream."

"A dream…or a vision?"

"…He'll correct himself and call it a nightmare…" Oomphga chuckled pathetically, looking around the room.

His bag of things sat an arm's length away from the bed. Ready to leave, he stood up and tried to pull his backpack up and over his right shoulder, but a wave of dizziness hit him like a club to the face and he dropped back down onto the cot.

"Easy there. Easy. You just woke up," Seirah said, pressing his hands against Oomphga's upper chest and back to hold him steady. "The aura coming off of you…"

"What?" Oomphga cocked his head to the side.

"The aura. The magic. The divinity. Whatever dream you had was no mere dream, but a message. I could sense Laniarra's company emanating from you. The Mistress of Misfortune's as well. Oomphga…" Seirah suddenly got down onto Oomphga's level, his silver-plated eyes burning a hole into Oomphga's sense of judgment. "Did you not feel the same presence?"

"Oomphga felt…something. On account of the baby and the threat of being murdered, anxiety was probably the most prominent thing he felt."

"A baby, you say?"

"Yes. A little girl. She had cutest little grey cheeks and the tiniest bear-" Oomphga paused. How could he have forgotten the half-giant company directly in front of him. "Fangs. Weird things. You should've seen them. They were nasty, but all other half-giant features she had were…great! The finest features a half-giant could have!"

Seirah raised a brow, his lips morphing into a questioning pout as Oomphga awkwardly fidgeted his fingers and fumbled for words, trying to paint a picture that showed distaste against the bearfolk people he secretly adored. Just the mere attempt at insulting them left a sting on his tongue and a heaviness in his chest. He knew Seirah could see through his poor attempt at deception. Seirah was no old fool.

"Oomphga…" Seirah sighed, firmly patting Oomphga's shoulder. "I think you and I should have a talk. Here. Alone."

Oomphga clutched at himself, his skin itching with discomfort. Despite the glistening smile Oomphga wore, he could feel his internal organs convulsing when, sluggishly, Seirah drew back his wrinkly palms.

"Don't worry. You're not in any trouble. I would just like to…*enlighten* you on a few things and *remind* you of others."

"If this has to do with bearfolks being bad-"

"No…no this doesn't have to do with bearfolks being bad. You hear enough of that from your cousin and uncle. I'm sure."

"So…what is it?"

Seirah stood tall and pulled a few things from his shelf: a book with a torn-up leather cover, a small pouch, and…a ram's horn! Oomphga's eyes lit up as Seirah brought these three items over to the crippled druid's bedside. He first opened the dusty, hand-made book and flipped through the parchment pages, his fingers tracing along the words.

"This book is a collection of all the chieftains, shamans, and famous warriors in this tribe," Seirah uttered.

With curled lips and youthful wonder, Oomphga flipped to a page where, upon it, appeared an illustration of a middle-aged, battle-ready warrior that shared an uncanny resemblance to Oomphga (minus the bear ears, of course), but his brutalized eye, the long hair, the rune-carved handaxes he wielded...

This must be the half-giant Elder Goat was talking about! And...that handaxe.

Oomphga reached for his waist-side and drew forth his mother's handaxe. Looking between the black and white painting and the weapon in his possession: it was undoubtedly the same.

"Who is that?" Oomphga asked.

"Oomphgor Thundrak. Whenever I think of you and Tuthjorn, I think back on him. He was a fighter, brave and courageous, but unlike your cousin, he always had a level head. An untraditional charm. A strange mentality that it didn't matter who you were or what you were, he would've protected you all the same. He had all sorts of allies: orcs, dark elves, shapeshifters, elementals, dragonfolk. He was the half-giant that once famously said, 'a tribe isn't the race, the village, nor the lineage that you were born into, but the community, companions, and company you recruit yourself'."

"Great grandpa sounds like a very popular guy, but...what does this have to do with Oomphga?"

"He was the last good man this tribe had, and he wasn't even present all that often from what I can recall," Seirah closed the book and held it close to his chest, his head hanging low. "He should've been chieftain, but he wasn't. He passed off the mantle to his brother who then passed it onto Oomphgor's son, Tuatung, and Tuatung...he was just another Tuthjorn. Strong, but cocky. Arrogant. Grounded in his biased assumptions. He's the one that the bearfolk suspected got us into this mess, and I don't blame them given the kind of person he was.

"Oomphga, when I chose you to be my apprentice, I could sense untapped potential, the same potential your great grandfather had many years ago. Though you're no warrior, you're a sage. A leader. A true protector of the people. You're a hero in the making the way I wish I could be. You have the very essence of your great grandfather's magic living inside of you when you were little. So, no matter what Mortium or Tuthjorn or your mother says about who you are and what you do, remember that you are so much more than they could ever imagine. You cannot afford to take another injury like that. Understand?"

Oomphga nodded, smiling a bit more sincerely.

"Oomphga understands. Thank you, Seirah."

"Good. Now, I want to give these to you. These are all of the things that kept your great grandfather safe and alive for all those years." He placed the ram horn and the pouch of what felt like rocks into Oomphga's palms. "Take them and take caution on the journey ahead. I don't know what kind of quest the gods have in store for you, but if they are speaking through you, it must be urgent."

Oomphga brushed his hand over the ram horn and toiled with the pouch filled with stones. The gentle clicks cleared his thoughts, making room for courage.

"Seirah."

"Hm?"

"Remember the crystium catastrophe you told Oomphga about a long-long time ago?"

"The flower planted atop of High Peak Mountains by the first druid? Yes, I remember."

"Well, if something bad were to happen to that flower – if it began to wither or if it fell into the wrong hands – what would happen? Hypothetically, of course!"

"Hmm…then the entirety of the Nature Faction would fall into ruin and chaos. War and discourse would be prevalent among every race, the forests would be set ablaze, the wildlife would bring about its own demise, and all life as we know it would either come to an abrupt end or become so corrupt, peace would become a distant prospect – a figment of our imaginations."

Visions of the Calamity immediately came to mind. Through the eyes of Aymus, Oomphga saw the meaning of destruction overwhelming the little amount of innocence still occupying his headspace.

"And, theoretically, if that were the case, could the effects be reversed in any way?"

"Only by some miracle of magic through the current druid, but for a druid with the skills to match a spellcaster as powerful as the first druid…it's impossible. Why, the current druid would have to be no older than you, and thirteen years isn't nearly enough time to acquire such strength and wisdom."

Without warning, Seirah squinted his eyes at Oomphga.

"Why do you ask? Do you…know something, Oomphga?"

"He knows that doesn't give Oomphga a lot of time to think about things." Kicking his feet out from under the blankets, Oomphga clambered from the bed cot and collected his belongings. "Oomphga appreciates the wisdom, but now, Oomphga has to investigate some things on his own!"

"Hold on! You wouldn't happen to be the-!"

"Hypothetically,…yes! Yes, he is!" Oomphga beamed. "Bye, Seirah!"

Putting one aching foot in front of the other, Oomphga shakily picked up his things, marched out of Seirah's cottage, and surveyed the snowy hills for his traveling companion, Marigold. Luckily for him, he didn't have to look very far to notice her and Tuthjorn both standing side by side, leaning against the wooden pillars holding up the deck of

Seirah's abode. The second Oomphga closed the door, Marigold turned her head and bolted over to him eagerly.

"Oomphga! You're alright," Marigold cried. She coiled her arms around his neck and planted her face into his chest. Her embrace was warm, her voice soothing. She let out a playful chuckle and drew back from the hug a bit sooner than Oomphga would've liked. "I...I didn't doubt your survival in the slightest," she added.

"I did," Tuthjorn chimed in, seizing his opportunity to pull Oomphga in close for a rough hair ruffling. "Thank the gods you proved me wrong!"

Wind escaped his windpipes as Oomphga let out a hearty laugh and a squeal. "Hey! Hey! Careful with Oomphga! He just woke up!"

"It's about time," a deep voice mumbled.

Looking towards the direction of the voice, Oomphga's body tensed against Tuthjorn's. There, within an arm's reach of Oomphga, suddenly appeared Mortium next to his mother. He seemed - strangely enough - more exhausted than angered by Oomphga's recovery. The wind hummed, snow sweeping between Oomphga's three close companions in the adults' shared direction. All eyes fell on Mortium, the violent uncle and tribe chieftain, who lumbered forward covered in fresh bruises and scars of his own.

"I apologize, Dearest Nephew," Mortium said, bowing his head respectfully. "To draw my own blood with my ancestral blade...is shameful at best and unforgivable at worst."

Oomphga held his hand over his heart, his expression softening.

"Wow. Oomphga is greatly appreciative of-"

"However,..." Mortium eagerly added, "I do need you to swear to me that I will never catch word of you in the company of those scarlet-furs ever again."

Those. The grinding and screeching of that word in Oomphga's eardrums numbed his senses. *Those.* He brushed back his hair and flashed Mortium a toothy grin.

"Well, we're going to cross paths. That's inevitable. We see them all the time on the battlefield, so-" Oomphga trailed off, kneading his hands together, folding and twisting them. "Uncle Mortium is going to have to be a bit more specific."

"You know what I mean, Oomphga!" Mortium roared. "Your mother refused to swear to this promise on your behalf, so I need to hear it from you. And I don't know who this friend of yours is, but if I find out she's an ally of theirs that you brought here knowingly and willingly, I will not apologize again for whatever happens to her then..."

His silvery blue eyes left scars on Oomphga's skin and peeled away his defenses without mercy, leaving his empathy on full display. His sensitivity, his greatest strength, was being weaponized against him by one of the few family members he thought he could trust.

What happened to you, Uncle Mortium?

"Father, please," Tuthjorn sarcastically cooed, putting his hands on Oomphga's shoulders defensively, "Oomphga may be aloof and sensitive and a bit of a...uh...a strange member of the tribe, but there is one thing he isn't, and that's a threat! Just look at his baby-face! Look at his scrawny little arms! Look at his hands! Does this look like a man that could or would do any harm to his own family? Oomphga wouldn't hurt a moose let alone a fellow man!"

"Your son speaks truth, Brother," Vergaia added. "My son didn't raise a hostile hand towards you even after you struck him first. Even in the face of death, he did not rebel. Is that not loyalty enough?"

Mortium reeled back but maintained his composure.

"Violent or not, it doesn't matter if he's going behind our backs and rallying the scarlet-furs against us!"

"Do you hear yourself?!" Vergaia swiftly retorted, her voice booming and defiant. "Nobody, not half-giant nor bearfolk, would hear out my son if he cried wolf! You're living proof of that, and you're the reason why that is!"

"I'm the leader, but I'm not-!"

"You're the one setting an example, Mortium! Where were you, our brethren, *my* people when I was in labor? Where were you and our people when my son nearly died to an archer? Where were you and our people when my son took your axe to his side?! They were by **your** side! Not mine, and not his!"

"MAYBE IT'S BECAUSE I KNOW WHAT'S BEST, AND YOU DON'T!!!" Mortium snapped.

Oomphga felt the blood rushing through his veins. Fists clenched and eyes alight, he was ready to put down his foot and stop playing Mr. Nice Guy, but deep within the rousing rage was still little Oomphga praying for answers and begging for resolve.

"You're my sister! I'm the tribe's chieftain! You're the tribe's chef! Nothing more!" Mortium continued. "You cook our meals and mother your child! One of those two things, you can't even handle, and here you and your son are corrupting *my* boy?! Twisting his genius mind into supporting your ignorant, little, two-timing traitor?!"

"The bearfolk got their paws on a secret weapon!" Oomphga blurted. His eyes widened and his hands raised for his lips to clasp them shut. Finally, there was a moment of silence, but at what cost? Mortium, Vergaia, Tuthjorn, Marigold…they all wore different expressions - disbelief, disappointment, excitement, intrigue - and yet all Oomphga could sense was shame of the highest order.

Snake. He condemned himself to this title. *You little snake…*

Gazing up at Mortium, Oomphga caught a devious flicker of hope. *Perhaps trusting this "two-timing traitor" wasn't a bad thing after all,* is what he probably thought, but this was no fun uncle that Oomphga wanted to talk to anymore. Standing before him: a hulking behemoth with slits for eyes, rigid fangs, and one large, razor-sharp claw hanging from his waist side. Suddenly, Oomphga could feel his heart palpitating, his senses closing themselves off to the outside world.

Aymus looked up at the dandelion sky, his body still and at rest as Laniarra's light brought a familiar warmth to his skin. She descended from the heavens with a flock of birds carrying her brightly colored figure down onto the blades of grass with grace and eloquence unmatched. Turning her attention down to the side of her bare feet, an inky puddle of sludge appeared. It expanded until, from it, a tall and slender woman with a raven cloak covered in blades and an ivory mask stood alongside the nature goddess.

"Laniarra. The Maiden of Misfortune."

A flash of fire. A wave of force. A third, hulking entity appeared. His fiery hair thrashed as his stone-skinned body remained perfectly still.

"And...Neodashkus. It's...a surprise to be blessed with your company all at once. Do you bring good news? Anything you'd like for me to share with Martin? He's...he's at his wits end. He could really use your insight."

"He could use discipline," Neodashkus huffed.

Aymus froze, the divine's words rendering him speechless. "What? But...he's the best warrior we have. What do you mean he could use some-?"

"You can't hide anything from us. Through Omen, I have my senses, and I can sense a great pain coming from you that is holding you back from reaching your full potential."

"Oh, that? It's...it's nothing," Aymus blurted. "Honest."

"Aymus...as the druid, I trust your judgment. You know the mortal man far more than I. If you truly fear Martin given all he's done-"

The memories of Martin's crueler nature burrowed into the core of his mind. His mercilessness on the battlefield, his radiance scorching flesh off of bone, and the pride he held in his blade as he heartlessly slaughtered a little girl has all equated to an aura of fear that he carried everywhere with him. Every devil slain, every demon demolished under his boots, brought another horrible flash of second-hand agony on Aymus's psyche.

That girl. That poor girl. She was a little trickster and a bit of a brat, but she was just a kid, one cursed with horns and a tail. Whenever she dragged Aymus around, she always looked back with a bright look in her eyes. Whenever she spoke about the world, it was always with a sense of wonder and excitement. She was an inquisitive imp, but a good girl all the same.

And to think Martin ignored her plight so effortlessly.

She did not have the same mercy Camellia did, dying in ignorance. Instead, she stared up at her attacker with puffy, red eyes and wept.

Martin is no hero. He's a ruthless exterminator, an angel blessed with a weapon and a divine title, but not an ounce of sympathy towards the very souls that need saving. If only he could walk in a devil's hoof steps, then maybe…

"It can be done, you know," the Maiden of Misfortune interjected.

"Should it? I mean, Martin…he's my friend. But these devils, these demons, they're…" Aymus tore his attention away and looked on at the ghosts of people of all shapes and sizes that had their eyes on him from the tree lines. "They're people too. I want Martin to see that so bad, but I can't reason with him anymore."

"So, you wish for him to be a devil as a means to understand."

"What?!" Aymus looked back at Laniarra with wide eyes. "No! I don't-! Maybe! I don't know! If it were only for a brief amount of time, then perhaps, he would-"

"...Then it shall be done."

Upon his request, Neodashkus stepped forward and raised his flaming blade up towards the sky. The wind lashed around the four of them, the earth shattered at their feet. Everything felt like it was changing.

Lightning flashed and thunder roared.

"AAAH!!!" Martin's deafening screams rang out.

"Martin!" Aymus ran at the call of his friend's cries. When he found Martin, he was curled up on his hands and knees. His feathered wings were malting to reveal the jagged skeletal remains underneath; his skin, once light and pale, was now covered in patches of burning red; lastly, his head, like bristled weeds sprouting from the earth, horns broke through flesh and bone, twisting and turning. The ripping, the crackling, the popping, the screeching...it hurt Aymus as much as it did Martin to bear witness to his best friend's torment. And yet, despite the horror unfolding before his very eyes, all Aymus could think of was one thing: *Was it worth it? Was any of this necessary?*

"Martin..?" Aymus approached the divine devil with caution.

Once the wailing subsided, Martin looked over his boney, crimson hands and scythe-shaped claws, his huffs tense and raspy.

"What did you do, Aymus..?"

"Martin, I-...it'll only be for a short while! I promise!"

"WHAT DID YOU DO TO ME!?!"

Martin's head snapped back over his shoulder, and, in a flash, he turned and violently lunged at Aymus in a blind frenzy.

Oomphga thrashed, hands on his head as Mortium pointlessly tried to question him further on this "secret weapon". His body shifted and reformed into that of a large moose with horns twice the size of his head. Mortium reeled back and reached for his blade as Tuthjorn rushed to pull his father away.

"Impossible!" Mortium hissed.

"Run, Cousin! Run!" Tuthjorn hollered.

Mortium brutally made an attempt to shove Tuthjorn aside, but Tuthjorn (as stubborn as he is) never let go. Vergaia aided Tuthjorn in this effort, gazing upon her son's new form with urgent eyes.

"Get yourself to safety, Oomphga! I won't let him hurt you again!" Vergaia pleaded.

Oomphga let out a deep honk and turned towards Marigold. She looked just as worried as Vergaia did. Vigorously swaying his head and stomping his hooves, Oomphga turned his body and aligned his backside with Marigold's chest. In the heat of the moment, he dipped his head and urged Marigold to hop on. She hesitated for a moment but then nodded and finally clambered onto Oomphga's backside. Huffing and grunting, he bounded away from the fray, only stopping once to look back.

Seirah had gotten involved. He was much calmer, all things considered, but spoke with some degree of urgency. However, when his eyes met with Oomphga's - that thousand-yard stare - that's when the fear of the gods struck him again, sending him off on his urgent trip through the mountains.

Chapter 17:
Hope at the Highest Peak

THE FRIGID WINDS pelted Oomphga's thick brown coat as he stumbled across the snowy cliffs until he returned to the familiar trail he used to follow many years ago. He didn't stop his traveling until his hooves met the cobblestone road leading to the church. With wild eyes, Oomphga looked to the skies, his attention falling upon Omen as he sat perched atop shingles and arches. He extended his wings and took flight, circling around Oomphga and Marigold like a vulture before finally landing between them and the church doors.

A flick of the feathers, a flash of light, and Omen stood erect in his more familiar humanoid form. His hands brushed against the edges of his ebony coat.

"Oomphga. Miss Marigold."

"Omen!" Marigold cheered. "It's good to see a familiar face in these mountains."

Oomphga wiggled and belted a tired honk, giving Marigold the signal to hop off of his back. The second, her feet touched the ground, Oomphga shifted back into being the same half-giant bearfolk he always was, only now, he had legs that refused to work. Wobbling aside, Oomphga rushed to the snow, ready to face-plant into that puffy cloud of frigid relief.

"It's good to-"

Poof!

"Hi, Omen," Oomphga muttered.

"...It's good to see you both. Not a moment too soon, I might add."

"Why? Is something wrong?" Marigold asked.

"Yes. Very. I was actually hoping you'd arrive soon so I could speak with the both of you about that," Omen uttered. "Come, let me show you."

Omen scooped up Oomphga with one arm and hauled him towards the church's wounded double doors clinging to battered hinges. With a gentle shove, they flung open revealing the sanctuary long since abandoned by man. The wooden bleachers have all since worn away into chips, the ground was almost completely blanketed with snow, and specks of colored light fluttered in through some of the stained-glass windows that were somehow still in-tact.

Marigold danced ahead, Oomphga's fuzzy blanket trailing behind her with each step. Her eyes sparkled and her mouth hung agape.

"This place...it's incredible!" She ran to one of the stained-glass windows and took in the craftsmanship. The one that caught her particular interest depicted Obak, all-father of giants, greataxe in hand and intertwined with the scaly body of a pearlescent dragon during the infamous Battle of the Highest Peak: a war between a god of giants and a goddess of dragons to see who would claim the High Peak Mountains as home for their kin. Those blessed to live on the mountains would be blessed with the best view of the rest of the world.

Maybe that's where the half-giants get their pride from.

"Look at all of these windows. It's like they tell a story. I wonder what happened here..."

She paused at a broken window but soon moved onto the next and then the next, the tale of the half-giants unfolding before her very eyes. She frequently spun her heels, her attention then following the stained-glass story of mankind. The first portrayed the creation of every race and every animal in the world, the second, the destruction of life and civilization, and the third, unity. Rebuilding. Rebirth. A new age. This last window was represented with the treaty between humans and animalfolk, celestials and infernal.

Walking alongside Omen, Oomphga watched Marigold with delight, basking in some of the excitement radiating off of her. After she got to a particular stained-glass painting of a long-haired half-giant with hair extending from heaven to earth, she turned around, face wrinkled with curiosity and a twinge of sass.

"You don't seem particularly excited by any of this."

"It's half-giant history. It's - uh – it's a something!"

"And you're not the least bit interested in the fact that **you** are in one of these paintings?"

"Hm? Oomphga? Are you talking about that guy?" He pointed to the burly man depicted in the window. "No. That's probably his great grandpa, Oomphgor. Oomphga was named after him, you know. He was this big-named hero from a looong time ago."

"But the subliminal message to nature - to being the druid - your naturally long locks! Come on, Oomphga, you can't deny it! That's you!"

"Impossible. This church was made-" Oomphga paused and looked to Omen. "The church was made *before* the Calamity, right? When the humans came together to worship Obak. Then that would mean-"

"Your great grandfather wasn't alive either." Omen replied. "The craftsman behind the church was a shaman, one that could depict the future through his art."

"A half-giant shaman?"

"A *human* shaman."

Omen walked up to the stained-glass portrait and extended a feathery hand out towards the colored lights before turning his attention to the famed crystium catastrophe, nothing more than a wilting flower covered in frost. Eyes sunken and expression grim, Omen approached the flora cautiously and dropped to his knees helplessly before it. Back turned to Marigold and Oomphga, he let out a strained chuckle.

"You were the one that got excited to pass the torch when the shaman said you'd find your future here. Do you remember, Aymus?"

A flood of insight struck Oomphga like lightning, sending his body into a painful paralysis. He writhed and reeled, wanting to deny himself - just this once - of his own visions, but the drowned-out, familiar voices echoed with deafening precision through his ears.

○ ═══════ ○ ○ ✿ ○ ○ ═══════ ○

Aymus, Omen, and Martin stepped inside of the abandoned church, the sight of fallen worshipers greeting them at their feet. Their remains were made recently judging by the cloaks and robes still attached to their bodies.

Martin froze up and remained close to the entrance while Omen and Aymus continued down the row of shattered pews.

"Remind me why we needed to come here again," Martin inquired.

"Neodashkus told us to find the shaman for guidance, right? And the shaman said we'd find the secret to stopping the calamity here," Aymus replied.

"But…there must've been some mistake. There's no one to talk to here. Not a soul alive, not a weapon to be found, no magic, and no tomes. Just a bunch of cobwebs and rubble. What answer will we find amongst the dead; dead that we have seen plenty of over the past decade?" Martin griped. "Gah! Are you telling me we fought through waves of the undead and fled from that…that ungodly dragon for nothing?!"

"Steady yourself, Martin. Maybe the solution to our problem isn't something that can be found, but something that we make ourselves," Omen cooed.

He looked between Aymus and Martin. While Martin crossed his arms and sulked at his friend's theory, Aymus reflected deeply on it. He looked around at the stained-glass art lining the walls. A few things stood out to him. One, the emphasis on nature and civilization. Second, the transition from barbarism to unity. Third, upon the final wall at the end of the church. Upon it were four distinct entities no one would ever expect to be unified under one banner: a half-breed, a devil, a dragon, and a frog with colors surrounding them that resembled the four elemental factions.

Standing before the dusty stone altar, Aymus brushed his hand across a visible patch of snow-covered grass amongst the floorboards. With the faintest brush of his fingertips, a white camellia sprouted, growing more and more into a blossoming majesty before his very eyes with gemstones that adorned its petals and absorbed the light that seeped in through the cracks of cobblestone. Drawing back, Aymus smiled and admired his work created amidst his enlightenment.

"Martin, Omen, come here. I'd like for you both to do something for me."

"Hm?" Martin knelt down beside Aymus, Omen gracefully doing the same. The moment he saw the faint glow clinging to Aymus' fingers, Martin snorted. "Planting flowers? Here? Bit of an odd spot, don't you think?"

"I think I've created a solution to our problem, and I'd like for you both to bless it."

"A flower. The solution to our problem is a flower? A flower that you made for - what - fun? Your own mortal sense of amusement?"

"The shaman said we'd find the answers. Omen said we'd make the answer. I'm doing both."

"So...you're making a flower."

"I'm making a beacon of hope. One that will last an eternity. All I need is for you two to bless it."

The two religious entities stared at one another, before returning their attention to the flower Aymus lovingly created.

"O-kay," Martin replied hesitantly, "I...bless this flower with my divine strength. May it have a strong body, capable of carrying the weight of the world and a blade forged in a thousand tales that it may wield in battle under Neodashkus' banner."

"That's perfect. Omen?"

"I bless this flower with wisdom. With this wisdom it will keep itself safe from future dangers and learn valuable lessons from the past. Its mind will be an impenetrable fortress, and yet, its gates will open to foreign knowledge that it will then use to create something as magnificent as its creator."

"Thank you, Omen. That's really sweet," Aymus cooed.

"And you? What's your gift, Aymus?"

"Life."

"Life? That's it?"

"Yes. A life to live happily, a life to love, a life to protect, a life full of magic and merriment, and a life to be whatever it wants to be. Life."

Martin cringed and stood up, fingers clutching his temples. "Uugh!" he groaned. "I can't believe we're wasting time on a flower. We have no time for sightseeing! We have a world to save! I suggest we go dungeon delving. Let's investigate that cave on the north side of the mountain to see what we find there that could help us."

Aymus chuckled and pulled himself onto his feet, Omen loyally remaining by his side.

"Do you think those four on the window is what the shaman wanted us to see? The answer to our problem that we need to find?" Omen asked.

"Mayhaps. We'll keep an eye out for them during our travels. For now, let's report back to the shaman and tell him what we found here. Maybe he'll bless us with a bit more advice."

The three friends collected themselves and began their journey back down the mountains. Seconds after they were out of the church, Martin began rambling aloud. While Omen intently listened to their knightly comrade, Aymus let his thoughts trail off into a land of imagination. When he paused to look back at the church, all he could see was his creation sitting at the foot of the altar.

"I believe in you, little one. Stay safe," he whispered, his voice carrying through the howling winds.

○ ═══════ ○ ○ ✸ ○ ○ ═══════ ○

Without realizing, Oomphga now sat alongside Omen, his hands brushing along the flower. A warm, golden light on his fingertips danced to life, returning health and wellness to the flower. A refreshing wave of tranquility and a new sense of freedom washed over him, his eyes longingly fixated on the flower he never imagined he'd ever see in all of its glory. Its silver petals sparkled, a rainbow of light washing over the shining beacon of hope resting between his thumb and index finger. His other hand brushed against the strange, crimson roots of the flower. He could feel them thrumming with life-energy much like arteries harboring a pulse…Oomphga's pulse.

"Could Marigold grab Oomphga's gardening tools from his backpack?"

Waiting on her to return, Oomphga looked up before the altar, his softened gaze falling upon the stained-glass art taking center-stage. Within it, a rainbow of colors, shapes, and light intermingled to create a work of art that depicted four individuals. Not three, (like Aymus, Omen, and Martin). Four. The same four Aymus perceived all those years ago.

Hands filled with bags of dirt, shovels of different sizes, and topped off with a purple and yellow painted pot, Marigold brought it over and laid it between the two of them. Together, as a team, they laid out the soil and tucked in the crystium with delicate touches. Then, when it was all over, Oomphga took the flowerpot into his palms and held it out towards Marigold.

"The crystium catastrophe" Oomphga said. "Here."

For a moment, she seemed perplexed as if she had forgotten the reason for their trip together. Eyes alight and midnight-painted lips curled into a gentle grin, she accepted the generous gift and extended her arms out towards him.

"Oomphga-" Omen interjected. "Is this what you wish to do with it? Even now knowing what it is? Knowing Aymus' intentions?"

"Yes," Oomphga stated. "Yes, he would like to give it to her as long as Marigold promises that it's in safe hands."

"I doubt they're as safe as yours," Marigold let out a breathy laugh, "but...I'll do my best with this gift I've been given. I swear on my life, I won't let anything bad happen to it."

Oomphga slowly stood up and happily pulled Marigold onto her feet with him, face alight with a warm glow.

"Glad Oomphga was able to be of service. Now, Marigold should probably head home before - you know - Oomphga's uncle tracks us down and tries to kill us or something."

Nodding, Marigold made her way across the sanctuary, admiring the stained glass one last time. Her movements were graceful, elegant beyond description. Shoulders pressed against the door, she stopped to look upon the flower she held curled up in her arms.

"Will I ever see you again?" she asked, voice fainter than a whisper.

Oomphga rubbed his neck bashfully, his heart telling him the answer better than his mind ever could.

"Of course. Oomphga will always be somewhere around. In the mountains, in the forest, at his Papa Sergei's house, at the Autumn Festival, mayhap. Anywhere around these parts, really. Marigold will run into Oomphga again! He just knows it!"

Marigold curled up; her softened gaze fixated on Oomphga. "Perfect. I'll be holding onto your blanket until then, if that's alright."

"Keep it if you must. Marigold owes Oomphga no favors. Consider it a gift."

"A gift..." she faintly repeated. "Thank you."

Her voice. Something about it sent heat rushing through Oomphga's body all concentrated in his face. Slipping through the crack between the doors, she vanished from sight but not from spirit. Despite being unable to physically see her there, Oomphga felt her presence lingering in the air, filling him with this powerful excitement like never before. Only when he finally accepted her departure did the feeling fade, a simple question inheriting its place: what now?

With the crystium catastrophe's potential restored, maybe it was time to finally do some talking with his uncle - maybe it was time to come forward and take his first big step towards peace as the fabled druid.

"Omen, Sir, do you think-" Oomphga's voice crackled, but he coughed, trying to fix it. "Do the gods think...Oomphga is ready to be a true druid like Aymus all those years ago?"

"Oomphga, they knew you were ready when you were a young boy with a heart filled with nothing but love for a world you hardly knew anything about. The moment you could speak, you expressed joy for *all* life. You had that deep-rooted connection with people, with animals, with Laniarra's greatest creation, nature itself. The moment I saw your face in the woods - when you were little - I knew Aymus' successor had been born, and I-...*we* are all eager to see what you do to make the universe just as great of a place as he did, as your parents did, as your great grandfather did."

Omen gazed upon Oomphga with thoughtful eyes and heartwarming smile. He threw his arms around Omen and embraced him tightly.

"It's your turn to write a legacy," Omen continued, voice warm and soothing. "The question is: where do you want to start?"

Oomphga knew what he wanted. He wished for it day in and day out. *Unrealistic*, they called it.

"He wants to start with his people. He wants to make things right between them. If their fighting really is nothing but misunderstandings and misconceptions, Oomphga wants to fix it. He wants his extended family and friends to experience peace for the first time in years. That's what Oomphga wants."

"I'm afraid I can't let you do that," a raspy voice echoed from above.

Oomphga looked up at the cracked wooden boards looming above them where the second floor was. He looked over to the silhouette on the stairs, eyes sharpening.

"Martin-" Omen hissed under his breath.

"That's **Marcuth** to you, and Morbius to my accomplices~"

The strange voice made his appearance, stepping down to their level with head held high. His body was shrouded in a black cloak that flowed freely behind him, and his expressions were concealed with an obsidian mask. Bright crimson eyes broke through the thin slits on either side of the nose bridge and skewered Oomphga's memories with deftly precision, leaving him paralyzed in place, huddled up against Omen.

"Who would've thought - in all of history - there would be not one, not two, but **three** bearfolk half-giant half-breeds I would have to get rid of?"

"What are you rambling on about now, Martin?" Omen snapped back.

"Marcuth," the man repeated with annoyance growing in his tone. "The name is MARCUTH now; angel-born and devil-transformed thanks to you and *Aymus,* and you'd best remember it, because it's going to belong to the new god you'll be worshiping in three years once that little cretin is out of the picture-"

"Th-three years? What's going to happen in three years?" Oomphga squeaked.

"A second calamity, of course. The gods are growing very impatient with the mortals on this planet. *Pity for them.* It's only a matter of time now before they start everything over again, but don't worry your little head about it! You'll be long gone by the time it happens."

"That's not true!" Oomphga retorted.

"You can't be serious..!" Omen snapped. "First you kill Aymus because he gets in your way of stopping the calamity and now you threaten to kill his successor because he somehow interferes with you starting up another?! Have you lost your mind?!"

"I've lost my faith, Omen - faith in deities and agents of the divine. I've learned my lesson. Don't worry. I'm fully capable of taking things into my own hands. *The prophet said we can't have any half-breeds in the picture. I thought killing the first would prevent that from another one showing up again, but it would appear that I miscalculated my approach.* ...Oh, well. It shouldn't be too hard to remedy that~! If I have to kill a thousand half-breeds, I will~! It doesn't matter to me~!"

Raising his hands, a gold-accented, obsidian scepter appeared on one side while a scythe appeared within the other. Atop this staff was a bright red pulsating gemstone: a hemogem, one sharing an aura very similar to the one Mr. Swiftclaw had in his possession. Meanwhile, his scythe stood to be about the same height as he with a long, crescent-like blade much like the dreadwalker's claws.

In response to this threat, Oomphga thrashed out his hands sending a wave of snow and stone congealed together in Marcuth's direction, trapping him against the wall. Oomphga and Omen made a rush for the door together shortly after. The two hardly made it out the front doors when a loud blast sounded, glass, rocks, and woodchips exploding in every direction behind them, some pelting the two in the back. Oomphga dropped down, covering his head. Flashes of light slipped through the gap between his body and the ground seconds before a massive shadow appeared, blotting out the sun.

"Oomphga..!"

Oomphga looked up, eyes wide as Omen - in the form of a massive raven - extended his wing. "Hop on!"

The weight of his options held him back. Pulling himself to his feet, Oomphga turned around to face Marcuth as he stepped out of the rubble in perfect condition.

"No... Get Marigold to safety! Oomphga can take care of himself!"

"You're exhausted! You look like-"

"He'll be fine."

"But you're just-!"

The young druid gazed up at Omen with large, round eyes and a hopeful expression. Even if, deep down, he understood his life was on the line, he still clung to that small sliver of confidence he had in himself.

"I will trust your judgment, but you had best be careful," Omen scurried off down the mountain leaving Oomphga behind to face Marcuth alone. "If anything happens to you-!"

And like a whisper in the wind, the sound of his voice was only audible for a mere moment and then gone along with its source. Oomphga shifted his focus onto the threat ahead. He let out a tense sigh and cracked a shaky smile in his direction. Putting a name to a masked face, Oomphga understood exactly who he was facing. The angel Martin, the murderous king, Morbius, and the devil Marcuth. All three appeared not much different from the men Oomphga's visions, but something felt off about him. Maybe it was the maddening fire in his glowing red eyes or the sadistic chuckle that escaped him every so often as he pointed his scythe directly at a mere child; the slightest twitch in his muscles, the stiff way he stood. He was mad, yes, but just as nervous as Oomphga.

Why is that? Oomphga pondered.

"Mr. Marcuth, Sir," Oomphga stuttered, "could you hear Oomphga out for a minute? If you please-"

His grip on his golden staff tightened, unstable magic crackling from the gemstone fixed to the top.

"Oomphga understands your situation to some extent. He knows a lot about you," he lied. "A…good amount about you," he corrected himself not quite fully. "Enough. He knows enough about you, and he knows that life was very unfair to you over the past hundreds or thousands of years, but life is unfair for a lot of other people too right now: Oomphga's family, his people. It'll be unfair for everyone if another calamity happens! Think of all the people you swore to protect that will be getting hurt! Think of all the innocent lives that will be lost to your bloodshed! Doesn't that make you upset or sad knowing that the world you tried to save all those years ago will see Mr. Marcuth as the man that swore his blade would be used to protect people only for him to use it against them?"

Marcuth let out another breathy chuckle beneath his cloaks and behind his false bravado, overwhelming Oomphga with a feeling of dread.

"The world should've thought about that before turning me into a devil before I even had the chance."

"Had the chance to…what?"

A blast of red. A flick of the wrist, and Oomphga put up a wall of stone in front of himself to protect himself from the blow.

"Before I had the chance to be someone – ANYONE. And it's all because of Aymus." Another blast. "Because of you..!" And another. "Because of EVERYONE!" And another yet again. "But Aymus, that arrogant swine, betrayed me and just when we were so close to saving the world *together*. I lost everything that made me a paladin of Neodashkus, the backstabber lost his life, and Omen…he got out good. The nameless wonder. A mainstream mystery. A deity in disguise. *That*…will be *me* before you know it."

There was a much louder blast that pelted the wall and sent pebbles and dust fluttering down from the cracks onto Oomphga's face. He backed away; muscles tense. He prepared every inch of his mind and body for the next shot to break through.

"Big words coming from a guy using blood gems harboring other peoples' magic in place of his own!"

"Oh, I have so much more than magic at my disposal~"

Looking up, there he sat - that dexterous demon - legs dangling over the side of the wall. Marcuth connected both ends of his scythe and his staff together, making a polearm of a weapon where both sides were equally as dangerous. In a flash, he dropped down in front of Oomphga and swung his crescent blade at Oomphga. Oomphga stumbled back and recovered quickly; just in time to recognize his opponent trying – this time - to bash his skull in with his scepter like a club. Oomphga raised his palms and curled his fingers tightly around the end, trying to hold it in place while he uttered through an incantation, eyes fixed on the hemogem at the end of the staff. It crackled with dangerous energy, while the ground beneath them rumbled…

…and not in the way that Oomphga had intended.

What would've been nothing more than a harmless tendril of rock and snow coiling around Marcuth's waist to hold him back turned into an earth-splitting tremor that opened up a massive, icy chasm beneath Marcuth's feet. He tried to step away, but Oomphga still held on tight to his scepter, refusing to let go out of fear of getting beaten or shot with whatever dangerous arcane energy remained trapped within the hemogem.

But what options did he have? It was either let go and become cornered or fall into the pit and cling to Marcuth for dear life, hoping he would bring the two to safety without a fight. Terror and helplessness struck through the young druid's chest as the chasm widened, exposing the deadly, dark depths below. Stones plummeted into the seemingly bottomless pit, the echoes of the descent fading into an eerie silence. Marcuth and Oomphga were truly trapped with only a thin sliver of earth separating them from the ever-expanding void. No thanks to Oomphga, Marcuth had no room to spread his wings with the wall of stone at his back.

Marcuth snarled and flashed Oomphga a vengeful stare seconds before he lashed out, his heavy boot connecting with Oomphga's stomach, sending him reeling. Taking the desperate leap, Marcuth attempted to clear the widening chasm, but his foot slipped on the treacherous edge at the other side. He tried to use his scythe to attach himself to the earth, but the thin blade slipped through the stone, and - with little room for recovery – he plummeted into the darkness, his screams swallowed by the icy abyss.

The agony of his fall reverberated through Oomphga's bones. He couldn't imagine the terror and the torment that Marcuth must've felt in those final moments. Swallowing his guilt, Oomphga reminded himself of his purpose. He had to live. He had to survive. He clambered to his weary feet and carefully tried to sidestep around the hole. Slipping. Limping. Caution controlled his every move, but the snow made for unreliable foundation. With one misplaced step, the ground beneath him crumbled. Oomphga lost his footing, his arms windmilling as he desperately grasped for something, anything to hold onto. Catching a ledge, he clung to it tightly, his nails becoming claws that dug in between creases in the rocky ground.

"OMEN!!!" Oomphga's voice cracked amidst his desperate plea echoing through the desolate landscape. "Please, come back! Oomphga needs your help! He really really REALLY needs it! PLEASE!!!"

But there was no reply. Not even the comforting flutter of wings or a bird's cry could be heard. He was alone, teetering on the brink of oblivion with only the biting wind and encroaching darkness as his only companions.

Chapter 18:

The Devil and the Druid

INEVITABILITY GREETED OOMPHGA with a twisted grin. His fingers slipped and down…

…down…

…and down he fell, helpless to the gravity that seized control over his body. Watching the light above him stare back at him as he plummeted into the depths made Oomphga feel so small in comparison. *Small…*

That's when, suddenly, an idea hit him. He spread his limbs and let his body take shape - the shape of a small, brown bat. He flailed his arms, beating them against the sky to hold him up for just long enough to get his feet ready for the landing but heard a painful howl ring out nearby. Looking around, he spotted Marcuth dangling from a jagged spear of ice along the wall. His wing was impaled, blood seeping down onto his back and shoulder as he hung above the ground.

Oomphga pounded his arms up and down trying to get over to Marcuth and the thick blade of ice that held him in place. When Oomphga finally made it, he clutched onto the girth of the ice with his wings and clambered up towards Marcuth before changing back to his usual self.

Marcuth looked up, spotting Oomphga in a heartbeat.

"You-!" He let out in a pained hiss.

"Oomphga's not here to hurt Marcuth. He's going to help him get down, okay?"

Without much fuss, Marcuth waited very patiently as Oomphga warmed his hands and melted away the ice starting at the end. It took a few minutes, but when he finally got to the bit where Marcuth was hanging, he gently pressed his hand against his wing.

"Does Marcuth think he could make it down safely from here?"

"He can," he grumbled.

"Alright. On the count of three Oomphga is going to push Marcuth off of the icicle. One...two...three!" Giving his wing a strong nudge forward, Marcuth dropped onto a cluster of rocks and slid the rest of the way down, Oomphga hesitantly following him. He let out a long sigh of relief and calmly rested his hand across the sheath hanging from his waist.

"You've made a big mistake, kid," Marcuth huffed, casting a scornful glance over his shoulder at the little boy wandering aimlessly behind him, his attention fixed on the intricate patterns scattered about along the cave's walls.

"He has," Oomphga admitted shamefully. "Shouldn't have opened up the ground like that. Looks like we're both stuck in this cave because of him. Oomphga can't fly out and Mr. Marcuth can't fly out either with a hole that big in his wing."

Oomphga looked upon it. With a little bit of magic, Oomphga could mend it easily, but the idea of giving back the power of flight to a man determined to see to the end of his life made him sick (moreso than he felt staring at the wound). So, just this once, Oomphga kept his healing magic to himself and summoned up the courage to negotiate with the winged terror instead.

"Oomphga can heal Mr. Marcuth, but if he's going to leave him here for dead, he's not sure if it'd be a great idea considering his plans. ...BUT if Marcuth was *nice* to Oomphga, then maybe-"

His words were abruptly cut short by the soft hum of a blade being drawn. Its chime rang throughout the cavern as the steely tip of Marcuth's scythe hovered beneath Oomphga's chin. His chest tightened and his heart plummeted.

"Well, *half-breed*, since you were so kind to me, I'll give you a choice," Marcuth sneered. "Would you rather die now, quick and easy, or would you rather wait and die slowly and painfully above the mountains and forest you call home?"

Oomphga's eyes widened in terror as he looked down at the reflection of the young boy staring back at him in the glistening steel inches away from his throat. His mind raced, trying to comprehend the gravity of the situation. To think he had considered the choice so carefully as if there was any doubt what his answer would be. With trembling hands, Oomphga patted himself down and pulled out his plant journal, a source of comfort and familiarity. He clung to it tightly, his fingers tracing around the worn edges as he spoke.

"Oomphga and Mr. Marcuth are both going to make it out alive and okay. No one has to die. Whatever Mr. Marcuth thinks Oomphga is going to do to hurt him or ruin his life in the future isn't going to happen. All he asks is that he spares him here and then…and then Oomphga will make his wing all better and he'll stay out of Mr. Marcuth's way as long as Mr. Marcuth promises he won't seek out Oomphga to hurt him or ruin his life in return."

Marcuth grimaced, clearly dissatisfied.

"…Your choice, half-breed," Marcuth repeated.

"That-…that is his choice," Oomphga shakily replied, voice trembling. "What's yours?"

The two paused, breaking away from each other's skepticism to take in their surroundings. In the center of the clearing lay Marcuth's staff, the hemogem at the end still intact, but scarred and cracked, the magic once inside of it completely empty. Glancing up from the snow-covered floor, the walls of their prison stood erect, a few dozen feet in height, with runic carvings and jagged spires of ice in every direction except one where a slender crawl space resided. A wisp of ancient magic hung in the breeze that circulated through the opening. The unknown lay in wait for them on the other side.

Marcuth let out a tired sigh, slipped his scythe into a sheath on his back, and slowly approached his magic staff. Looking over it, he removed the broken hemogem and haplessly tossed it aside before refocusing his attention onto Oomphga who silently stood in place all the while.

"*I hate children-*" Marcuth hissed under a heated breath. "Alright. Lead the way."

Quick on his feet, Oomphga more than eagerly ran on ahead, brushing his warm palm against the ice, melting some away to reshape the crawl space into more of a tunnel that comfortably fit their sizes averaged out. Marcuth trudged close behind, his breaths tense and a bit shaky. Step after step, Oomphga lead the venture, alert and attentive to every natural detail they came across.

On the other side of the slender tunnel was a sizable open space with rocks trailing upwards along the wall like a spiral staircase. The gap between rocks was fairly steep, and the snow covering them made each step hazardous, but taking great caution, Oomphga and Marcuth began their ascension.

"So, if I overheard Omen correctly, you're Aymus' little flower boy," Marcuth cooed with a twinge of ennui in his tone.

"But Oomphga isn't a flower. He's a-"

"Half-breed. Yes. I'm well aware." Marcuth hovered behind Oomphga, peering down over his shoulder like a shadow tied to his waist. "One with Aymus' memories, it would seem. *I suppose that would explain some of your competence using magic.* Tell me, what all has your insight revealed to you? Anything of note?"

"Nope," Oomphga said instinctively. "Well-…nope. Nothing to note. From what Oomphga knows, Aymus and Martin were just two good friends that didn't see eye-to-eye."

"Is that all?"

"Yes. Besides, Oomphga can't make an opinion on Martin - *sorry* - *Mr. Marcuth* based on Aymus' perspective. Oomphga would like to get to know Mr. Marcuth for who he is now! And right now...Oomphga thinks...Mr. Marcuth is a little too close for comfort considering all the threats he's been spewing to Oomphga up until this point."

Marcuth slowed his pace, allowing Oomphga to gain some distance between the two of them, watching him with a cold glare as he clambered up the steep pile of rocks and snow.

"Can't blame me for trying to make the trip with you more tolerable-"

"Can't blame Oomphga for not wanting to be right next to the man that wants him dead."

"...Fair point."

Step by step, clutch by clutch, the two made it to the top where a large arch holding two heavy, stone doors resided. Oomphga pressed against it, putting his full weight into his shoving, but to little avail. It wasn't until Marcuth helped that they managed to push it open just enough for them to both squeeze through. Oomphga's eyes widened shortly after at the sight of ashen bricks strewn about in piles along the open trail leading further into the cave. Ignoring the red glow coming from beyond the icy wall on his right side, he gleefully approached the remnants.

"These are the same bricks that make up the church on the surface at the top of the mountain..!" Oomphga cheered.

"So?"

"So maybe they're connected somehow! What are the odds that if we follow the trail of rubble, we'll find a staircase or a ladder leading up into the church?!"

"We would, but the exit inside the church is covered in debris from long before our arrival. I remember that much. But there's another way..." Marcuth shifted his gaze away from Oomphga and crossed his arms in a huff. Oomphga followed his attention and looked at the reddened walls of the cave once again. There were claw marks and skeletal remains hugging the corners with stone and snow covering most of the remnants. "...through the dragon's lair."

"A dragon?" Oomphga gasped, pressing his hands firmly against chest. "On High Peak? But...Oomphga hasn't heard of any dragon-"

There was a low, guttural growl coming from the other side of the red wall. It was beastly, but unlike anything the druid had ever heard of. Instead of heightening Oomphga's fears, the droning noises sounded almost like a sleepy purr. No more did it sound like a dragon than it did an innocent bear sleeping away a long winter.

"Shun your denials... It's him," Marcuth audibly hummed as he approached the wall by Oomphga's side. He traced his hands along its surface and occasionally tapped his finger against the ice to find a hollow spot. "This is our ticket out. Right here."

Oomphga slowly glanced over his shoulder, and, beyond the semi-transparent barrier, he could make out the rough silhouette of what definitely appeared to be a dragon judging by the spikes emanating from its massive figure and the rumbling sounds that escaped from it. There was no doubt about it now.

The moment Oomphga inched close enough to the wall, Marcuth snatched his wrist and pinned his hand against the surface. He let out an audible yelp that Marcuth swiftly shushed, but he hardly eased Oomphga's worries. The way his claw gripped onto his skin, cutting off the circulation in his arm. He was hardly trying to hold onto Oomphga, and yet he was hurting him, making the magic all harder to flow through him.

Thanks to Marcuth's death grip, it took much longer to melt away the ice and reveal the dragon's resting place, but Marcuth hardly cared for the boy. Once a passage had been opened to him, he stepped inside, eyes alight at the spectacle of crystals that surrounded them.

Dozens of corpses that have been bled dry laid intertwined with hemogems of impressive size. Without hesitation, Marcuth plucked one of the smaller gems and traced his hand along its surface.

"Hm...could use a good carving, but this will have to suffice," Marcuth uttered under his frigid breath. Then, effortlessly, he forcibly pressed the new hemogen against the end of his obsidian staff. Holding them together, Marcuth's magic crackled to life. Abusing the power of the hemogem, he tapped into its magic. Helfire consumed his skin and with this controlled element of evil flowing through his fingertips, he welded his arcane focus onto his glorious scepter.

A raspy, perverted chuckle escaped him as he admired his handiwork.

"Wonderful. This will work beautifully~"

He looked around at the corpses, his brow raising at the sight of one in particular. As nervous as Oomphga was, he averted his attention to gaze upon the same body, one that belonged to a half-giant warrior from ages past. The figure, as recognizable as the sun and the moon, lay petrified in crimson ice. He appeared to be about two dozen years old with long, half-shaved, brown hair and bore scars that enveloped the right half of his face, exactly wear Oomphga's bear eye was.

Slowly and hesitantly, Oomphga weaved through the field of hemogems and approached the man, dropping down to one knee before him.

"Oomphgor..." Oomphga whispered.

"Who?"

"Oomphgor," Oomphga repeated, darting his eyes over his shoulder at Marcuth. "He's Oomphga's great grandpa. He was a hero of his people. Seirah said that Great Grandpa Oomphgor was a warrior, one with the strength, the magic, and the heart to do amazing things. So...this must be what happened to him. This is how he disappeared."

He shifted his focus back onto his great grandfather, still and silent as the ice that preserved his bloody and battered remains.

Great Grandpa, Oomphga doesn't know you much, but...he wishes you were here. Maybe things would be better. Maybe you could stop everyone from fighting. Maybe...

Hidden beneath the snow by his foot was the glint of something shiny. Something magic. He could feel it coursing through the ground beneath him.

Brushing aside the pearlescent powder, Oomphga uncovered a large greataxe covered in primordial runes and frost that melted away the moment Oomphga held it in his hands. Its arcane energy hummed to life and sent a refreshing wave of familiar ancient magic into Oomphga's small frame.

So, this is the magic Oomphga felt earlier!

Like whispers on the wind, his great grandfather's greataxe called to him, beckoning him to be its next bearer.

"That's great, kid. Lovely story. Now, let's follow the rocky trail leading up to the surface, and we'll be-"

The dragon let out a loud huff and suddenly opened one of its gigantic, glowing, red eyes, staring daggers into Marcuth's backside. With its claws, it forced itself to full height and stared down upon the two mortals, blood congealing into a sentient mass of fangs and spikes, all blades of past heroes morphed into its form.

"So...how did Marcuth and company handle *their* confrontation with the dragon?" Oomphga asked in a whimper.

"We...we didn't. Aymus *tried* to negotiate with it, but after that failed, we kind of just-"

The crimson dragon let out a mighty roar, specks of blood shooting out onto Marcuth. For a brief moment, Marcuth stood frozen, his face pale and eyes wide, but grip firm on his staff and teeth grit, he lunged forward and swiftly turned around, shooting a mass of crackling energy at the dragon. While it was reeling, Marcuth burst through the air, sprinting at full speed towards the exit. Oomphga followed his steps as quickly as he could, but his great grandfather's greataxe was heavier than anticipated, and along with his quarterstaff, he could hardly get a good foot in front of the other. It made Oomphga wonder how Marcuth could get away with a staff in one hand and scythe in the other during fights.

Suddenly, a sharp, burning pain radiated throughout his spine as the dragon's talons tore flesh from bone. He fell to the ground, crying out in agony. The pain paralyzed him. As he clawed at the rock and snow, the dragon lowered its head close to him, but then jolted its head in a different direction, and swiftly refocused its efforts on stopping Marcuth. It let out a serpentine hiss. One blink of his beady eyes and several tendrils of blood lashed out from his torso up the rocky path and yanked Marcuth back into the pits with Oomphga.

Oomphga watched on in sickening horror as the tentacles of blood burrowed in through his wounds, drinking the life out of Marcuth's still living and breathing body. His panicked screams rung in his ears, echoing his agony throughout Oomphga's skull. Eager to intervene, Oomphga grabbed the greataxe in his possession, and frantically used it as a crutch to stand upon.

With his footing secure, he sprinted forward with all his might. Muscles aching and heart pounding, he swung his blade at the tentacle of blood as hard as he could, severing the tether between Marcuth and the dragon. To his surprise, a trail of ice followed down the tentacle attached to the dragon, but before it reached the torso, the dragon tore the tentacle from himself with his teeth. A waterfall of blood poured down onto the snow from his self-inflicted amputation. Marcuth, still mostly in-tact, looked between a battered, wheezing Oomphga and the screeching dragon.

"Come on, kid. Stay with me. Show me what else you got!"

Dizzy and lightheaded, Oomphga leapt at the dragon a second time. Every muscle in his arms tensed and strained. His axe sluggishly met with the dragon's hide, the arched blade driving in deep into its gelatinous mass. When ripped from the body, a geyser of liquid scarlet exploded in front of him for some time until the frost covered it up like a scab - no - an infection.

The ice spread across the dragon's body, slowly climbing across his liquid form until he ejected the chunks of blood and ice onto the floor. This ejection caused the dragon to thrash and roar, knocking Oomphga back. He slid across the ground, stone and snow burying deep into his wounds. However, it was far better to be in crippling pain than to be dead.

"Not bad, mutt. Not bad," Marcuth snickered.

Readjusting his stance, Marcuth seized the opportunity to exact his revenge. Despite his one wing being inoperable, he used it to propel him across the ground. Dexterously, he evaded the dragon's slashing and snapping. After a few seconds of dodging, Marcuth worked up the strength and the magic to strike back. With an elegant swing of his staff, a blinding beam of light shot out and enveloped the dragon's gigantic frame. The beast paused as if its own, ticking clock of motion had stopped. His jaw, filled with hundreds of hungering daggers, remained unhinged. Now was the perfect – if not his only – time to react.

With the last of his strength, Oomphga pulled himself to his feet and approached the dragon as it stared blankly back at him, blissfully unaware of its fate. Stone and ice shot up underneath Oomphga's feet, launching him up almost high enough to reach the roof of the cave. He steadied his breath, tightened his grip, and brought down the greataxe of Oomphgor with deadly precision.

The gods guided his axe head directly between the monster's eyes. He could feel the shattering of bone. It burst into tiny bits by his blade. Bone and flesh and everything a mortal man had exploded from the wound. Just as the dragon regained its ability to move, so too did it die.

Holding on tight, Oomphga embraced the tumble down upon the blanket of red and white beneath them.

Chapter 19:
Brothers in Arms

THE PLUME OF SNOW CLEARED, the dragon laid silent as the grave. The rune-covered greataxe in Oomphga's possession clung to the mushy contents between the dragon's ridged brows while Oomphga laid alongside the creature's toothy maw. After taking a minute to rest and recuperate across the ground, the cold numbing the wound on his back, Oomphga sat up. His head throbbed and his vision spun circles around him. Marcuth grabbed ahold of Oomphga's arm and firmly pulled him onto his feet. His limbs quivered and ached. He could hardly stand on his feet by himself. Luckily, Marcuth stood by patiently to hold him up upright until the dizziness and nausea had passed.

Once his senses had returned, Oomphga looked upon the dragon inches away from him. With a shaky step, he trudged forward until Oomphgor's greataxe was within reach. Then, he lunged his hands forward and grabbed it firmly by the handle, dragging it out of the dragon's head and back towards the safety of his embrace.

"Come on, kid," Marcuth quietly barked, hands firmly pressed against Oomphga's sides to hold him upright while he faltered from the excessive weight. "You did good – real good – but how about we get out of this cursed place. Yeah?"

Oomphga's body trembled. He choked on his own heart caught in his throat, but despite being so weak and vulnerable, Marcuth carried him and the axe and his quarterstaff along up the rocky tunnels and into the light on the other end where they were met with a tall, vertical ledge reaching upwards past Oomphga's vision.

"No more," Oomphga spewed between heavy breaths. "No more no more no more…"

Marcuth smiled and shook Oomphga to and fro gently.

"Don't worry. I think…I think we might actually be at the end of this death trap-"

Marcuth knelt down and pulled Oomphga behind him. Without question or remorse, Oomphga sprawled himself out across Marcuth's back, his arms coiled around his neck just enough to hold himself steady. He could feel his pulse slowing down for a brief moment before suddenly spiking back up during the climb. Marcuth's grip was unsteady; the veins running up through to his chin bulged. One devil claw after another, he carried the weight of the druid on his winged back.

And then, when they finally made it to the top, a flood of hazy memories came back. Memories of peace among pain; a miracle among a massacre. It was hard to pin down the feelings that invaded Oomphga's subconscious, whether pleasant or terrifying, but this particular clearing in comparison to all the others brought Oomphga the most relief. Watching the stars in the night sky beyond, feeling the gentle midnight breeze brushing against his cheeks, taking in a deep breath of fresh pine…

Giddy smile plastered on his face, Oomphga rolled off of Marcuth's back and fumbled out of the cave. They were still very high up on a side of the mountains that Oomphga had never seen before.

Marcuth walked up to Oomphga and looked out at the mountain range that extended far to the north. A moment of blissful silence rolled through the pyramids of earth as the unlikely pair sat down in the snow next to one another. Oomphga set aside his frosted greataxe and Marcuth laid down his hemogem staff.

"You know…I remember this view from a looong time ago." Marcuth hummed. "Not much has changed since aside from the skies being blue and the forest being green again…"

"Beautiful, isn't it?" Oomphga asked but received no immediate reply. He wasn't expecting one. It was rhetorical, of course, but in time, Marcuth answered.

"Yes. Some might say it's…a view to die for."

"Oh, Oomphga would disagree because…because then you wouldn't be able to enjoy the view anymore if you were dead!"

"I-" Marcuth sputtered. "I suppose so."

His eyes shifted from the sights onto the half-giant bearfolk sitting beside him. Oomphga could feel the sting of his crimson gaze from the corner of his vision, but when he looked up into them, he couldn't help but smile. Before him was not an enemy nor a stranger, but a man - one whom Oomphga felt pain for. He could feel the burden of his misdeeds hanging off his shoulders, the crippling pain of his wounds masked by layers and layers of robes, but there was one wound Oomphga saw more blatantly than the rest.

Letting out a quiet grunt, Oomphga pulled himself back onto his battered feet and side-stepped behind Marcuth.

"What are you-?"

Before Marcuth could question him, Oomphga pressed his palm against the back of Marcuth's wing. His fingers traced around the punctured rim left behind from the fall. A familiar warmth enveloped his hands and from the edges of the hole, new flesh was formed, weaving and intertwining together. Within a matter of seconds, the gaping hole in his wing had completely healed. Marcuth glanced back over his shoulder, a snicker escaping him.

"You're a good kid, Oomphga." Marcuth reached back to playfully pat Oomphga's abdomen. "Heh. Oomphga. I don't think I'll ever be able to forget that name nor what you've done for me today. Besides, I'd like to know who to thank for fixing me up and saving my life…at your FUNERAL!!!"

Oomphga's instincts screamed an ear-ringing warning at the first glimpse of Marcuth's hand coiling around his hemogem staff to cast a spell. His eyes snapped open and, with a burst of adrenaline hitting him like a streak of lightning, he leapt back and shifted the earth into a fist that knocked Marcuth's staff out of his hands and over the edge of the cliff, but the devil had other tricks up his sleeve.

His scythe, intended for gutting Oomphga, sliced through the air and missed his stomach by a fraction of an inch. Oomphga rolled onto his side, the snow cushioning his fall. In one fluid motion, he snatched his quarterstaff from the ground, rather than his great grandfather's greataxe, and planted it in the snow, using it as leverage to spring back. His thighs burned with exertion and his arms throbbed with each step and motion in desperate attempts to evade Marcuth's violent swings.

"Don't think I've already forgotten about why I'm here, half-breed. You may very well be innocent, you may very well be a nobody, and you may very well be the most gullible person I've ever seen, but you…you are a thorn in my side that needs to be purged..!"

Once there was enough distance between the both of them, Oomphga turned his heels and faced Marcuth head on, holding his quarterstaff firm across his chest. His hands twitched, his breathing shaky. The two circled each other, the tension crackling in the air like a storm rolling in from the west. Oomphga, his heart pounding in his chest, knew he was outmatched. Marcuth was a warrior, his movements honed by countless battles and bloodlust. Already, Oomphga was panting, losing his strength with each cautious step he took.

"Was nice knowing you, kid. Will be even better forgetting you ever existed!"

Marcuth lunged, his scythe a blur of steel. Oomphga parried with his staff, the impact jarring his arms and leaving scars in his oversized stick. He swung again, but Oomphga danced back, narrowly avoiding another strike. The clash of weapons echoed through the still night air, a deadly symphony of survival.

"'No more! No more!' GAH!!! You're putting up such a fight for a kid that wanted to call it quits earlier!" Marcuth snapped.

"NOT ON HIS LIFE!!!" Oomphga squeaked back, tears of agonizing terror blurring his vision.

Now, all he could hear was the dreading ringing of the blade cutting through the air. He could feel the breeze from each swing pelting him stronger and stronger the closer Marcuth got to him as he continued to thrash his body in different directions blindly. His heart pounded, begging to be free of its intense pulsing, but Oomphga denied it. The world revolved around the flashing blade before him, the burning in his muscles, and his ragged gasps of breath. Whenever an opportunity presented itself, Oomphga tried to brute force magic into being. He prayed for a blade of ice, a blinding puff of snow, a barrier of stone, but nothing. His exhausted hands fumbled each gesture, and his words became a plethora of vowels without meaning. Oomphga, energy waning, knew he couldn't keep this up forever.

One wrong step, one slip of the ankle, and Oomphga fell prone, curled up with his quarterstaff in the snow overlooking the ignorant and chaotic world beyond. Desperation clawed at his chest as his limbs ignored his demands to move. Marcuth approached slowly, watching Oomphga sprawled across the ground, a sadistic expression plastered across his rugged face.

"Ah, finally!" Marcuth crowed, raising his sword high. "The sweet relief of death!"

Oomphga couldn't see his attacker anymore, but he could envision his fanged smile and fiery eyes staring daggers down upon him. Now, in his eyes, all he could see were hazy reflections of the past. His birth atop the mountain, his father and mother swooning over him in the comfort of Sergei's cottage, spending the half-giant celebration all those years ago with Buppy, the many games he played with his cousin Tuthjorn and his friends, Eladda and Faith, all while they playfully made fun of him for talking about plants and rocks. Then…everything that he remembered happening just a month ago came into view: meeting Bear

Friend and Small Bear, meeting Marigold for the first time in Bristlethorn Forest, and…

Marigold…

Her…

Her smile. Her laughter. Her wide-eyed enthusiasm. Her delicate, dark elf hands intertwined with his. That beautiful face. That kind soul. That warm, relieving feeling he felt through his chest whenever she was near him. It was all he could think about. In his final hour, it was all he ever could've wanted and more.

His visions faded, leaving the cold, harsh reality: being alone at Death's door on top of the world, but now, he felt different. Weakness evaded him, leaving him with a pang of determination rushing through his veins.

Shifting his hands on his quarterstaff and gritting his teeth, he slammed the base of the stick as hard as he could against Marcuth's kneecaps. There was a sharp *SNAP,* and then, Marcuth came crashing down. Oomphga rolled to the side to evade the devil's fall, but there was no stable ground left to roll to. Only the cliff's edge of which he carelessly flung himself off of.

For a heart-stopping moment, he plummeted through the air, the icy wind tearing at his bare chest, but instead of being greeted by jagged rocks or broken bones, he felt his body being enveloped by a soft cushion of ebony feathers. His eyes shot open, and a smile crossed his face.

"OMEN!!! You came back!!!" Oomphga cheered, looking over his bruised shoulders. "Oomphga…is…*really* glad you underestimated him!"

"You may be the druid, but even the druid couldn't take on a threat like Martin all by himself!"

Omen, eyes gleaming with fierce determination, spread his wings and soared back towards the mountain peak. With a graceful arc, he landed on the snow-covered ground, Oomphga safely cradled in his mahogany arms. Meanwhile, Marcuth, consumed by a whirlwind of frustration, shakily caressed his kneecap with one of his gnarled claws. He cussed in a devil's tongue under his breath, but the moment he looked over his shoulder, eyes falling upon Omen and Oomphga, a twisted grin spread across his scarlet face.

"Ah, I see how it is. Even beyond the workings of Death, you still choose to side with Aymus..~" he laughed spitefully.

Omen gently lowered Oomphga, allowing him to carefully readjust to the feeling of being on his feet. Numbness and tenderness flooded through his heels up to his hips but swiftly vanished the longer he stood still.

"This path you tread…" Omen began, his tone solemn yet firm. "There's still time to change, Martin."

"*Marcuth,*" the devil in paladin's armor spat back.

Omen's face contorted with a mixture of pain and frustration. "No matter what name you go by, you're still no different from the monster you used to be. Blinded by destiny, by this…tough-guy facade, by a twisted desire to kill anything that you deem a threat to whatever your current scheme is-!"

"I've watched the divine scheme against me for far too long. That child…must…be…silenced," Marcuth seethed. "And in his silence, so too with the gods cease to taunt me!"

Oomphga looked up at Omen, his eyes shimmering with the faintest trace of hope. Both he and Omen shared a silent understanding. They knew what had to happen: Oomphga had to live.

Same as before, Marcuth was the first one to take the initiative, bolting forward with his scythe trailing by his side. However, the moment he swung his arm to strike, Omen parried it with a longsword he pulled from its sheath. Noticing Marcuth's attention fixed onto Omen, Oomphga seized the opportunity to bat at Marcuth's legs with his quarterstaff. Feeling the wood bludgeon his skin, Marcuth reacted by kicking Oomphga in the shin, knocking him down onto his back, but before he had the chance to strike him, Omen deftly interfered once more. The clang of steel rang out loudly in Oomphga's ears, leaving him stunned until a beacon of an idea revealed itself to him.

Hands and feet burrowing into the snow, Oomphga shifted into his familiar dire wolf form, barking and growling. His yellow eyes locked onto Marcuth's limbs even as they moved at a lightning-fast pace. When a good opportunity presented itself, Oomphga leapt up and buried his fangs and claws into Marcuth's dominant arm, clamping down with ferocity.

The pungent taste of blood and sweat overwhelmed Oomphga's senses - the daggers burrowing into his skin, the gore, the raw rush of adrenaline, and the power coursing through his youthful body. All the while, Marcuth roared in agony and thrashed his arm back and forth fearfully, same as Tuthjorn when he got bit, only in this instance, Oomphga felt far less sympathy.

Marcuth backed away and slammed Oomphga against the jagged mountainside, locking Oomphga in a suffocating chokehold. Oomphga's throat clenched, his lungs pleading for air. He clawed desperately at Marcuth's arm, his arched nails breaking uselessly against his skin.

"Let. GO. You dumb, mutt!" Marcuth snapped.

Oomphga unhinged his jaw to gasp and whine. The second his fangs reeled back, so did Marcuth, and with an agile flick of his heel, he brutally kicked Oomphga in the face, sending him reeling back into a pillow of snow. Omen seized the brief window of opportunity - while Marcuth was distracted with Oomphga - and he lunged at his opponent, but Marcuth elegantly parried his swing, holding a steady position. His wounded arm tensed, blood gushing from the bite Oomphga left, but his expression remained tame, eyes locked on Omen's intently.

"And you," he purred. "I expected more from you, Omen~"

Omen growled, twisting his wrists to adjust his grip, but no matter what he did to reinforce his hold on his blade and the force behind it, nothing could compare to the strength, the power, and the foul play Marcuth concealed beyond his slender, devilish front.

Marcuth reeled back, clenched his fist and, more than happily, punched Omen square in the face with a sickening *THUD*. Within the blink of an eye, Marcuth disarmed Omen of his sword, kicked out his feet from beneath him, pulled his head back by yanking on his dreads, and pressed his blade against Omen's neck.

Their eyes screamed their desires:

One for divine intervention, and one for blood…

"In the end," Marcuth panted, "I don't think anything - in any life - will bring me more pleasure, more satisfaction, than watching the light drain from your eyes. Just. Like. Aymus."

A blind fury consumed Oomphga's mind listening to Marcuth prattle on. His back jolted, his muscles bulged, and his body grew. He snapped his head forward, small pupils dilated. Pounding his paws against the snow, Oomphga barreled over to Marcuth, and yanked him back away from Omen violently with his teeth. Marcuth jolted and flailed his arms, annoyance rising in his groans of pain. When he realized who or what was behind him, he twisted his grip on his scythe and drove it deep into Oomphga's shoulder, but he hardly felt a thing.

His bear pelt was thick, and his grizzly rage suppressed his senses. Marcuth kept swinging his arched blade into the same shoulder repeatedly, ripping skin from his flesh and wrestling for control over his movement, but Oomphga's grip was too strong. He tossed Marcuth back over his shoulder and threw his entire weight onto him. 600 pounds of meat and fuzz. While Marcuth struggled to sit upright, Oomphga threw all of his weight on top of his attacker. His bear claws dug into Marcuth's wrist, causing his hand to contract and his fingers to twitch.

Omen slowly stood up behind Oomphga and leisurely walked over to retrieve his weapon from the clouds of windswept frost coating the ground. His attention directed itself to the display before him.

"Oomphga!" Omen called out, his voice echoing over Marcuth's cries of pain, "If he truly wishes to bring about a second calamity, then we must stop him *now* before it's too late!"

Marcuth and Oomphga - their eyes never left each other's. Marcuth frantically dug his heels into Oomphga's belly, batting it over and over trying to break free all while staring deep into the dilated, amber pupils of the brown-furred beast.

"Finish him," Omen commanded.

Oomphga froze, the wrinkles across the bridge of his nose fading. His mind ceased to function. The idea of killing a man; Oomphga never imagined. Not once. Not ever. However, Omen quickly caught onto Oomphga's hesitation.

"Oomphga, you cannot spare him. You cannot show him any mercy. Not now. Think of what he did to Aymus. Think of all the things he'll do to you, your people, and all the innocent people out there if you let him live!"

He did imagine those things. He imagined Marcuth in the same position Oomphga was in when his body failed him and his consciousness spoke to him. Oomphga refused to believe that deep down, inside of this devil's heart of misconception and delusion, there was something worthy of redemption - a second chance. There had to have been a love he fought for, or a family he cared about. There had to have been someone out there waiting for him, a *life* waiting for him past the confines of that singular day. Otherwise, why would he fight so hard? Why would he fight for *nothing*?

Nothing. Oomphga couldn't even comprehend the idea of it. *Nothing.*

"I knew it." Marcuth's voice snapped Oomphga out of his trance. "You really are quite the softy. As harmless as they come."

Looking upon the marks Oomphga left on his body…

Oomphga is anything but harmless…

The shakiness in Marcuth's voice was evidence of the agony, even if he tried to mask it with this "tough-guy facade" Omen spoke of.

"Well, what are you waiting for? Finish me."

Oomphga's breathing intensified.

"FINISH ME."

Oomphga lunged his head forward and grabbed a chunk of Marcuth's wing, biting and gnawing through it until a gaping hole remained. After it was ripped up well enough, he grabbed onto the base by his spine, readjusted his footing, and threw him against the mountainside. The sudden impact knocked the wind out of the helpless devil, and his body toppled to the ground, lying still aside from the reflexes of his pitiful groaning and hoarse breathing. A moment of painful silence hung in the air as Oomphga's body slowly contorted and shifted back to its original form.

Still tasting the meat and blood hanging from his lips and coating his tongue, Oomphga gagged and clung to his quarterstaff desperately to hold him steady. A wave of nausea and dizziness hit him like lightning, his stance and grip loosened up, and helplessly, he fell onto his back. His senses caught up to him, even if his limbs were numb to the touch. He could taste the sickening concoction brewing in the back of his throat. He could feel the snow seeping through his skin and clothes. He could hear heavy wings pounding against the sky and the crunch of frosted powder against leather boots followed by a familiar, melodic call.

Relief approached swiftly and relentlessly.

"Ooomphgaaa! Oooh, Ooooomphgaaa!"

That voice…Tuthjorn?!

Despite having his head and ears cradled by the ground, Tuthjorn's approach made itself known, and, despite his eyes closing against his will, he could still feel his Marcuth's vengeful gaze fall upon the worn-out druid.

"You toy with me, mutt. You think you're so kind and so compassionate. You think, by showing me mercy, that I'll do the same," Marcuth pulled himself to his feet, limping up to Oomphga with bloodlust in his voice and malice in his gaze, "but the world is cruel, kid, and irony is the cruelest thing about it."

A twisted claw grabbed onto Oomphga by the neck and hoisted him aloft over the icy ridge extending from the mountain's winding path. Unable to see the height or the land beyond High Peak, he instead frantically looked around for Omen, but saw him nowhere. Even Marcuth's sideways glance and malicious laughter affirmed that he had vanished.

"Well, now, isn't this a familiar sight~?" the devil cooed.

Oomphga sputtered, gasping for air and spitting out consonants that vaguely depicted his pleads for mercy.

"Let this be one last lesson to you, half-breed: the gods are vicious onlookers with their own agenda, and you…they don't care about you."

His grip uncoiled from around his neck and Oomphga plummeted down the ridge, jagged edges of rock tearing through his flesh on the way down. He hit the snowy base with a crack and a thud that rang through his ears. Helplessly, he tried to bring a hand to one of the many wounds lacing his body, but he couldn't move. Not one inch. He was completely paralyzed from the neck down. Shortly after his tumble, his great grandfather's greataxe followed him down. It must've been kicked over the edge by Marcuth. The blade nearly sliced open his arm, but even still, he didn't have enough feeling to instinctively recoil.

Left to the mercy of the Maiden of Misfortune, he lied in wait for something to happen. Whether it be his own demise or help from his cousin, Tuthjorn, he waited.

Just then, he spotted something lumbering down the path, a pack of wolves, saliva dripping from their jaws, but coming from the other direction, he could hear Tuthjorn calling out to him, more panicked than he was earlier. The wolves retreated but silently acknowledged that the druid was no more than a pathetic child.

As Tuthjorn crested over the hill, he spotted his cousin and swiftly raced towards him, fear and concerned written across his face.

"Oomphga?! Hold on, buddy! We're coming!" he hollered.

Oomphga's lips shuddered, and his words came out as little more than whispers upon his growing exhaustion. Life or Death, it mattered not anymore, so long as all would be alright in the end.

Chapter 20:
A Kindred Spirit

THERE WAS ONLY DARKNESS. For a long time, the only thing that existed was a black, inky void that stretched out as far as the eye could see. Oomphga could not see or hear or feel in this place. Not until pain struck him suddenly in the gut.

"Wake up, little druid," a muffled voice demanded.

Oomphga yelped and jolted underneath the base of the staff that battered against his abdomen just above his groin. His eyelids separated and soon, the cloak of shadows parted, revealing a kind, familiar face.

"Aymus?" Oomphga asked. "Is...is Oomphga...dead?"

"No. You've merely been sleeping...for a while."

"So, is this a dream? Can Oomphga wake up now?"

"No. Not exactly," Aymus extended a hand and grabbed Oomphga by the wrist to pull him up onto his feet. "Firstly, I wanted to thank you for sparing my friend earlier. I know the gods may be displeased, but it always brings me great pride seeing my druidic brethren show the same amount of compassion for others as I would."

Oomphga watched Aymu's lips but could hardly focus on a single word. If anything, the new world he found himself in caught more of his interest. So, peeling his attention away momentarily, he took in the sights of the bountiful forest that surrounded them. A diverse selection of wildflowers bloomed in patches, the trees connected the earth with the peachy sky above, and leaves of ruby, citrine, and jade fluttered in the wind and littered the sun-kissed ground where they stood.

"Secondly, I would like to-"

Aymus stopped mid-ramble, his eyes following little Oomphga as he trailed over to a patch of peace lilies. A soft, white light radiated off of their petals and stamen. From behind him, he could hear Aymus chuckling to himself.

"I had…almost forgotten how young of heart and mind you are," Aymus noted aloud.

Oomphga's bear ear twitched; he cocked his head over his shoulder. "Pardon?"

"Nothing. It's just-…watching over you, sending you visions, seeing you grow. I thought time had flown by faster. Your mannerisms, your compassion, and your optimism suggest youth but…your environment, your wisdom, the fuzz on your chin, and the weapon you carry at your waist. I assumed you were older. As old as I was right when…"

"…The calamity happened?" Oomphga asked.

"Yes."

Aymus looked off towards the rolling mountains and let out a long sigh. Oomphga's big eyes stayed on Aymus. His heart ached for the man, one he never even knew in life, but one he understood in passing. Pulling himself to his feet, Oomphga joined Aymus' side and took in the beautiful view of the world that wasn't even his own. He breathed in the fresh, floral scented air and took in the rare, refreshing feeling of breeze that never ended on a warm, early-autumn day.

"Oomphga is…sorry Aymus didn't get to live beyond the calamity." Oomphga looked to his hands and began fidgeting with them above his stomach. "If Aymus were around…Oomphga bets everything would be perfect. Oomphga's people wouldn't be fighting each other and…maybe he'd be able to talk some sense into his friend Martin so he doesn't start another calamity and hurt even more people."

"Maybe…but…what happens in the present is no longer in my control. As a druid, I did my best to bring the change the world needed. Then, whatever happened just…*happened*. I can reach out beyond the veil to speak to you and the other druids - that much I can do - however, what happens now rests in your hands."

"But Oomphga's just a kid," Oomphga retorted. "A kid that's born different, and nobody wants to listen to him."

"I think you'll find that being *different* isn't a bad thing at all."

Aymus and Oomphga locked eyes with one another, holding their stares for a soothing minute. It gave Oomphga time to think and breathe - to contemplate and to realize the genuine, heartfelt honesty in Aymus. The way he smiled, not estranged by Oomphga's company, it made him feel seen and heard. Oomphga liked that feeling.

"Druid Oomphga," Aymus resumed, "there are three things I wish to tell you before we depart. One: don't ever be afraid to fight for what you believe in."

With dexterous hands, Aymus reached for Oomphga's handaxe, drawing it from the makeshift holster of rope around his waist only to return it to him. He gazed upon the handle, the hilt, and the blade, admiring every detail as if it were new since his mother gave it to him all those years ago.

"For family, for friends, for lovers, for happiness, or merely for survival. Your heart always knows what's right," this Aymus explained.

Oomphga hummed affirmatively, placing the axe back into its proper place at his side.

"Two: one small act of kindness will always spark another."

From Aymus' hand appeared a beautiful marigold, similar to the one Oomphga gifted away when he first met Marigold. He wove the stem between Oomphga's matted locks and bear ears, so it remained in place upon his head.

"Even if you can't see it, your sweet and generous nature will always make the world a better place."

Oomphga smiled, plucking a peace lily for Aymus, only further proving his point. Aymus happily took the lily into his grasp and stuck it into his leafy vest pocket.

"And three - this is the most important one: live your life however you wish. Don't let me, the gods, or anyone dictate what you do. You only get one life, so be happy. Laugh a little. Let loose. Be a kid while you can and be the best you that you can be when you're older. Always stay open-minded, but…keep being yourself."

Tears welled up in Oomphga's eyes. Tears of fear, sorrow, and joy - tears filled to the brim with emotion. Feeling them…he couldn't have felt any more alive (despite being where he was). When Aymus laid a ghostly palm upon Oomphga's shoulder, a comforting warmth that reminded him of everything he held dear brought him a peace like no other.

"You're a good kid, Oomphga Silverblood."

From the trees beyond and foliage beyond, a faint rustling could be heard. Oomphga peered past Aymus to try and find what was making the sound. Then, there *he* was, bouncing and prancing out of the bushes towards Oomphga.

"BUPPY!!!"

Oomphga rushed to Buppy and picked him up into his grey-skinned arms, holding him tightly against his chest. His fur was just as soft and just as wild as Oomphga remembered it being. Waterfalls of immeasurable joy streamed down Oomphga's cheeks atop Buppy's head and between his two, pointy, grey ears. He felt awful, looking like such a sappy mess, and yet, Oomphga couldn't have been any happier. With a toothy smile, Oomphga dropped down onto the grass and ran his hands across Buppy's head and neck, giving him as many pats and rubs as he could.

"Who's been a good boy? Who's been the BEST boy in the world?!"

Buppy yipped and hooted, his tail frantically wagging back and forth as he hopped up and down.

"ME!!! Me?! Is it me?! Oh, I hope it's me!" Buppy cheered. His voice was high pitched and squeaky, cuter than anything Oomphga would have imagined. It was enough to make Oomphga sob and bury his face into Buppy's fur.

"Yes! Yes, you!" Oomphga wept.

Surprisingly, Buppy didn't seem to mind Oomphga's bawling. Instead, he laughed and smiled.

"You've been a really good boy too! Really REALLY good!" Buppy added. "I saw you do many MANY good things and make lots of people happy! You're so spectacular and amazing! I wish I was cool, and strong, and brave just like you! Maybe one day, though!"

Oomphga's eyes burned, and his throat clenched. It hurt terribly to cry, even if this was nothing more than a dream. He clung on tight to Buppy, never wanting to let go.

"Oomphga misses you," he cried.

"I missed you too! Nobody in this world can give headpats and neck rubs the same way you do!"

Arms trembling, Oomphga scooped up Buppy into his embrace and let the pup rest his head on his shoulder. To him, holding Buppy in his arms again, it felt like holding a fluffy baby. He traced his hand up and down Buppy's back, his tail tickling his chin. Amidst the pause in the conversation, Oomphga found relief and comfort. He took deep breaths and steadied his whimpers. Aymus looked upon the too with a patient, heartfelt expression.

"Whenever you're ready…"

Better to do it now while he still had some peace of mind.

"Oomphga…has to go now, Buppy."

"Oh! That's right! You have a family and friends that are probably worried sick about you!" Buppy chirped. Reluctantly,

Oomphga pulled Buppy away, giving the wolf pup a chance to lick the tears off of his cheeks and look him in the eyes this one last time.

"Don't worry, Friend. Aymus and I will keep a close eye on you! Everything will be okay!"

Oomphga nodded, forcing a painful smile from a genuine place. He lowered his hands, allowing Buppy to hop out of them, and then slowly got to his feet. With one last sigh, he looked to Aymus.

"Oomphga's ready to go home. He's ready to…to face whatever the world has in store for him."

Aymus beamed. "That's the spirit."

Aymus raised his hand and flicked it across the sky. The forest - once crisp and clear - became a hazy mesh of colors blending and weaving into darkness once more.

"Good-bye, Oomphga! Be a good boy!" Buppy called out. His voice became hazy, echoing and muffling until not a sound could be heard.

"You too-!" Oomphga uttered in reply.

Congestion. Exhaustion. What a welcome back to reality. Every bone in Oomphga's body screamed bloody murder and every inch of his face burned despite the liquid relief covering his cheeks and clinging to his eyes.

"Hey, bud," Tuthjorn cooed, overlooking Oomphga from a chair by his bedside. "Are you alright? Are you feeling okay?"

"Oomphga-"Oomphga hissed as, carefully, he sat up in his bed. "Ugh…he feels like…-"

Before Oomphga had a chance to voice his feelings, Tuthjorn extended a wooden bowl towards his cousin. It was filled with orange, yellow, and white honey-glazed vegetables.

"Your mom made this for you."

Oomphga cracked a small smile and took the bowl, relieved that - after not eating for what felt like days - here in his lap sat one of his favorite meals: cooked root vegetables with honey, rosemary, and thyme. He took an eager, heartfelt bite, letting the sweet and savory taste of carrot, parsnip, and beets run across his tongue.

"Oomphga...feels a lot better being home again."

"Glad to hear it," Tuthjorn leaned back in his seat and cocked his head to the side, ear turned towards the door. While he wasn't looking, Oomphga brushed back his bear ears, but turned to listen in as well to the conversation going on just outside of the room.

"I apologize on his behalf. He's not usually this reckless."

Oomphga could immediately recognize the disappointed tone coming from his mama (as if he hasn't heard it a million times before).

"Does he run-off a lot?" an unfamiliar voice asked. *"Does he always act so...strange?"*

"He doesn't run off. No. He leaves the tribe to train. He wishes to be a shaman and a great warrior just like his grandfather, and his father before him. As for him acting strange...he just-...he has different interests from everyone else, that's all."

"I see. So that's why he acts differently..."

Tuthjorn let off an irritable groan. His muscles bulged and his teeth clenched.

"Gah..! Can people just shut up about you for one second..?! I can't stand hearing person after person ramble on about you behind your back like this! Seirah, my father, my brother, Kina, my friends, your own mom..! The moment you come back, all of a sudden, everyone starts yapping like...like-!...Ugh! It isn't fair. If people are going to talk badly about you, they should do it to your face!"

"Who's Kina?" Oomphga asked, tilting his head to one side. "And...who are these other friends of yours?"

Tuthjorn clasped his lips shut and suddenly turned to Oomphga. At first glance, he appeared no more lost and afraid than a deer at the snap of a stick. The way he looked with his eyes wide and his mouth agape with all but a reason why. Oomphga was only a little curious. Being gone for weeks at a time, he always fell out of the loop with his half-giant brethren, but now...now it felt as if he's been gone for a whole year and the world had forgotten all about him until only yesterday.

"Well, she's-...they're-...while you were gone, I found new people to train with me. Kina, the girl from the Violet Sun tribe, she's the newest addition to that group. (The one I was telling you about before you left). I was hoping I'd be able to catch you the moment you arrived to introduce you two more formally, but-...I-...you know," Tuthjorn stuttered and stumbled, his movements as sporadic as his gaze. "Everything that's been happening with you-...it's scary. And finding you so-...so beat up, I can't help but wonder..."

Tuthjorn bit his tongue and looked over his shoulder again. It was almost as if Oomphga's bruised, bandage-wrapped appearance struck some kind of nerve with him. Their shared discomfort consumed the room until Tuthjorn finally asked the question most appropriate given the circumstances.

"What...happened? And...how did you get your hands on our great grandfather's greataxe?"

Oomphga stared vacantly; thoughts pertaining to the actual question evaded him.

Gee...that sure is a lot of "great"s Tuthjorn just said. To be fair, isn't it accurate because of all the great things great grandpa Oomphgor did? He fought dragons, made allies with a lot of people outside of his tribe, and he did it all on his own! Wow...that's...

Finally, in that moment, Oomphga remembered all that he did a few days to a few weeks prior: taking on a dreadwalker AND a dragon, making friends with animals, an elf, becoming acquainted with one of the fabled three that stopped the calamity, and to top it all off...he did those things all by himself (with the exception of Marcuth that one time). Even still, he's done so much. He couldn't help but wonder - if Oomphgor knew Oomphga or saw the things he did - *would he be as proud as Buppy?*

He looked over at the greataxe of Oomphgor Thundrak standing tall propped against the wall in the corner. The frost that clung to its edges hissed. From his bed, Oomphga could feel an unnatural chill running down his spine. It swirled and weaved in a pattern over his skin, tracing - what felt like - runes across his back.

Slowly, Oomphga reached for his handaxe lying next to his bowl of food on the small, wooden table by the head of his cot. Some of the runes matched...but not all of them.

What does this mean? Great grandfather...what are these runes and why does their magic call to Oomphga?

"Gods!" Tuthjorn cut through his cousin's inner thoughts deftly, his voice echoing with alarm. "What did you do?!"

"Huh?!" Oomphga's attention snapped back onto Tuthjorn, who sat patiently waiting an arm's reach away from him. "Oh, uh...Oomphga merely got into a scuffle with someone in the mountains. A man showed up and started attacking Oomphga out of nowhere, but it's alright! Oomphga's feeling much better now that he's home and in his cozy bed with a nice, warm-"

"So, how did you get your hands on our great grandpa's axe?!"

"That's...a long story that can be summed up with one word: ...wandering."

"...Wandering?"

"Yes."

"So, you were just...*wandering* around when you just so *happened* to stumble upon..."

"Yes."

"And what - pray tell - are you going to do with it now?"

Oomphga let out a faint hum. "Nothing."

"Nothing? You find Oomphgor's legendary blade before or after getting attacked by some stranger in the mountains and you choose to do NOTHING with it?! If I were you, I'd wield it! I'd use its magic to protect our tribe, save our people from the scarlet-furs, and maybe end this war with it. Wouldn't you?"

"No…Oomphga wouldn't." Oomphga froze up, Tuthjorn's offended expression driving an icy stake through his chest the second his verbal disagreement left his lips. "W-what Oomphga means is that…he couldn't! He can barely withstand its weight, much less use it to its full potential. It's bulky. It's impractical. It's-"

"Dangerous. And that's why we need it!"

"That's why it can't fall into the wrong hands and - Oomphga's hands -…" He looked down upon them. Though battered and bloodstained, they trembled even as he clutched onto his handaxe. He put his blade back down onto the bedside table and curled up in his blankets. "…they aren't made to carry weapons."

Tuthjorn sighed and patted Oomphga on the back.

"Cousin, if you're not going to wield it…" He rose up from the ground and strode over to the greataxe. The moment his hands coiled around the handle, the axe sprung to life. Shards of ice sprung from the blade's sharpened edge and a surge of magic crackled from head to pommel. "…then I will."

The chill running under Oomphga's skin intensified, and his heartbeat's pace quickened.

"Tuthjorn, you're a good warrior, but…this isn't right. We can't keep fighting the bearfolk like this! Every day doesn't have to be another battle. Every life doesn't have to be put on the line. We don't need axes or swords or bows. We need to make peace with them. The next time we see them, we need to try and-"

Tuthjorn swiftly turned his attention towards Oomphga, his eyes igniting with a vicious, silver flame and yet his crooked brows expressed feelings of betrayal.

"Are you…siding with them?"

"Oomphga is siding with no one or he's siding with everyone. He is done fighting. Look at him…"

The two looked over the druid. His appearance looked the same as it always had appeared aside from the bruises and the bloodstains clinging to his clothes, but while this appearance of his made Oomphga's stomach knot and his body tremble, it was clear - judging by his cousin's confused expression - that Tuthjorn saw through the crimson. He was completely oblivious to Oomphga's frantic gesture.

"What was it Tuthjorn said before? 'Look at his scrawny little arms! Look at his hands! Does this look like a man that could or would do any harm to his own family? Oomphga wouldn't hurt a moose let alone a fellow man!'"

Tuthjorn sighed. "And yet…here you are. Blood-soaked."

"Yes! Against his will! How do you think Oomphga feels? Someone from our tribe is dead because of him! He left his attacker in the mountains greatly wounded! HE SLAYED A DRAGON, and yet Oomphga feels so so bad! If only he were a little kinder, maybe-!"

"So, what you're saying is, you feel remorse for the scarlet-furs?"

"Yes. For them. For our people. For everyone and everything that had to suffer the consequences of Oomphga's actions..!" Oomphga curled up on himself, tears welling in the corners of his eyes. "He's…so… sorry..!"

He pressed his face against his kneecaps and suppressed the urge to weep violently in front of his cousin. He expected him to brashly walk out on him or snap at him the same way Uncle Mortium did, but not a sound came from his cousin. The only thing Oomphga could hear was the faint opening of the door.

"Oomphga?" A warm voice called out to him.

Brushing away his tears, Oomphga slowly lifted his head and looked over towards the door only to see his mother standing in front of Kina, the new girl, and behind her Seirah loomed.

"Is everything alright in here?"

Chapter 21:
Mama's Heart-to-Heart

OOMPHGA HID HIS SEETHING AGONY and nodded towards his mother. Despite drying his eyes and cracking a crooked smile, his face clung to the burning sensations radiating through it. He prayed in silence, hoping his mother wouldn't reveal his façade, but the moment he saw her gaze soften, he knew she recognized his grief, and yet, she continued to waltz into the room with a bucket of water hanging from her burly, tattoo-covered arm, ignoring the company they kept. Tuthjorn, Kina, and Seirah all stood by patiently as Mama Vergaia stole Tuthjorn's seat by Oomphga's bed.

She dipped her hands into the water bucket and brought a seething hot rag to Oomphga's battered face to wash the crimson off of his cheeks.

"Leave. Everyone except Seirah," she commanded.

With reluctance, Tuthjorn propped the greataxe against the wall and joined Kina's side.

"Come on, Kina. I apologize on my cousin's behalf for the concern..." Tuthjorn jeered, his voice fading the further he got from Oomphga's room.

Guilt gnawed at his chest. Between every word insulting him and the deafening quietness, Oomphga preferred the quiet. Even if he was left alone with his guilty consciousness, it paled in comparison to the spite - the verbal assault - he bore from his cousin.

"Oomphga. Oomphga, look at me," Vergaia requested.

Despite Oomphga's attempt at refusal, Mama Vergaia pulled his face towards her own.

"Everything is going to be alright. Understand?"

"How do you know that? Oomphga messed up really really bad, and now it feels like everyone is out to get Oomphga and Mama. He...he didn't mean to get someone killed, but when he was with Papa, they..."

"Oomphga, it's not your fault. Given your situation - your position - things happen. That's war."

"But Oomphga doesn't like war! Oomphga doesn't like getting people killed nor does he like killing people! He'll never-! He...he won't-!"

"I know. I know."

Vergaia let out a long, exhausted sigh and, after cleaning Oomphga's face, she began washing his clammy hands. With so much red staining the white cloth, Oomphga was surprised it came off in the water, but the more she scrubbed - his arms, his neck, his chest - the darker the rag became until it was a muddled mess of scarlet stains. All the while, Seirah stood by, leaning against the door frame with his arms crossed over his chest.

"So..." Mama Vergai faintly cooed. "Do you...wish to tell me anything about this elven lady friend of yours?"

"She's not-"

Oomphga, how dare you dismiss her so suddenly.

Oomphga's thoughts cut through his speech with deadly precision, unveiling the beautiful reality staring him right in the face, begging for his acknowledgement. How could he keep denying his own feelings so relentlessly? There was no hiding it. Heat spread throughout his cheeks and his heart picked up the pace to compensate for the fantasy-laced excitement creeping up on him.

"She...was looking for a flower in the mountains, and Oomphga wanted to help her. She helped Oomphga when he was in a bad spot and...she's really really nice. She likes a lot of things Oomphga likes and she's fun to talk to, but..."

The druid gazed out at the snowy landscape filled with brawny half-giants and serious faces all going about their busy day, working hard in preparation for another invasion or another attack. As much as he longed to believe they'd meet again by chance, one thing stood in the way:

"…war," Vergaia stated plainly.

Oomphga nodded. "Yeah. War. He wouldn't blame her if she stepped away from it all. If Oomphga could…he would too."

An icy breeze hit Oomphga's face and directed his gaze over towards the greataxe sitting alone in the corner. It called to him. How or why the young boy couldn't fathom. With Vergaia's hands drawn back, Oomphga pulled himself onto his aching feet and approached the vile weapon and gently pressed his fingertips against the blade. It was cold as ice but soothed the cursed agony that infected his muscles.

"*Do as you must, not as you wish,*" an aged voice whispered, his cadence resonating deep within. "*But whatever you do, do it as yourself, not as I.*"

As Oomphga's fingers traced down the shoulder of the fabled axe, he could sense the energy flowing through the darkened wood that made the handle - the years this greataxe has experienced since the day it was forged in the heart of a blacksmith's home located in the farm village of Alamagus. The intention? Noble. The history? Prosperous until the very end. Hand on the haft, he took the greataxe into his grip and clung to its craftsmanship firmly. Aside from the weight at the head, holding the greataxe felt little different than holding his quarterstaff. It brought a sense of relief intertwined with a magical aura. Even still, something felt terribly wrong as fear-reincarnate buried its vicious claws into Oomphga's skin. He returned the axe to where it was and shuddered.

"You seem troubled wielding your great grandfather's weapon," Seirah noted aloud. "Is something amiss?"

"Everything. Everything is a-miss, Seirah. Oomphga doesn't-...He can't-...It doesn't feel right. Even if this weapon is meant to be carried by Oomphga's hands, they don't want to hold it. They don't want to use it for its intended purpose."

"Maybe you are to find a new purpose for it. Maybe it's not meant to be used, but to be protected just like everything else in the world. Either way, it's yours and it's your decision what is done to your great grandfather's legacy."

Oomphga reached for his plant journal. It was battered and bloodied, but every part of it remained in-tact. He held it between his twitchy fingers and gazed longingly upon it.

"Why Oomphga..?" the druid uttered. "Why not Tuthjorn? Why not Mama? Why not Uncle Mortium?"

"Because..." Mama Vergaia sighed and reached a hand out towards Oomphga's shoulder. The weight made him tense, but the familiarity brushed away the pain and anxiety. "Because there is no one else like you in the world. You're...different, but - I think - that's what our people need."

Seirah hummed and nodded along.

"No one is expecting you to do this alone, sweetie," Mama Vergaia continued. "You have me, your father, Seirah, your cousin, your friends, maybe even this elven lady you like."

Oomphga let out a quiet chuckle. "He - *ahem* - he supposes."

"It'll be okay. I can't vouch for your cousin or friends, but Seirah, your father, and I...we'll always be here for you, and we'll always love you no matter what. You're our special, beloved, little, Oomphga."

She coiled her arms around Oomphga and pulled him against her breasts for a firm embrace.

"Thanks, Mama..."

"Now, you finish up your dinner before it gets cold and get plenty of bedrest. I'm sure you'll have a long day of looking for new plants tomorrow morning."

Oomphga waddled over to his cot and hopped back onto the warm, fuzzy pelts that covered it. Some of his equipment dug itself into his waist side the moment his bed hit the frame, but he hardly minded. He was far too relieved to be safe at home even if it was merely for a few minutes or a few hours until daybreak. Despite the worries still lingering in his head, he enjoyed the peace. He munched on his room temperature vegetables and snuggled up underneath his blankets.

Then, until nightfall, he scribbled and doodled away in his two journals, weaving together strings of knowledge and vivid imagery into his pride and joy by candlelight until Mama Vergaia came in to ready herself for bed. She trudged over to a large chest and pulled off layers of pelts and leather until the only thing left clinging to her body were the matching black cloths wrapped around her chest and hanging down from her hips. The moment she dropped down onto her cot, Oomphga understood that it was time to finish up his scrawls and turn off the lights.

"Good-night, Mama," Oomphga whispered. "Maybe tomorrow morning, we could go out looking for plants in the mountains together after breakfast?"

She let out a long, raspy groan in response.

With a smile and a nod, Oomphga flicked his hand through the air and extinguished the flame beside him, leaving nothing but the faint glow emanating from the stars and moon beyond the open window as his only source of light.

"Good-night, Obak, Laniarra, Neodashkus, and the Maiden of Misfortune. Good-night Marigold, wherever you are. Sweet dreams~"

A yawn escaped the young half-giant bearfolk as he burrowed underneath layers of heavy pelts. Blissfully entwined and eyes heavy, he succumbed to exhaustion without a care in the world.

Everything changed. Twisted visions of a grim future filled with anarchy and destruction had all since vanished. Finally, there were no divine voices, no haunting imagery of the dead, and no dark memory to relive. This dream was different. Far more pleasant than the norm.

Before Oomphga's eyes was a moonlit clearing where wisps danced amongst the trees, laughter echoed from far off into the distance, and a catchy, jovial tune played in Oomphga's ears despite there being no instruments or musicians in sight. Here was an open space where Oomphga could do as he pleased. With a brush of his foot and a wave of his hand, flowers began to blossom between blades of grass, with a melodic whistle, he could beckon squirrels, rabbits, and birds to him, and with a singular, well-considered thought, *she* could appear.

With elvish grace, she weaved between the youthful oaks and waltzed into view. Her short, ebony locks sat upon her shoulders and the Crystium Catastrophe remained embedded between them above her pointed ear.

"Mari-...Mari-...Mari-..." Oomphga stuttered, rendered helpless by her enthralling, raven-feathered dress and cloak.

"Is something the matter, Oomphga? Did the titmouse catch you by the tongue?" she asked, her innocence outweighing her insight.

A shiver went up Oomphga's spine, rendering him helpless to fate. "His-...He's not-...You're very...very-...um..."

He wanted to explain his feelings in depth to her, but he couldn't. The frog caught up in his throat wouldn't let him. While he stood anxiously in wait, Marigold inched closer until she was directly in front of him. She raised her hand up towards his lips only to gently push his jaw upwards to close his mouth. He hardly realized it was hanging open.

What a dog...fawning over a pretty lady like this. Oomphga's no better than Tuthjorn.

But he couldn't suppress his primal, pubescent instincts. Looking upon her softened gaze, her bittersweet smile, and her sultry eyes: he saw nothing but the girl that saved his life and the blossoming woman he wished to share passages of plant and animal knowledge with for the rest of his years. If ever he had a moment in time to escape from the war, he'd be more than willing to do so with *her*.

Oh, to wake up every morning like the one: Marigold clinging to him, embracing him in a warm hug he felt once in a blue moon. To share every ounce of wisdom and emotion he had with her every second of every day. To finally be able to whole-heartedly laugh like a child again.

He hoped…one day…that his fantasy could be a reality.

Taking his hand into her own, Marigold pulled him even closer. Her attention rested on him as she adjusted Oomphga's grip. One hand on her waist, another in her clutches.

"Know how to dance, druid?" Marigold purred.

"N-no. He's never-"

"Then let *me* teach *you* how to dance."

"F-Fair enough, Oomphga supposes. Although, despite being a good learner, he has…bad coordination-"

"All you have to do is parrot me~"

Hesitant step after hesitant step, they began to move in tandem. Oomphga's feet dragged along, but he watched each step closely, so he didn't trip over her. (If he did, he assumed it would end up disastrous given their size differences). One thing Oomphga didn't understand about Marigold's dancing was that she counted a lot, and she never went past three. It sounded nice along with the faint traces of music that filled the air, but what was it all for?

"Why is Marigold counting?" Oomphga asked bluntly.

"It's to keep track of our steps. Haven't you noticed?"

Oomphga watched closely. Their steps were on time, and they moved in a pattern. A few steps later and they were roughly back to where they started, but now, doing it repeatedly, Oomphga finally got the feel for the motions. Realizing the secrets of dancing, his eyes lit up and a breathy chuckle escaped him.

"He's...he's dancing! Oomphga is dancing with Marigold!"

"You are! Look at you!"

1, 2, 3...1, 2, 3...currents of vigor flowed through his arms and legs. Every motion, every passionate gesture, happened with ease. The need to watch his footsteps vanished in a flash as he fixed his gaze onto the love of his life. Somehow, even as Oomphga started getting creative with his movements, Marigold followed in perfect tandem, their eyes never departing. They weaved through the air, feet brushing across the soil beneath them. The longer the two partook in such intense and vigorous waltzing, the harder it was to catch their breaths in-between steps.

When his legs finally caved, he dragged Marigold down to the earth with him. The weight of her torso kept him pinned amongst the grass and the blossoming flowers, but Oomphga didn't mind. Not one bit. He accepted her as she laid across him and felt nothing more than an innocent joy long forgotten amidst the discordant realm of his feuding people. As Marigold rested her head across his chest, she took deep breaths - not too dissimilar to Oomphga's - and let out the faintest giggle his ears could perceive.

"This is nice," she whispered.

"Yeah," Oomphga affirmed, his voice just as quiet. "Oomphga wishes Marigold and him did stuff like this all the time. It's really fun and Oomphga doesn't get a chance to have fun too often."

"Well, as long as I'm around, we will."

"Promise?"

Marigold glanced up at Oomphga, her cheeks rosy and her lips curled towards the heavens.

"I promise."

Oomphga readjusted himself, still supporting Marigold's back with his arm. Then, letting out a quiet purr, he pressed the side of his face up against her soft head. Her warmth mesmerized him, her voice soothed him, and soon, he found himself lost in her dreamy existence.

○ ══════ ○ ○ ❀ ○ ○ ══════ ○

"Oomphga! Oomphga, wake up!" his mother demanded. "Wake up, now!"

Clinging to the satisfaction of sleep, Oomphga let out a scratchy hum. He could feel her palms violently press up against his lanky frame to shake him, but he remained resistant, determined to live in his fantasies for an hour more. She ripped off his blankets, leaving his grey-skinned body exposed. However, instead of being greeted by autumn morning's relentless chill, he felt warm. Almost scorching hot. When Oomphga finally had the energy to force his eyes open, he saw his mother looming over him with a mortified expression. He could see the dance of the firelight through the window at her backside and hear agitated warriors hollering at one another through the walls.

"Mama..!" Oomphga cried, sound barely escaping him. "Another attack?!"

"Grab your handaxe and your quarterstaff. I got your greataxe. The bearfolk have arrived, and they're looking for you!"

Chapter 22:
He, Who Claims the Traitor

OMPHGA FRANTICALLY SCOOPED UP EVERYTHING HE COULD into his possession: his journal, his pack of herbs, his quarterstaff, and then his greataxe - but despite all of this, there was one thing he nearly had forgotten: the ram horn. He needed it more than anything, and he needed to use it now.

Gods, please, look out for Oomphga...

Stepping out into the open alongside Mama Vergaia, Oomphga stayed close by her waist for protection, not knowing what lies in wait for the mother and her druidic son. Then, in fires lighting up the mountains, there they stood: a whole crowd of familiar faces looking upon the two with varying expressions.

Eladda and Faith were at the head of this small bearfolk army with Mr. Swiftclaw sandwiched between the two of them. Father and daughter looked upon Oomphga, shocked and shaking their heads in denial while Faith couldn't see a thing and therefore had no extreme reaction to seeing her friend wearing different clothes and dawning an unfamiliar mask.

Tuthjorn and Kina were close to one another - close enough to hold hands. Kina spoke quieted words to Tuthjorn while Tuthjorn himself gritted his teeth in a blind fury, his attention jumping between Oomphga and his father, Mortium.

Seirah hovered next to the flames that danced across the long, pine panels that extended across their neighbor's home. His hazy eyes reflected no sign of resistance or urgency. With lazy steps, he trudged over to his chieftain's side and muttered something under his breath before disappearing into the dense cluster of half-giants.

And there, Uncle Mortium stood by. He was separated amongst the masses, with his chest puffed and greataxe of his own outstretched directly towards Oomphga. He stared daggers into his own kin, not a trace of familiarity in them now. The child he once called nephew was far too grown - far too dangerous. Oomphga was a traitor to his people...all of them.

He unhinged his mouth to speak, but a man's loud yet lilted cry rang out, the foreign accent echoing through the snowy hills.

"MY LITTLE OOMPHGA!!!"

Papa Sergei!

He barreled through bear and boulder alike to get to his son. Extending his padded paws, he reached out to pull Oomphga in close, his arms twitching and heartbeat drumming loudly against Oomphga's cheek.

"Papa-!"

"It's going to be okay, son. You and your mother are going to be okay. We'll keep you safe."

For some odd reason, Oomphga believed these words. Despite the teeth-baring beasts and barbarians amongst the crowd, there were still some that gazed upon the estranged family with awe.

"Well," Mortium finally began, "there is the Oomphga you seek. Take him, if you wish, although...judging by your expressions-..."

"Nobody will be taking Oomphga away from us," Mama Vergaia interrupted, raising the frosted greataxe in her possession with ease.

Her stance, her rippling muscles, the way she held the unbalanced weapon so easily in one hand; it all made her look stronger than Tuthjorn and Uncle Mortium combined. Maybe Papa Sergei was right after all, and everything would be okay in the end. Ear still pressed against his father's chest, he could feel a similar relief through him. Though his pulse still skipped, his eyes were alight with nothing but love and excitement for his wife. Even though he opposed the use of violence (as much as Oomphga did), this was the mother of his child, ready to defend the two of them 'til the bitter end.

Looking out at the large group of people, Oomphga refocused his attention on Eladda and Faith. Eladda snorted and huffed, her grip tight on her spear, but Faith remained as calm and collected as ever.

"WE TRUSTED YOU, OOMPHGA!!!" Eladda finally snapped, slamming the butt of her spear into the snow and rock next to her fuzzy feet. "You were such a good-hearted, and nice guy, and all along, you've been LYING to us!!!"

"Oomphga hasn't been lying to his friends! Not...not on purpose!" Oomphga shakily hollered back.

"But you kept this a secret from us for years! We've known each other practically since we were-...since I was a cub! When were you going to tell us? Were you *ever* going to tell us?!"

Tears flew from Eladda's eyes, her voice quivering on every word.

"I still don't understand..." Faith uttered, blind to the source of such hostilities. "What's the issue exactly?"

"Don't you see?! He's one of them!!!"

"I don't *see* anything," Faith replied coldly. "And what do looks have to do with anything? He's still our friend, isn't he?"

"He's one with our enemies!"

"It doesn't sound like it. Seems to me like they're trying to get rid of him, our friend, our non-aggressive, non-threatening friend."

Eladda sulked, but Faith cracked a faint smile as she stepped forward towards Papa Sergei and Mama Vergaia with little guidance or aid. Oomphga approached to meet her half way. Before bumping into Oomphga's chest, Faith suddenly stopped and reached out a paw towards her friend's face. She felt his cheeks, and brushed her fluffy, padded fingers through his long hair to feel the round protrusions coming from his head.

"You still feel like a bearfolk to me in some parts, but maybe a half-giant in others. Even still, you're the same, soft Oomphga I remember…"

"Thank you, Faith, for believing in him," Oomphga pulled Faith in for a warm embrace and laid his head on top of hers. "Oomphga didn't want to lie to Faith and Eladda, but…if they knew when they first met Oomphga, would they have let him be their friend?"

Neither Faith nor Eladda replied initially.

"I don't know," Faith uttered. "That, I couldn't say."

"I wouldn't." Eladda stormed over to the two and pulled Faith back towards the other bearfolk. "Nor do I want to be your friend knowing what I know now."

"Eladda, you're being petty."

"I'm keeping you safe, Faith."

Oomphga tried to follow after his friends, but Eladda held out her spear. The head shimmered in the light, the sharpened tip rising about an inch away from his chest.

"Chieftain Mortium!" Mr. Swiftclaw hollered, catching Mortium's immediate attention. "We leave the boy with you. He has committed a greater crime against your people than he has ours. Although he stuck his nose into places where it didn't belong, he never got one of his own kin killed, and therefore, (and I can't believe I'm saying this) but I trust you to execute the proper punishment."

Execute?! What?! No! Don't execute Oomphga! It was an accident! The NFC were the nameless warrior's executioner, not Oomphga! He didn't-…THEY are the ones that need punishing!

"With pleasure…" Mortium purred. "Men, hold my sister and her lover back for me please…"

Papa Sergei shrunk down behind his wife as a giant's handful of battle-worn warriors approached them. Mama Vergaia dashed forward and drove her grandfather's greataxe into the side of one of the men, but the moment she ripped the blade apart from his flesh, ice began consuming the wound, going so far only as to mend it before stopping. Seeing that she did nothing but cause him momentary anguish, she hesitated, and, in her hesitation, she was swiftly apprehended by three of her kin. Two others walked to Papa Sergei's side and held his arms steady. He hardly put up a struggle with them. Only the slightest shimmy to make their grasp on him more comfortable.

Now, left to his own devices, Oomphga stood alone, face to face with the behemoth he once associated. Slowly, his uncle lumbered forward, his steps causing the faintest tremor in the earth beneath Oomphga's feet. His hollowed-out eyes, his toothy scowl, and his iron grip on his weapon made him appear more monster than man. Oomphga gulped, his throat tense. No dragon, devil, nor demon could compare to the wretched mortal known as Mortium Thundrak, Chieftain of the High Peak Mountain tribe, son of Tuatung and grandson to Oomphgor.

Oomphga's hands trembled, magic flickering between his fingers. He didn't want to die. He couldn't. He was too young to go. He promised Marigold they would see each other again. He still had a civic duty to become the druid to bring about balance to his homeland and to the unknown territories beyond the emerald glades and rocky peaks. His journey could not end here.

"May Obak, Creator of the Giants and Eternal Chieftain of the High Peak Mountain Clan, oversee Oomphga and the legacy he bore as a shaman in his birthplace and a druid in the groves of his bearfolk kin."

"Praying are we, Oomphga?" Mortium growled, propping his greataxe against his shoulder as each step brought him closer to his trembling nephew.

"May Laniara, Mother of Nature and Creator of the Land, protect Oomphga as his beloved uncle threatens his life and his loved ones."

He raised a brow at Oomphga. *Was he somehow confused about that one?* Regardless, he shook it off with ease and swiftly returned to looking just as furious at Oomphga as he did before.

"May Neodashkus, General of War and Champion of Combat, grant Oomphga the strength and the courage to confront whatever fate befalls upon him."

There was no stopping him now. Mortium towered above Oomphga, body at the ready to easily deliver upon the young boy his just punishment.

"And the Maiden of Misfortune, a goddess whom Oomphga knows so very little of..." the greataxe had reached its full height, blade cresting over the mountaintops. "...may she grant Oomphga swift relief..!"

In the last few seconds he had of consciousness, Oomphga stared up at Uncle Mortium and - for a brief moment - he thought he caught a glimpse of remorse. Of sorrow. Of regret.

"...STOP!!!" a female voice cried out.

But Mortium did not hesitate. Just as Oomphga dropped down to the earth to curl up into a ball, his uncle brought down his greataxe and severed...

...a mound of snow by Oomphga's head.

Oomphga peeled back his fingers from over his face, still gripping onto his bare chest. Fear paralyzed him, but, oh, how thankful he was to be alive! How grateful he was to see his own uncle spare him. Even if his expression remained iron-clad, his actions sang a new tune.

"Uncle Mortium!" Oomphga cheered, "you...you didn't-!"

His eyes widened as he came to notice an arrow embedded into his uncle's shoulder. Mortium ripped it out from his flesh, seemingly unphased, and crushed it in his hands. Only briefly did he glance over his shoulder at the crowd. None held a bow. He looked to the mountains. Not a soul in sight. He huffed and returned his focus to Oomphga, his eyes far gentler than they were moments (and days) ago.

"I meant what I said, Oomphga. Never again will I spill the blood of my own kin, even if he shares it with a scarlet-fur. You, your father, your mother...you are no longer welcome here, so if I catch you on these sacred grounds again, I will wish death upon you. Do you understand, Nephew?"

Oomphga clambered to his feet and, without saying another word, he threw his arms around his uncle and hugged him. Face pressed firmly against the pelt wrap around his uncle's waist side, he wept, the thick furs and fabrics absorbing his tears.

"Thank you! Thank you! Thank you!"

Uncle Mortium hesitantly wrapped a burly arm around Oomphga's back, the pads of his fingertips meeting with the faded remnants of the wound he buried in his nephew's body. He hardly gave himself a minute to reminisce before pushing little Oomphga away.

"Okay. Okay. That's enough," he growled. "Now, collect your things and get out of here. I don't...I don't want to see you ever again..."

Oomphga nodded, disheartened but overwhelmed with relief nonetheless. Heart still racing, he turned back towards his house and rushed inside, his mama and papa trailing close behind once their guards had let them go.

Now, this was the first time Papa Sergei had ever seen Vergaia's house. Despite having a far better (and far cozier) cottage, he still traced his paw across every piece of furniture delicately as if it were his own.

"This place is...very beautiful, my love. Did you make this~?"

Vergaia grunted. "With my bare hands."

"And...these?" He picked up - between his thick, fluffy fingers - a small figure made of sticks tied up with different colored strings around a flower petal that somehow, miraculously, hasn't lost its color.

"No, no. Oomphga made those. Night charms, he calls them. Keeps away bad dreams."

"Ooh. I see. Uh...what does one do with these?"

"Wish for a certain kind of dream, I suppose. They don't always work, but..."

"But...sometimes?"

"Mhm. Sometimes. And sometimes, they even come true."

Papa Sergei's ears perched high atop his head. "Oh?"

Mama Vergaia let out a deep hum and leaned against Sergei's prosthetic arm, her fingers intimately coiling around it.

"I suppose we're going to find that...safe home far away from it all. Where our son can be happy. Where we can be happy. Together as a family," Vergaia whispered, looking up at Sergei.

Sergei, in response, let out a quiet chuckle and pulled his wife against his chest to embrace her. "Together...as a family~"

Chapter 23:
The Oomphga That Cried Wolf

VERGAIA LOADED UP THE WAGON with two heavy chests filled to the brim with her belongings. Blankets, rations, and her cooking cauldron were all piled up and crammed into these old, wooden crates while Oomphga's things fit neatly in only one with the exception of his greataxe, his quarterstaff, and his backpack full of traveling gear that he always kept with him.

As he sat curled up in the back of the cart with all of his mother's stuff, Oomphga took this time to add personal notes on his nature journal page dedicated to his research of the crystium catastrophe.

"Oomphga. Add this to your pouch," Vergaia said coolly.

A quiet clattering sounded by Oomphga's feet. When he moved his book aside to peer over his thighs, he noticed a golden medallion of some sort with a large, jagged "X" etched into the center. He picked it up and looked it over carefully.

"What…is 'this', Mama?" Oomphga asked.

"A medal. It's your birthday gift."

"Uh…thanks! So…what is it from?"

"I don't know. I found it pinned to the chest of a dead body when I was a little girl. Looked pretty, so I kept it and wore it, but your uncle said it was too - *what's the word?* - too 'distinguished' for a woman of the tribe to wear. So, I respected his demand, and I put it away, but now that you're older and more 'distinguished', I believe you should have it."

Oomphga examined the medallion closer and flipped it over. On the back were words written in a strange, foreign language Oomphga had never seen before, but judging by the alien-like intricacies of the patterns and the dotted markings connecting the lines, one could assume that this was the language of the divine: celestial. Now, Oomphga was no astrologer nor a god-spoken saint, but he recognized one of the written constellations. It belonged to Neodashkus when his warrior soul transformed into a memoriam among the stars as a manifestation of his ascent into godhood, but what were the others? What did it all mean?

He lifted his head and gazed upon the night sky. So many stars littered the deep, blue sea above. He'd have to stargaze for hours if he wished to find the five constellations embedded on the back of this medallion. As he stared upon the map of constellations, a faint shadow danced across his peripheral vision. He turned to look towards the mountain peaks and...*there he stood.*

It was Marcuth, and he wasn't alone. Wolves, a whole pack of them, standing on two legs with their backs hunched and jaws unhinged: their piercing gaze hyper-fixated on their target below.

They're the strange wolves Elder Goat spoke of. But the crystium catastrophe is safe. So...that must mean...

"Alright, that's the last of everything," Mama Vergaia huffed. With a lazy hand, she patted the most recent wooden chest she loaded onto the cart, her sapphire eyes drifting onto Oomphga

"Ah! Perfect!" Papa Sergei dreamily sighed. "All things considered; this is actually pretty nice! It's like we're getting an official pardon to live out our lives in peace. No more hiding or keeping secrets. We're free. Free to be happy, my love~"

While Papa swooned over Mama, leaning against her and clinging to her larger mass, Mama Vergaia remained focused on her beloved son.

"What's on your mind, Oomphga?"

"Oomphga...wants to talk to Tuthjorn real quick before he leaves! He'll be right back!" Oomphga blurted as he stuffed the medallion in his pack of things, tucked his handaxe into the leather carrier around his waist, and hopped off of the cart.

"Wait, why is Oomphga grabbing his handaxe?! Little Oomphga! Oomphga, wait!" Papa Sergei cried, but his hollering fell on deaf ears.

His legs buckled, still exhausted from the day prior, but Oomphga cut through the frigid winds and the icy snow to make it back into the heart of his village. He had to warn his people - his cousin, at the very least.

He'd listen. Out of everyone, he always listened to Oomphga. Oh, please, gods and goddesses of the realm, don't let that be past tense!

He kept his attention fixed on the cliff edges where Marcuth loomed. His arms were crossed behind his back as his pack of wolves began their advance. With shaky hands, Oomphga drew forth the goat horn from his waist side, took the deepest breath he could, and let it ring. The deep bellowing sound it made echoed loud and clear. Both half-giant and bearfolk heads turned from all directions, directed towards Oomphga and his noisy horn.

"Wolves attacking from the north! Mean, nasty, terrible wolves! Protect your loved ones! Ready yourselves!"

But no one seemed to believe Oomphga. Not one soul. The bearfolk all rolled their eyes and began their trek home while the half-giants resumed their gossiping in the village streets only slightly more annoyed after being interrupted by Oomphga's obnoxious horn-blowing.

"Come on! Anyone! They'll be at our doorstep any minute! Can't you all see?! Won't anyone-?!" Oomphga's yapping was swiftly met with a ruthless fist to the cheek that sent him reeling.

"Crawling back to your tribe already, Oomphga?"

Oomphga recognized that snarky voice and the cackling choir of young men behind him.

"Your mouth doesn't seem to be cooperating with your eyes, Tuthjorn," Oomphga spat back, gritting his teeth. He never spoke ill of his cousin's thick-headedness, but he didn't care anymore. Gentle words and acts of kindness got him nowhere.

"Oh, really? Considering all the trouble that you've caused, Mr. Advocate-of-Peace, I'd say that you're the blind rambler here."

"All the trouble that Oomphga has caused?" Oomphga brushed away the pain clinging desperately onto his cheek and pulled himself onto his feet. "All the trouble that OOMPHGA has caused?! Oomphga has been nothin'...NOTHIN' but nice to you, and none of that matters because - what - he was just born DIFFERENT?!"

"Look at him, Tuth!" one of his new friends jeered. "I think the half-blood is starting to cry!"

They laughed. At the pit of grief festering in Oomphga's stomach they laughed. Oomphga pulled back the cloth wrap covering his bear eye and wiped the tears away with it before tossing it aside. They spit insults and names at him from every direction, filling the young teen with nothing but a newfound hatred - not for them - but for himself. Oomphga had never hated himself, but try as hard as he might, he couldn't bring himself to hate his cousin or his people. They were godsends, all of them. Perfect fits to their cruel worlds and the crueler lives they led in the cruel little game they called 'life'.

"I hope you die." Tuthjorn's words cut Oomphga deep, its blade leaving a gaping hole in his throat and chest that bled a thousand times over. "I hope you take another axe to the side and you die."

As if saying it once wasn't awful enough, there he went repeating himself over and over again. If ever there was a word worse than "those", it was that...that infamous three letter word with redemption miles away from it. Never has a sentence been spoken to Oomphga that held "D", "I", and "E" together under a positive light. Until the day he died, he'd never rid himself of that gruesome, gut-wrenching command, and...in that brief moment...he considered the dreaded "what if" as if it were an ingenious plan, a grand scheme, he neglected to consider.

If Tuthjorn had known better, he'd know Oomphga's poor sense of differentiating the literal from the meaningless, and he'd realize the irreparable scar left on his cousin's psyche that day, one that could not be healed and one that wouldn't fade fast enough.

"Tuthjorn…you don't-" Oomphga, fueled by denial, reached out towards his cousin, a blur amongst his sights, but Tuthjorn kicked up his heels and sauntered off proud of himself for threatening a weak, defenseless soul. "Tuthjorn…"

Once again, Oomphga was alone, the threat of death swiftly approaching with its fangs bared, its claws unsheathed, and its inevitability clear as the moon and stars in the night sky. Staring deep into the glowing, monstrous irises of several half-men-half-wolves bounding down the winding slopes with violent intentions.

Suddenly, Oomphga felt himself being swept off of his feet and flopping down onto his back across a warm, fuzzy arch. When he adjusted his stance and sat up, he finally realized what had saddled him.

"Elder goat! What are you doing here?!"

"You called for us!"

Oomphga returned his attention to the beasts drawing nearer. They all appeared different from one another, each a different, quantifiable mix of wolf and man from one another. While some looked much like the tall, lanky assassin (Cinth) from Oomphga's nightmare, others looked like mutant wolves with arms and legs, yes, but jagged fangs hanging from their maws the size of daggers. There were a rare few regular wolves, however, their howls and barks were not battlecries, but cries of agony. These were not creatures acting by their own volition. If anything, it seemed as if, the more animalistic their features, the more physiological manipulation required.

Oomphga looked to their commander, Marcuth, looming above the village with his new scepter in hand. The hemogem at the crown crackled with dangerous energy as he spoke. His glowing, crimson eyes locked onto the army he commanded, but one among his ranks remained. It was a wolffolk, one much like the one that Oomphga swore he saw once before in a dream…

Suddenly, from the edges of the village, a half-giant gave the warning - the same one Oomphga gave with little difference in word choice.

"Wolves attacking from the north! Get the women and children to safety! Warriors, ready your blades!"

"Stand at the ready along the edge of town!" Mortium added. "I'll signal for a return attack if they get too close!"

Meanwhile, the bearfolk paid the wolves and the half-giants no mind. They were far more focused on getting Vergaia and Sergei ready to leave, but without Oomphga, they couldn't do much aside from patiently wait and rest up for the long journey back down the mountains.

"What's the plan, Druid Oomphga?" Elder Goat asked.

"We…we join forces with Oomphga's tribe and we…"

The clashing of steel, the cries of battle echoed at the heart of Oomphga's most vivid and gruesome memories. Barbarity. Bloodshed. *So much bloodshed…*

"We…we should-"

Every inch of his body denied him the command. The painful familiarity of anguish and needless violence tormented him in ways unimaginable. His youth was stolen from him because of this, so why condone the one thing he wished to put an end to?

Swallowing his traumas, he reached for his handaxe and forced his voice to repeat the words his heart kept him from saying since the day he was brought into the world.

"We fight. Elder Goat, Oomphga will watch your back. He'll be using a lot of magic, so keep your distance and be ready for anything, okay?"

Elder Goat cocked his head to the side and gave a resolute nod to his mountain goat brethren before they began their slow trek towards the outskirts of the village.

"Oh, I know what to expect, little one. I've seen druids work their magic before. Guaranteed, whatever power you have up your coat won't hold a candle in comparison to theirs."

"Oomphga!" Mama Vergaia cried out.

Oomphga turned to look at his mother anxiously, half-expecting her to have some sort of blunt or instigating remark to make. With Oomphga's gnarled quarterstaff in one hand and his great grandfather's frosted greataxe in the other, she tossed Oomphga the quarterstaff. The stick flew between his arms and hit him in the face, but he coiled his arms around it afterwards tight enough, so it didn't slip out of his embrace.

"Be safe out there. You know I'll be keeping a sharp eye out on your father, but you...I believe in you. Make me proud, son."

Quarterstaff firm in his grasp, he looked to the skies and took a deep breath, letting relief wash over his thrumming muscles. Then he shifted his eyes over to Marcuth, still an onlooker to the war he orchestrated recklessly and carelessly.

The wolf pack was a few strides away by now and the mountain goats were picking up their pace, ready to batter any living creature before them with their twisted horns, but before any contact could be made, Oomphga reeled back his quarterstaff, holding it alongside Elder Goat by his rump, and he swung it upwards as quickly as he could. A peaking wave of rock and snow shot out from Elder Goat's front hooves and tripped up more than half of the pack by shoving them back.

"Knock them unconscious, if you can!" Oomphga hollered, his voice painfully cracking.

A few stragglers ran up to Oomphga and Elder Goat, but before they could get too close, he hit them with another wave of molded earth. One or two broke through, their leaps too high and wide for them to be affected, but quarterstaff gripped tight, Oomphga slammed the blunt edges against their heads with deathly precision.

Not long after, a cluster of wolf-like beasts formed and charged all at once from the side. Elder Goat made a wise call and approached with caution from an angle that allowed Oomphga to make a cloud of frost cold enough to stun them.

"Permission to ram?"

"Permission granted."

Letting out a hearty laugh, Elder Goat charged into the frigid air and flailed himself around. He kicked up his hooves and thrashed his head and torso separately. With one hand on his staff and another on the neck of his mount, Oomphga fell off, hitting the ground with a gentle thud.

"Need a hand?" Oomphga looked up, and there was Marigold riding on the backside of another mountain goat.

"Marigold!" Without hesitation, Oomphga reached out and grasped onto Marigold's outstretched palm. "W-when did you get here..?!"

"I caught your friends scaling the mountains looking for you during my trek back to civilization. I went along with them because - knowing your luck - I had a sneaking suspicion something bad was going to happen to you."

"Knowing his luck, indeed. You would not believe all the terrible things Oomphga has been through..! That guy up on the mountains is one of those terrible-"

But when Oomphga looked to the mountains, Marcuth had since vanished without a trace and yet - for one reason or another - the wolves continued their fight. One of the more humanoid creatures tried to lunge at Marigold from behind, but Oomphga swiftly got between the two, his quarterstaff stretched across his chest as a shield. With one powerful thrust forward, Oomphga knocked the half-wolf, half-man back, but twisted blades glinting between his fingers, he buried them into Oomphga's upper arm, inches away from his neck.

In a flash, Marigold unsheathed her own knife, maneuvered her mount behind the attacker, and slit the back of the wolf-man's leg just above the knees. He dropped down, blood pouring from his legs into a thick, red pool that encapsulated the skin and earth around him. Oomphga knew, within a matter of minutes, he'd be dead if not properly treated.

"Gods...!"

"Come on, Oomphga, we have to keep moving, lest another isolated pack of them gang up on us!"

Oomphga clambered onto Elder Goat's back and followed Marigold wherever she led him. Whenever a wolf or a wolf-like monster got close or leapt for Elder Goat from behind. Oomphga would do his best to knock them out or trip them up, but not every whack of the quarterstaff felt right. Some felt incredibly off and resulted in a loud cracking sound or a yelp that shook Oomphga to the core. Brief moments like that passed by so fast, he could hardly tell if, by the time their bodies tumbled to the ground, they were left dead or alive.

Meanwhile, Marigold let arrow after arrow fly from her woven-oak longbow. Never did she miss a mark as each one of her targets received a jagged head that embedded itself deep into their flesh, killing them instantaneously. Hearing them soar, the echoes of their cries. Man, beast, or monster, it didn't matter.

"How does...Marigold do that?" Oomphga asked,

"Do what?"

"Kill...living creatures without - you know - feeling bad?"

"Who says I don't feel bad?"

"You-...you do? But...isn't Marigold?"

"There's a difference between killing out of anger or for fun versus killing for survival. It's okay to protect yourself. I would hope that you, especially, would not be scared of fighting to stay alive, because…because I couldn't imagine-"

A flash of fangs. A deafening bark. A massive figure of meat and fur shot out from the corner of Oomphga's vision and barreled into the side of Marigold and her goat. Only a few seconds had passed and already this creature had its jaw clasped around Marigold's shoulder.

"MARIGOLD!!!" Oomphga cried out.

She violently struck the monster with her dagger over and over again, screaming bloody murder all the while, but to no avail. Oomphga tossed his quarterstaff aside and swiftly took his handaxe into his grasp. Then he jumped onto the back of the beast, blade pressed against its neck, and with a sudden flick of the wrist, the creature fell still, covering Marigold with its thick hide. With all of his strength, Oomphga shoved the corpse off of Marigold to examine the damage dealt.

Looking closely at her shoulder, he could barely see the bite through all the blood. The fangs must've been buried deep enough into her skin that a major artery was struck. She was bleeding out fast, her skin gradually turning blue in that brief amount of time.

"Hold-hold on, Marigold..!" Oomphga stuttered. "He…he got you..! You're going to be okay..!"

He held her close to his body for warmth, brushing his palm against her wounded shoulder. She winced and clenched her fists against his chest at his touch. She was in pain even if the magic seeping through the pads of his fingers were the cure for her suffering.

"Elder Goat, keep Marigold and Oomphga covered the best you can. He promises he'll be quick."

His goat companion gave a resolute nod and trotted around the vulnerable couple, gaze sharp and horns at the ready.

"Oh, Marigold, Oomphga should've been better. He should've been more careful. From now on, Oomphga is going to keep a closer eye on-"

"Oomphga…" Marigold whispered between staggered breaths.
"Yes?"

"I'm…afraid. F-for you. For us." She spoke through rugged breaths. In her voice, Oomphga could discern the faintest trace of - not worry - but sorrow as she then asked the question without an answer: "Why? Why must it be like this?"

"Marigold knows all that Oomphga knows; has seen almost everything he's seen. If anything, there are probably a thousand reasons why but…" Whether out of anxiety or desperation, Oomphga let out a painful chuckle. "What can Oomphga do about it? Nothing he does will change anything. He was just…born this way, and…and that's okay! No matter what he looks like…at least Marigold will still be his friend…right?"

Marigold carefully lifted her other hand and laid it across Oomphga's on top of her shoulder. Her touch was so delicate, so shaky. He could feel the tremors running through her fingertips upon his thick, grey skin. She awkwardly patted him and responded with a faint chuckle of her own. No words followed.

Poor girl is probably just exhausted, Oomphga reassured himself. *She's been traveling for so long. She needs rest. Oomphga can't let her fight for him anymore.*

Slowly, he rose up from the ground, Marigold still coiled in his arms. When he drew away from the embrace, he looked over her shoulder. Blood still covered her skin, but the wound had all since vanished. Turning towards Elder Goat, he whistled as loud as he could to catch his attention and beckon him over. Battered in blood and scars, he approached, stumbling a little as he walked, but he still held up his head with pride and attentiveness, even if his body portrayed otherwise. After assessing the damage and discomfort, Oomphga carefully hoisted Marigold up onto Elder Goat's back and adjusted the crystian catastrophe she had thoughtfully placed in her hair.

"Elder Goat, I want you to get yourself, your herd, and Marigold to safety. Oomphga will take care of the remaining wolves the best he can. And…Marigold?"

Oomphga's and Marigold's eyes were drawn to one another as he spoke. His heart fluttered and his breathing staggered, but all of his muscles were at ease. He felt himself lean in close, temperature rising until his cheeks were a bright red. Time became non-existent in this one moment, giving Oomphga plenty of time to think on this one impulsive feeling that cried out louder than all the others. He watched Marigold's expression closely. Her brows lifted in innocent curiosity, and she shifted her hands in preparation for whatever Oomphga had in mind.

Cracking a heartfelt smile, Oomphga pulled Marigold in close to his chest for another warm embrace and held her tight.

"Be safe," he whispered. "Oomphga doesn't know what he'd do without you."

Gradually, she lifted her arms and gracefully folded them around his upper back. He let out a sigh in relief, happy knowing that he didn't cause the girl of his dreams discomfort approaching her like this, and feeling her hug him back filled him with a newfound reassurance that maybe she felt the same way. Without warning, however, Marigold let out a quiet giggle and turned her head slightly to look upon her friend.

And then…that's when it happened:…she kissed him.

Her lips pressed against his cheek for more than a few seconds; long enough to leave a lasting impression on his face. Even after she drew herself away, Oomphga mirrored Marigold so he could get a good glimpse of her cheeky countenance while he was left looking flustered and doey-eyed. He could feel his smile growing twice in size from excitement as he eagerly did the same, pressing his own lips against her cheek. When he pulled back again, he let out an audible *MWAH* and beamed brighter than ever before.

He didn't know what to do now. He brushed his fingers through his matted hair and clumsily collected himself. His handaxe that was still lying in the snow? He picked it up and put it away. His quarterstaff he tossed aside? He took it into his hands and pressed it up against his breast.

"Oomphga - uh - after all of this, he promises he'll-! And then…and then Marigold and Oomphga can-! Next week! Autumn festival! He'll see Marigold there~?!"

Without even batting an eye, she replied. "Yes~"

Oomphga hopped back, his steps lighter than air. Sounds of all sorts left his vocals. He couldn't control his ecstasy. He probably looked like a fool to anyone watching the chaos that ensued, but he didn't care.

"Oomphga-! He-! I-!" It felt bizarre, speaking in the first-person for the first time, but in the moment, it just…felt right. "I love you!"

And every word rang true. I…loved her.

His energy was immediately revitalized. He was ready for anything life threw at him knowing that he had such a bright future to fight for. The wind carried him across the white, powdered fields and guided him into the heart of the canine company. By now, there were two or three dozen still conscious and fighting tooth and nail with the intent to kill. But no more.

Oomphga pushed past the mountain goats that retreated back to their elder, his eyes alight with determination. With no one present to help him, Oomphga was on his own.

He reeled back his quarterstaff and within a few steps of the cluster of wolf creatures and mauled corpses, he firmly planted his feet into the ground and put as much force as he could into waving his staff. Another ripple of ice, snow, and rock shot out from his feet and knocked the wolves back, separating those remaining into individuals that lunged at their earliest convenience. Attacking one by one, Oomphga had plenty of room to work his magic. Slashing, flicking, and swinging his quarterstaff were the only gestures necessary for the earth to bend to the druid's command. Gusts of wind repelled the wolves on all fours, small trails of fire repelled the wolffolk, and bursts of stones were required to knock the wolf-like monstrosities unconscious.

One by one, the pack was depleted. Some had died, some laid seemingly "asleep" in the snow, and the rest turned tail to flee.

"We did it! Oomphga and the mountain goats and Marigold, we all did it!" Oomphga cheered and laughed aloud, not realizing that the only one left among the carnage and destruction was him. The goats retreated, Marigold's condition after the bite left unknown.

He turned to the half-giants, wide-eyed and bushy-tailed in the hopes that they would acknowledge the return of peace to their tribe, and they did, but there was no celebration or acknowledgement of all that Oomphga had done. Only plain, grey faces minding their own business with the exception of Tuthjorn and Mortium who continued to watch Oomphga very closely. Their eyes ordered for him to return to his mother and father without delay, and Oomphga - now robbed of pride, relief, and that giddy feeling he still had inside from that brief kiss with Marigold – begrudgingly obeyed.

He trudged back to the wagon silently and plopped down in the back next to Papa Sergei who sat uncomfortably among the stacks of wooden trunks. Seeing Oomphga in his seat, the bearfolk finally began the trip back towards the forests they called home. The view of Oomphga's birthplace faded from view, and yet, a spark of hope remained deep in his heart.

"Marigold...Oomphga will see you again soon. He just knows it."

Over the mountain's peaks, Oomphga could make out the faint, fuzzy silhouette of Marigold sitting atop Elder Goat's back. She waved good-bye to Oomphga, but all Oomphga could think about was seeing her again as he sunk comfortably into his papa's torso.

Chapter 24:
Fallen on Deaf Ears

PAPA SERGEI MADE A VERY COMFORTABLE PILLOW during the trip. His warm fur, his heavy, brown coat, and his steady heartbeat lulled Oomphga into a trance. This allowed his thoughts to drift in and out of a land painted in autumn's vibrant hues where he, his family, his people, and Marigold all lived in harmony.

Ah…Marigold…Oomphga misses her already.

Many nights would pass by where she would be the only thing that existed in his dreams and every vision of her that danced across his imagination left him feeling particularly warm. Being frequently huddled up to Papa in the back of the wagon, he was the first to take notice of this change in temperature.

He brushed the back of his bear paw against Oomphga's forehead, gazing upon his son with concern.

"My son, you are heating up. Are you feeling well?" Sergei asked.

"In all of his life, despite everything that happened at home? He…feels pretty great!" Oomphga chuckled aloud and let it drift off into nothingness shortly after. "It feels good being able to get plenty of sleep with little to worry about. No more secrets. No more being in the middle of a war. No more…being alone. It's nice~"

"Even still, you could've easily caught an infection," his father insisted. "It is almost that time of the year."

"Sergei," Vergaia interrupted. "Relax. He's an apprentice to the shaman. He-" Then it hit her. Her son wasn't a shaman's apprentice anymore, since they've been ex-communicated from the tribe which, unfortunately, meant old man Seirah was on his own. Both her and Oomphga realized this and shared similar expressions to one another. And here they thought nothing was lost on their path to freedom.

Sergei batted his brown eyes between the two curiously.

"Vergaia, dearest? Oomphga? Is something the matter?"

Vergaia looked over to the bearfolk guiding their humble carriage through Bristlethorn Forest. She didn't want to say anything aloud. She couldn't. Otherwise, they'd see an opportunity to strike their opponent, a weakness in their defense, that could be their key to winning the war and slaughtering the half-giants like cattle.

Oomphga carefully stood up while the wagon was still in motion, and he walked over to the bench on the other side where Vergaia sat. He then put a hand on hers and smiled.

"Obak will protect them," Oomphga whispered.

"He will," Vergai replied.

Finally, Papa Sergei caught onto their discussion and glanced over his shoulders at the dozens of bearfolk that walked alongside the cart. Seeing their ears twitch and their hemogem spears at the ready-made Sergei more than a little nervous. He brushed his prosthetic arm, attention darting from soldier to soldier.

Then, there was a loud, monstrous screech that cut through the evening air and echoed a thousand times over. The wagon came to a sudden halt, the horses reeling back in fear. Oomphga could hear the animals screaming out the name of the creature they dreaded like bloody murder.

"It sounded close," Eladda noted aloud. Her body erect and at the ready, she turned to her father. "Permission to investigate?"

"Permission denied. I'm going to investigate. You hold down the fort here." Mr. Swiftclaw ordered.

"Dreadwalker," Oomphga quietly blurted.

"Pardon?"

"It's the dreadwalker. Oomphga would recommend avoiding a fight with it, if at all possible. He's seen it up close. He knows what it can do. One bite of its fangs, one cut of its claws, or one touch of its flesh and you're dead."

"Pfft...you're just overreacting," Eladda sassed.

"Are you willing to gamble your father's life on that doubt?" Oomphga replied calmly. "Please, Mr. Swiftclaw. Let's just focus on the road ahead, yeah? Before someone gets-"

"Enough. Both of you," Mr. Swiftclaw promptly interjected before adjusting his spear in his clutches, "I'm going to investigate and that's final. If this beast poses a threat to our journey home, then it's my duty to ensure that it is dealt with. Faith, keep an ear on your friends."

"I will do my best, Sir."

Giving an affirmative nod, Mr. Swiftclaw sauntered off towards the wall of towering pines and disappeared in the darkness leaving little more than a trail of pawprints behind him.

"Mr. Swiftclaw..! Please..! You don't know what you're going up against..!" Oomphga warned more desperately.

He felt Papa Sergei's paw on his shoulder. When he turned to face his father directly, Sergei shook his head and silently beckoned Oomphga to take his seat. He did so reluctantly and let out a sigh. Shortly after, he cocked his head to the side to look upon Eladda. Eladda looked to Faith, and Faith looked to no direction in particular, so Oomphga, praying nothing bad would happen, turned to his nature journal and paged through every entry. To think all of his studies under Seirah would be for naught.

"For being a 'friend' of ours, you sure don't seem too eager about following my father into the woods to confront this so-called dreadwalker," Eladda jeered.

Oomphga sighed. "It's not Oomphga's place to intervene if no one listens to him. Besides, he's going to...put his trust in Mr. Swiftclaw."

"So, assuming you're right about how dangerous this dreadwalker is, which you're probably not, you still don't feel an ounce of urgency?"

"He does, but he's not going to argue. He really doesn't want to make Eladda mad. He already has enough people angry at him as it is, don't you think? Besides, Oomphga doesn't see Eladda going after him either, so…"

Eladda let out an annoyed huff and stood against the wagon with a paw tucked under her spear arm. "I…guess…"

Hesitance. Beats aggression or a sarcastic remark.

Suddenly, another loud screech came from beyond, commanding the forest to silence itself and listen to its cries. As haunting as it was, one could not help but be entranced by such an unfamiliar beckoning.

Eladda clung to bated breath. She didn't want to admit it, but as distrusting as she was to Oomphga, as much as she didn't want to believe him, something inside of her festered. He could see behind the shifting of her feet and the swaying of her spear arm. Her ears fluttered at every sound, curious to know if any of them belonged to the beast. Once again, Oomphga looked upon Eladda and Eladda looked upon Faith. Faith hardly stirred an inch or uttered a consoling word to either of them.

The second a more excruciating cry of the dreadwalker rang throughout the hills, Eladda bounded forward into the depths of the woods before Faith even had a chance to react. Oomphga followed shortly after, hopping over the side of the wagon without sparing a second of waiting. He recognized that wail - that deafening screech.

Running as fast as their feet could take them, Eladda, followed by Oomphga and Faith, made their way to the scene of the attack. Oomphga's chest and throat tightened, making his breathing heavier and louder than ever before. Helplessly, he followed Eladda into an ignorant oblivion on a one-way trip towards a beckoning Death. He could feel determination and longing flooding from her strides, but Oomphga could sense something far more sinister amiss: the gods were weaving a vacant space in the afterlife for a new addition. Loss was inevitable.

By the time the three companions got there, it was already too late. Not long after spotting Mr. Swiftclaw beside them with the dreadwalker straight ahead, shimmering scythes plummeted from the moonlit sky and sliced open Mr. Swiftclaw's chest. The blades slipped under his metal plates, burrowing into his bones and flesh, impaling and intertwining themselves on most of his organs and all the while. A flick of the mangled, ebony hand and, suddenly, the front half of Mr. Swiftclaw's body was gone. However, despite the odds, he still stood alongside them, innards on display for two of the three children to see in full detail. He sputtered out a few breathless noises, blood pouring from his body onto the grass, and only when his mind recognized all it lacked did, he finally toppled to the ground with a thud that echoed across a thousand lifetimes.

It took an eternity before Oomphga could tear his eyes away from the gruesome remnants of his body, his gaze finally settling upon the active threat towering above them. The dreadwalker, a monstrosity of bone and sinew, unleashed a hiss that echoed the hunger of the grave. With a grotesque fascination, it admired Mr. Swiftclaw's still-beating heart, impaled upon its crescent-shaped nails, his intestines dangling like cushy rings between its skeletal fingers. In a horrifying slow-motion ballet, the creature unhinged its jaws, revealing rows upon rows of jagged teeth. Its tongue, a slimy, writhing tentacle, unfurled and snaked out from its maw. Then, with an agonizing slowness, it lapped up the blood and organs that adorned its macabre form, savoring the taste of despair in one's final moments alive.

"Is everyone alright?" Faith whispered.

No one replied. Neither Oomphga nor Eladda could process the life desecrated and eaten away by the lumbering beast. However, Eladda came to a conclusion far quicker than Oomphga and lunged forward with her spear at the ready, letting out a thunderous warcry. In the blink of an eye, the dreadwalker snapped its head downward to watch Eladda swiftly approach.

"Eladda! Wait!" Oomphga hollered. "Get back!"

Thrusting his arms out and throwing them to the side, the straight path she had curved underneath her feet, turning her around completely. The dreadwalker screeched and, in response, Oomphga separated a hefty rock from the earth that he, (with some ease) kicked in the direction of the monster. It stumbled back, the ground rumbling under its weight.

"Oomphga, what are you-?!"

"One touch of that thing and it'll kill you!"

Instinctively, Oomphga transformed into a horse and ran between Eladda and Faith. He neighed, catching Faith's attention. Without question, she obeyed, leaving Eladda standing alongside him. Her attention flashed between the angered dreadwalker and a desperate Oomphga. With a trembling whine, Eladda grabbed her father's spear and hopped up onto Oomphga's rump, her back pressed up against Faith's. Kicking up his hooves, he made a mad dash away from the danger that lunged for his tail. Legs aching and pulse flaring, he galloped through the treeline, evading every log and rock in his path.

Don't look back. Don't look back! DON'T LOOK BACK!!!

The unsteady beast tore through the forest, releasing its rage in a mighty howl. Oomphga couldn't help but wonder if the creature recognized him from their last encounter, however, his quizzicalness soon subsided as it snapped its jaw at the three. Either the dreadwalker had gotten faster or Oomphga had gotten slower on account of the riders that mounted him.

Eladda swept her spear to and fro, to keep the creature at bay. There was a ripping sound. It sounded like her jagged tip made contact with the little flesh on its face, granting Oomphga a moment of reprieve to expand the gap between him and the gluttonous creature.

Stumbling over his own hooves, Oomphga wrenched his body in another direction and burst into a sudden sprint to evade the dreadwalker's bite. Death hovered a few feet away, eager to satisfy its hunger for revenge against the half-blood that evaded him days prior. Though he couldn't see it, he could sense the beast's festering appetite.

"You're doing good, Oomphga!" Faith reassured the panicked stallion over his panting and wheezing. "Keep going! Maybe, he'll leave us alone if we get past the edges of Bristlethorn!"

"And what about our fellow bearfolk back at the cart?!" Eladda snapped back.

"That's true. And Oomphga's family is back there as well…"

A flash of gore. A rush of unwanted visions. Oomphga belted a sudden, loud neigh at the terrifying idea of his family in imminent danger as he tore through the forest as quickly as his body would allow. His lungs strained; his throat burned.

"Who cares about them?!" Eladda laughed hysterically. "If it weren't for them, none of this would've happened! Hels, if it weren't for Oomphga here-!"

"Enough, Eladda! Now is not the time to beat up on our friend..!" Faith retorted. "Besides, he may be a horse, but he can hear and understand you just fine."

"Good, because he needs to hear this!"

Oomphga dropped his long ears and prepared for the worst.

"Oomphga, you are the most reckless, annoying, and self-centered guy I've ever met! You are nothing but trouble, and I wish you were never brought into this world because, by the gods, it would be such a better place without you!"

"ELADDA!!!"

His heart beat more intensely than the rest of his body could handle, and a surge of magic flooded through his veins. He didn't want to let his emotions get the better of him. Not now, when one outburst could cost everyone their lives, but her demeanor, her tone, her choice of words…she was practically begging for a fight. Whether out of grief or anger, she edged Oomphga closer towards the breaking point with her vile confessions. By now, Death had never felt closer. It whispered sweet nothings into his ears, confessing its appetite for a misguided young druid, but Oomphga pushed on, treading down his own path. The road became clearer now thanks to the dagger of insults Eladda embedded into Oomphga's back.

Eventually, the three arrived at a clearing where the infamous cliff edge stood tall overlooking a large lake. The location of Aymus' demise and the birthplace of anarchy amongst his own people over the death of a newborn; a notorious sight indeed. The ground was covered in hemogems, each reflecting the glistening remnants of the bloodshed that had happened here. Dashing to the side, Oomphga reared up onto his hind legs, knocking Eladda and Faith off of his back so he could change back into his natural form. The dreadwalker stopped a few paces away, its shimmering gaze piercing through Oomphga's chest as if to target the source of its next meal.

Oomphga panted and wheezed but shot the dreadwalker a dangerous gaze. Forcefully, he embedded his feet into the ground, standing resolute. He readjusted the red ribbon holding back his hair and looked to the horizon. Though lit by pale starlight, Oomphga could perceive nothing but the flames of years past that consumed Bristlethorn on the night an infant was slain. To think: all that death happened here.

The dreadwalker slowly approached, its eyes alight with the same familiarity. It's met Death a thousand times over and remained unphased by it. The closer it got, the louder Oomphga's heartbeat grew. Despite the history the land bore, Oomphga didn't want to die, and yet, here he stood facing the epitome of his fear head on. In this very moment, nothing could negate the relief he'd feel vanquishing the terror of his life like a hazy memory in the face of the future. Not even thoughts of Mama Vergaia, Papa Sergei, or Marigold could soothe the tremors coursing through his muscles. Against his body's own will, Oomphga took a deep breath and stepped forward, his fingers and arms the most tense they had ever been.

"Faith, come on," Eladda whispered as she brought herself to her feet with the aid of her spear. "Let's get to safety. I'll deal with this dreadwalker personally some other time, but for now, you and I need to-"

"Eladda…" Faith murmured, voice shaking. "Eladda, you have to do something, because…because if you don't…I will..!"

Oomphga reached for his handaxe, but there was no handle to grasp onto.

Had he…forgotten it?! Did he drop it?!

His attention returned to the weapons the dreadwalker bore. Daggers protruded from his gums, scythes were embedded into his fingertips, and a rack of spears adorned his crown. All the while, here were Oomphga's palms: empty of defense. The only thing he had at his disposal was the spark of magic at his fingertips, and even then, it would only last him for so long before it began leeching away all the energy he had left after several perilous days.

With the dreadwalker a few steps ahead, Oomphga stopped dead in his tracks. Firmly adjusted his stance, he took one last deep breath and thrust his hands outwards from his chest. A thunderous wave erupted from around him and knocked the dreadwalker back a bit, but the dreadwalker snapped back, jaw unhinging to full length as he thrust forward to bite one of Oomphga's hands, but Oomphga narrowly dashed to safety. He flicked and swirled his palms in different directions, causing flowers and grass to stretch and weave around the limbs of the beast, but aside from pestering the salivating monstrosity by tripping it up, it did little to stop it.

Noticing the cliff at its backside, he tried to use a wave of earth to knock it back while it tore through the emerald coils that restricted it, but it wasn't strong enough. There was little else he could do aside from restrain the creature the best he could. He focused all of his efforts on tightening the bindings that held it back.

Just then, a faint clattering rang through his ears. He looked down and there, by his bare, ashen foot, was a sword: Faith's sword. The moonlight kissed the length of its oil coated steel. Oomphga took it into his grasp and held it with resolve.

Glancing up from the weapon, Oomphga's eyes fell upon Eladda, standing in front of Faith defensively as she used Eladda's spear to stand. Her sharpened features reflected her resilience to aid her enemy, but they were all equally as vulnerable here. Even if it was everyone out for themselves, Death wouldn't have stopped after one morsel when more sat before it on a silver plate.

Eladda confidently twirled Mr. Swiftclaw's hemogem spear in her paws as Oomphga, with a snap of his fingers, ignited Faith's sword with fire that danced to life. However, with both of his hands occupied fiddling with his newly acquired weapon, the terrain began losing its hold on the dreadwalker. It thrashed its limbs, but just before it got free, Eladda's spear flew from Faith's fingertips into Death's skull. Somehow, it lodged itself through the eyes on either side of its head, leaving it completely blind by the time it was freed.

Nodding to Oomphga, Eladda seized the opportunity and ran towards the dreadwalker, Oomphga following her lead. Letting out a thunderous cry, she sunk the hemogem into the beast's thigh, while Oomphga buried Faith's sword into the molting fuzz just above its cloven hooves. It kicked its leg out towards Oomphga of which he narrowly dodged. On the other side, it brought down its claws onto

Eladda, but she held out her spear above herself. The crescent blades nearly brushed against her forehead, but Oomphga rushed around to the dreadwalker's frontside and shot a wave of fire out from his blade. It hit the monster's arm, causing it to yank its hand away from Eladda.

She joined Oomphga at the front and gave him an affirmative nod. Then, like an executioner bringing down swift justice, Oomphga plunged the sword into the ground where he stood. The cracks in the soil erupted alongside the flame and sent the disoriented dreadwalker tumbling off the edge.

A few seconds later, a sickening *splat* echoed, along with snapping and crunching.

Faith stumbled over to Eladda and Oomphga.

"Is it-?"

"Yes..." Oomphga huffed. "It is..."

Taking one last shaky breath of fresh air, Oomphga extinguished the fire and handed Faith back her scorched sword. Silence met the battlefield, bringing relief and life's value along with it.

"We should..." Eladda sniffled. "We should get you back to your family...huh?"

"Oomphga...thinks he would like that-"

Chapter 25:
Worth Its Weight in Suffering

EVERYTHING FELT OFF after Mr. Swiftclaw's passing. With the dreadwalker nothing more than a stain on the minds of those who bore witness to its feast, a peaceful funeral was held in the darkened woods of Bristlethorn. Being the heir to her family's authority, all eyes rested upon Eladda, yet despite all of the attention, she spoke not a word about it. With the mutilated remains of Mr. Swiftclaw - the bearfolk's current commander - buried under layers of soil, they turned to Eladda for answers. Even though she was a young girl, she still held a level of maturity and authority that even Oomphga couldn't oppose now. Under her guidance (accompanied by Faith and her wisdom), Oomphga and his family arrived safely at their destination: the old cottage where the first bearfolk and half-giant couple lived in harmony.

Without complaint, Mama Vergaia began unpacking her and Oomphga's things from the carriage. She didn't seem to mind the change in house. Neither would Oomphga, however, imagining this accursed place as his new forever home wasn't easy considering the history the land had and reputation it continued to obtain. While Oomphga aided his mother in unloading the carriage, Papa Sergei spoke with the bearfolk. By the sounds of it, he was only working out more moving technicalities with the other adults.

After Oomphga had finished helping his mother unload all of her things into the house, she proceeded to help him carry his belongings to the abandoned bedroom upstairs next to the nursery.

"Look at that, Oomphga. Your own room. No more shared bedroom. No more attic. Just imagine all of your things in one space," said Vergaia.

Oomphga cracked a smile at the thought. He placed down his chest of things at the foot of his new bed and looked everything over. The room was much bigger than the attic, perfect for a growing boy such as himself. Admiring the builder's craftsmanship, he traced his fingertips along every piece of furniture he now had to his name. A dresser big enough to fit far more than three changes of clothing, a desk to sit and craft to his heart's content, and a bookshelf to display all of his work. His plants, his journals, everything he had ever created would fit perfectly here.

Papa Sergei hesitantly approached the doorway where his wife stood and smiled upon his son, eyes glinting with a cruel mixture of love and sorrow.

"Little Oomphga, I need to ask a favor of you before you get too comfortable," said Papa.

Oomphga approached and stood at the ready, still smiling all the while. "Yes, Papa Sergei?"

"I need you to give something to Eladda for me."

"W-why can't you give it to her yourself, Papa? She's still outside, isn't she?"

"Yes, well…you see…I am not good with handling people's feelings during such hard times, and you are very VERY good. Besides, I believe she's more likely to listen to you than she is me."

Oomphga doubted his father's words, but reluctantly nodded in agreement. "Alright. He'll do it."

He dug his paw into his coat pocket and carefully unveiled a glistening gemstone about the size of his thumb. Then, he placed it into Oomphga's hand allowing him to examine it closer.

"A moon opal! What was Papa Sergei doing with this in his pockets?"

All attention fell onto Papa Sergei, who uncomfortably rolled his arms and adjusted his stance.

"It was a gift. A long, long time ago - after moving away from Old Country and after losing my arm to the leviathan, I came here to the Nature Faction to settle down and live my life, but before becoming the Papa Sergei you know now, I was...not a great guy. Quite the troublemaker, as a matter of fact, and the one person that got me out of trouble most of the time, was Artyom. Artyom Swiftclaw. He was a nice guy! Loved his gemstones! Never usually parted with them, but...one day, he did.

He gave me his favorite gemstone of all time, this moon opal.

At first, I had thought something was wrong, but turns out, it was merely a thank you gift after he had gotten married!" Sergei let out a jovial laugh that faded away in seconds. "But...considering all that has happened and all that he had lost - all that Eladda had lost - I think it's only fair that she holds onto such a beautiful reminder of her papa. Besides, if Papa Sergei were to pass away, he would want Oomphga to-"

Oomphga swiftly tucked away the stone and covered his ears. He never liked hearing his Papa Sergei talk about such things. Even if it were possible that it happened tomorrow or the next day or the next week, he denied the reality with every fiber of his being. Why entertain the thought, especially when all was just about to get better for the family? They were free from oppression, free from the threats of execution.

Everything is going to be just fine, Oomphga convinced himself. *No more bad stuff from now on.*

A bit forcefully, Vergaia pulled Oomphga's cupped hands from his head.

"Oomphga, show a bit more respect to your father when he's talking to you," Vergaia noted sternly.

"Please. Please, no more. No more talking about death," Oomphga whined back. "It's done. We're safe. We can start over together..! We can finally be a happy, NORMAL family, and that's all that matters!"

Papa Sergei walked up to his son and brushed back his long, brown hair and pulled him in for a loving embrace.

"Oh...it's okay, Oomphga. You are right. I'm sorry if I made you feel like - you know - the world was coming to an end, but..."

"War," Vergaia interrupted. "It's still happening and will still happen for who knows how long."

"But..!" Sergei swiftly added, "we will still be here. For you, for each other, we will stick together from now on. I promise, Oomphga."

"Tell him it'll be okay, Papa..." Oomphga muttered, eager to dismiss the shuddering in the back of his throat.

"We will just have to-"

"Please!" Oomphga wailed. Suddenly, the kid – no longer really a kid - burst into tears. He clutched onto his father's shirt tightly, the hesitation and skepticism Papa Sergei presented pulling at his heartstrings until his chest was on the verge of exploding. Oomphga craved an answer, one that would reassure him. All he wanted was to be told that nothing else would go wrong; that no one else would have to die because of Oomphga's good intentions.

But he didn't respond. Papa Sergei was an honest man. He would beat around the bush, but he always told the truth. Him and Vergaia both, and the fact that they couldn't dismiss Oomphga's fears made him frightened all the more.

Taking great care, Sergei drew himself back and looked deep into Oomphga's sparkling, russet eyes.

"Now, remember...I am entrusting you with giving this rock to-"

"Gemstone," Oomphga quietly corrected, shuddering as he spoke.

"-gemstone to Eladda. Do you think you can do that?"

Oomphga nodded and pushed past his parents, rushing ahead to complete his task so he could finally drop his duties and responsibilities to be young again for once in a long time. Hand on the front door, he paused to catch his breath and steady his whimpering. If no one else would console him, then he had no choice but to console himself.

Pressing against the door, there was little more that he could do than silence his cries with forcible words of reassurance. However, it became more difficult to ease his anxieties while listening to his friends conversing and gossiping amongst one another a few steps away from the house.

"Eladda, you know it's alright to grieve," Faith said with deep sincerity lingering in her cadence. *"No one is expecting you to be heartless and unfeeling. We'd all be more than understanding if you needed a moment to cry. If anything, it'd be very noble and honorable of you to drop your guard as much as it'd be wise of you to listen to your emotions, not self-set expectation. Not only are you losing a father, but you are losing a friend, twice in the same day."*

"I'm not sad, Faith, and I don't need to cry. Not anymore," Eladda spit back, *"I've shed enough tears over the course of my life. For my older siblings, for my mother, now, for my father. I have nothing left for a backstabbing, two-timer! Why, if I were any wiser, I'd wish my mother took him down with her all those years ago when she confronted that…that Chief Mortium and tried to avenge my brother, Silas!"*

Oomphga drew back. All too suddenly, his senses flung him into the past to that fateful day when the bearfolk's unyielding flames of vengeance engulfed the mountains, when carefree lives of all races and creatures present that day, were stolen of their prosperous futures, and when Oomphga first felt the anguish of clinging onto innocence beyond saving. Born with a heart open to the pain and sorrows of his bearfolk and half-giant kin, Oomphga had experienced all their anguish and turned it into a glistening beacon of hope for a better future for everyone, but now that he was an exile…

Gah! What's the point in offering aid to his people when they don't even want it? Who would want to keep fighting for barbarians blinded by their own selfish hatred for every living thing that opposes them?! TO THE NINE HELS WITH THEM!!!

Oomphga looked upon his body. His feet were battered, his legs and arms were bruised, and his chest bore dozens of scars new and old. He took a beating fiercer than any game of ramball his cousin made him endure. He experienced heartache more crippling than all of the times Eladda had ever shut Oomphga down from talking about the things he loved, and yet, even despite all of the abuse he endured, not once could he truly hate the people he grew to love and the strangers he longed to know.

Through tears, Oomphga looked down at the moon opal in his clutches. He gently pressed it against his lips and bowed his head submissively to the heavens.

"Maiden of Misfortune, please spare Oomphga's friends from further torment. If you must, Oomphga will endure their burdens on their behalf, but…please…grant them peace, even if only for a while." He paused, waiting patiently for some kind of feeling in his chest that his words were received, and his prayer was answered, but not a single stirring sensation met with him. "If there is anything he could do to save his people…please, give Oomphga a sign. An obvious one, preferably. He's…not very good at decoding subtle hints or picking up on small clues…"

The warmth of his new home enveloped him. Despite the silence, he could hear the clashing of steel, wood crackling under immense pressure, fire roaring louder than its victims cries for mercy, but then, a cool breeze swept across his skin, making way for a snowy dreamscape created out of his own, childish imagination.

○ ══════ ○ ○ ✦ ○ ○ ══════ ○

Wide, open fields - stretching as far as the eye could see and covered in blankets of white - were laid out before him. Soft, hazy lights flickered in the distance, beckoning for Oomphga to follow. Before taking a singular step forward, he looked to his sides. His great grandfather's greataxe lie unattended to his right and the quarterstaff he chose as an extension of his magic lie to his left. Dexterously, and with ease, he took both into his grasp and began his journey towards the light.

The winds whispered echoes of the past, reminding Oomphga of every precious word ever said to him, but he remained unphased, determined to reach his destination of greater interest. Even the animal spirits that inhabited this plane of visions seemed entranced by the soothing glow on the horizon. Prancing, leaping, slithering, or crawling, the spectral entities traversed the rolling hills with him.

Eventually, they all met up together at the base of a hill, and resting at the top was the familiar cottage of his dreams' own design. Despite the steep ascent, Oomphga clambered up the rise, using his great grandfather's greataxe and quarterstaff as tools to steady himself. Then, when he had finally made it, he stopped to take in the joy emanating off of the house.

Its cozy interior called to him. Tracing his hands along the oaken walls reminded him of those firm embraces from Papa Sergei and Mama Vergaia; their muscles and bulkier figures always made him feel safe; and the soft hum of music inside bolstered his anticipation for the autumn festival. It was only a week or two, and Oomphga was more than excited to see Marigold again.

She made him really happy.

I love her. Gods, do I love her.

Working up the courage, Oomphga dared himself to look inside. He strode up to one of the windows, and there it was: paradise. Plants littered the quaint, country-style house, a golden retriever lay on a well-cushioned dog bed by a bookshelf standing five shelves tall, and sitting on the couch was an older gentleman (mayhaps a gardener, farmer, or florist of sorts judging by the way he dressed) with long, waves of chestnut locks streaming down his backside and over his shoulders. No doubt about it: this was the same person Oomphga saw in the stained-glass painting up in the mountains.

If what Marigold says is true, then that's-!

"Oomphga, sweetie, I have something for you~"

Oomphga's heart skipped a beat. He recognized that mellow voice from anywhere, and so it was.

An older Marigold sat down next to this older interpretation of Oomphga and immediately began brushing back strands of his hair, placing them delicately over the bear ear protruding from the top of his head. After a moment of fiddling and fidgeting with his hair, she wove the stem of a pink camellia into the mix, so it sat perfectly.

"Camellias are Oomphga's favorite~" both Oomphga's younger and older self-remarked.

Reluctantly, the thirteen-year-old druid turned away from the window and looked out over the snowy fields, surprised to see the ghostly faces of everyone he's ever met, and ever seen, standing at the base of the hill. Some people (like Papa Sergei) tried to climb up the steep incline, but their efforts were in vain.

"Rest, my child," a womanly voice hummed - the very same that echoed in Oomphga's eardrums many years ago when his magic was first gifted to him. *"You have done enough. Step away, rest your muscles, and return again."*

"Step away? You mean..." Oomphga could hardly utter a word. "No. No, he can't leave! Not yet! He can still stop the war! He can fix this! If he keeps trying to politely reach out - if he keeps making an effort to be better - then everything will be-!"

Thunder boomed; lightning crashed down close to him, sending a jolt of fear through his limbs and into his core. Despite all of this being nothing more than a vision in his mind's eye, the shock felt real.

"Your acts of good-will and pacifism will only get you so far. Evil shows no mercy, and you've barely the defense to protect yourself. You must leave this place you call home. You must rest your weary muscles. You must return a new druid, 'lest you wish to die young, at the claws of Marcuth - or worse, your own people - before you get the chance to bring about the **change** *you so desire."*

Oomphga thought back to Aymus, Omen, and Martin. They were all fairly young adults, and yet two of the three broke under the pressure and died before they got to see the world recover from years of death and endless suffering. Oomphga did not want to end up like them.

"So…you want him to run away from home? Is that what he's supposed to do?"

"Would you rather leave by your own will, or would you rather be forced out by circumstance?"

The druid looked down upon the false re-envisionments of his mother and father. To leave them after they had recently moved away from the fighting, to look them in the eyes and tell them directly that the gods told him to abandon hope, or to sneak off in the middle of the night with little more than a note made out of grief; none seemed like pleasant options. However, if this was the answer he sought, then who was he to argue with the divine, much less the Maiden of Misfortune?

"He'll…work up the courage to leave…eventually."

And there it was: the front door. At least it wasn't time to depart just yet. After all, he had a stone to deliver.

So, taking a deep breath and recollecting his thoughts, he exited the house and took a few steps out into the open, making his presence known. Eladda paused herself mid-sentence and turned to look at Oomphga.

"What do you want?" she spat.

Without batting an eye, Oomphga extended his hand and presented the moon opal to Eladda.

"What? Do you think a rock from you is going to make me feel-"

"It's not from Oomphga. It's from Papa Sergei. It belonged to your dad at one point." Oomphga froze up out of nervousness but pushed through his worries. "Apparently, he really liked gemstones. This was his favorite."

In a heartbeat, she changed her demeanor. Eyes once filled with malice were now filled with disbelief and silent mourning made known only by the tears along her lower eyelids. She hardly spoke a word as she scooped up the small gemstone into her paw. Never has anything of this size held such significance to her until now. Hearing her sniffle, and seeing her nearly drop to her knees, Oomphga couldn't help but extend his arms. Eladda crashed into his embrace and wept into the crook of his shoulder.

"I...I hate you, Oomphga. I hate you..!" Eladda whined amidst her whimpers and cries.

But like Tuthjorn, Oomphga couldn't hate her back, especially not now realizing that this may very well be the last time they'd see each other again.

Faith eased over, clearly concerned for their friend's well-being. "Is she-?"

"She'll be alright," Oomphga whispered, patting and brushing Eladda's back reassuringly. "You'll be okay, Eladda. And if you ever need someone to talk to, you'll always have Faith. Faith is a really good listener."

"Yeah," Faith affirmed, "and if you need a place to stay, you could stay with me and my family. They'd be more than happy to take you in. You know Mama already sees you as family."

Eladda made a few noises that sounded like hums of agreement, but still couldn't quite collect herself. It took a few reassuring words and faint humming, but eventually, she settled down enough to pull herself away, wipe her eyes, and stifle her whimpers.

"Come on, Eladda. Let's get you to my place. You look like you could use some food and rest."

Faith gently put a paw on Eladda's arm and walked back towards the other bearfolk, but before leaving, Eladda stopped to look over her shoulder at Oomphga. She parted her lips as if she had something to say, but she let out a tired sigh and continued to walk alongside her best friend in silence.

Satisfied himself that he managed to do one last generous thing for his bearfolk friends, Oomphga turned tail and went back inside the house. He didn't mind his parents who were conversing with one another in the kitchen. He didn't mind the unfamiliar and unwelcoming decor. He was tired, and as such, longed for his cushy bed and a long night of rest.

Chapter 26:
Night of the Autumn Festival

THERE WERE A LOT OF LEGALITIES involved with moving homes due to our somewhat political affairs. Not only did Papa Sergei have to sell his old, hand-made cottage, but he also got a lot of visits from people on behalf of the N.F.C. Representatives asked him and Mama questions, they offered assistance with the move where they could, and they even promised special protection to avoid further conflicts between the two warring races, of which Papa Sergei politely accepted.

While Papa Sergei and Mama Vergaia worked out the specifics of our societal future, Oomphga grew more and more excited for the Autumn Festival swiftly approaching. To think, a few weeks ago, the event was first brought up to him, and now, it was only a few minutes away.

Oomphga burrowed through his chest of belongings, only finding a few pairs of pants and oversized sweaters to his name. He didn't own anything particularly nice or fancy for such a festive event aside from the medallion his mother gave him and the white bedsheets he could fold like a toga…if he knew how.

So, helplessly, he fidgeted and flailed around, creating something that resembled a nicer than average appearance. With his newly-made toga wrapped to cover most of his chest (an over the shoulder wrap was the only thing he could figure out on his own), brown, baggy pants fluffed to perfection, and his everyday essentials hanging from the rope wrapped around his waist (i.e. his handaxe, handmade journal, ram horn, and pouch of herbs), Oomphga deemed himself fitted and well-prepared for the festival. He eagerly raced out of his room, and swiftly joined his parents in the living room where they sat discussing the future amongst themselves. However, they paused the moment Oomphga made his appearance.

"Well, look at you, my little Oomphga!" Papa Sergei cheered, "You look like a little gentleman! And you don't smell strongly of salty sea water! …That is not a sarcastic remark!"

"What your father means to say is that you look very nice," Mama Vergaia clarified.

"Thanks, Papa. Thanks, Mama," Oomphga replied, nodding to each of them respectfully. "Say, you wouldn't happen to have something to cover - you know," he gestured to the right half of his face, "would you?"

"Oomphga, my son, what are you talking about? Your eye? Why would you ever want to cover your eye? It's one of your most amazing features!"

"Yeah, but…" Oomphga hushed himself.

It was hard to explain, but there was something about his eye that didn't feel normal. Granted, nothing about him could be considered "normal", but there was still this nagging voice in his subconsciousness, a desperate yearning sensation that wanted to look as much like everyone else as possible, and no one else that Oomphga had ever met had fur consuming their eyelids stretching from their brow to their cheek.

Besides, seeing himself years into the future as this muscular, burly behemoth with natural, long, flowing hair and a cool eyepatch was – well – cool. If Oomphga hadn't a slight inkling of his own future, he would've thought that he became a pirate with enough bounties to last an eternity or a retired veteran far beyond Death's grasp. In short, Oomphga wanted to look like *that*.

Mama Vergaia took notice of Oomphga's shyness and spoke out on his behalf. "I'm sure he merely wants to look his best for this particular event. That's all it is."

"Very well," Papa Sergei sighed, "I might have an old eyepatch lying around with all of my sailing things. Would that-?"

"Yes!" Oomphga eagerly chimed. "Yes, that would work perfectly! Thank you, Papa!"

Reluctantly, Papa Sergei pulled himself up out of his chair's warm embrace and lumbered over to his and Mama Vergaia's shared bedroom. Oomphga followed close behind and peaked his head inside. To Oomphga's surprise, it wasn't much different from Papa's old room when he still lived blissfully ignorant and alone in his cottage, aside from the accompaniment of his mother's belongings intertwined with his. Before he managed to get a good look inside, Papa Sergei pulled forth an eyepatch from one of his dresser drawers and handed it over to Oomphga. Eagerly, his fingers started toiling away at the eye patch, adjusting and shifting it to fit perfectly. Resting comfortably across the right half of his face, he turned to his parents and smiled, but neither truly seemed too thrilled.

Was the eyepatch too much? Were his makeshift robes paired with the medallion his mama gave him too flashy? Were his baggy, tan pants not flashy enough? Admittedly, looking over himself a second time, it did seem odd to mix comfort and style in such a bizarre way, but if anything, mixing the style of his cultures in a way that felt as formal as it did casual felt right.

"You look great, son," Sergei hummed.

"Whatever makes you the happiest, Oomphga. This is something you've been looking forward to for the past month or so after all, and after all that we've been through, you deserve to have fun," Vergaia added sweetly.

"Have fun, at your festival thingy!"

Sparing not a moment more, Oomphga snatched his quarterstaff propped against the wall, waved "good-bye", and bolted out the door.

○ ════════ ○ ○ ✿ ○ ○ ════════ ○

He slid down the steep incline leading up to the house and broke into an eager sprint down the winding trail, his body feeling lighter than air all the while. As fast as he ran, he hadn't realized that he caught the attention of the local wildlife until he began hearing birds whispering to one another on branches above and rabbits giggling amongst themselves in the bushes and burrows that lay low. A few daring deer even ran up alongside Oomphga, staring at the half-breed with a deep curiosity, but all he could do at the time in response was flash the inquisitive creatures a jovial smile that grew larger as he drew closer to the familiar city of Endinerose.

As he neared the edges of Bristlethorn Forest, the sounds of music, upbeat and lively, became more audible the closer Oomphga got. Hurdy gurdies, viols, and panpipes all played in perfect unity. Atop a hill overlooking the rolling fields, Oomphga paused to take in the splashes of color on the horizon. The animals around him mirrored his astonishment, their eyes sparkling as they, too, gazed at the spectacle before them.

"The Autumn Festival," he cheerily huffed aloud to himself, looking to either side at the critters crowded by his sides. "Oomphga can't bring all of you into the town with him, but if anyone would like to join him, they're more than welcome! Just gotta promise to be on your best behavior!"

Butterflies, moths, beetles, and ladybugs swarmed his hair by the dozens, field mice and squirrels scurried into his pants pockets, and birds perched themselves onto his shoulders. An owl sat atop his quarterstaff. Their closeness to him filled him with a sense of belonging in nature.

"Anyone else~?"

One last stoat climbed up Oomphga's backside and stole a spot curled around his neck. The birds, understandably, kept their distance, but the stoat didn't disturb them. Oomphga remained steady and still, awaiting any other critters to join the coup, but none seemed eager to walk among the land of two-legs.

"Alrighty! Be good, everyone!" Giving an affirmative nod, Oomphga carefully approached the city, a couple of stray birds guiding his way in the skies above.

People of all races gathered together in the town square to dance harmoniously to the rhythm of a different kind of drum than the ones Oomphga grew most accustomed to. They drank in excess and dined like kings, consuming the festival's greatest bounties, but this was a commoner's world where they could make as much of a beautiful fool out of themselves as they wished. Every wandering passerby, every street vendor, and every musician scattered up and down the streets was a smiling, gleeful soul that welcomed Oomphga into the charming atmosphere like sirens luring a sailor into the watery depths, but Oomphga tossed aside his caution long before his arrival. He came to indulge; he came to make merry. And make merry he did.

Not long after becoming acquainted with a few of the townsfolk, a little bearfolk girl approached him shyly.

"You…are a half-giant, but…you have ears like mine," her lilted voice hardly carried over all of the chatter, but Oomphga could still hear her. *Bless his sense of hearing.* "Who are you?"

Oomphga stood still as stone, his mind drawing a blank on the simplest of questions, but he could tell there was something special about this girl. She was the first child to ever approach him in a world that only repelled the outcast. Knowing well that it'd be rude to ignore her question, Oomphga carefully dropped down onto one knee and smiled.

"My name is Oomphga and…Oomphga is the druid," he replied, voice as soft as hers. "Nice to meet you!"

Her irises expanded, taking in the stars of an autumn night. She let out an excited gasp as if she had found something never before seen in a billion lifetimes.

"So, that's why all the little animals are on you! Are they friendly?"

"Yes, very!" Oomphga laughed.

"Can I pet one of the birdies?"

Oomphga turned to a small, song sparrow sitting on the edge of his shoulder. "May the little girl pet you?"

It sang its approval and hopped closer to the girl. She was very gentle with the bird, brushing her index and middle finger across its tiny head.

"Mr. Druid don't tell anybody, but…I have a friend up in the mountains. She's a half-giant girl about my age. Her name is Calla. Can you…make sure she stays safe until the war is over?"

Oomphga had never heard of this half-giant girl, but if she was anything like the young one standing before him, he knew he'd be able to recognize her in a heartbeat…if he could ever return to his tribe.

Letting out a sigh, he looked to the High Peak Mountains and opened up his heart to the comforting memories of his half-giant brethren. Though they were brutish in nature, they cared for their kin immensely. If not for Uncle Mortium, Seirah, Tuthjorn, and his Mama Vergaia, Oomphga would not've been strong enough to endure the weight of his position bearing down on him. One day, he wished to speak with them and his bearfolk family once again. With hope as his witness, he would unify them under the gods. They'd put war to rest and experience peace.

Oomphga turned his attention back to the little girl and smiled. "He will do his best."

She waddled closer and wrapped her little arms around him. "I believe in you, Mr. Druid."

She then swiftly drew away and ran back to her bearfolk family, already telling them all about her brief encounter with Oomphga. Listening to her ramble on about how friendly and sweet he was, made Oomphga experience a pleasant nausea that sent him reeling and squealing, but there was something else hidden amongst the crowd of people ahead of him that heightened this elation: Marigold.

It was easy to find her. She rode through town on the back of Bear Friend, Omen by her side, and Small Bear held up high. She wore a crown of marigolds atop her head with the crystium catastrophe being the highlight, and for her attire, she dressed in a long, flowing blue and black gown with ornamental golden swirls coiled around the sleeves, neck, and base. Somehow, despite all this eloquent decorum, she still bore a charming ruggedness with the way she tied back her medium-length, black hair into a messy bun, and fashioned her ebony, leather quiver with her longbow attached across her back.

"Fuzzy!" Small Bear squeaked, squirming excitedly in Marigold's hands.

Marigold looked towards Oomphga and rode through the crowd of people separating the young lovers.

"Oomphga!" Marigold cheered, lowering Small Bear into her lap. "You made it, and I see you brought the entire forest with you~"

"Oh, this~?" Oomphga gestured to himself and chuckled, "Naaah, this is probably more like…a fifth of the forest? Maybe less, though he doubts the rabbits were very active this year with the dreadwalker still on the prowl. At least, until recently."

Her jaw dropped and she cracked the faintest hint of a grin. "No-! You-! Did you-?!"

"He did, actually. …Marigold is talking about slaying the dreadwalker, right?"

She nodded. "Well, I feel like that's something worth celebrating, isn't it?"

"Uh…is it?"

Oomphga looked between Marigold and Omen. And there stood Eladda and Faith. Poor Faith had beeswax filling her ears. Under her own volition, she probably wouldn't have come to such a noisy event, but Eladda wanted her company. Oomphga can remember the time when she was just as excited as he was, and she was eager for Faith to be by her side. Although, looking at them now, neither of them seemed very happy aside from the brief glimpses Oomphga caught where they smiled at one another and ruffled each other's fur.

"You're still alive," Omen intruded, his words cutting between Oomphga's sight and hearing. "That's a good thing, Oomphga."

"Huh! So, he is! Oomphga supposes it is worth celebrating! Well, that and the fact that he-" Oomphga froze up, remembering his own reason for his eagerness to come to the autumn festival. His eyes locked onto Marigold's. His face lit up; a rush of warmth spread through his body. "He's…getting pretty hot. Must be from…all the…lanterns lit up around the city~"

"Maybe. Oh! There's going to be a big dance in the open fields outside of town! Would you like to check it out later?"

"Absolutely! Anything for Marigold~"

Omen took a deep breath. Eyes narrow, he turned to Oomphga and bobbed his head respectfully.

"Young druid, there are tea samples a little ways in. Why don't you and I go try some before you scurry off with your girl-friend, hm?"

Every animal coiled around his body turned to look at his flustered expression. "Ooooh~"

"Shh..!" Oomphga hushed them. "Yes, yes! He'd be delighted to join, Omen! Could…Marigold wait for Oomphga here?"

"I've been waiting for you here all evening, haven't I?" She giggled cutely. "What's a little while longer?"

Suddenly, Omen began guiding Oomphga along, separating him from the only thing he could think about without hesitation. His focus remained fixated on the brief journey ahead to a small wooden stall where a silver tray where a plethora of tea samples sat before him.

"I recommend you try the chamomile," Omen abruptly suggested, handing the small cup to Oomphga daintily.

"Oh, thank you." Desperate to not seem rude, he took a sip. His discomfort rose quicker and quicker by the second but faded seconds after he took his swig of this herbal remedy. "So...what does Omen wish to speak with Oomphga about? If it has anything to do with what happened in the mountains-"

"Oomphga," Omen quietly interjected and discretely, dragged the druid to a secluded alley nearby to speak in all the more privacy, "you know Marcuth will stop at nothing to see your head on a silver platter, correct?"

"Oomphga knows. He, unfortunately, knows all too well. Him and...everyone else."

A chill ran down his spine at the mere mention of the cloaked devil. Despite being who knows how far away from him, he could still feel his steely, cold gaze and a ghost of his grip on Oomphga's neck.

"Well, what you don't know is...I can't keep being your guardian raven. Not physically. The Maiden of Misfortune has given me strict instructions to guide you, not to baby you on your endeavors."

"So...is that why Omen left after Oomphga spared Marcuth?"

"I left at that moment to keep myself from interfering with you and your destiny. The divine insists upon it, upon you becoming a druid worthy of stopping Marcuth and his plans for a second calamity."

"Why Oomphga? Why only him?"

"It's not only you. I promise. If anything, the stained-glass mural at the head of the church should've told you that."

That's right. The mural illustrated three others: a devil, a dragonfolk, and a frog-man of some sort...

"Look," Omen continued, "I only wish to tell you this before I depart: no matter what happens, you will not be alone. For as long as you live, someone as nice as you will always have someone at your side. Whether it's me or your family or Marigold or the gods, there will be someone to look out for you. Everything will be alright as long as you stay vigilant and stay wise. Understood?"

Oomphga looked to the stoat around his neck that turned its head towards him. Content, he brushed his half-giant finger between his ears, cracking a hint of a smile.

"Understood."

"Now, you go enjoy your happiness. Treasure it for as long as the moment lasts because that moment may be brief."

With a dash of his arm and the unfurling of feathered wings, he took to the heavens above and disappeared into the darkness. Then, finding himself left to his own devices, Oomphga giddily ran back to Marigold and hopped up onto Bear Friend's back behind her.

"Alright! Which way is the dance~?"

Chapter 27:
Dance of the Exile

OUTSIDE THE CITY'S WALLS were lanterns and ribbons draped across the trees, illuminating the stage for energetic intimacies. Couples of all types skipped and frolicked under the moon, kicking up their heels and clapping along to joyous tunes played by a group of four women: a satyr, an elf, an orc, and a foxfolk. They had their own makeshift stage under a canopy woven of silk and leaves entwined. As eloquently as he could, Oomphga hopped off of Bear Friend's back with his quarterstaff and extended a hand for Marigold to take.

"My, my. It's hardly been a few days and you've grown into quite the gentleman~"

"Yeah! It's...been a process!" Oomphga stated proudly.

Together, they found the perfect spot in the grass to rest their belongings. The animals hopped, crawled, and flew off of him, so they could watch over the two love birds without the excessive motion blurring their vision.

"Now, you be a good druid," the stoat purred. "We'll be keeping sharp eyes on you two."

Stifling a laugh, Oomphga laid down his quarterstaff and handaxe next to Marigold's bow. Then, he politely escorted her to the center of the emerald fields.

"You know, despite not knowing how to dance, I'm really excited to try - for the first time - with you," Marigold silently confessed.

"You...you don't?" Oomphga asked. "But...Marigold is so wise and so graceful! Just the way she moves, it's like-"

"It's that hard to believe, huh~?"

"Oomphga-" he paused, thinking back to his dream. Yes, it was only a dream, but his dreams always felt genuine. If anything, these dreams of his were becoming messages or visions from the gods, so why? Why would the dream - of him learning how to dance - be disingenuous? Unless...

"Oomphga could teach Marigold how to dance," he whispered shyly, his fingers coiling around hers as he spoke.

"You? Whenever did you learn?"

"Well, he never said he was a master at it!" Oomphga laughed. "He knows the basics. As funny as it sounds, Marigold taught him...in a dream."

"So, that's why you thought I could dance~"

"Just follow his movements closely, and if you mess up, don't worry! Oomphga will make sure you don't fall."

One hand in her own and another resting across her back underneath her shoulder blade, Oomphga leisurely began taking the first steps of the pattern he vaguely recalled. Both he and Marigold stared down at their feet, watching them move in tandem with one another. The music started off slow, allowing the two a chance to grow accustomed to the cooperative movements they made.

"Miss Marigold?"

"Yes, Oomphga?"

"While you and...I...are dancing, Oomphga would like to teach you a bit of magic, if she'd be interested."

"*While* we are dancing?"

"Yes!"

"And...how do you intend to do that?"

"Simple. Relax yourself and let yourself soar! It'll happen on its own. You'll see~!"

The rhythm picked up and so did their tango.

"1, 2, 3…1, 2, 3…!" Oomphga quietly counted aloud, bouncing a little as he moved until he was practically skipping along to the beat, still holding onto Marigold.

"What's the counting for~?!" Marigold laughed.

"To attune to the rhythm!"

Merrily, the two youngsters frolicked in the fields, giggling and gazing upon the sparks of light in each other's eyes. Lost in the melody, their minds and souls weaved into one. Blades of grass brushed across their ankles, their bodies cut through the wind, and the magic buried deep within them surfaced as a link between them and the earth at their feet. With each step and each stride another flower blossomed, leaving behind a floral trail of beauty wherever they went.

By now, the two had completely lost themselves in the magic. A kick of their feet, a swing of their arms - every gesture a glorious reflection of their freedom, their exhilaration, their love for the dance. As the song reached its climax, they broke from each other's grasp to be their own individual, making up whatever gesture came naturally to them. Never too far did they stray before, at last, reuniting in a passionate embrace on the strike of the last note.

Their breaths were heavy, their arms and legs ached, and all the while, they stared longingly into each other's eyes. Then and there, in that moment, they had everything they ever could've wanted right there in front of them.

"Marigold," Oomphga uttered.

"Oomphga," Marigold giggled in reply.

"M-may he-?"

"He may~"

Face heated and glowing, he leaned in near to his grinning girlfriend and planted a heartfelt kiss upon Marigold's lips and drew back. Warm, exhausted, flustered, and madly in love, he cracked the biggest smile his face would allow.

"Oomphga- He- If Marigold would- If she's tired, he'd be more than willing to-"

Marigold fluently pulled Oomphga over to their things and sat down. Happily, Oomphga sat down next to her and took in the view of the fields, once barren, but now covered with a wide array of autumn flowers from daisies to alyssums. Marigold hadn't realized until now, but when she did, her face lit up.

"Did we…make that happen?"

"We did. Marigold and Oomphga both used their magic and made the flowers grow~" Oomphga sighed dreamily. "So, how…did that feel, casting magic for the first time?"

"Easy. A bit too easy, if you ask me. How can I be so sure that you didn't do it all by yourself and are saying 'we did it' to make me feel better?"

"Well, to make flowers grow, you just gotta…think happy thoughts, and brush the ground where you want them to sprout."

Oomphga guided Marigold's hand to the grass and the moment it touched the surface, a daisy sprouted. Marigold's face blossomed with awe until it was all rosy. It was cute, watching her light up with happiness in Oomphga's company. If anyone else could see her face that night, they'd find that no firefly could compare themselves to the glow of her cheeks; no branch could bend to the shape of her smile.

Slowly, Oomphga drew his hand away and let Marigold bashfully run her fingers through the grass and over the dirt around her, leaving a trail of small flowers.

"See?! Marigold did it all by herself~"

*"Well, I **am** still thinking about-"*

"Hm?"

"Nothing..!" She curled up into a ball and threw herself against Oomphga's side. Feeling her hair tickle his arm and her elbow bat his side forced a playful laugh out of him.

"Aww! Marigold is really cute when she's shy~!"

"And you're just as adorable whenever you're all sunshine-y and cheery and sweet and…gah! All the time! You're cute all the time!"

Suddenly, Oomphga snatched Marigold into his arms and held her close, letting her hide her face in his chest and her figure in his arms. Resting his head on top of hers, the druid couldn't have been more comfortable enveloped in the aura of her presence. Together with their bodies intertwined, they both lounged in the fields, taking in the colorful, celebratory atmosphere.

"Oomphga…I…" Marigold murmured, drawing Oomphga's attention to her faltering expression. "I'm glad I traveled so far to find you."

"You know…Marigold never told Oomphga why she needed to find the crystium catastrophe so bad. O-of course, he didn't want to pry."

He couldn't deny he still wished to know the answer to his burning question. He wanted to know all he could about Marigold. His inquisitive mind yearned to understand the girl he found his feelings completely helpless to.

Marigold shyly brushed her fingers across the petals of the crystium catastrophe nestled amongst the other golden flowers in her flower crown.

"But, no matter what the reason, Oomphga would've been more than happy to help her find it~!"

"Thank you, but…" Marigold trailed off, her voice fading into the music. "It feels wrong. After we parted ways in the mountains, I'll admit…I got selfish. For a moment, with the crystium catastrophe - the miracle of Hope in my hands - I almost debated on going back to my homeland to mend what was broken right then and there. I felt awful. I…I couldn't just leave you! I didn't want to feel like…like a…bad person for wanting-"

She practically choked back her woes, words sputtering out of her control. Her thoughts were left to the mercy of Oomphga's insight, and he could read it in her eyes. He could recognize the agony resonating in her whimpers. Glancing over her silver skin, that's when the dark reality of Marigold's history came to light.

Gently, Oomphga brushed his fingers along the scars she so expertly kept concealed for so long. They stretched across the edges of her shoulders and down her back, a place that Oomphga dare not reach for without Marigold's consent.

"Marigold…needs to put Marigold first," Oomphga whispered.

"I don't just want to survive anymore, Oomphga. I want to live..-!"

"Well, Oomphga's no…miracle worker, but he'll do his best to help Marigold's dream come true. As long as he's around, as long as Marigold is around, they'll work something out together. …It's going to be okay~"

In his words, Marigold found the comfort she so desperately needed. She steadied her breath and melted against Oomphga, heart drifting back into a soothing rhythm, but the comfort didn't last forever…

A lone wisp, floating astray from the forest, drew Oomphga's attention to Eladda as she spoke with a familiar individual.

Marcuth..!

Though he bore the body of a bearfolk, Oomphga could see through the disguise. The way his ruby eyes shimmered with malicious intent, the stiff way he stood with his muscles clenched around where an injured wing resided, and the sharpness of his mask of expressions all revealed him too easily. From afar, he watched them, friend and foe, speak casually in the sincerest of forms to one another. Over the music, Oomphga couldn't hear a concise word of their conversation, but judging by the exaggerated gestures Marcuth made towards the mountain and Eladda's resolute grip on her spear, one could draw the assumption that trouble was on the horizon. Then, with an elegant bow and a twisted smirk, Marcuth vanished into the tree line, leaving hardly a trace of his presence.

"Oomphga?" Marigold caught Oomphga's attention by surprise with her voice being nearer than the conversation he tried to listen in on. "...If I may, I'd like to request that we make our way back to Bear Friend's den so we can enjoy ourselves more privately. How does that sound?"

"That...sounds lovely, Marigold," he anxiously chuckled in response.

Oomphga looked upon the animals surrounding him. They gazed upon him with divine judgment, curious as to his next course of action given the situation at hand.

"Oomphga, is something wrong?"

"Uh, well-" he murmured. He didn't want to ruin the moment, but all the while, gazing at his two friends hastily making their way away from the festivities, he couldn't hide the wicked truth of the matter. "He'll...tell her everything on the way to Bear Friend's den because - hoo, boy - Oomphga has *a lot* of explaining to do-"

One shared cup of chamomile later and they were off on their way, but the relaxing brew did very little to ease the nausea. As they rode back to Bear Friend's den, Oomphga fidgeted with his journal, fingers tugging and rubbing the parchment bound within. He gazed over years of work, analyzing every word he marked and every stroke of the paintbrush to illustrate the flowers and herbs he lovingly described. Before Marigold, this was his joy, and he needed every ounce he could to take his mind off of the storm on the horizon.

"You had something you wanted to tell me about?" Marigold asked, glancing back over her shoulder at Oomphga who sat behind.

"The instigator is at it again..." he spewed.

"What? What does-"

"*All these years of fighting…it all makes sense to Oomphga now.* There's this devil that's been following him. His name is Marcuth. He used to go by Martin-"

"Friend of Omen and the first druid?"

"Yes. Him."

"And he's been…following you?"

Memories of his visions aligned themselves all too well. Each one danced and intertwined into a tight-knit theory that rang true all the way to the heavens above.

"Does…Marigold believe in prophecies?"

"I believe in the *concept* of prophecies - same with destiny and same with fate - I believe things just happen and sometimes people get lucky in their predictions. Some predictions are more accurate than others, but unpredictable things happen, and they happen a lot, sometimes even out of the control of the gods…"

"Marcuth…he said that-…he said that Oomphga needed to be-" Oomphga shook his head and buried his fears deep. "When Oomphga told Omen that his dream was to unite his people, Marcuth interrupted and told him he couldn't. Now, Oomphga didn't understand a lot of adult talk between Omen and Marcuth at the time, but what he did gather was that - for some reason - Marcuth wants Oomphga gone. Something about a half-breed being responsible for unraveling his plans; plans to start a second calamity."

"A second calamity? He *wants* to trigger another cataclysmic event? Why?! I thought Martin was one of the good guys that sought to put an end to the first calamity all those years ago!"

"He was, but Oomphga thinks, after Aymus got him in trouble with the gods, and after they turned him into - well - a devil, Martin got mad at Aymus, Omen, and the gods for changing him from an angel to the one thing he despised more than anything. Now, out of spite-"

"He wishes to start another calamity."

"Exactly. The one thing Oomphga *doesn't* understand is why he needs the half-giants and bearfolk to be in this war or what he hopes to gain from their conflict…"

Both Marigold and Oomphga let out a mindful hum.

"Oh!" Marigold chimed. "You said Marcuth believed, in this prophecy, that you would be the one to keep him from starting a second calamity, right? Or…a half-breed or…something."

"Yes..?"

"What if he wanted the half-giants and bearfolk to fight one another so that, because of their conflict, *you* wouldn't be born? After all, think of everything your parents went through just so you could be here!"

"That's true! And in one vision or dream or nightmare or…whatever it was that Oomphga had, Marcuth killed a child and a baby that were part-bearfolk and part-half-giant just like Oomphga! *Why he went by a different name in his nightmare, Oomphga doesn't understand*, but regardless, since the bearfolk and half-giants were both people that put tradition and family above all else-"

"War ensued, and as long as it continues-"

"Oomphga remains the only one that matches the prophecy's description."

As all the pieces came together, a sickening horror overcame Oomphga as he realized that every move he made mattered. Every choice up until this point - to live or to die, to fight or to flee - sent a ripple through the tides of time and would carry on to a brighter or bleaker future. It was in this moment, the day before his coming of age, that it finally occurred to him the cost of his own life and the price he'd have to pay for peace.

But the nausea and jittering came to a halt soon after taking his first, deep breath in a long while. The skylight illuminated the divine presence that hung above them, and the faint wisps of the evening breeze made for loyal and supportive company. Despite the axes, spears, and bloodshed on the horizon, Oomphga reassured himself:

Whatever it takes, whatever you ask of Oomphga,…

…Miss Laniarra, Sir Neodashkus, Maiden of Misfortune,…

…he will do as he must. He is ready.

"Let's make our way towards the mountains, Marigold. There's trouble afoot," Oomphga stated.

"And what about your bear friends?"

"We'll need all the help we can get."

During their ride, Oomphga thoughtfully returned his nature journal to his side and drew forth the ram horn. Bringing it to his lips, he let the ivory ring loud and clear.

The sky, once filled with music, was now filled only with the battering of war drums, the thumping of heavy footsteps, and the clattering of steel as more than a dozen half-giant warriors gathered beneath the autumn leaves one step away from a battlefield-sized clearing with little debris aside from the occasional hemogem embedded in the soil. Slowly, Bear Friend and Small Bear crept through the edges of the field with round eyes focused on the quietest route to the center.

"Wow. I've never seen a whole pack of grey-skinned hairless before," Small Bear squeaked quietly.

"I have. Now, make sure to stay close, sweetie, and stay low. We don't want them seeing you."

Oomphga's attention darted from one end of the forest to the other, keeping a close eye out for Marcuth, the bearfolk, or any sign of movement from the half-giants. Marigold did the same, all while making sure her bow was primed and ready.

"Marigold," Oomphga whispered, pressing his palm against the back of her hand. "We're not going to hurt them. Oomphga wants to talk to them first."

"Are you sure? They don't look to be in a talking mood."

Oomphga looked upon the half-giants, assessing their chosen carefully and, with ease, he was able to spot the leader of their raid.

"Oomphga knows their general. He's Tuthjorn's older brother, Okradash. He's not a hot-headed guy and he knows Oomphga…kinda. He knows Tuthjorn at least, and he knows Tuthjorn is Oomphga's friend."

"Are you *positive* that he's still your friend?" Marigold asked. "Even after everything that happened?"

"Well-"

He **hopes** *they're still friends, although…*

He *did* wish Death upon Oomphga.

"Oomphga has to try." He dismounted from Bear Friend and began his approach, cautious and hesitant. "Wait here. Oomphga will be right back. He promises."

Chapter 28:
By the Will of the Gods

O NE SHAKY STEP AFTER ANOTHER, Oomphga could feel his body turn against him. His breathing became unsteady, his throat clenched, and his side ached with the same sharp pain he felt after taking an axe to it. The scar still remained, but nonetheless, he resumed his trek up the winding path, over fallen trees and jagged rocks that burrowed into his heels.

When he finally made it to the small band of half-giants, he froze where he stood. As much as he wished to approach them as friends, he knew very well that they saw him as no friend, but as the opposition. Mind focused on the task at hand, he stepped into their view and, immediately upon sighting, one of the half-giants - swifter than light - drew their bow and fired an arrow that nearly struck Oomphga's cheek. He threw himself behind a tree, heart pounding, veins pulsing as he clung on tightly to it.

"Hold your fire..!" the familiar voice of Okradash ordered. "We are – technically – on his family's safe grounds."

Soon after, Oomphga could sense him approaching. His bear ears twitched in response to each crunch of the leaves and sticks beneath his older cousin's feet.

"Oomphga..? What are you doing here?" Okradash questioned coolly.

"Oomphga...wishes...to request...a ceasefire," Oomphga huffed in response.

"A ceasefire? ...Then, you understand why we are here. Who told you?"

"No one! Oomphga swears! He just...noticed all on his own! That's all!"

"You're shaking. It's okay, Oomphga. You can be honest. No one here is going to hurt you. We have direct orders from Father not to. You're going to be alright as long as your stay here is brief. I cannot guarantee that those scarlet-furs won't tear you to shreds when they arrive, but-"

Those.

"Those scarlet-furs? Th-those scarlet-furs are Oomphga's friends and family just as much as you are! So, please, don't fight! It's all Oomphga asks!"

"It's a big ask coming from an exile."

Okradash brought his hand up above Oomphga's head. Oomphga held his breath, waiting for him to strike, but instead, he ruffled Oomphga's hair - bear ears and all, the same way Tuthjorn did - and took a step back towards the others.

"I'm sorry, Oomphga, but it's Father's orders."

"Wait!" Oomphga interjected suddenly. "Wh-what if...what if the druid told you not to fight?! Would Okradash listen?!"

Okradash paused, his interest piqued. He looked around at the nature that surrounded them. Surprise evaded him, but curiosity crept onto his face.

"You spoke with him?"

"Spoke with him..?" Oomphga, hand on his chest, took the deepest breath he could to steady his vocals. "Oomphga is-"

"General Okradash," one of the warriors interrupted. "They've arrived."

"I must get ready now, Oomphga."

Okradash drew away from his cousin before Oomphga could get a word in otherwise, but he refused to let a turn of the heel or a lack of eye contact interfere with his urgent request.

"Oomphga is the druid!" Oomphga blurted, following close behind.

"…You are not."

"Yes, he is! Okra- he-…You have to believe him!"

"You were the *shaman*. That's not the same thing."

"Can a shaman make flowers bloom in the harshest of conditions? Can a shaman send out waves of rock and earth from his feet? Can a shaman control the eb and weave of the wind?! Can a shaman change into an animal?!"

Oomphga stared at his hands, twitching with magical intensity fueled by the whirlpool of emotions overtaking him. If he refused himself another breath, he would've drowned in them. If he transformed into an animal now, he would be throwing away the opportunity to state his case.

"The answer is 'no'. No, they can't. …just in case you wanted to know."

"I can see why Father banished you from the mountains. You're one wild child."

"He's-…he just-…Oomphga wants peace. So do you, so do our people, so do the bearfolk, so do the animals, and so do the bystanders of our conflict. The half-giants and the bearfolk were able to reach an agreement when it came to my exile, so why not now? You can unite over your hatred for Oomphga - that's fine - but think of the younger generation that has to grow up during these times. Think of Tuthjorn. Think of the children too young to understand why their fathers and brothers are here fighting against strangers they hardly know, risking their lives in a war they hardly understand, and not at home spending every waking moment with them…"

"What do you know about war, Oomphga?! You're just a kid. A kid with a close-minded view on what it is we fight for. All you know is that good things are good, and bad things are bad with little understanding of why things are the way they are."

"He knows why! He knows both sides are killing and fighting each other over a misunderstanding. A MISUNDERSTANDING. All those years ago, the bearfolk didn't-"

"But they do now! For as long as you and I have been alive, they've been invading **our** homeland and killing the people **we** love!"

"So, you think it's right to do the same?! Look at yourself! You're doing it like a-"

"I'm doing it to protect us!"

"No! You're doing it out of blind hatred because that's all our people are taught to feel! Since the day we were born, our fathers told us, 'Oh, those scarlet-furs are evil! Those scarlet-furs will eat you and your babies alive! Rawr! Grr!'"

"Shut up-"

"Well, guess what?! Oomphga loves his papa, and his mama loves his papa too because he taught Oomphga how to be sweet and kind and happy while *your* papa-!"

"SHUT. UP."

Okradash grabbed Oomphga by the toga and yanked him in towards his bearded chin and gritted teeth. Fingers intertwined with the fabric and, grip tight, he dragged Oomphga along towards the clearing.

"Druid or not, you listen to me, and you listen to me good, Oomphga. If I send you over there and you're somehow able to get them to come out with their paws raised and claws unsheathed, then I'll think about your request, BUT…if they turn on you…don't you dare come crawling back to us begging us to do what they won't..!"

With a shove, he sent Oomphga stumbling into the big, wide-open space with a clear view of the bearfolk gathered on the other side. Eladda's armor stood clearly amongst them. Shaking out his arms and rolling his neck, Oomphga hyped himself up to talk to the bearfolk, hoping and praying for the best as he awkwardly closed the distance between the two feuding races.

"Eladda!" Oomphga called out, catching her disinclined attention. "Oomphga needs to talk to her!"

She greeted him with a spearpoint aimed at the crook of his neck.

"Go. Away."

"No."

Oomphga batted her spear away, using the back of his hand to do it swiftly without giving her a chance to impale him, but she quickly returned it to where it was prior and inched it even closer to his jugular.

"I'm not playing around, Oomphga! Stay out of this. It's none of your business."

"Eladda, just…listen to Oomphga, please. He knows Eladda. He knows, part half-giant or not, she thought Oomphga was a good friend,…right?"

"Good friend? You lied to me and Faith. You played us for a fool..!"

"What else did Oomphga do?"

Eladda paused. Her muzzle wrinkled, the edges of her lips twitched, and her paws trembled. She tried to hold onto her tough-girl attitude, but logic betrayed her. Gradually, she lowered her spear, drawing it back towards her body to hold onto.

"You-…you were always-"

Her voice broke. Her eyes welled with tears. She hid this from him and turned herself around.

"You were always so stubborn…"

"Well, Eladda is too when she's fighting for the people she cares about."

That's when it hit him: with that singular line, Oomphga broke her. Eladda curled in on herself, sniffling and trembling while her grip on her spear remained strong. She could hardly speak, and whenever words managed to break through her sorrowful cries, they were completely unintelligible. Trying as hard as he might, Oomphga made an honest attempt to listen to her pleas. He longed to know what cut her so deeply, but he didn't understand the mix of vowels and consonants she spewed.

Eventually, she found the strength to form a tangible thought aloud, and when she did, she did not hold back.

"It's their fault!" she cried. "It's all their fault! If half-giants never existed, my family would still be alive! My brother, my mother, my father would still be here!"

"But...But Oomphga wouldn't-"

"And I'd be glad! You and your family have caused me enough trouble! You got my father kill, so..." she thrashed her spear across Oomphga's face, nearly slicing open a bloody rift from one eye to the other. "Get out of here, Oomphga! I NEVER want to see you again, and if you try to convince me to spare the half-giants one more time, I'll...I'll KILL you!"

"Eladda wouldn't-!"

But she would. Both hands fixed onto the handle of her spear, she swung it like a club, the spearhead cutting through the air. If Oomphga hadn't thrown himself backwards onto the rock and dirt at his feet, she would've reopened the wound Uncle Mortium left across his side. Eyes wide, Oomphga clambered onto his feet and ran back towards the clearing. Her steel rang out after it had severed the earth where Oomphga's head once laid.

"SPARE NOT A SINGLE GREY-SKIN!!!" Eladda screeched. "KILL THEM ALL!!!"

Bearfolk rushed after Oomphga onto the field and the half-giants charged in from the opposing side shortly after. From the corner of his sights, Marigold charged in with her bow drawn on Bear Friend's back along with Elder Goat tailing close behind.

The clashing of iron and steel was inevitable, leaving little room for choice on Oomphga's part. Negotiations went out the window a long time ago, and if Oomphga didn't pick a side in the fight, he'd be taking his neutrality to the grave along with him. Question or doubt lost its vacancy in his skull. In a huff, Oomphga retreated to Marigold and hopped onto Elder Goat's back.

"I'm sorry, Oomphga!" Marigold hollered. Her voice strained in volume.

"Sorry? Sorry for what?!"

Her bow crackled, the sound echoing through the forest. The arrow, a blur of silver in the twilight, whistled through the air and plunged into to Eladda's shoulder. Its pointed edge pierced through her flesh with deathly precision and dug out a burrow in her shoulder. Eladda roared with pain and fury. Had her focus not been entirely consumed by Okradash's relentless assault, she would've returned the favor right back to Marigold. Luckily for her, the chaos of the battlefield, a maelstrom of steel and blood, held Eladda's attention captive.

The absolute chaos...

Battle cries overshadowed the gut-wrenching wails of physical anguish as the tormented souls of warriors, young and old, dragged Hope to the afterlife with the last of their strength. One by one, grown men and women were dropping like flies into the crimson rivers at their feet.

As many times as Oomphga bore witness to such a familiar sight, the trauma and the torment never faded. Each helpless body branded its final form into Oomphga's memory and consumed his every waking thought. If it weren't for Elder Goat, Oomphga would've been as helpless as a rodent caught in the talons of a falcon, stunned until the beak of Fate claimed him. And to think this all could've been prevented by Oomphga. Maybe if he were more prepared, more likable, more charismatic, more...anything that wasn't who he was now, things could've turned out different. If only he had killed Marcuth in the mountains. If only he had been closer with Eladda. If only...

"Druid Oomphga!" Elder Goat wheezed. "I don't mean to order *you* around of all people, but don't you think it's about time to do...something?!"

Something, yes, but what should he do? He can't kill his own kin, he can't negotiate a peace, - not anymore - so what CAN he do?!

Everything was happening all at once. In the center of the field, Eladda fought to defend herself from Okradash's intense maneuvering. He used the curved heel of his bearded axe to knock away the length of her spear, but before he could get a strike in, Eladda parried. This back-and-forth contest of endurance lasted until Marigold intervened once again with her bow. One after another, she sent arrow after arrow at the two, each one making their mark in their skin, but their hungering vengeance kept them alive.

Okradash, with a flick of his wrist, sent his axe hurtling towards Marigold. Its straight edge embedded itself in her fingers with a sickening crunch. Her screams pierced the air. From across the field, Oomphga could feel her anguish fueling the flame until it grew to be a storm.

Driven by a primal fury, Oomphga ushered Elder Goat through the crowd of heavy bodies and swinging weapons. He needed to be by her side. He needed to assess the damage.

Up close, he could see just how much damage Okradash had done to her. Her hand was a mangled ruin, blood painting a sickening display on her delicate skin. Her flesh had parted to reveal her inner ivory.

Oomphga, his face a mask of fierce determination, channeled his healing magic with intensity that crackled and sparked. A radiant aura enveloped Marigold's hand as Oomphga's power surged from his chest. By his fingertips, her flesh and bone were mended with impossible speed.

"Oomphga-!" Marigold gasped.

Okradash barreled towards the two of them. Oomphga could see it in Okradash's eyes. His compassion had completely abandoned him leaving nothing but the violent husk of a half-giant warrior. Oomphga thrashed his palms outward. A wave of fire arose from the earth, harvesting into a dancing inferno that forced every half-giant and bearfolk to draw back.

"ENOUGH. ALL OF YOU," Oomphga snapped.

For once, a grave silence hung in the air as every living soul paused to listen to the young druid. How convenient that, now, when his mind was too overwhelmed with grief and aggravation to articulate his desires for peace, that people were willing to hear his cries. He dashed his hand across his chest and summoned a raging wall of fire around the battlefield.

"You want to fight?! You want to fight that bad?! Well, raise your weapons high, 'cause you've done the impossible - you've pissed off Oomphga the druid, and now..." Oomphga exploded with mad laughter. "NOW, there's no going back..!"

And everyone eagerly accepted the challenge. As alarmed as Oomphga was to be approached by several men with swords, spears, and axes aimed for Oomphga's head and his heart, he was prepared. He had an army of his own after all. Wolves, foxes, deer, badgers, hawks, Elder Goat, and Bear Friend stepped forward to fight back against their hunters in the young druid's defense, and - *Oomphga hates to admit it* - it was one of the most breathtaking sights he ever lived to witness.

Thunder roared, grown men cried, and the forest sang a glorious war song. Claws, teeth, talons, hooves, and horns broke the bones of the opposition in every direction. Following their lead, Oomphga charged into the living wave of destruction, handaxe drawn in one hand and magic crackling in the other. His body danced and weaved across the earth, his blade gliding across skin and fur, drawing forth a stream of blood in its wake. By his might, the world shifted to his design.

Rock and soil burst out from his feet to keep clusters of bearfolk and half-giants at bay, fire shot from his fingertips, burning any creature that ran into the scorching mass of light, and all the while, a current of electricity ran through his body, charging his magic and fueling his adrenaline. With each step and turn, he'd discover something new about himself and the winds of change that guided his every motion. Sometimes, his half-giant body would transform to reflect one of the creatures entwined in the fray. He stole his physical strength and endurance from the bear, his dexterity and elegance from the hawk, fangs from the wolf, and claws from the badger.

Once she had fully recovered, Marigold leapt back into the fight, firing arrow after arrow into any warrior that dared try to get the jump on Oomphga, Bear Friend, or Elder Goat. Together, the rag-tag band of nature's finest fighters conducted a symphony of screams.

Time passed all too slowly. Seconds felt like minutes on the hour; the clashing of steel and the ripping of skin from bone began to feel more like the ticking of several metronomes - chaotic and yet monotonous; the cries of agony and disbelief - as loud as they were - gradually faded into non-existence. As strange as it was, it almost felt as if Oomphga wasn't really killing anyone at all.

Though he could taste the blood from his swollen gums dripping onto his tongue and though he could feel the physical anguish with each swing of his handaxe as he burrowed it into the bodies of the half-giants and the scarlet-furs that opposed him, it didn't feel like killing. In fact, they hardly seemed like people anymore.

If anything these monsters and barbarians resembled WEEDS more closely, growing and festering where they didn't belong, suffocating and killing out the flowers that would be perfectly fine without them, and yet these weeds had dreams, mortal desires, and probably a wish for the war to end just as he did, so why..? *Why doesn't Oomphga feel anything cutting them down and running them through?*

*Because they **asked** for this.*

NO!!! The deeper voice of his subconscious replied. *No! They didn't!!! They **begged** for peace!!! They never asked for anything more than that!!!*

Oomphga had no choice.

OOMPHGA ALWAYS HAD A CHOICE!!! He just didn't pick a very WISE one!!!

*He's better than them! Oomphga is fighting out of self-defense! They wouldn't listen to reason unless it struck them in the face and made them bleed! If they weren't the ones **fueling** this stupid war with petty revenge and misconceptions, we wouldn't BE in this situation! Besides, Oomphga is the druid. The gods are on his side. **They** know that **he** knows what's right!*

WHAT DOES OOMPHGA REALLY KNOW!?! The bellowing voice roared in retaliation. *Sure, he knew that someone was orchestrating the war beyond the half-giants and bearfolks' knowledge. Fine. THAT'S. FINE. But why kill people over something that could've saved them!?!*

…Because no one listens to Oomphga.

And for once, the two voices agreed.

…

…It wouldn't stop. At this rate, the fighting would never stop. Not until either Oomphga or the warriors were dead, and it sure wasn't going be Oomphga.

In one last desperate attempt to end the suffering, Oomphga reached for the heavens and called upon the divine for one final lethal strike, but when he looked up and saw the rolling clouds and the darkening sky, he wondered if the divine knew something he didn't. Something far grimmer and darker than he could ever comprehend.

*Was this really the only way he could **save** his people?*

Regardless of the answer, a streak of lightning drew forth from the rolling voids above and struck Oomphga's palm. Pain shot through him, reminding him that he was alive when others weren't. He clung to the anguish and torment. He let out a guttural cry and wailed as the magic consumed his flesh and bone until the moment of release when he threw the electricity into the ground at his feet. A wave shot outwards from him and, one by one, all of the half-giants and bearfolk fell to the earth.

Still. Silent. Lifeless.

Was it worth it? Was any of this necessary?

Oomphga looked at his hands, scarred, battered, calloused, and bloodied. Trusting no one, he turned to himself for answers and found nothing but the slow realization that the dozens of mutilated corpses littering the fields at his feet were a product of his own reckless creation. Through tears, he examined the horror of the massacre. Bodies twisted and contorted in ways all too familiar. He just ruined the lives of thousands - mothers, fathers, sons, daughters, husbands, and wives all without realizing - but in the end, what did he do?

His esophagus clenched itself shut, locking him in an inescapable chokehold. Against his will, he cracked the faintest smirk and let out a maddened laugh in the face of his own anguish.

He clung to his handaxe and held it against the crook of his own neck. He longed so desperately to silence the deafening thump of his pulse. His story had to end here. He couldn't bear the thought of Oomphga - the fraud, the outcast, the tormentor, and the executor - trailing along for another page...

"Oomphga!" Marigold shot forward and grabbed onto Oomphga's wrist. "Oomphga...stop this..! You're...you're the only thing I have left to love and hold in this world. Please. Don't take yourself out of it. If Death wants you, make it fight for you, but don't surrender. Not now. Not ever. You're a good person, Oomphga. You're the druid. The world needs you. I...need you."

If it weren't for her, Oomphga would have obeyed his impulses in a heartbeat, but she gave him the pause he needed. She gave him time to mull over his choices, to reflect on what all he truly had to live for.

Killing himself. What a ridiculous thought.

And yet it was this thought that blinded his consciousness and silenced his reason. His grief puppeteered him. His hand twitched with an eagerness to spill more blood than necessary to be at peace again. Marigold's loving palm pressed against his wrist and guided his cursed weapon down to the grass at his waist side.

"Oomphga wants to hurt people..-" he blubbered.

No...

"No. He doesn't..." Marigold whimpered. Slowly, she dropped her head and fell against Oomphga's body, coiling her arms around him to hold him steady.

"Oomphga...is not a good person anymore. He's not fit to be a druid. He's killed so many people. So, so many people, and deep down, he thinks a part of him...liked it! If that isn't-! If he wasn't-! He's a-"

Marigold hushed him and held him near. When the roaring flames died down, silence took its place. Elder Goat dropped down by Oomphga's side and laid his weary head in his lap.

"Mama! Mama!" Small Bear cried, barreling through the grass to leap onto his mother's bloody pelt.

"It's alright, my child. Fuzzy and I are alright," she uttered into Small Bear's fluff.

She consoled him with his presence and carried him over to Oomphga so she could rest in the company of her half-breed son who continued to look on at the corpses littering the forest. He kept his attention sharp, desperately hoping for signs of life amidst the destruction that he caused.

Then, coming from Eladda, he saw her paw twitch around her spear. And Okradash. As battered and bruised as he was, he pathetically clambered onto his knees to crawl into the thick wall of trees. Oomphga quickly stood up and stopped by Eladda to brush his palm across her fur. Though he cured her wounds, he could still feel the tenseness in her muscles and the pain coursing through her. That's when Oomphga remembered. He still had his herb pouch hanging from his waist side.

He blindly reached into the bag and fished for a corydalis to offer to her.

"Eladda, if you can hear Oomphga, eat this if you can. It'll make you feel better."

He could see it in her swollen eyes. She truly did have nothing left to lose, so, abandoning her stubbornness, she reluctantly chowed down on the herb, nestling into the grass helplessly. When he turned to look for Okradash, eager to help him, he was gone.

"I know I heard it!" Faith's voice echoed from afar. "Fighting! Lots of it! This way!"

Suddenly, dozens of soldiers bearing the capitol's crest broke through the shadows and stood in shock, staring down a terrified, blood-covered Oomphga.

Chapter 29:

The Beast Behind Bars

STEP AFTER STEP, two rugged men approached. One grabbed Oomphga by the arms while the other patted him down. They picked up his quarterstaff, handaxe, and then reached at Oomphga's side for his herbal pouch. At first, he rolled it in his hands, examining only the bag's crudely sewn exterior.

"Are these...drugs?" one asked.

"No. They're herbs," Oomphga replied anxiously. "Be careful. Some of them are-"

He opened the bag and drew back, coughing loudly. Oomphga could smell the potent, bitter herb robert all too well to the point that he began gagging and wheezing. "We'll...*cough cough* we'll see what the apothecary has to say about that. Come along, now, and no funny business."

Bear Friend approached cautiously, ready to defend her grey-skinned bear son, but the soldiers showed no tolerance, drawing their weapons to step between Oomphga and the angry mama bear.

"It's okay, Bear Friend," Oomphga said serenely. "Oomphga and Marigold will be okay. You take care of Small Bear. Be safe."

"Come on..!"

With a firm shove, the one soldier forced Oomphga to step forward while one of the others holding Marigold guided her far more gently.

From the forest to the station outside of Endinerose, they endured Marigold's pleading for their freedom, but in the end, they ignored them and guided the two of them into separate holding cells where they shackled them in magic-suppressing manacles and left them there to their own devices.

No one said anything. Not a word. The soldiers, the guards, no one. Not until they were out of earshot to discuss - most likely - what was to be done next with the little killers.

"Oomphga?" Marigold caught Oomphga's attention with the uncertainty in her voice.

"Hm?"

"I'm…I'm scared."

"Oomphga is too. He's just-" *Trying to suppress it.* Swallowing his insecurity, he forced a smile and pressed his head against the course, brick wall behind him. "It'll be alright. What Marigold and Oomphga did…it was self-defense, right? Besides, we've been in worse situations, and it beats getting killed."

"I…guess you're right about that. I suppose I'm…more scared about you."

"About Oomphga?"

"Have you already forgotten? You almost tried to- you know- in the forest."

"Ah. Yes…" Oomphga reflected on his past-self. Between then and now, he felt like a completely different person. If anything, he felt like a soothing current of psychological insight and divine reassurance washed over him. "Oomphga's been mulling it over and - uh - he thinks he's feeling a bit better now. He's had time to think and he's almost positive that, despite everything that happened earlier, there wasn't a whole lot Oomphga and Marigold could really do. They were in danger. They were scared. People were attacking each other and then they started attacking them. What else were we supposed to do? Die?"

Marigold didn't reply. Oomphga didn't elaborate.

After an hour of sitting and waiting for something to happen, an armored minotaur stepped up to Oomphga's cell, towering over him with a bag slung over his shoulder and writing utensils in his hands.

"Name," he demanded.

"O-Oomphga Silverblood, sir," Oomphga murmured.

"Do you live with anyone?"

"His mama and papa."

"His?"

"Oomphga's."

"Their names."

"Papa Sergei and Mama Vergaia."

"They also have the last name of Silverblood?"

"Yes…"

He nodded, held a piece of parchment against the wall next to his cell, and scrawled a few words onto it silently. He folded it up, tucked it into his armor, and reached into the bag hanging down from his shoulder. He pulled out a few leather and metal devices that served unclear purposes at first glance. Then, drawing his keys, he unlocked the door and stepped inside.

Initially, Oomphga drew back, terrified by the way the soldier approached with the leather straps of these contraptions outstretched. He didn't know what they were for nor did the soldier take any time explaining in any detail.

"It's alright, kid. I'm not going to hurt you. I just need to put these on. Safety regulations."

Safety regulations?!

He pressed the metal cage of the larger devices against Oomphga's face. Upon contact, Oomphga jolted away, trying to fight the inevitable. Every inch of his nerves sent distress signals to his brain that he didn't like this kind of feeling: being forced to dawn on a mask labeling him a monster. The collar was no better. It coiled around his neck like a constrictor snake and cut off his airways. His gasping and raspy wailing served as the only indicator to the man that he had to readjust it to be a looser fit. The ruthless iron and leather clung firmly onto Oomphga's head and throat. As if shackles and manacles weren't enough..!

"There. Now, be a good boy and stay in your cell," the guard ordered.

He backed away from the petrified druid and closed the door, locking it shut all while little Oomphga laid sprawled across the ground to confront his own festering panic. It consumed him suddenly and aggressively. To be constrained, to be physically mishandled, and to be locked away in a cold, dark cell sent his conscious and subconscious mind into a spiraling frenzy.

"No more…" he silently begged. *"No more no more no more..!"*

"Oomphga! Are you okay over there?!" Marigold cried from the other side of a thick, cobblestone wall, but the guard interrupted her to ask her questions not too much unlike the ones they asked Oomphga before invading his cell.

"Name!" the guard hollered.

"…Marigold," she growled.

"First and last name, please."

"Marigold. I don't have a last name."

"Do you live with anyone?"

"Not anymore. I travel. I've been traveling with Oomphga for a while. He's been taking care of me. He's an innocent person! I'll have you know, he's the-!"

"Thank you for your cooperation..!"

There was a moment of pause, and then the guard walked off, heavy bootsteps echoing into nothing.

"Darn it…" Marigold cursed under her breath.

Oomphga could hear her pacing back and forth in her cage. Her chains rattled and her breathing was heavy.

"He's sorry," Oomphga uttered. "He's so, so sorry. Oomphga's roped Marigold into a terrible mess."

"What? No. No, Oomphga. Don't be sorry. We're going to be okay. Understand? We're going to make it out of here one way or another. You promised."

"You're…" *Oomphga did promise, didn't he?* "You're right. Whether it's in a few days or a few years, Marigold and Oomphga will be let go."

"I'm talking about today."

"Huh?! But, Marigold, we're not *really* guilty, right? And even if they declare we are, we'll still be together, at least. So…it won't be all bad."

"I've lived my life in cells like this for most of my life only instead of stone, it was rotting wood, and instead of a cot, it was a bed of straw, but…I wasn't allowed to leave - not unless I was told - and my sisters watched over me with their scrying eyes all the while. Prison is an improvement, yes, but…it's not the same as being out there: roaming free, hiking up mountains, riding on a *bear*-back, and…dancing under the stars~" she chuckled quietly to herself. "Don't you miss it already, Oomphga?"

Oomphga reflected on his childhood: staring out the window and hiding behind one of two masks on the daily. However, on those days when he was free to explore his desires in emerald glades and snowy peaks alone from the prejudice - oh, the euphoria. It was of the purest kind.

The forest was his paradise with Laniarra's luxuries sprawled out between the highest mountain peaks to the deepest depths of the ocean. It was a blessing that Obak fought for High Peak, for a view overlooking Laniarra's most beautiful creation. To think, the only thing separating them from the freedom they long sought after were brick walls and a few, dense metal bars along a slender opening just an arm's reach above their heads.

"If…Marigold wishes to get out of here, we're going to get out of here. Oomphga promises, and Oomphga never breaks a promise."

A whole night of planning and scheming with little action to be had. Eventually, the two wore themselves out and slept the night away. *Better to sleep on the plan that night than be weaker and dumber the next,* they agreed.

The next morning, Oomphga woke up to a loud clattering and an aching back.

"Get up. Your parents are here to speak with you."

The one thing Oomphga hoped to avoid if at all possible: his parents finding out.

He rolled half of his body off of his wooden cot and stretched his muscles, still tense from sleeping on a bed that was a foot too small for the growing boy. When he looked over towards the soldier, he froze, mouth agape.

"Mama…Papa..!" Oomphga raced to the bars, but tripped as the shackles around his ankle tightened, pulling his foot out from under him.

"Oomphga, my son! Are you okay?!" Papa Sergei got down onto his knees. "What happened last night?! Are you hurt?! Are you bleeding?! Please, tell Papa you haven't been completely scarred for life..!"

"Papa! Papa…Oomphga is alright…all things considered."

"So, what went wrong?" Mama Vergaia asked sternly.

"He-…Oomphga-…" Oomphga stuttered and stumbled over his speech, digging deep for the right words to say that didn't undermine the situation, but didn't weave a lie. "He tried to talk to Okradash and Eladda, Mama. They were going to fight each other, and Oomphga…he had to stop them! So, he tried to talk to them, but they didn't listen, and then…they started killing each other in front of Oomphga! Oomphga didn't want to hurt anyone, but…!"

There it was. *The lie.* He could deny it all he wanted, but he could never mask the truth of his adrenaline induced desires. He was desperate to be heard, and desperate to be obeyed. A selfish, wretched want this was, gnawing at his innards until it hit him - that flash of grief so powerful, it nearly cost him his life, and all in exchange for a cure long sought.

"…he had to, Mama."

"Why didn't you run?" Papa Sergei asked.

"Because Oomphga is so…so tired of running! He wants to help people! He wants to make a difference! He wants his people to be friends with one another again! Is that so much to ask?!"

"Oomphga…" Papa Sergei cooed, reaching beyond the bars with his warm paw to pat Oomphga's bruised shoulder. "I know you want to help unite everyone under the same sun and moon, we do too, but there are just…some things you can't fix, my child."

"So, Oomphga's supposed to give up? On the bearfolk? On the half-giants? On himself..?" Oomphga's voice trailed off into near nothingness.

"Oomphga," his mother interrupted, "listen to me and listen to me well: you did your best, but sometimes…your best won't be good enough. When it isn't, you have to accept that fact, even if it's hard, and you move-"

"Maybe that wasn't Oomphga's best, but Oomphga can do better! He'll make everything better! If not today and not tomorrow, Oomphga swears, one day, he'll make it better for everyone! For Mama, for Papa, for Marigold, for his friends, for the Nature Faction, for everyone in the world! One day-!"

"Oomphga, sweetie, I hate to be the bearer of bad news, but don't you think that's a little…*unrealistic*?"

A flood of tears broke through Oomphga's tear ducts and poured down his pale cheeks as he pictured Tuthjorn and Eladda standing in his parents' place. Their disappointment couldn't be measured in words. And their expressions. They looked down upon Oomphga, the failure that was unable to become the strong, wise, charismatic, and powerful druid fabled by the masses and the divine to bring balance between man and nature…

But a failure Oomphga refused to be. He wiped away his tears, buried his sorrow, and grabbed ahold of the small ounce of joy hidden within his heart. Voice shaking and smile stretched wide across his face, Oomphga opened his mouth to speak to his parents one last time:

"Yes. And?"

Mama Vergaia slowly drew back from Oomphga to cover her mouth. Perhaps she realized something new about her son or, perhaps, she remembered something about him that she had long since forgotten. Whatever it was that twisted her perception tore her up and mangled her expression into a tragic one. Papa Sergei pulled himself to his feet shortly after noticing his sad wife and he wrapped his arms around her.

"Sweetheart, what is it?"

But she didn't speak. Not a word. She buried her face into her husband's shoulder and wept the hardest Oomphga had ever seen. The minotaur guard politely tried to intervene to let her know that it was time to leave, but Vergaia didn't move an inch. She needed time to collect herself, and when she finally managed to, she peered over Sergei's shoulder and uttered:

"I love you, Oomphga, my little miracle~"

Strength and stubbornness fading, the guard and Papa Sergei escorted her out, both of them making sure to comfort her down the long hall leading to Oomphga's cell.

More time had passed. Another hour, maybe. By this point, it was becoming impossible to tell if not for the slight changes of light seeping into the room through the slender arched window hanging above him.

The door at the end of the hall had been opened again and a different guard from before came to pay the two a visit. This one was a human. He had a soft face that smelled faintly of rum and sandalwood, a soothing scent that outweighed that of the meal he so kindly presented Oomphga with through a little hatch at the bottom of the door.

"Good morning, children. Uh, here's your breakfast. I know it's not much, but it's all we have at the moment to keep you fed until your interrogation."

Oomphga looked over the display. Before him laid a bowl of steaming gruel, a wooden cup of water, and a slice of rye bread. He gave Marigold the same.

After delivering their meals, he nodded to the both of them politely and left the room.

"Oomphga likes that guy. Way more than the night guard, at least," Oomphga said aloud, picking up the one slice of bread lying on the tray.

"Oomphga, the plan?" Marigold gently reminded.

"Oh! Yes."

Pulling himself up onto his feet, he walked up to the window in the back of the cell and slid the piece of bread through the bars. He watched it closely in the meantime, waiting patiently.

Suddenly, two mockingbirds dropped down next to the bread, and Oomphga let out a trilly whistle to catch their attention. One after another, they peaked their heads between the bars to investigate.

"Hello. Hi. It's Oomphga again. Listen, he could use your help."

"Oh, no. Not this kid..." the male on the left grumbled as he turned to leave. "Let's get out of here. I hear this hairless is nothing but trouble."

"No! No! Wait! He's not asking for bird friends to fight for him. He needs them to deliver a message to the bears. They live in the cave at the base of the mountains. They're very friendly. Tell them that Oomphga and Marigold are in the station outside of the big city, and that Marigold needs her things. She has a small bag of things and a pretty flower that belongs to her. Got all that?"

"And why should we help you?"

"Darling, be nice to the boy-" the female interjected.

"Because Oomphga wants to help you too. He knows many things, terrible things. He knows bearfolk and half-giants hunt your kind, and what's worse, there's a bad man out there that wishes the whole world were in ruin. He plans on starting up a second calamity.

Oomphga's on a quest to stop these things from happening. He wants to protect the forest and all its inhabitants. He wants people and nature to live in harmony. He's sorry for any harm he's caused, but…he wants to be a good boy and do good things if he is able. So…could you help Oomphga? Please…and thank you?"

"Aww…" The female bird turned to her partner and let out a melodic coo. "He sounds like our little hatchlings, sweetie."

"Rambling on about the end of the world?"

"No..! I-" she sighed and shook her head. Then she fixed her gaze upon Oomphga and smiled. "Don't worry, hun. We'll help you out as much as we can."

"Thank you. Oh, and one more thing!"

The two mockingbirds leaned in closer, dandelion eyes widening.

"Fetch all the field mice you can, and make sure they're living, please and thank you."

Chapter 30:
Escaping the Confines

OMPHGA SAT PATIENTLY on his cot, sipping on water and watching the bread piece he left out in the grass get eaten up by ants that passed by. As much as Oomphga would've loved to ask them for help, he didn't want to disturb their hard work.

"Hey, Oomphga?"

"Yes, Marigold?"

"Let's make a bet. Actually, let's make two."

Oomphga looked over at the wall between them, grinning from ear-to-ear.

"Alright. What are they and what are we betting?"

"I'm betting my feathery cloak."

"Then...Oomphga will bet his blanket that you still have."

"Sorry for not giving it back."

"No worries. If Marigold wins this bet, she'll get to keep it anyways~"

"Very well. The first bet is I'm betting the field mice are going to show up before Bear Friend. Poor girl is probably tired and desperate for a good night's rest, so she'll probably take her time getting here."

"Oomphga'd beg to differ. She's a strong girl, and a dedicated mama bear. Plus, considering all that's happened, he's not sure Bear Friend would be able to sleep knowing well where we are. Oomphga accepts this bet. And the other?"

"Second bet is that, after you and I get out of here, I bet you'll be asking me to spend the rest of my life with you~"

Oomphga's face lit up and he curled up in his cot. If he could, he'd roll up into a little ball the way hedgehogs do and disappear, but that was an ability he lacked all thanks to the magic suppressing manacles on his wrist, and the cage on his mouth made it all the harder to hide his face.

"Oomphga…can't accept that bet," he murmured.

"Well, why not?"

"Because…because it's true. Oomphga would ask Marigold to spend the rest of her life with Oomphga if he could. Since we'll be exiles on the run and since Marigold has been the best company Oomphga has ever had in - well - ever, of course he'd want to be with her. For company. For safety. For happiness. For comfort. He loves her a lot, after all."

Oomphga could feel the tension in the air, but it vanished at the sound of Marigold giggling, and it wasn't a laugh filled with malice or discomfort, but of pure innocence.

"And she loves him too."

"So…does she? W-want to stay with Oomphga, he means."

"I do," Marigold hummed. "I want to live a free life. Here. There. Anywhere. As long as I'm with you, Oomphga."

Suddenly, a faint chittering rang out from overhead. Dozens of field mice crowded by the bars, looking down upon Oomphga while munching on the ant-infested bread.

"Looks like Oomphga's blanket is Marigold's now. The mice are here."

"Druid Oomphga," a familiar voice called out.

"Elder Goat..!"

Wrinkles cresting across his fuzzy face, Elder Goat lowered his head towards the window. His eyes were wide, his expression grim.

"I'm here to help see to it that you kids get out of here, and fast."

"Fast? Why? What's the rush?"

"I don't know a lot of hairless words, but I saw a powerful looking individual talking to a couple of wolf creatures much like the ones we saw in the mountains, and they were talking about an execution and your name came up in the conversation."

"Marcuth-" Oomphga growled. He looked back over his shoulder at the door to his cell quizzically and returned his gaze to the group of mice to count how many were present. Two dozen. "Alright, Oomphga needs all of you to work together for this assignment. He needs half of you to distract the soldiers and the other half of you to scope out the station. He wants you to find, 1.) the exit and 2.) a special kind of storage room. It'll be filled with wooden chests, and in those chests are Oomphga and Marigold's things. Once you do that, report back to Oomphga and Marigold. They'll need you to guide them there and then swiftly guide them to the exit immediately after. Did you get all of that?"

They all squeaked an agreement and scurried between the metal bars, down the ridged, stone walls, and across the floor.

"And me. What would you like for me to do?"

"Stay here. You'll be Marigold's ride to safety if we somehow manage to get out of here before Bear Friend shows up."

And almost as if on cue, she arrived with Small Bear sitting like a toddler on her back. Sitting between Small Bear's paws was the crystium catastrophe in the same flower crown Marigold wore at the Autumn Festival, and hanging from Bear Friend's jaw was a somewhat empty-looking satchel that she dropped down into Marigold's cell.

After a bit of digging, Oomphga could only assume she found something useful in her pack because she started banging something made of metal against her binds, and with a faint *tink,* they clattered to the floor.

"There we go…" she sighed. "Now, for the door…"

Commotion stirred. Guards were starting to take notice of the rat infestation just outside the hall of holding cells.

"Looks like we might have to get our belongings back ourselves, huh?" Oomphga asked, his voice and hands trembling with anticipation.

"Looks like it, but…no worries, Oomphga. Once I get your magic-suppressing handcuffs off, nothing will be able to stop us from getting out of here."

"Are you sure?"

"Positive."

Click.

Marigold grabbed her things and rushed over to Oomphga's cell to fiddle with his lock. Oomphga monitored her closely, examining the ornamental hairpins as she dexterously maneuvered it between her fingers. Watching her work, Oomphga couldn't stop himself from falling more in love with her.

What a talented lady Marigold is. Oomphga's so lucky to have met a girl like her.

Fear and doubt vanished more with each heavy heartbeat. The soft tapping of metal soothed him, and Marigold's closeness enveloped his field of vision in the most pleasing of ways. Lock by lock and buckle by buckle, she freed him from his confines and fueled his flustered state of mind. Her presence, her appearance, and her expression all had Oomphga drowning in his own innocent daydreams.

"Earth to Oomphgaaa-!"

"Huh..?!" He snapped out of his stupor.

"Now's not the time for goat-staring. We have to go."

She grabbed him by the hands and pulled him to his feet.

"Uh, Bear Friend, Elder Goat, you wait right there. Oomphga and Marigold will meet you two outside..!"

Marigold took the lead and Oomphga followed toe-to-heel after her down the hall and out the door. Though both were frightened and extremely tense, they were determined to escape - they were determined to face whatever lay in wait for them on the other side, but nothing could've prepared them for the spectacle that unfolded before them…

Mice littered the room, capturing the soldiers' attention. They taunted and teased them as they skittered about. Two sprinted over to Oomphga and crawled up his baggy pants and tucked toga until they sat comfortably on the medallion across his shoulder.

"Third room on the right is all the stuff. When you head out, take a left, take a right, take another left, and there's the exit," the one mouse squeaked.

"Thank you, friendly field mouse~!"

"You're welcome!"

"This way, Marigold. Come on..!"

Oomphga dashed forward, keeping a sharp eye on the rooms along the right wall and the wooden signs hanging on the wall next to them.

"Privy",... "Dining Hall",... "Evidence"..!

With a swift flick of his wrist and a haphazard step, he stumbled into the room and swiftly shut the door behind Marigold, taking great care to lock it as well. The loud thud of the heavy oak rang through Oomphga's sensitive ears. Body tense and eyes darting from one side of the room to the other, Oomphga wondered if anyone noticed.

Marigold, unphased by the danger, navigated the room, gently picked the locks, unhinged the latches, and hoisted open the lids of the boxes and chests that littered the available space. She peered into each container and checked them thoroughly before moving onto the next.

The commotion outside got louder as the guards got more irritated with their own poor pest control. Any minute now, they'd start to get suspicious of foul play, surely.

"I found it..!" Marigold exclaimed.

"You did?" Oomphga stepped away from the door and joined Marigold's side. Lo and behold, there it all resided, piled haphazardly together in a chest. While Marigold fished out her belongings, Oomphga did the same with his. His handaxe, his quarterstaff, and his journal were all here. The only thing missing were his herbs. No matter. Their freedom came first, his material possessions came second.

Suddenly, a loud thud rang out. The soldiers were pounding at the door.

"Come quick! The convicts are in here!" the man behind the door shouted.

Oomphga stepped back towards Marigold defensively, eyes tracing over each wall of the room. There were no windows or doors, just chests, closets, and boxes. They were trapped and cornered. Marigold readied herself, strapping on her archery glove, slipping on her quiver, and readying her bow, but Oomphga held a firm hand over hers.

"Hold on, Marigold. Oomphga doesn't think we'll be needing that," he whispered.

"Open this door right now, children, lest you wish a longer and more resolute sentence for your crimes of mass murder and resisting arrest!" the soldier demanded, clearly growing more impatient by the second.

"Alright! Alright. Oomphga will open the door, as long as Mr. Soldier Guy promises that no harm will come to Oomphga and Marigold if he complies..!"

A lingering silence followed his request. "...Very well."

"Better take a deep breath, Marigold. Oomphga's about to do something dangerous."

Marigold nodded and did as ordered, Oomphga doing the same for his own sake. The small storage room was suffocating with very little air circulation, but there would be enough. Swishing and swirling his palms in front of his chest, he conjured a small, circular whirlwind in his hands. Then, holding it as if it were a ramball, he threw it as hard as he could out in front of him.

The door before them flew off of its hinges and slammed two soldiers against the wall on the other side. Seizing the opportunity with a faltering huff, Oomphga grabbed Marigold's hand and made a mad dash for their destined escape route. Once they were out of the room, he pulled Marigold against his back, and let the gods dictate his form.

His features shifted. His hands became claws, and his body gained more mass. He was a dire wolf. Marigold sat mounted on his back along with the two field mice that accompanied them. Her weight on Oomphga's back caused his legs to grow tense; he panted louder and heavier. Fighting the urge to crumble, he pushed onward and dexterously weaved down the halls as smoothly as his thick, furry body could muster. Crowds of armored guards made way for the druid as he barked and howled vicious warnings to them to keep their distance. Obediently, they parted in waves and revealed to him the double doors that marked their exit.

Oomphga reached up and desperately clawed at the handle, his paws slipping off the metal ring.

"Oomphga..! Oomphga, it's a push, not a pull!"

Letting out an embarrassed whine, he forcibly pressed his head and chest against the heavy, oak doors to lodge them open and step out into the open where Bear Friend, Small Bear, and Elder Goat greeted them. Swiftly, Oomphga hoisted Marigold up onto Elder Goat's back and hopped up onto Bear Friend's, his body shifting back into its original form. With his humanoid arms and legs again, he pulled Small Bear in close to his abdomen and held onto him somewhat firmly.

"Alright, Bear Friend. Let's get out of here..!"

Eagerly, Bear Friend and Elder Goat kicked up their heels and ran off towards the trees. From behind, Oomphga could overhear the soldiers' panicked prattling only for one, most likely their commander, to cut through their conversing.

"Let them go," he ordered. "It would appear the boy is our new druid. Drop his charges, and send an informant to the N.F.C."

Chapter 31:

Starting a New Story Together

AFTER FLEEING FROM ENDINEROSE, they sought refuge in Bear Friend's den. Weary and tired, they camped under stalactites, bathed themselves in the cave pond, and survived off of whatever nature provided them within a mile of the mountains. Days grew shorter, and the autumn nights grew colder. The bitter chill in the wind spared Marigold's temperature-sensitive skin no mercy, and soon she found herself painfully ill.

One night, after an evening of gathering fruits, herbs, and grass, Oomphga returned to the cave and sat down by the fire where Marigold spent most of her time sniffling and coughing. The animals, exhausted and dreary, kept her company while he was away and took turns serving as her pillow. Tonight, it was Bear Friend's turn, and she was already fast asleep beneath Marigold's head.

Taking quiet steps, Oomphga approached the fire and knelt down next to the love of his life. He gave her a soft-spoken greeting and gently held the back of his palm to her forehead. It was scorching hot, same as it has been a few days after they escaped the guard station.

"I'm sorry, Oomphga," she murmured.

"Sorry? Sorry for what..~?"

"You've been working hard for the both of us, and I've been lying around thinking for days on end."

"Don't be so hard on yourself, Marigold. Thinking is hard, and Oomphga's thankful he hasn't had to do too much of it," he chuckled. "What has Marigold been thinking about?"

"Let me-" she coughed into her arm and slowly sat up straight. "Let me answer that question with another question: how would you feel about seeking out sanctuary in the Fire Faction?"

His eyes lit up in interest. He never contemplated the idea before. However, given everything that he's been told and everything they've been through, it'd most likely be for the best since it'd hide them well from the world. The majority of the Fire Faction consisted of cities with tall buildings that blocked out the sun and fully paved streets that covered the earth in a thick layer of rock and cement. Rumor has it that trees only existed in dedicated parks and animals only thrived under their owner's roof or in a homemade of waste, but Oomphga couldn't say anything on a personal basis. He's never been there.

In the end, what did it all matter anyway if he'd be happier there than trapped in the invisible barrier of a war?

A warm smile revealed itself across Oomphga's face as he reached for Marigold's hand.

"As long as Oomphga and Marigold are happy and safe together, that's all that matters, so if Marigold would like to move there with Oomphga, then Oomphga will do whatever it takes to get her there. Even if he has to carry her on his back, he'll do it~"

Marigold let out a hum fainter than a whisper. "We'll find the place of our dreams one day, Oomphga. I promise~"

"What about us?" Small Bear chimed in, waddling up to Oomphga and Marigold. "So that's it? You're just going to leave us? We'll never get to see each other ever again after all Mama and I have done for you?"

"Fret not, young one," Elder Goat calmly interjected from the other side of the campfire. "He wouldn't just up and leave you and your mother like that without consulting with her first. Although, it would be going against nature if you two were to migrate with them into civilization, especially during the winter."

"So why can't he just stay with us, huh?" Small Bear barked back and then turned to Oomphga. "Why can't Fluffy stay?!"

Oomphga reached for his shoulder and slowly pulled the medallion that his mother gave to him off of his toga. He stared deeply into his reflection and the constellation etchings engraved on the bottom.

"But it's not fair! Why do people that didn't do anything wrong have to get hurt?!"

"It's not…normal for kids like you to grow up hiding who they really are all the time. I get doing it around your friends on the rare occasions that you see them, but to do it out of fear in the big city where there are far more people and far more dangerous things that could happen if you get caught?! I…I worry for you, my little Oomphga."

"Oomphga, it's not your fault. Given your situation, your position, things happen. That's war."

"The moment I saw your face in the woods - when you were little - I knew Aymus' successor had been born, and I-…we are all eager to see what you do to make the universe just as great of a place as he did, as your parents did, as your great grandfather did."

"Don't think I've already forgotten about why I'm here, half-breed. You may very well be innocent, you may very well be a nobody, and you may very well be the most gullible person I've ever seen, but you…you are a thorn in my side that needs to be purged..!"

"You're a good kid, Oomphga Silverblood."

"Your acts of good-will and pacifism will only get you so far. Evil shows no mercy, and you've barely the defense to protect yourself. You must leave this place you call home. You must rest your weary muscles. You must return a new druid, 'lest you

wish to die young, at the claws of Marcuth - or worse, your own people - before you get the chance to bring about the **change** *you so desire."*

"I hope you die. I hope you take another axe to the side and you die."

"Get out of here, Oomphga! I NEVER want to see you again, and if you try to convince me to spare the half-giants one more time, I'll…I'll KILL you!"

"Oomphga would ask Marigold to spend the rest of her life with Oomphga if he could. Since we'll be exiles on the run and since Marigold has been the best company Oomphga has ever had in - well - ever, of course he'd want to be with her. For company. For safety. For happiness. For comfort. He loves her a lot, after all."

"And she loves him too."

Oomphga nodded along to his memories as he fiddled with the medallion in his hands. Marigold was right. They couldn't stay. It wouldn't be safe. Even though he'd be proving everyone's doubts correct, he'd rather be alive and happy than spend another day trying to live up to the heartless and cruel expectations of his people. The things they asked - no - *demanded* of him: *that*…was *unrealistic* for a kid like Oomphga to comply.

"Fluffy needs to step away from the bad things," Oomphga finally replied, petting Small Bear's head. "He needs time to be happy. He wants to settle down with Marigold, one day. Fluffy wants to-…If it's okay with Marigold, he-…Oomphga wants to be…Marigold's 'mate' and roam the world with her. If Bear Friend and Small Bear wish to join them, they may, but…this is what Fluffy wants."

Small Bear let out a defeated sigh. "You are one weird hairless. You know that?"

"It's genetic..~" Oomphga chuckled. "Now, everyone, let's fill our bellies with some vegetation and get some rest. We still have a long journey ahead of us~!"

Reluctantly, Small Bear scooped up a handful of berries and herbs that he snacked on while Elder Goat ate away the grass at the bottom of the basket. Whatever remained Oomphga and Marigold shared with one another.

The next morning, Oomphga spoke with Bear Friend about their plans to move into the city. To Elder Goat and Small Bear's surprise, she agreed to give up her den and travel alongside the young couple as a "measure of assurance to make sure us kids didn't get into trouble". So, with Bear Friend, Small Bear, Elder Goat, and Marigold, the four began their long and tumultuous journey across the Nature Faction.

They crept with caution in their step through Bristlethorn Forest, turned a teary, blind eye to the Silverblood house, evaded a town of soldiers (appropriately named Paladin's Rest), and followed the branching road through a farming village called Alamagus. At first, they swore to only stop for food and drink, but were instead surprised to find a friendly blacksmith that offered up shelter in exchange for some questions answered.

His dwelling was humble yet accommodating. Though the remnants of his trade, soot and debris, lingered, a welcoming hearth fire warmed the five travelers. Each was afforded a comfortable chamber for repose. The blacksmith, known as Wallomir, proved to be more than a generous host; his wisdom and talents were evident. Despite his awareness of Oomphga and Marigold's identities, he harbored them graciously and even assisted Oomphga in tending to Marigold's afflictions.

One night, lying by Marigold's side, Oomphga denied himself a well-earned night of rest in favor of daydreaming by the faint glow of the crystium catastrophe.

"Marigold, do you know if there's a place like this in the Fire Faction?" he whispered, his voice echoing in the silence of night.

"Only one located in the city of Starfall on an island off its coast. Why?"

"There. That's where Oomphga and Marigold will be. That's where they will make their happily ever after come true. They'll make a camp. Maybe start up a farm. Live off the land. Be alone with nobody to lock them up or boss them around."

Marigold hummed thoughtfully, her voice fluttering into Oomphga's petite, brown-furred ears.

"I'd really like that, Oomphga~"

Mornings came and mornings went, each hour invested in the ground they covered with their footprints. Despite this, boredom was non-existent as the young lovers joined the whistling winds with riveting conversation.

"You know, Oomphga's parents used to tell him stories about war and peace," the druid rambled. He flicked his thumb, popping one wild berry after another into his mouth between each sentence. "They were lovely, but now that Oomphga thinks back on them, Oomphga doesn't know if they were fictional tales based on the real world or real events overshadowed by fictitious elements meant to shed light on some kind of predetermined reaction. Either way...bringing about harmony...it is not as easy as legends and fables have you believe."

"Well, you must take into account, back then, they probably didn't have a sharp-tongued shrew driving a stake through everyone's hearts. Man, giant, dragon, animal - they were all simpler. Now, everything's gotten to be..."

"Complicated?"

"Exactly. Back then, they didn't even have classes or nobility or politics. They definitely didn't have civilization the way we know it now. If anything, they knew good was good, bad was bad, and change was inevitable whether they wanted it or not. But now…"

"Now…nobody really knows what they want. They just want things to be good again…"

Marigold nodded and let out an affirmative hum.

"Things will be good again. One day. You'll see~"

Together, the two gazed off into the distance. They crested over the top of the hill and took in the view of the big city with grey towers reaching towards the sky. A long, brick wall - lit up with several torchlights equally spaced - separated the citizens inside from the wilderness beyond.

In never occurred to Oomphga how far he's strayed from home. His mother and father, he never told them of where he went. Already, he could imagine the earful he'd get from Mama Vergaia if she ever found out about him scampering off so far away from home. He glanced back at the line of trees and the watchful eyes that filled them. None were truly familiar to him.

They will be blind to our presence here beyond the walls and across the sea. Good. Wouldn't want Marcuth to learn of where we've gone…

Abandoning the forests' calls proved no easy task for the apprentice druid, but the gods firmly reminded him of his role in the grand design. Feathery silhouettes pointed straight ahead and straight ahead they would venture. Oomphga tapped his heel against Bear Friend's side and led the march up to the hulking, wooden gates.

As they approached, two humans dawning red, cloaked armor poked their heads over the parapet and stared down at the wandering youths.

"Halt. Who goes there?" asked the one.

"Children, it would seem," chimed in the other. "Where are your parents?"

"We...we came alone. We've traveled all the way from Endinerose and we seek refuge in your kingdom. My name is Oomphga and this is Marigold."

"Oomphga and Marigold," the other repeated. "Do you have any relatives here? Any friends? Anyone you'll be staying with?"

Oomphga shyly brushed the back of his neck. "Well, we were sort of hoping that-"

"Lord Penumbra," Marigold interjected.

To which Oomphga wondered...*who the heck is that?*

Then, to further Oomphga's shock, one of the wall-watching guards shouted an order to the gate operator to raise the lead portcullis. Then, giving a bow, the other cut the silent air with three highly anticipative words:

"Welcome to Starfall."

Note from the Author

Thank you, kind adventurer, for spending time to read my book! It's crazy to imagine that a character lovingly designed for a brief tabletop roleplaying campaign (from a little more than three years ago) would evolve to have his own story with conflict, culture, and finding love in unexpected places. This book has been a passion project of mine for well over a year, and it brings me great joy knowing that I can finally share tales of his journey with others. I couldn't have done this without the help of my family, friends, and co-workers that aided me in the process from start to finish.

I would really appreciate it if you could:

Connect with me. I'd love to hear from you! Your thoughts on my writings would be greatly appreciated and could even be helpful in writing future novels (maybe even a sequel). Please take a look at Oomphga's Instagram **Oomphga Silverblood** or feel free to email me at **theoomphgasilverblood@gmail.com** with questions or comments.

Share this. If you liked this book, share it on social media. It allows more people to discover this story, and helps debut authors, like me, reach an audience with interests similar to their own.